"It's very nice o⬥ W9-BPM-942
stay." Savannah regarded

"But," she continued, "I'm sure that when your sister offered you a place to stay, she wasn't expecting you to pass it on to a random stranger."

Savannah wasn't a stranger. Carter had carried her photograph around in his pocket for two months.

For a moment it looked as if Savannah was wavering. But then her chin came up.

"You don't have to worry about me. I know you were Rob's friend, but I'm not your responsibility."

"When I make a promise, I keep it."

"And you did. You delivered Rob's message—"

"Not that promise," Carter interrupted. "I'm a marine, ma'am. And we never leave a man—or a woman—behind."

* * *

**Texas Twins: Two sets of twins,
torn apart by family secrets, find their way home.**

Her Surprise Sister—Marta Perry
July 2012

Mirror Image Bride—Barbara McMahon
August 2012

Carbon Copy Cowboy—Arlene James
September 2012

Look-Alike Lawman—Glynna Kaye
October 2012

The Soldier's Newfound Family—Kathryn Springer
November 2012

Reunited for the Holidays—Jillian Hart
December 2012

Books by Kathryn Springer

Love Inspired

Tested by Fire
Her Christmas Wish
By Her Side
For Her Son's Love
A Treasure Worth Keeping
Hidden Treasures
Family Treasures
Jingle Bell Babies
*A Place to Call Home
*Love Finds a Home
*The Prodigal Comes Home
The Prodigal's Christmas Reunion
*Longing for Home
*The Promise of Home
The Soldier's Newfound Family

*Mirror Lake

Love Inspired Single Title

Front Porch Princess
Hearts Evergreen
  "A Match Made
  for Christmas"
Picket Fence Promises
The Prince Charming List

KATHRYN SPRINGER

is a lifelong Wisconsin resident. Growing up in a "newspaper" family, she spent long hours as a child plunking out stories on her mother's typewriter and hasn't stopped writing since! She loves to write inspirational romance because it allows her to combine her faith in God with her love of a happy ending.

The Soldier's Newfound Family

Kathryn Springer

Love Inspired

Special thanks and acknowledgment
to Kathryn Springer for her contribution
to the Texas Twins miniseries.

Recycling programs
for this product may
not exist in your area.

™ LOVE INSPIRED BOOKS

ISBN-13: 978-0-373-87776-8

THE SOLDIER'S NEWFOUND FAMILY

Copyright © 2012 by Harlequin Books, S.A.

Printed in U.S.A.

We ought always to thank God for you, brothers,
and rightly so, because your faith is
growing more and more, and the love
every one of you has for each other is increasing.
—*2 Thessalonians* 1:3

This book is warmly dedicated to my continuity cohorts—Marty, Barbara, Arlene, Glynna and Jill.

For wisdom, grace, patience and a sense of humor while we linked the Texas Twins books together.

It was a blessing working with you!

Chapter One

*"**A**nd this one's Asteroid Man..."*

Another plastic action figure landed on Sergeant Carter Wallace's lap tray, adding to the growing number of soldiers that had formed a perimeter around the coffee cup the flight attendant had set down in front of him.

"I got him for my birthday." A pair of eyes the color of Texas bluebonnets regarded Carter solemnly, waiting for his opinion.

"Cool." Just like the coffee he hadn't taken a sip of yet.

A wide, gap-toothed grin rearranged the pattern of butterscotch freckles on the preschool boy's cheeks. "He can fly, too. And the bad guys can't see him coming because he's *inbisible* when he lands."

Across the narrow aisle, the boy's harassed grandmother caught Carter's eye and mouthed the words *I'm sorry* as she tried to calm the fussy toddler in her lap.

The frustrated looks the woman had been receiving from their fellow passengers had only compounded her stress. Which explained why she hadn't noticed her grandson unbuckle his seat belt and commandeer the empty seat beside Carter after the beverage cart rattled past.

Without an invitation, the kid had settled in next to him

and announced that his name was Josh and that he was four years old.

"Are you a real soldier?" he'd whispered, staring at the patches on Carter's camo jacket in open fascination.

Carter wrestled back a smile. "Yes, I am."

"I like soldiers."

Those three simple words had derailed Carter's plan to get some shut-eye. Josh had plunged both hands into a backpack and proceeded to pull out his action figures, an eclectic blend of superheroes and guys in camouflage, all working together to save the world.

The kid might have prevented Carter from the luxury of a long-overdue nap, but he'd also kept the nightmares at bay.

At least for a few hours.

"This is Mike." Josh carefully placed another action figure behind a Lego bunker. "When he's in trouble, Asteroid Man does this—" The action figure came down right in front of Soldier Mike with a thump that rocked the lap tray and sent coffee sloshing over the side of the cup. "See? He saves him 'cause they're friends."

Carter felt beads of sweat pop out on his forehead as a memory slammed against the barricade he'd built around it. Josh's chatter was muffled by the deafening blast that sucked Carter back in time. He felt the sun-baked ground shudder beneath his feet. Saw a fireball bloom in the distance, reaching so high the flames licked the clouds. By the time he'd reached the scene, two trucks in the convoy had been reduced to smoking metal skeletons.

Along with the buzzing in his ears, Carter had heard shouts and the pop of gunfire from a sniper who'd moved in to finish what the roadside bomb had started.

You'll be nominated for a Silver Star, Wallace.

Carter didn't know why. Sure, he'd saved three men that day. But he'd lost Rob.

His closest friend.

He hadn't reached him in time. And God hadn't bothered to intervene....

Carter was almost relieved when the seat belt sign blinked on a few minutes later and the flight attendant told the passengers the plane would be landing soon. Josh's soldiers retreated to the backpack once again, and he scrambled back to his grandmother's side.

Carter stared out the window as the wheels came down and the plane began its descent. Sheets of gunmetal gray clouds began to unravel, offering a teasing glimpse of the city below. It had been over a year since he'd stepped on Texas soil.

A lifetime ago.

The plane rolled to a stop by the gate, and the child's grandmother smiled at Carter across the aisle. "I can't thank you enough for keeping Josh occupied."

A smile hooked the corner of Carter's lips. "Not a problem, ma'am. Marines are trained to handle all kinds of situations."

"Are you home for good?"

Carter hesitated, not knowing quite how to answer the question. He chose the safest response.

"For a little while."

The woman frowned. "But someone will be here to meet you?"

Carter nodded, touched by her concern. "My sister." In her last email, Maddie had promised to pick him up at the Dallas/Fort Worth airport, but that had been several weeks ago and he hadn't been in touch with her since then.

She'd hinted that she had something important to tell him, but insisted the news be shared in person. Carter couldn't imagine what it would be, but there were times he'd been grateful for the distance that separated him from family drama. Besides that, she had Grayson, their older brother, to confide in. The two had always been close, bound together by some invisible thread that Carter had never been able to grab hold of.

There was a flurry of movement around them as the passengers collected their bags. Josh grinned up at him. "Bye."

"Take care, bud," Carter said.

"I will." The boy's thin arms locked around Carter's leg and then he was gone, swallowed up in the line of passengers exiting the plane.

Carter slung the camouflage duffel bag over his shoulder and made his way toward the baggage claim. A businessman glanced up from his laptop and gave him a respectful nod. A woman on the escalator caught his eye and tapped the tiny yellow ribbon pinned to her collar.

Carter had learned that when he wore his uniform, he wasn't just a soldier named Carter Wallace. He was someone's dad. Brother. Son. Across three time zones, people had sought him out. Smiled at him. Thumped him on the back. By touching him, they were touching someone they loved.

It was strange. Humbling.

At the bottom of the escalator, he began to look for Maddie. She was the kind of woman who stood out in a crowd. Stylish and sophisticated...

"Carter!"

Out of the corner of his eye, a blur of movement began to take shape.

Auburn hair. Big brown eyes...and cowboy boots?

Carter had only a split second to brace himself for impact before Maddie dived into his arms. His throat swelled shut when she clung to him. He couldn't remember his older sister ever being so demonstrative.

"I can't…breathe," he managed.

The choke hold around his neck loosened. A little. "Sorry. It's just—" Were those tears in her eyes? "I'm glad you're here." Sniffling, Maddie stepped back and clasped his shoulders. "Let me look at you."

Carter's lips quirked. "I haven't changed since the last time you saw me."

Not on the outside, anyway.

"You, on the other hand…" His gaze skimmed the Western-style plaid shirt and jeans and paused to linger on her feet. "Nice boots. Are you on some kind of undercover assignment for *Texas Today?*"

"I'll leave the undercover stuff to Gray—and I'm not working at the magazine anymore."

"Not working… I thought you loved your job."

Maddie flashed a wobbly smile. "I told you there have been a lot of changes."

"That's an understatement."

Carter's head whipped around at the sound of a familiar drawl. His brother, Grayson, sauntered up, hand in hand with a beautiful, dark-haired woman and a small boy sporting a cowboy hat and a Dallas Cowboys T-shirt.

Carter had come home on leave several times since he'd enlisted, but he'd never been greeted at the airport by both his siblings before.

"I didn't expect to see you here." He extended his hand but Gray ignored it and hugged him instead, adding a manly thump to his back for good measure.

The lump in Carter's throat doubled in size. Had the plane landed in Fort Worth or *The Twilight Zone?* Because things were getting weirder by the second.

"Carter, I'd like you to meet my fiancée, Elise Lopez,

and her son, Cory." Gray smiled down at the woman, an expression on his face that Carter had never seen before. Identical to the one he'd seen on Rob's face whenever he'd talked about Savannah…

He thrust the memory aside.

"Congratulations." Carter glanced at Maddie. "I guess this must be the big news you had to tell me about in person."

A look passed between his siblings.

And that's when Carter felt it. The prickle of unease that skated up his spine and lifted the hairs on the back of his neck. He recognized the signs, similar to the ones he'd experienced trudging through the mountains of Afghanistan.

Suddenly, this no longer felt like a reunion. It felt more like an ambush.

"Let me get this straight. There are *two* of each of you?" Carter leaned forward, staring at his siblings in disbelief.

His *half* siblings, if what Gray had just told him was true.

"We thought it would be better if we waited until you got home to break the news," Maddie said softly.

It would have been better if they hadn't told him at all, Carter thought, still trying to wrap his mind around the fact that his mother, Sharla Wallace, hadn't given birth to Maddie and Gray. They'd spent the past hour explaining that a woman named Belle Colby was their biological mother and both Maddie and Gray had an identical twin.

Which meant their dad had never bothered to mention that he'd been married once before. Brian Wallace might be a distant father—more available to the missionary patients he served than his own family—but he wasn't the kind of man who would keep something like that a secret.

Unless there was a good reason.

Maddie reached for his hand across the kitchen table. At least they'd chosen the privacy of Gray's condo to drop this bomb on him. Gray had left Elise and Cory at Maddie's apartment, where they'd been staying now that his sister was living at the Colby Ranch near a small town named Grasslands.

Carter's older brother was apparently tying up loose ends in Fort Worth before starting his new job at the Grasslands Police Department. Gray and Elise planned on making a permanent move to Grasslands after they were married.

Carter had barely recovered from the news that his brother was engaged when Maddie spilled the rest of the story. Starting with how she'd recently reunited with Violet, her identical twin.

According to Maddie, Violet was the one who'd set things in motion. Her mother, Belle, had been badly injured after falling off a horse last July and she'd set out to find her biological father. A search that had led her to Maddie, instead.

"I know it sounds unbelievable—"

"Unbelievable?" Carter interrupted, shifting just out of Maddie's reach. "How about impossible? You both have an identical twin that you didn't know about. Dad was married before he met Mom. I think we've gone straight from unbelievable to a guest spot on the Dr. Phil show."

No one smiled. Probably because they knew it was true.

"We've been having a hard time accepting it, too," Gray said carefully. "Unfortunately, Belle can't answer our questions until she comes out her coma. And...Dad." He stumbled over the word, which suddenly made the story more real than fantasy. Carter wasn't used to seeing his big brother, a tough undercover cop, lose a grip on his emotions. "I'm still trying to track him down."

Carter tried to put himself in Gray's position. While

tracing their roots to an old address in Fort Worth, Maddie had met a woman named Patty Earl who'd cast doubts on the fact that Gray and his twin, Jack Colby, were even Brian Wallace's sons. Her late husband, Joe Earl, had claimed that *he'd* fathered the twin boys.

Carter had always felt like the odd man out in his family, but if the woman's claim was true, it meant that he was Brian's only son by blood.

He wanted to talk to his father, demand to know why he'd kept all this a secret. But according to Gray, their dad had disappeared while traveling near the Texas-Mexico border and no one in the family had been able to reach him for several months.

Brian wasn't expected to return until Thanksgiving, but his wallet and cell phone had turned up recently and there was a growing concern that something had happened to him. Another piece of information that Gray and Maddie had waited to tell Carter until he was back in the States.

"I know it's going to take some time to sort all this out," Gray said. "We're still working on it. It's been just as hard on Violet and Jack."

The names meant nothing to Carter. He tried to picture another Maddie. Another Grayson. The "country" equivalents of his big-city sibs. Under different circumstances, the thought would have made him smile.

"I'd like you to meet Ty." Maddie touched the engagement ring on her finger. The last Carter knew, she'd been engaged to Landon Derringer, a Fort Worth CEO who'd been a close friend of the Wallace family for years. Carter was having a hard time keeping up. "And Violet and Jack have invited you to stay at the ranch until we hear from Dad."

"Why?" Frustration sharpened the word but it didn't faze Maddie.

She lifted her chin. "Because family should stick together."

Family? Is that what they were? Because Carter had no idea how to define this tangle of relationships.

"Come on, Carter." Gray met his eyes and Carter saw a glint of stubbornness there. Or maybe he was seeing his own reflection. "What would it hurt to hang out at the Colby Ranch for a week or two?"

"You'll love it there," Maddie said earnestly. "I promise."

I promise.

Carter's hand closed around the photograph in his pocket.

"Give me a few days."

Maddie's expression clouded. "Carter—"

"There's something I have to do first."

"Did you see the guy who just sat down at table four? Because he sure can't take his eyes off *you*."

"That's your section." Savannah Blackmore brushed aside her coworker's sly comment as she continued to restock the shelves behind the counter.

Libby hadn't been working at the diner very long, so all she knew was that Savannah was single, but not the reason why. Not that it mattered. The "cosmetology student by day—waitress by night" fancied herself a modern-day Emma, matching up people with the hope they would find their own "happily ever after" ending.

Over the past seven months, Savannah had learned there were endings, but they weren't always happy ones.

"He has broad shoulders, too." Libby fanned herself with the order pad.

Some girls noticed a man's smile or the color of his eyes. Libby judged a man by the width of his shoulders. Savannah doubted she could find a pair strong enough to carry her burdens. Guys avoided women with baggage and she had enough to fill up the cargo hold of a Boeing 747. The delicate flutter below her rib cage reminded Savannah there was someone else to consider. Someone *she* needed to be strong for.

That's why she wasn't even tempted to look at the guy at table number four.

"I'll be in the kitchen."

"You can run but you can't hide," her coworker teased.

"Watch me." Savannah made a beeline for the swinging doors that separated the kitchen from the dining area.

Come to think of it, the canned goods in the pantry could use a little organizing, too....

"Order up." Bruce, the diner's owner and self-appointed cook, pointed to a platter piled high with ribs, mashed potatoes drenched in butter and a generous helping of coleslaw.

It was Libby's order, but over the top of the doors, Savannah could see she'd been waylaid by a group of tourists wearing matching T-shirts with the words I Brake For Rodeos emblazoned on the front.

"I'll take it." Savannah grabbed the plate and caught Libby's eye as she rounded the counter. "Where does this one go?"

The impish light that danced in the younger girl's eyes answered Savannah's question even before she could say the words—

"Table four."

With a sigh, Savannah counted the scuffed tiles as she made her way to the back of the diner.

Part of her knew that Libby must have misunderstood the guy's interest. The past few months had taken their toll. She felt—and probably looked—as wrung out as the mop hanging in the utility closet.

Savannah summoned a polite smile as she approached the table.

Okay, so maybe Libby hadn't been exaggerating. The guy's close-cropped hair was the pale gold of winter wheat, a perfect setting for a pair of deep-set, cobalt-blue eyes. A gray T-shirt stretched across the broad shoulders Libby had gone on and on about....

Savannah's gaze locked on the familiar insignia and her mouth went dry.

A soldier.

He rose to his feet as she reached the table. "I'm Sergeant Carter Wallace, ma'am...."

Savannah felt a tingling numbness spread down her arms to her fingertips. The plate wobbled. As a river of barbecue sauce carried the ribs toward the edge, it was gently plucked from her hands and deposited on the table.

The soldier's gaze dropped to the apron tied around her waist, lingering there until Savannah felt the color rise in her cheeks.

What was his problem? Hadn't he seen a pregnant woman before?

"Your waitress will be back in a few minutes to see if you need anything else." Savannah whirled toward the kitchen.

"Savannah? *Wait.*"

How did he know her name?

She slowly turned around, reluctant to face him again.

A muscle worked in the sergeant's jaw. "I know— *knew*—your husband. Rob."

Bitterness and sorrow clashed, splashing over the walls of Savannah's grief. She swallowed hard against the lump that rose in her throat and managed a smile.

"I'm glad one of us did."

Chapter Two

Carter watched Savannah disappear through the swinging doors that separated the kitchen from the dining area.

In his mind, this had played out differently.

Savannah had been happy to see him. Touched by the message that Rob had entrusted him to deliver. Instead, she'd looked at him as if he'd lobbed a grenade in her direction.

Maybe you did.

It occurred to Carter that he shouldn't have chosen a public place to introduce himself, but Rob had never given him their home address, only mentioned the name of the tiny diner in Dallas where Savannah worked.

Carter dropped into the chair again and pressed his fingers against his temples, an attempt to ward off the headache that had sunk its talons behind his eyes. When he'd stepped off the plane, he'd naively assumed that time would slowly begin to sand down the jagged edges of his memories and life would return to normal.

Normal, he remembered his nanny, Rachel, saying with a laugh, *is just a setting on the dryer.*

Carter finally understood what she'd meant. Because so far, nothing had gone the way he'd planned.

He'd spent a sleepless night at Gray's condo, fighting jet lag and the realization that everything he'd believed about his family had been based on a lie.

Breakfast with Maddie and Gray the next morning had been awkward; no one seemed to know how to fill the silence. Carter had politely declined their invitation to church. His brother took off shortly after breakfast to pick up Elise and Cory. After the service, Maddie planned to return to Grasslands so she could check on Belle Colby at the convalescent center.

Carter had welcomed the time alone to regroup. He'd decided to help Gray search for their father, the only person who could tell them the truth about the past. But first, he'd been honor bound to deliver a message.

If the woman the message was intended for decided to cooperate.

"How are those ribs tastin'?" Libby, the waitress who'd been so attentive when Carter had walked into the diner, bounded up to his table.

"Great." Once Carter tried them, he'd know for sure.

"Okaay." She glanced down at his plate and frowned. "Anything else I can getcha?"

How about an explanation for Savannah's parting words? *I'm glad one of us did.*

The statement hadn't made sense. She was Rob's wife. Of course she knew him. Savannah's reaction—and her abrupt departure—didn't quite match up with the woman Rob had described. A woman with a sweet smile, a sense of humor and a strong faith.

Carter understood how grief could do a number on someone, but wouldn't she want to talk to someone who'd spent time with Rob?

Been with him at the end?

His gaze shifted to the kitchen, where Savannah was

hiding out. If he could outlast a sniper for ten hours, he could certainly wait out a pretty green-eyed waitress.

"I'll take a piece of pie and a cup of coffee."

Libby followed the direction of his eyes and grinned. "Coming right up."

A half hour ticked by and the dining room emptied as the lunch crowd dwindled. Carter finished off the pie and started on his third cup of coffee but there was still no sign of Savannah.

"Excuse me?" He motioned to Libby as she emerged from the kitchen, armed with two coffee pots. She changed direction, navigating through the maze of tables until she reached his side.

"Do you need a warm up on that coffee?"

He needed to talk to Savannah. "No, thanks. Just the bill." Carter reached for his wallet. "Is Savannah busy?" he tossed out casually.

"No." The smile dimmed. "She left a little while ago."

"Left?"

"She said she wasn't feeling well."

Savannah had slipped past him. Admiration and frustration battled for dominance. Frustration won.

Carter released a slow breath. "Will she be back tomorrow?"

"She's not scheduled to work again until Tuesday."

Great. Before she'd left, Maddie made him promise he would drive to Grasslands to meet the rest of the "family" as soon as possible.

"Would you mind giving me her home address?"

Libby looked uneasy with the request. "I don't know—"

"Her husband and I served together in Afghanistan. He introduced us." It was the truth. Sort of. He and Savannah might not have met until today, but Carter felt as if he knew her. He knew that she hummed when she was nervous and that her favorite color was blue. She liked yellow roses and coffee-flavored ice cream and black-and-white movies.

And she was more beautiful in person than she was in the photograph Rob had given him.

Carter set that thought firmly to the side.

"I didn't know Savannah was married to a soldier," Libby breathed. "She never talks about him."

"He talked about her." Twenty-four seven. "And he asked me to deliver a message."

"That's *so* romantic."

Only in the movies, Carter wanted to say. The reality hadn't been quite so warm and fuzzy.

He and Rob had been shoulder to shoulder in a shallow ditch, caught in the middle of a firefight. Under attack from both the ground and the air.

If anything happens to me, promise that you'll find Savannah and make sure she's okay. Tell her that I loved her.

But Rob hadn't told him that Savannah might not *want* to be found.

Or that she was pregnant.

"Going somewhere?"

Savannah whirled around at the sound of a deep male voice.

It was him. Carter Wallace. The soldier who'd shown up at the diner that morning. He filled the doorway, arms folded across his chest in a casually deceptive stance. The set of his jaw warned Savannah that she wouldn't evade him as easily this time.

She didn't bother to ask how he'd found out where she lived. He must have sweet-talked Libby after she'd left the diner.

"Your landlady let me in." Those intense blue eyes

scanned the living room and narrowed on the hedge of cardboard boxes that separated them.

"Look, Sergeant Wallace." Savannah heard a catch in her voice. "I don't know what you want—"

"That's because you didn't wait around long enough to find out." The corners of his lips kicked up in a rueful smile. "I'm sorry if I upset you when I showed up at the diner today. Rob told me where you worked but not your address."

Rob told him.

Savannah's throat tightened. She couldn't deal with this right now. Not when she'd spent the past few hours packing up her things, each box she taped shut one more reminder that she was closing the door on the past with no idea what the future would bring.

"Do you mind if I come in?"

Yes, she did.

"I'm really busy." To prove it, Savannah bent down and snatched up one of the boxes. A muscle in her lower back protested the suddenness of the movement and she winced in pain.

"Hey—take it easy." Carter Wallace was at her side in an instant and he plucked the box from her hands. "Should you be lifting stuff?"

Color flooded Savannah's cheeks when she saw his gaze drop to her rounded stomach, something that even a loose-fitting sweatshirt couldn't hide.

"I'm not an invalid." She was just...tired. And not prepared for unexpected company. Especially a handsome, blue-eyed soldier who'd claimed to be friends with her late husband.

"Where do you want this?" Carter stared her down.

Good job, Savannah. Instead of convincing him to leave, she'd unwittingly given him a reason to stay.

"Really, you don't have to—" She saw his eyebrows dip together and realized there was no point in arguing. "By the door."

Without a word, Carter strode across the room and deposited it near the entryway. And then proceeded to do the same with the rest of the boxes.

As he set the last one down, Savannah didn't miss his swift but thorough assessment of the cramped upstairs apartment she'd briefly shared with Rob after their wedding.

"Thank you." Savannah glanced at her watch, hoping Carter would take the hint.

He did.

"I'll only take up a few minutes of your time," he said quietly. "It's important."

Savannah sighed. Maybe the best thing was to get this over with as quickly as possible and send Sergeant Wallace on his way.

"All right." She motioned toward a chair and sent up a swift, silent prayer for strength as Carter sat down. The flimsy wood creaked under the weight of his solid frame, the floral slipcover an almost comical backdrop for a guy who looked as if he could bench press the sofa.

It didn't matter that Carter Wallace wasn't in full uniform. His faded, loose-fitting jeans and a gray T-shirt with the marine insignia that stretched across his muscular chest proved to be just as intimidating. He looked as if he were born to be a soldier.

Savannah perched on the edge of the sofa and waited. But now that he had her attention, Carter didn't seem to know what to say.

"You mentioned that you knew Rob—" Savannah's voice cracked as grief sliced at the threads of her composure. She'd barely begun to accept the fact that her husband had walked out on their marriage when a military chaplain had knocked at the door and informed her that Rob had been killed in a roadside bombing.

Carter nodded. "He was assigned to my unit. We worked together. He talked about you."

Savannah's fingers knotted together in her lap. "He did?"

Carter looked surprised by the question. "All the time." He paused. "That's why I'm here. A few days before Rob… He asked me to give you a message."

Savannah heard a rushing sound in her ears. Spots began to dance in front of her eyes. "A message?"

This wasn't what she'd expected. She'd assumed that Carter had sought her out because Rob had owed him money. After the funeral, she'd received calls from some of his former buddies, asking if she would "make good" on the loans they'd given him.

Each one a reminder of how gullible she'd been.

"He was a good man. A good friend." Carter leaned forward. "And he…he loved you."

Savannah felt the color drain from her face. "You don't know what you're talking about."

Carter frowned. "That's the message that Rob asked me to deliver. He wanted me to tell you that he loved you."

Savannah's breath collected in her lungs, making it difficult to breathe.

"Sergeant Wallace, Rob *left* me."

Carter stared at Savannah, more shaken by the words than he let on. Rob hadn't mentioned that Savannah didn't support his decision to become a soldier.

"To serve his country, yes," he said carefully. "Rob thought he was doing the right thing, but he couldn't wait to finish his tour and come home to you. It was all he talked about."

Savannah vaulted from the chair and then swayed on her feet. For a split second, Carter was afraid she was going to pass out. Instinctively, he reached out to steady her but she spun away from him, one hand pressed protectively against her belly, the other one palm up, as if trying to keep him at a distance.

"Please. Just go."

Carter sucked in a breath, the flash of pain in those green eyes landing with the force of a physical blow. It was obvious that Savannah was still grieving. He fumbled for the right words, something that had never come easily. Unlike Rob, who'd entertained everyone on base with his anecdotes.

"Savannah, I know this must be difficult. Have you talked to someone—"

"I didn't mean that Rob left when he enlisted. I meant that he left *me*. A week after we were married," she choked out. "He sent one letter when he finished basic training saying that he'd made a…mistake. After that, I never heard from him again."

The words hit Carter broadside. "I don't understand."

"I think you do." Savannah's gaze didn't waver. "You just don't believe me."

Carter opened his mouth, ready to argue, and then realized she was right. What Savannah had just told him clashed with the man that Carter knew. The one who'd been devoted to his wife.

Rob had bragged about their plans for the future. Buying a piece of land. Building a home. Raising a family.

Why would—

Carter's heart plummeted to the soles of his boots,

weighted down by a sudden, unwelcome suspicion. "The baby—"

Emerald sparks flashed in Savannah's eyes. "Is Rob's. But he…he never knew."

"You didn't tell him?" Carter regretted the question the moment Savannah started toward the door.

To see him out.

But Carter didn't move. Wasn't going to move until he got some answers. "Rob never mentioned that you were separated. In fact, all he talked about were the things the two of you were going to do when his tour ended."

"Then he lied to you, too."

Too?

The band around Carter's forehead tightened. "Rob and I were friends. Why would he do that?"

He had looked up to Rob. Admired him.

Envied him.

Carter had dodged serious relationships for years, never going out with the same woman more than once or twice. Knowing how hard it had been on him and his siblings every time their father left on a mission trip, he was determined not to subject someone he cared about to a relationship marked by uncertainty and goodbyes. Something the wife of a soldier had to accept. But listening to Rob talk about Savannah had made him question his decision to remain single. Made him wonder what it would be like to have a woman like her in his life.

Now she was trying to convince him that it had all been a lie?

Savannah opened the door, which didn't answer his question but guaranteed there wouldn't be an opportunity to ask any more.

Carter didn't know what—or who—to believe. Savannah? A woman he'd just met. Or Rob, the guy who'd laughed with him? Encouraged him to pray, even though every mile Carter had hiked through the rugged hills of Afghanistan had taken him that much farther from the faith he'd professed as a child?

The guy that Savannah claimed had abandoned her.

What he *did* know was that she wanted him to leave.

"I'm sorry," Carter muttered, although he wasn't quite sure why he was apologizing. Or even who he was apologizing *to*. "I won't take up any more of your time."

As he started to move past her, she touched his arm. A gesture that stopped Carter in his tracks.

"Sergeant Wallace? Thank you for keeping your promise," she whispered. "I am… I'm glad that Rob had a friend over there."

The words brought Carter up short. He had kept his promise—but not all of it.

Find Savannah and make sure she's okay.

For the first time, he noticed the lavender shadows below her eyes. Being the youngest in the family, Carter didn't have a lot of experience with kids, but he figured that working at a diner wouldn't be easy on a pregnant woman.

Savannah's grief might be coloring her perspective about Rob's feelings for her—maybe she'd somehow misinterpreted the reason he'd left—but Carter couldn't simply walk out the door until he knew that she wasn't alone.

"Are you moving back home?" he asked abruptly.

"Home?"

"Back to your family."

"I'm staying in Dallas." An emotion Carter couldn't identify flickered in Savannah's eyes. "But my landlady's nephew needed a place to stay so she asked me to find something else."

She was being *evicted?*

"Don't you have a lease?"

"Mrs. Cabera only agreed to let me stay here because Rob and her son had gone to high school together. It was a verbal agreement."

Carter didn't like the sound of that. "But you have somewhere to go, right?"

Savannah hesitated just long enough to make him suspicious. "Of course."

"Where?"

Her pink lips compressed. "This isn't your problem."

In a roundabout way, that answered his question.

"What are your plans?"

Savannah was silent for so long that Carter didn't think she was going to answer the question.

"I'll check into a hotel for a few days. Until I find something else," she finally said.

"Isn't there a family member who can put you up for a while?"

"No."

Funny how one simple word could complicate a situation, Carter thought.

"Well, I happen to have picked up a few extras recently," he said lightly. "And one of them owns a ranch near Grasslands. My sister, Maddie, offered me one of the empty cottages on the property, but you can stay there—"

Savannah's eyes widened and Carter felt a slow burn crawl up his neck when he realized how that sounded. "—and I can bunk in the main house," he added quickly. "You'd have a place to rest up. Until you find something else."

Color swept into Savannah's cheeks, filling the faint hollows beneath her cheekbones.

"That's very nice of you." She regarded him warily, as if she wasn't sure it was nice of him at all. "But I can't just quit my job at the diner. And I'm sure that when your sister offered you a place to stay, she wasn't expecting you to pass it on to a random stranger."

Carter could have argued the point. Savannah wasn't a stranger. He'd carried her photograph around in his pocket for the past two months. Memorized the heart-shaped face and delicate features.

But how could he tell her that without coming across as some kind of stalker?

"I heard someone say that sometimes, a change of scenery can change your perspective."

Carter decided not to mention Rob was the one who'd told him that.

For a moment it looked as if Savannah was wavering. But then her chin came up and Carter saw the answer in her eyes.

"You don't have to worry about me. I know you were Rob's friend, but I'm not your responsibility."

Find Savannah and make sure she's okay.

Whether Carter wanted it to or not, that *made* her his responsibility.

"But it's not just you anymore, is it?" he reminded her. "You have your baby to think of, too."

Savannah flinched. "Goodbye, Sergeant Wallace."

Carter battled his rising frustration, not sure how to get through to her. "When I make a promise, I keep it."

"And you did. You delivered Rob's message—"

"Not that promise." Carter interrupted. "I'm a marine, ma'am. And we never leave a man—or a woman—behind."

Even though he was serious, Carter flashed a smile, letting her know that she could trust him.

A smile Savannah didn't return.

"You aren't leaving me behind, sergeant." The door began to close. "I'm *asking* you to go."

Chapter Three

"So, when will you be here?"

Carter sighed into the phone as he entered the post office. "Soon."

"How soon?" Maddie wanted to know.

"A few more days." Long enough to give Savannah time to change her mind.

Carter had jotted his cell phone number and the Colby Ranch's address on a piece of paper and tucked it under the windshield wiper of her car after she'd shut the door in his face the day before.

He hadn't been able to stop thinking about her. Wondering what had happened between her and Rob. None of the things Savannah had told him lined up with the claims his friend had made, but Carter couldn't shake the feeling that *she* was the one who'd been telling the truth. Unsettling, given the fact he'd trusted Rob with his life.

"Jack said he might be able to find some work for you around the ranch now that you're out of the service," Maddie continued. "You love being outdoors. You helped Dad build that playhouse in the backyard when we lived in Appleton, remember? Once it was finished, you told everyone that you wanted to live there. I had to lure you into the house with chocolate chip cookies when it was bedtime."

Maddie's low laugh flowed over him, stirring up memories from the past.

Carter remembered handing his dad the nails, one by one. It was one of the few times they'd actually worked on a project together. Once his dad had started medical school, he'd left Rachel, the full-time nanny he'd hired, in charge of the family. Carter had heard the words "don't bother your father" so often over the next few years, he'd eventually taken them to heart.

"I'll come to Grasslands and meet Violet and Jack—" Carter still couldn't think of them as family. "But I can't promise any more than that right now."

"I just want us to be together," Maddie whispered. "With Dad gone…"

Dad is always gone, Carter was tempted to say. He knew that Gray and Maddie were concerned that something bad might have happened to their father, but knowing Brian, he'd probably just got caught up in his work and assumed everything back home was fine. Thanksgiving, the day he'd promised he would be home, was still three weeks away.

Gray had explained they couldn't file a missing person's report because technically, Brian Wallace wasn't considered missing.

"I'll be there." Carter inserted the key into the post office box he'd kept in the city. "By the weekend—" A package tumbled out with an avalanche of junk mail. He winced as it hit the tiled floor. "I hope that wasn't something breakable," he muttered.

Maddie heard him. "Breakable? Where are you?"

"I'm at the post office and there's a package in here that didn't get forwarded for some reason."

"A package," Maddie repeated. "What does it look like?"

"Um…like a package?"

"Well, open it!"

Carter rolled his eyes. Bossy older sisters. But there was a tension in Maddie's voice that hadn't been there before. Not even when she'd been pestering him about coming to Grasslands. He dumped the letters onto a nearby counter and cut through the tape on the package with his pocketknife.

"Did you send this?" Carter stared at the small, leather-bound book swaddled in tissue paper. "Because I already have one."

Not that he'd cracked it open for a few years.

"What is it?" Maddie whispered.

"A Bible."

"Is there a note inside?"

Carter thumbed through the delicate, gold-tipped pages and found a piece of paper. "How did you know?"

"Because someone sent a Bible to me and Gray. And to Violet and Jack."

Carter quickly skimmed the contents of the letter and then read it out loud.

"'I'm sorry for what I did to you and your family. I hope you and your siblings can find it in your hearts to forgive me.'"

It wasn't signed.

"What is this about? Who sent it?"

"We don't know," Maddie admitted. "At first we assumed it was a mistake because whoever wrote the other letters specifically mentioned a twin. But Gray thinks it might have something to do with the reason we were separated."

"Maybe it has something to do with Dad's disappearance." Carter read through the words a second time, trying to make sense of the cryptic message. "Why didn't you mention this before?"

"We didn't think you'd—" Maddie stopped.

"Get one." Carter filled in the blanks.

Because at the moment, he was the only one in the Wallace-Colby puzzle who actually knew where he fit. Which, the irony wasn't lost on Carter, made him the odd man out. Again.

"I'm sorry, Carter." Maddie sounded on the verge of tears now. "Gray will want to see the letter and compare the handwriting, but it has to be from the same person. Maybe if we put all of them together, we'll find something that we missed."

Carter held back a sigh.

"I'm on my way."

"I have to admit I'm not happy with the numbers I'm seeing this morning."

Savannah felt a stab of fear as Dr. Yardley set the paperwork down on the desk and took a seat across from her in the examining room.

"Is there something wrong with the baby?"

"The baby seems to be fine. It's *you* I'm worried about," the doctor said bluntly. "Your blood pressure is elevated, and you've actually lost weight since your last appointment."

"I'm feeling fine," Savannah protested. "A little tired, that's all."

"Mmm." Dr. Yardley looked skeptical. "How many hours did you work at the diner last week?"

Savannah silently tallied them up. "Between twenty-five and thirty." Give or take a few. She'd volunteered to cover for one of the waitresses who was standing up in a friend's wedding so she would have money to cover the security deposit on a new apartment.

The apartment she still hadn't found.

After being on her feet all day, she just couldn't seem to summon the energy to search for a new place to live. Savannah assumed it was normal to feel this way but the concern in the doctor's eyes told her otherwise.

"That's what I thought." Dr. Yardley shook her head. "I want you to cut back to half that amount. Effective when you walk out of this office today."

"But I promised my boss that I could fill in on weekends and evenings when I wasn't working my regular shift." Savannah stared at her obstetrician in dismay. "It was the only reason he hired me."

"You've been under a tremendous amount of stress throughout this pregnancy, Savannah, and you still have three months to go. If you end up on complete bed rest, you won't be able to work at all." The doctor's stern words were tempered with a smile. "You need more rest and a little TLC. Two things that I'm afraid modern medicine hasn't figured out how to put in a pill yet."

Savannah laced her fingers together in her lap to stop them from shaking. "I'll talk to him." Although Bruce didn't exactly have a reputation for his easygoing disposition.

The doctor gave her a shrewd look. "Is there anything else going on that I should know about?"

"I've been looking for a new apartment," Savannah admitted. "But I'm sure that I'll find something in the next few days."

Dr. Yardley's pen tapped the clipboard. "Isn't there a family member you can stay with until the baby is born?"

"I don't have any family." One of the reasons she'd been so quick to fall for Rob's charm.

"All right, then. How about a friend?" the physician persisted.

Even as Savannah was shaking her head, an image of Carter Wallace's face flashed through her mind.

No. Way.

She didn't want to accept his help. Carter had been stunned when she'd told him that Rob had left her. Savannah hadn't really expected him to believe her word over Rob's—but still, it had hurt. Why, she wasn't sure.

She wasn't sure why Carter had offered her a place to stay on his sister's ranch near Grasslands, either. The sergeant had been Rob's friend. She, on the other hand, was simply an obligation. One he had probably been relieved to cross off his list. There was no way she was going to show up on his doorstep like an orphan puppy in search of a home.

She'd viewed Rob as a knight in shining armor, swooping in to rescue her, and look where she was now. A single mother on the verge of being homeless.

God, I know that I'm not alone. I know that You're with me. Show me what I'm supposed to do.

"I know things are difficult right now, but you have to do what's best for you and the baby," Dr. Yardley was saying. "If I could, I'd write you a prescription for a change of scenery. I think that's what you need more than anything right now."

A change of scenery can give you a change in perspective.

The words chased through her mind, stirring the memory of someone else who had said the same thing.

Savannah didn't know whether to laugh or cry. Because even though she'd just asked God to show her what to do, she wasn't ready to acknowledge that Carter Wallace just might be the answer to her prayer.

* * *

"Earth to Carter. Come in, Carter."

Maddie's teasing voice yanked Carter back to the present.

"Sorry." He cocked his head to one side. "Reception is still a little fuzzy between earth and *The Twilight Zone.*"

Laughter rippled through the dining room and once again, Carter had to adjust to the sound. To the faces of the people gathered around the long plank table. Gray and Jack. Violet and Maddie. Identical but…not.

"What's *The Twilight Zone?*" Eight-year-old Darcy Garland's lively, brown-eyed gaze bounced back and forth between the adults.

"It's not real," Ty Garland, the little girl's father, explained. Carter saw him wink at Maddie across the table.

Yeah. That was another thing. His siblings hadn't only found each other, they'd found, in Maddie's words, "their soul mates." Carter was still trying to wrap his brain around that, too.

"That's what you think," Jack Colby muttered. "You don't have to get used to a guy walking around with *your* face."

"Wearing a shirt and tie," Violet added, her eyes dancing with mischief.

"She's right." Jack flashed a wicked grin in Gray's direction. "When you start working for the Grasslands Police department in January, Sheriff Cole will have you trading in those fancy city duds for a pair of Levis and Tony Lamas in no time."

Their easy banter ricocheted around the table and Carter felt a stab of envy. Violet and Jack Colby had gone out of their way to make him feel welcome since his arrival, but Carter still felt as if his life had become a jigsaw puzzle in which the pieces no longer fit together.

But at least he *had* family. More than he was comfortable with, at the moment.

Carter's gaze drifted to the window. Again.

Almost a week had gone by since he'd left the city and he still couldn't stop thinking about Savannah.

He lay awake at night, scrolling through past conversations with his friend. Searching for scraps of information that verified what Savannah had told him. Rob had talked about her constantly…but had he ever talked *to* her? Sent an email or letter? Received one?

That's what Carter couldn't remember.

Lupita Ramirez, the ranch cook and housekeeper, bustled into the dining room. She rapped a wooden spoon against the palm of her hand to get everyone's attention.

"Who has room for chocolate cake?"

A collective groan followed the question.

"No one—" Jack started to say.

"But we'll take some anyway," Maddie and Violet sang out. At the same time. And then they laughed. In unison.

"Weird," Ty Garland muttered.

Carter had to agree.

"I'm going to have to start working out more." Gray sighed when the housekeeper left the dining room. "Lupita makes enough food to feed the entire county."

"That reminds me, Pastor Jeb wants the church to host a special harvest dinner the weekend before Thanksgiving," Violet said. "He's been calling around, asking members of the congregation to volunteer to help, but he wants to invite the whole community."

Unbidden, an image of Savannah's face swept into Carter's mind. Again. The flash of anger in those expressive green eyes when he'd asked about the baby. The vulnerable curve of her lower lip.

Did she have plans for Thanksgiving? Or would she be alone?

Carter shifted in the chair. In his mind's eye, he could see her standing by the door, arms wrapped protectively around her middle. Proud. *Scared.*

She made it pretty clear that she isn't your concern, he reminded himself.

But that didn't stop him from wondering how she was doing. Had she found an apartment yet? He hated to think of her staying in a hotel with a baby on the way, even for a few days.

Carter had made Rob two promises before his friend had died. He'd promised that he would always have Rob's back and he'd promised that he would make sure Savannah was okay. So far, he hadn't kept either one of them.

"I'll see if I can't round up a few of the boys from the teen center to help with setup or something," Landon Derringer was saying. "They're always complaining they don't have anything to do."

"Round up?" Violet grinned at her fiancé's choice of words. "You're starting to think like a cowboy already, sweetheart."

Gray shook his head in mock sorrow. "Another victim."

Across the table, Derringer smiled at Violet, confirmation that he'd been a willing one.

Carter had been stunned to find Landon, Maddie's former fiancé, at the ranch when he'd arrived. The guy had followed his sister to Grasslands and fallen in love with… Violet. And apparently no one but Carter thought that was strange. But in light of the other things the family had experienced lately, maybe it hadn't even made the list.

"I think a harvest dinner is a great idea." Violet handed a pitcher of cream to Maddie a second before she reached for it. "We have a lot to be thankful for."

Carter couldn't believe a murmur of agreement followed the statement. Maybe if they'd witnessed some of the things that he had over the past five years, they would have a different perspective. And given what they'd been through lately with Belle's accident and Brian's disappearance, Carter didn't think there was a whole lot to be thankful for, either.

Maddie's expression turned pensive but she smiled at Violet. "This is the first Thanksgiving we'll all be together."

"Mom loves holidays," Violet said wistfully. "She pulls out all the stops.... I know she'll be home by then. She *has* to be."

"There are a lot of people praying for her," Maddie whispered.

But Carter noticed that everyone sidestepped the real question. Whether his father would be in attendance. Carter had managed to corner Gray for a few minutes and his brother had finally admitted how worried he was that something had happened to Brian. Their dad ministered to transient people in remote areas along the border, and the last person Gray had been in contact with had noticed that he seemed ill. Carter tried to convince himself that a physician would certainly know what to do—where to go—if he came down with something.

Unless he was alone and didn't have access to the medicine he needed to fight the illness. His dad's cell phone had been recovered a few weeks ago, but there were other ways he could have maintained contact with the rest of the family. Why hadn't he used them?

Carter felt the walls begin to close in and suddenly felt the need for some fresh air.

"No dessert for me." His chair scraped the floor as he rose to his feet. "I think I'll take a walk."

"Sure." Maddie frowned.

So did Violet.

Carter blinked but there were still two of them. Oh, yeah. He definitely needed some fresh air.

He could feel everyone watching as he walked out of the dining room. The second the door closed, he would be the next topic of conversation around the dinner table.

Carter wasn't used to that, either. His older siblings valued and encouraged independence. Other than exchanging brief updates now and then, Maddie and Gray had pursued their own interests and left him alone. Carter wasn't quite sure what to do with the sudden interest they were showing now. Add Jack and Violet into the mix, and Carter was beginning to feel like it was four against one. Odds he didn't care for.

He stepped outside, back against the door as he made a swift but thorough sweep of the property. Searching for possible threats.

You're in Texas, remember?

It took a moment to let his soul adjust to the newness of his surroundings. The rustle of the wind through the pecan grove. The scent of the mesquite trees. Miles of blue sky. A place that Maddie and Gray were both ready to call home.

And yet Carter was tempted to reenlist after they located his dad. In the military, he knew exactly who he was. What he was supposed to do. Now, it felt as if he'd stripped of his identity along with his uniform.

Nipper, Jack's Australian shepherd, bounded up to him, and Carter reached down to scratch the dog's velvety ears.

"I suppose you want to go for a walk?" Roaming the property together had become a nightly ritual when Carter couldn't sleep.

The dog's tail slashed the air and he barked. Carter took that as a yes.

Restlessness drove him toward the creek where the

cottages were located. In spite of Violet's generous offer, Carter had decided to stay in the main house and bunk in the guest room that Gray occupied when he visited the ranch, leaving one of the cottages empty in case Savannah changed her mind. A possibility that had begun to shrink over the past few days.

Savannah hadn't exactly welcomed him with open arms. What made him think she would accept his help?

Just as Carter reached the creek bank, his cell phone rang.

An unfamiliar number appeared on the screen and Carter's heart slammed against his rib cage. Had his father finally discovered they'd been trying to contact him?

"Hello?"

He heard a crackling sound. And then a tentative but familiar voice. "Hi."

"Savannah?"

"Yes." A long pause followed. "I hope I'm not interrupting anything."

"Not at all." Carter's hand tightened around the phone. "Is everything all right?"

"I'm sorry I didn't—" The line crackled, distorting her words. If they lost the connection, Carter was afraid she wouldn't call back.

"Savannah? You're breaking up. Where are you?"

"I'm…here."

"Here?" Carter repeated.

"At the gate."

Chapter Four

Savannah's heart performed a little Texas two-step as Carter Wallace approached.

In faded jeans and a long-sleeved black T-shirt that accentuated his athletic build, Carter was even more attractive than she remembered. His loose-limbed stride and the set of his broad shoulders conveyed the fierce confidence of a man who faced life head-on. A confidence Savannah couldn't help but envy.

Once again, she contemplated turning the car around. Something that had crossed her mind at least half a dozen times since she'd left Dallas.

Her boss hadn't exactly been thrilled when she'd stopped by the diner after her appointment with Dr. Yardley and told him that she had to reduce her hours. The next day, when Savannah checked the schedule, she saw that not only had Bruce honored her request, he'd given *all* her shifts to a new waitress he'd hired over the weekend.

Leaving her with no choice but to accept Carter's offer to stay at his sister's ranch for the time being.

But doubts began to creep in as Savannah parked between the massive stone columns that stood like sentinels on either side of the driveway, guarding the property from outsiders. Like her. She wasn't sure what she'd expected, but the Colby Ranch was obviously a large, prosperous operation.

It only reminded Savannah how little she knew about Carter Wallace. Was she really welcome here? Maybe he was already regretting his impulsive invitation.

Rob had made a lot of promises, too, and he'd only kept one of them.

I'm leaving, Savannah.

Savannah's fingers closed around the shift stick but the passenger-side door opened before she could put the car in reverse. Carter hopped in beside her, his large frame folding almost in half to accommodate the passenger seat of her compact car.

Savannah took a deep breath. If he looked at her with pity, she'd turn the car around and head straight back to Dallas....

"It's about time." The crooked smile that Carter flashed in her direction coaxed a dimple out of hiding, an unexpected but charming contrast to the man's ruggedly handsome features. "If you didn't show up within the next twenty-four hours, I'd decided to round up a posse and find you."

He'd planned to return to Dallas? For her?

No, not for you. For Rob, she reminded herself sternly. An internal dash of cold water on the warmth his words stirred in her heart.

It would be a mistake to forget the reason she was here. To Carter, delivering Rob's message had been a duty. An obligation. But Savannah had an obligation, too. To do everything she could to protect the health of her unborn child. Even if it meant swallowing her pride and accepting help from a stranger.

"I hope this isn't a bad time," she stammered. "I probably should have called first."

Except that if she'd dialed Carter's number any earlier, Savannah knew she would have lost not only her voice, but her nerve. She'd packed her suitcase that morning and stowed it in the trunk of the car, giving God what she hoped was ample opportunity to send some kind of sign that He had another plan. One that *didn't* include Carter Wallace.

Yet here she was.

"I didn't call before I showed up at your door that day, either," Carter said easily. "So I guess that makes us even."

No, they weren't. Not until he understood that she didn't intend to be a charity case or outstay her welcome here. She'd scheduled another appointment with Dr. Yardley in two weeks. If the test results proved that she was obeying orders, Savannah planned to ask for an increase in her hours at the diner again and continue her search for another apartment.

"I can pay rent." Savannah didn't look at Carter as she put the car into gear and continued down the long gravel driveway. "I don't expect to live in the cottage for free. Or I can help out around the house or in the kitchen. I'm a pretty decent cook."

At one time, she'd dreamed of attending culinary school. Before she'd met Rob.

"Chicken and dumplings are your specialty, right?"

"How did you know…" Savannah's voice trailed off, leaving an awkward silence in its wake.

Rob must have told him.

The day they'd met, Carter had claimed that Rob talked about her all the time when they'd served together in Afghanistan. Savannah hadn't believed him—until now. The thought that Rob's friend knew more about her than she knew about him was a little unsettling.

And what else had Rob told him? The truth—or more lies? Less than twenty-four hours after they were married, Savannah had discovered that her new husband didn't seem to know the difference. She'd been so tired of being alone that she'd let Rob sweep her off her feet.

Believed everything he'd said…

"Don't worry about things like paying rent or washing dishes right now." Savannah could feel the weight of Carter's gaze, studying her profile. "How about I show you where you'll be staying first? You can unpack your things. Settle in and get a good night's sleep."

Which could only be, Savannah thought ruefully, a tactful way of saying that she must look as exhausted as she felt.

"All right." Self-consciously, she looped a wayward strand of hair behind her ear. She knew the past few days had taken a toll on both her health and her emotions. The stress of apartment hunting during the day. Wrestling with her fears at night. Savannah had been reading through the New Testament every morning, taking comfort in the fact that other believers had faced difficult situations, too, and God hadn't abandoned them.

She trusted Him. Men, not so much anymore.

"Keep going past the main house," Carter instructed.

The simple description didn't do the place justice.

Savannah tried not to gawk as they passed a magnificent two-story home fashioned from native stone and brick. The setting sun winked off the mullioned windows and painted the glass with a rosy, welcoming glow. Trumpet vine wove through the spindles of the wrought-iron fence that separated the landscaped lawn from the rest of the property.

Everything was neat and well cared for. The Colby Ranch could have easily been featured on the cover of *Texas Today* magazine.

"It's beautiful," Savannah murmured. "Did you grow up here?"

"No."

Savannah tried not to flinch at the sting of Carter's curt response. Although he seemed to know a lot about her, it was becoming clear that Carter wasn't going to be very forthcoming about his own life.

Carter saw Savannah's hands tighten around the steering wheel and realized the word had come out a little sharper than he'd intended. He tried again.

"No," he said more softly.

One-syllable words were okay on a military base, but if he wanted Savannah to stay at the ranch, it was clear to Carter that he would have to brush up on his people skills. He could coax a disabled vehicle back to life and make an engine purr like a kitten, but he'd never been much for small talk.

Especially when the woman sitting next to him took his breath away.

The photograph hadn't done her justice. Savannah's honey-brown hair fell loose around her shoulders, a perfect frame for her delicate features and wide green eyes.

The only thing missing was the smile.

Carter still hadn't seen one of those.

When he'd heard her voice on the phone, he couldn't believe that Savannah had actually accepted his invitation. Not until he'd spotted her car parked at the gate. Both hands gripping the steering wheel, ready to turn around and exit his life as quickly as she'd entered it.

He wasn't sure why Savannah had changed her mind, but now that she was here at the Colby Ranch, Carter was going to make sure she stuck around for a while.

It's what Rob would have wanted.

Carter was certain about that, no matter what Savannah had said about their marriage. Why would Rob fake devotion to a wife that he'd abandoned? What would he have to gain?

Savannah might need a place to stay, but Carter needed some answers. And the woman sitting next to him was the only one who could provide them.

Another light winked on in the house. Carter hoped no one would glance out the window and see an unfamiliar vehicle nudging its way up the drive. Typically after Lupita served dessert, everyone pitched in and cleaned up from dinner and then gathered in the family room to watch a movie or play a game. Ty and Maddie would help Darcy with her homework. Jack and Gray would take part in what had become their favorite pastime—giving each other a hard time—while the women planned their upcoming nuptials with all the intensity of a military strategist.

And they insisted he join them.

Bonding, Maddie called it. Carter figured it was easier to bond with people who shared your DNA. He'd never had much in common with his siblings before, and now he was no longer sure he and Gray had *that* in common.

Carter would count the seconds until he could come up with a reasonable excuse to slip away. But now, for the first time, he hoped they followed standard protocol again and did not show up at the cottage to meet the newest visitor. It might overwhelm Savannah and give her a reason to bolt.

She didn't trust him, that much was clear.

But Rob had. Which meant that Carter was honor bound to shield her from potentially stressful situations.

Meeting his family definitely qualified.

Savannah fixed her eyes on the driveway.

The sudden drop in temperature inside the car made

her wonder if there was some family dynamic going on between Carter and his sister that she should know about. The last thing she wanted was for her presence to add tension to an already strained relationship.

"You can take the first right behind the barn." Carter pointed to an enormous metal building with a green roof. Two chestnut horses stood shoulder to shoulder in a corner of the paddock, dozing under the branches of a cottonwood tree.

Savannah followed his instructions and saw a row of adorable little cottages scattered along a creek bed.

"I've been staying in the main house but the cottage on the end is empty. My sister had it all made up for me, but I never moved in. That means it's all yours," Carter said.

Yours.

In spite of her misgivings, the word flowed through Savannah, as sweet as a glass of tea on a hot summer day. Even knowing this was a temporary arrangement couldn't prevent the sense of wonder that swept over her.

The branches of two mature pecan trees formed a canopy over a cottage as whimsical as an illustration in a child's storybook. A sloping roof with patchwork shingles shaded an enclosed porch like the brim of a hat. Narrow wooden shutters trimmed the windows. Blue. Her favorite color. A hand-woven basket, overflowing with gourds and miniature pumpkins, sat on the top step like a welcome gift.

An Australian shepherd emerged from one of the outbuildings and ambled toward the car as Savannah pulled up in front of the cottage.

"That's Nipper. Jack Colby's dog." Carter shook his head. "Don't let the name fool you, though. The only thing that mutt might do is lick you to death."

"Is Jack part of your family?"

"That's the question of the day," he muttered.

Savannah frowned. "I don't understand."

But Carter didn't bother to enlighten her. Instead, he hopped out and jogged around the front of the car to open her door. His large hand gently cupped her elbow as he helped her out of the vehicle.

The warmth of his touch sparked something that sent Savannah's blood racing through her veins like a prairie fire.

She sucked in a breath, yanked her heart back in line.

It wasn't as if she were...*attracted*...to Carter Wallace. More than likely sleepless nights and low blood sugar had tipped her off balance.

Guard your heart, Savannah.

Savannah had forgotten her grandmother's advice when she'd met Rob. She wasn't about to make the same mistake again.

"Come on. I'll show you the inside."

Savannah balked. "You're sure that your sister won't mind an extra houseguest?"

Carter glanced in the direction of the main house. The flash of some emotion—*guilt?*—didn't exactly put her mind at ease.

"Sergeant Wallace?"

"It's Carter, remember?" That elusive dimple made an appearance again. A secret weapon designed to sneak through a woman's defenses and affect her ability to think straight.

Fortunately, Savannah had become immune to a charming smile.

"Now that we've got that cleared up...how about answering my question?"

Chapter Five

Carter realized he'd made a tactical error. He should have known that Savannah would see through his pitiful attempt to sidestep the question before she unpacked her suitcase from the car.

"No one will mind a bit that you're here." Carter hoped it was true.

According to Maddie, the Colby family had taken Keira Wolfe in after she'd been injured in a car accident and suffered short-term memory loss. The veterinarian was now Jack's fiancé and staying in a guest room down the hall until the couple exchanged their vows. Violet also made room for Landon Derringer and Elise and her son, Cory, during their frequent visits to the ranch. Even in the midst of their own problems, it seemed that Violet and Jack didn't mind lending a helping hand to someone in need. And Savannah definitely qualified.

He couldn't help feeling protective of her. It wasn't that she appeared weak and helpless. Just the opposite. It couldn't be easy to accept help from strangers, and yet Savannah had done the best thing for her and the baby. He respected that. He respected *her*.

Relief took some of the starch out of Savannah's slender shoulders. "That's good, because I don't want to take advantage of your sister's hospitality."

Carter decided this might be a good time to clarify a few minor details. After all, Savannah would find them out sooner or later. Although if he had his way, later—*much* later—would be better.

"Maddie doesn't actually own the ranch," he admitted. "She's a…guest…here, too."

Savannah, who'd started up the narrow sidewalk, froze midstep. Twisted around to look at him.

"A guest?" she repeated.

"Belle Colby actually owns the Colby Ranch. Maddie is spending some time with Belle's…daughter."

Violet. Maddie's identical twin sister. His long lost *half* sister. Carter could barely make sense of what had happened, let alone try to explain it to someone else. And something told him this wasn't the time to launch into a lengthy explanation about the Wallace family tree. The one that had sprouted a few branches since his last deployment.

"So Belle Colby gave you permission to invite me here?" Savannah asked slowly.

Carter drove a hand through his hair. "Belle is…recovering from a riding accident that happened last summer. She's in a long-term care facility in Grasslands right now, but the family is…hopeful that she'll recover."

Savannah's lips parted but no sound came out. She glanced down at the keys clutched in her hand and Carter realized she was only seconds away from getting in the car and driving back to Dallas if he didn't explain.

"It's complicated." Really complicated.

Savannah's eyes narrowed. "What exactly is going on, Sergeant?" she demanded. "Are you dispensing information on a need-to-know basis only? Because if that's the case, I need to know a whole lot more before I accept your invitation to stay here."

Carter suppressed a smile. Savannah was downright beautiful when she got riled up. She got some color in her cheeks and those eyes…as green as cottonwood leaves.

"Fine. I'll try to explain. But keep in mind that sometimes truth is stranger than fiction—"

"There you are!"

Carter slowly turned around. Great. Just great.

Walking toward them was the proof.

"Is that Maddie?" Savannah whispered.

Carter's eyes narrowed on the young woman striding toward them. Brown-and-gold-plaid shirt, complete with pearl buttons. A silver belt buckle roughly the size of a paperback novel.

And he still couldn't say for sure.

At some point over the past few months, Maddie had swapped her designer labels for Western wear. To make life even more interesting, the two women conspired together, taking an almost fiendish delight in making it difficult for people—like him—to figure out which one was which. Or who was who.

"Maybe."

"Maybe?" Savannah choked.

"I told you. It's—"

"Complicated?" A huff of frustration punctuated the sentence.

"Right."

"Darcy said she heard a car come up the driveway." The flip of a long copper ponytail provided the clue that Carter had been looking for.

Violet.

Once Maddie's hair got longer and she could copy her twin sister's hairstyle, he was going to be in big trouble.

"Now I know why you ran off before dessert." Violet gave him an I'll-deal-with-you-later look but smiled warmly at Savannah. "Who do we have here?"

Carter caught the brunt of Savannah's accusing gaze.

Okay. He already *was* in big trouble.

Knowing that Carter hadn't been completely honest left a bitter taste in Savannah's mouth.

She was going to have a few choice words with the man. But at the moment, Savannah had no idea what to say to the woman standing in front of her. The one whose eyes were bright with curiosity—and who obviously had no idea that Carter had invited a pregnant stranger to stay with them.

"This is Savannah Blackmore." Carter came to her rescue.

Nice of him, since he was the reason she was in this awkward predicament to begin with!

Good manners forced Savannah to clasp the hand the woman offered when what she really wanted to do was hide. "Hello."

"Savannah, Violet Colby—" For some reason, Carter stopped.

"Carter's sister." The woman nudged him aside and finished the introduction.

Savannah felt Carter stiffen beside her.

"You're Carter's…sister?"

And why hadn't he mentioned that when he'd talked about Maddie?

"When he wants to claim me." Violet smiled sweetly at her brother.

Carter shifted his weight, almost as if he were uncomfortable with the direction the conversation was going.

Well, good, Savannah thought. Why should she be the only one?

Savannah's gaze bounced back and forth between Carter and Violet Colby but she failed to find even the slightest resemblance between them. Carter was blond and blue-eyed while Violet's hair, as bright as a new penny, framed an oval face dominated by a pair of eyes the color of dark chocolate.

"Savannah lost her apartment a few days ago," Carter explained. "I was hoping it would be okay if she bunked in one of the cottages for a while."

"I'd like to rent it," Savannah interjected. "If that's all right with you."

Violet was already shaking her head. And even though Savannah had been ready to drive away a few minutes ago, the thought of leaving the Colby Ranch left her with a sudden, inexplicable chill.

"Renting is out of the question," Violet Colby said firmly. "We always make room for friends. And you and Carter are friends, right?"

Savannah didn't dare look at Carter. They weren't friends. She wasn't quite sure what they were.

"Savannah's husband, Rob, and I were stationed together in Afghanistan," Carter said quietly. "I promised him that I'd check on her when I came back to the States. Make sure she was doing all right. There was a misunderstanding with her lease and she needed a place to stay."

"Just for a few days," Savannah choked out, feeling the sting of Rob's betrayal all over again.

He'd asked Carter to check up on her?

Every letter she'd sent to Rob had been returned, unopened. At any time, he could have picked up the phone and called to find out how she was doing. But he hadn't. And then suddenly, it had been too late.

Savannah hadn't known there'd been another part to the promise Rob had held Carter to other than the one he'd delivered, but it explained why he'd offered her a place to stay. Left his number so she could get in touch with him if she changed her mind.

Violet's gaze dropped to Savannah's midsection for a split second before lifting again.

"You're more than welcome to move in for as long as you'd like." The genuine sincerity in her voice convinced Savannah more than the actual words. "My mom is one of those people who believes in sharing the blessings we've been given. She would want you to stay here. And so do I."

Savannah's grandmother had been the same way. Edith Callahan reached out to those in need whether they needed a hot meal or a hug. Or a place to stay. Savannah had witnessed it countless times, she'd just never expected to be the one on the receiving end.

"Thank you." Savannah felt tears sting the back of her eyes. "I…I don't mind helping out, either—"

"We agreed to talk about that later, didn't we?" Carter cut in.

"Was that an agreement?" Savannah tipped her head. "Because it sounded like an order to me."

"Well, I am a sergeant. So technically, I outrank you." Carter had the audacity to *wink* at her.

Savannah knew she should have been irritated by the outrageous statement. So why did she have to fight a sudden, overwhelming urge to smile?

A polite cough pulled her attention back to Violet. There was a speculative gleam in the chocolate-brown eyes; her expression disturbingly similar to the look Savannah had seen on Libby's face the day Carter had walked into the diner.

"Carter's right. We'll have plenty of time to talk about that later." Violet linked arms with her. "I'll show you the cottage and rustle up some fresh linens for the bed. If you don't think you'll be comfortable here, we can probably squeeze you in somewhere at the main house. But I have to warn you, there's a lot of hustle and bustle going on around the place."

Savannah didn't mention that she would welcome a little hustle and bustle. She'd lived a solitary life after her grandmother had passed away the previous year. The loneliness had briefly subsided during her whirlwind courtship with Rob, only to return with a vengeance when he'd left her a week after they'd exchanged vows.

Long days had slipped into sleepless nights. Until she'd found out that she was pregnant. An unexpected blessing but one that had turned her world upside down. Especially after any hope of reconciliation had ended with Rob's death.

Violet flipped on the porch light and pushed open the front door. "It's not very big," she warned. "But it's cozy."

Savannah felt tears sting the back of her eyes as she took in her surroundings.

The inside of the cottage was as quaint as the exterior. A pocket-size kitchen. Colorful rag rugs. Corduroy furniture with oversize cushions, as deep and inviting as feather pillows.

She'd dreamed of a place like this.

"Not quite what you expected, huh?"

Carter was suddenly standing beside her and Savannah realized he'd mistaken silence for disappointment.

"I didn't expect it to be—" She fumbled for the right description.

"So small?" Carter supplied.

Savannah shook her head.

"So...perfect."

"Perfect?" Carter's husky laugh rumbled out, wrapping around Savannah like one of the quilts that Violet was pulling out of the antique armoire in the corner.

"I know what you mean. I love the cottages, too." Violet shot him a quelling look. "But I love them even more when they're being used, so please, make yourself at home."

Savannah already felt at home. That was a problem she hadn't anticipated. She would accept the Colby's hospitality for one or two weeks. No longer. She would be gone by Thanksgiving. Gone before she grew too attached to the sunsets and fresh air and a blue sky that stretched for miles, giving her space to breathe.

Gone before Carter's smile had a chance to work its way into her heart.

Carter took a restless lap around the living room as Violet took charge. Compared to the apartment Savannah had been living in, he had to agree the cottage was an improvement.

"You should be warm enough tonight with a few extra blankets but I'll ask Jack to drop off a load of wood for the fireplace tomorrow. The weather around here can be as contrary as his favorite bull."

"Is Jack your husband?"

Violet's eyes widened in response to Savannah's innocent question. Which made him feel guilty. Carter didn't have to be an identical twin to know what Violet was thinking. If he and Savannah were close enough friends to warrant an invitation to stay at the ranch, wouldn't he have filled her in on some of his complicated family history?

"Older brother," she replied evenly. "Jack runs the cattle part of the Colby Ranch. I manage the truck farm and produce stand in town."

"I see," Savannah murmured.

Carter had no doubt about that whatsoever. Just like Violet, Savannah could see that he'd left out a few pertinent details when he'd invited her to stay at the ranch.

"I'll make up the bed while you unpack your things." Violet frowned and looked around. "Where is your suitcase?"

"It's still in the trunk of my car."

Violet looked at him now, eyebrow lifted, and Carter shook his head. No *way* he was leaving them alone. He didn't want to take the chance that Violet might accidentally ask Savannah questions that would open old wounds.

She ignored him—just like Maddie would have.

"Carter? Will you be a sweetheart and get Savannah's things while I find some fresh sheets for the bed?"

Carter had enlisted in the military five years ago, the ink barely dry on his high school diploma. In spite of the sugarcoating on the words, he recognized a direct order when he heard one.

"Sure." He spun toward the door. It wasn't that he didn't trust Violet. He didn't *know* her.

But if she and Maddie were identical when it came to busybody tendencies, Carter figured he had better hurry.

Flecks of rust rained onto his boots when he lifted the trunk. Through a gaping hole in the metal, Carter could see the ground.

Rob had hinted that life had been good. He'd bragged about the house that he and Savannah planned to build, bordered by gardens because she loved flowers. Yellow roses, in particular.

So why was she driving an old beater with close to two-hundred-thousand miles on it?

There were a hundred questions Carter wanted to ask, but couldn't. Not yet. He'd seen the look on her face when Violet introduced herself. Savannah had assumed that he had lied to her. But the accusing look she'd tossed his way hadn't been the worst part. It was the look of resignation riding in its wake. As if she'd been *expecting* it.

Rob, what did you do?

And why had he thought that Carter could somehow make it right?

He grabbed Savannah's suitcase, a plaid relic as ancient as the car she drove, and made his way back to the cottage before Violet had a chance to interrogate Savannah about her personal life.

As his foot touched the top step, Violet's cheerful drawl stopped him in his tracks.

"So, how far along are you, Savannah?"

Carter winced.

Too late.

Chapter Six

"I'm back."

Carter lunged through the doorway and held up the suit-case, hoping to distract Violet.

She didn't so much as glance his way. Neither did Savannah.

Carter had been afraid this would happen. He dropped the suitcase with a thud. That didn't have the desired effect, either, although Violet did hold up one hand. Carter wasn't sure if she was acknowledging his presence or trying to shush him.

"You can put that in the bedroom, Carter."

Definitely the second one. Carter wondered if the bandana dangling from Violet's back pocket could be used as a muzzle.

Violet nodded at Savannah with a smile that encouraged her to continue.

"I'm six months along." The faintest hint of pink stained Savannah's cheeks.

Violet tipped her head. "So that means your baby is due sometime in February."

Savannah nodded. "The fourteenth."

"Really? Valentine's Day?" The woman who'd just tried

to shush him released a piercing whistle, only several decibels lower than the one she used to summon her horse from the pasture. "That's awesome."

Carter silently did the math. Rob had been deployed the first week of June. The dates lined up with Savannah's claim that Rob had left her right before he enlisted.

The first time they'd met, his friend had bragged about his new wife. Her sweet personality. How beautiful she was.

But for some reason, Rob had neglected to mention that they'd been estranged before his death. Which meant that either his buddy's acting skills would have been worthy of an Academy Award—or Savannah was the one who wasn't being truthful about their relationship.

Neither possibility sat well with Carter.

"You must be pretty excited," Violet continued. "Do you know if you're having a boy or a girl?"

Carter cleared his throat. A less than subtle warning not to pry and one that Violet, of course, chose to ignore.

"I think—" Carter began. And then discovered that he couldn't. The simple ability to string several words together splintered under the impact of the smile that spread across Savannah's face.

Carter watched, mesmerized, as the woman in the photograph came to life right in front of his eyes. The sparkle in her eyes chased the shadows away until it looked as if she were lit from within.

"It's a girl," she said softly.

Violet reached down to plump one of the sofa cushions. "Do you have any names picked out?"

Carter opened his mouth. Closed it again. Not because he wanted to know if Savannah had any names picked out, but because she was *still* smiling. She didn't look uncomfortable or upset by Violet's questions. Questions that

Carter hadn't thought to ask. Until this moment, he hadn't thought of the baby as being a separate person. A child who was going to grow up without knowing her father.

Because of him.

"Her name is Hope."

"Is that a family name?"

"No." Savannah settled one hand almost protectively on the rounded curve of her stomach. "It's a…reminder."

Something passed between her and Violet then. A look of understanding that told Carter the two women shared the same strong faith.

A few years ago, he wouldn't have felt like someone on the outside looking in. At the age of five, with Rachel's gentle guidance, Carter had knelt by his bed one night and prayed a child's simple prayer, asking Jesus to come into his heart. But somewhere along the way, life had become more complicated. Carter had witnessed people doing terrible things to each other—seen things that still haunted his dreams. He'd begun to think that God was as distant and unapproachable as his father.

Savannah had been through a lot the past few months and yet she hadn't turned her back on God. If she ever married again, it would be to a man whose faith was as solid as her own. A man who didn't have more questions than answers.

Married again?

Carter mentally slapped himself upside the head for even thinking along those lines. He'd provided Savannah with a place to stay. He planned to keep a discreet eye on her— from a distance. It was all he'd promised to do.

It was all he *could* do…

"I think Hope is a beautiful name. Don't you, Carter?"

Carter realized that Violet was talking to him now. He'd

been distracted by the way the setting sun filtered through the curtains and picked out golden threads in Savannah's hair.

"Beautiful," he agreed absently.

Color flooded Savannah's cheeks and she averted her gaze.

Way to go, Wallace. Open mouth, insert combat boot.

Laughter danced in Violet's eyes. "I was talking about the name Savannah picked out for the baby. What were *you* talking about?"

"You and Maddie *are* alike," he muttered.

As if on cue, the front door swung open.

"Did someone say my name?"

Savannah's mouth dropped open as a young woman breezed into the cottage. A woman who, from the top of her shining copper hair to the silver tips on the toes of her cowboy boots, was the mirror image of Violet Colby.

"I thought I saw lights on over here. What's going on?" She parked her hands on her hips and looked around. Big brown eyes got even bigger when she spotted Savannah standing in the kitchen but she quickly recovered. "Hello."

Savannah glanced Carter's way, but he didn't seem inclined to rescue her this time. Call her crazy, but she got the distinct impression that *he* was the one who looked like he needed rescuing.

"Hi." Savannah scraped up a smile in response to the woman's cheerful greeting.

"This is Savannah," Violet interjected.

"Maddie Wallace."

So there really *was* a Maddie. Savannah supposed she should be grateful that Carter had told her the truth about that, even though he'd omitted a few other significant details about his family.

Like the fact that Maddie and Violet Colby were identical twins.

"Nice to meet you, Savannah." Maddie's smile grew and she turned to her sister. "I didn't realize we were expecting company this evening."

Carter didn't so much as blink, drat the man.

"That's all right." Savannah resisted the urge to cast a reproachful look in his direction. "Neither did Violet."

Maddie's forehead pleated, a sign of her confusion.

"Savannah is Carter's friend," Violet said helpfully. "She had some issues with her last apartment and needed a place to stay."

"Only for a few days." Savannah found herself repeating the words that were quickly becoming her theme song.

Violet pulled a set of bedsheets from another cabinet and the scent of lavender stirred the air. "I told her that we've got plenty of room."

"That's true enough." Maddie sauntered into the tiny living room. "Is there anything I can help with?"

"No, thanks. I think we're good," Violet told her twin.

Savannah cringed inwardly.

Although touched by their kindness, she didn't want Carter's sisters to feel like they had to fuss over her. Given the fact that Maddie and Violet hadn't known she was coming, they were handling her arrival with remarkable aplomb.

And neither one of them seemed to be in a hurry to leave.

Maddie reached for a stack of towels at the same time as Violet. They looked at each other and started to laugh.

In spite of her misgivings about Carter, Savannah couldn't help but be fascinated by the two women. She was an only child who had dreamed of having a large family someday, but to have an identical twin sister? She couldn't imagine what that would be like....

"Weird, isn't it?" Maddie grinned.

Savannah felt her cheeks heat up. "I'm sorry. I didn't mean to stare."

"That's okay." Violet gave Savannah's arm a friendly pat. "Most of the time, Carter can't tell us apart, either."

Shaking his head, Carter grumbled, "It might help if you didn't *dress* alike."

Maddie hooked her thumbs in the front pockets of her jeans and stuck out a foot. "Maybe it's the boots," she mused.

"Or the matching belt buckles?" Carter said under his breath.

"Well, it certainly can't be the Texas drawl." Maddie looked smug. "I've been practicing, *y'all*."

Carter rolled his eyes.

"That's right. You'll be speaking fluent cowgirl in no time," Violet teased.

Maddie turned to Savannah. "Where are you from?"

Carter shifted his stance, a movement that blocked Maddie from her view. Savannah got the distinct impression it wasn't an accident.

"I think we should leave Savannah alone so she can settle in. She's probably tired from the long drive." Carter's voice sounded strange. Almost as if he were gritting his teeth.

"You're right." Maddie peeked around his shoulder and smiled at Savannah. "How long of a drive *was* it?"

"I live in Dallas."

Carter cleared his throat.

"Catching a cold, little brother?" Maddie patted his arm.

"Lupita has a special remedy that will fix you up." Violet flashed an impish look. "But don't worry, it tastes bet-ter than it smells."

Maddie and Violet snickered. In harmony.

Savannah decided that she liked Carter's sisters already. "Is that where you and Carter met? In Dallas?"

Savannah nodded, wondering why Carter seemed tense. It wasn't as if the questions she was being asked were dif-ficult—

"How long have you two known each other?"

Except for that one.

Savannah swallowed hard, unsure of how to answer the question. What would Carter's sisters think of her if she told them that she'd met him less than a week ago? Would they think she was taking advantage of their hospitality?

"Not very long—"

"For a while."

Savannah's statement collided with Carter's in midair, leaving her momentarily speechless.

How could Carter stand there and tell his sisters some-thing that wasn't true?

Two pairs of matching brown eyes bounced back and forth between her and Carter.

Now that the two women stood side by side, Savan-nah could see subtle differences between the two. Violet's complexion tinted bronze from the sun, evidence of hours spent outdoors. And Maddie's auburn hair was an inch or two shorter than her sister's....

Savannah groaned when she saw Maddie grin at her twin. "I'm doing it again, aren't I?"

"Don't worry. Violet and I are still getting used to it," Violet said.

"Getting used to what?" Savannah asked curiously.

"Seeing each other. I mean, we met five months ago, but it's weird to see your face on someone else."

Savannah tried to hide her confusion. And her rising frustration with the one person in the room who'd only said that his family situation was *complicated*.

Violet looked at Maddie. Who looked at her brother. They folded their arms.

"You didn't tell her."

Carter had never seen a simple mission go south quite the way this one had.

"I thought she might want to wait for the movie."

"Ignore my brother, Savannah," Maddie huffed. "He has a warped sense of humor."

Carter gave her a look. "It certainly helps in this family."

"Violet and I met for the first time last summer," Maddie explained. "She *accidentally* found me. After Landon found her, that is."

"We were pretty shocked," her sister added.

Shocked wasn't exactly the word Carter would have chosen.

"You didn't grow up together?" Savannah pressed her hand against her lips the moment the words slipped out.

"Neither of us knew the other one existed. I grew up on the ranch and she grew up in the city, but we're hoping it didn't cause irreversible damage."

Carter knew Violet was teasing, her own attempt to lighten the moment, but the words hit too close to home. Whatever the circumstances had been that caused Belle and his father to part ways, they wouldn't be able to undo the damage they'd inflicted on their children. Maddie and Violet. Gray and Jack. None of them could recover the years they'd lost.

Something must have shown in his expression, because Maddie looked at Violet and shook her head.

"It's a long story," she murmured. "I'm sure Carter will explain everything when he has some time."

Savannah glanced at him, and Carter saw the doubt shimmering in her eyes. He'd had the time, when she questioned him on the way to the cottage.

Savannah grasped the back of a chair with both hands, a weary gesture that brought him to her side in an instant.

"Are you all right?"

Savannah's teeth sank into her lower lip. "A little tired, I guess."

"That's it. We're out of here." Violet gave the afghan draped over the back of the sofa a final pat.

"Is there anything else you need before you turn in for the night?" Maddie asked.

"I'll be fine. Really."

Savannah's smile was convincing. Almost.

"We'll see you in the morning, then. Lupita is making her famous buttermilk pancakes." Violet tossed a smile over her shoulder as she walked with Maddie to the door. "If you need anything, just give a holler."

Finally.

Carter tried to conceal his relief. Once Maddie and Violet were out of the way, he could do damage control. Although he couldn't shake the sneaking suspicion that he'd been the one responsible for the damage in the first place.

His plan was thwarted when Maddie reached out and grabbed his hand.

"You're coming with us, Carter. Violet and I need your help with something, too."

Before Carter could protest, Violet had taken hold of his other hand.

"Two against one?" he muttered.

He thought he heard someone laugh. But when he looked

over his shoulder, Savannah was already disappearing into the bedroom.

"You better get used to it." Maddie smiled sweetly.

Carter, who knew a dozen ways to extricate himself from a difficult situation, found himself being herded out of the cottage and up the driveway like one of Jack's stray calves.

Chapter Seven

Carter saw a light on in the kitchen and hoped it was Gray. His brother would recognize a hostage situation and intervene. After all, the guy *was* a professional.

Unfortunately, it was Keira, Jack's fiancée, who sat at the table, hands cradling a steaming cup of tea, a stethoscope still draped around her neck.

No help there. One of Maddie and Violet's allies, not his.

"Hey, ya'll." The veterinarian looked up as they shuffled past the doorway, Maddie and Violet attached to his side like a pair of amateur country line dancers. "Care to join me?"

"Sure," Violet sang out.

Maddie bobbed her head. "We'll be right back. We have to talk to Carter for a minute."

Talk?

Carter wasn't fooled by Maddie's bright smile. He was being hauled in for questioning.

"Aren't I entitled to a phone call?" he quipped.

"No."

Carter winced when the emphatic retort rang in both his ears at the exact same moment.

"My favorite meal?"

"Move it, soldier."

Violet kicked the door shut in some cowgirl-ninja move that left Carter inwardly shaking his head. Then he was free.

Sort of.

"Okay, let's hear it." They folded their arms, stared him down.

Carter felt like he was back in boot camp, under the gimlet eye of his commanding officer and resisted a crazy urge to salute.

"Everything," Violet said promptly.

"And don't even bother to waste our time with that name, rank and serial-number stuff," Maddie warned. "You know what she means."

Carter checked a smile. "You've been watching too many old movies."

"And you're stalling." Maddie's chin hiked up a notch. "Why didn't you tell us you invited Savannah to the ranch?"

"Because the first time I asked her, she turned me down." Flat. "I didn't think she would change her mind."

Maddie and Violet exchanged a look.

"That's why you moved into Gray's room instead of taking the cottage Violet offered," Maddie said slowly. "You were *hoping* that she would."

He couldn't argue with that, either. "Savannah didn't have anywhere else to go. She planned to stay in a hotel while she looked for another apartment."

Maddie continued to study him and Carter could almost see the wheels turning in her head.

"When we were at Gray's apartment the day you got back, you mentioned there was someone you had to see before you came to the ranch. Was it Savannah?"

Maybe Maddie should have been the detective in the family.

"Yes."

"You've never mentioned her before. How do you two know each other?"

Carter felt a hitch in his breathing.

"Her husband, Rob—" He managed to push the name out, past the lump that instantly formed in his throat. "He asked me to check on Savannah when I got back to the States."

"Then I'd say it's a good thing you did. Will he be home for Thanksgiving?"

Violet's innocent question landed like a punch to the gut. Pain radiated through his body, leaving Carter unable to do anything but shake his head.

He hadn't talked to his siblings about what happened to Rob. How did you put something like that in an email? Every time he said Rob's name, it was ripping the bandage from a fresh wound.

For the first time since he'd come home, Carter understood why Maddie and Gray had waited to share the news of their father's disappearance in person.

"You wrote that one of your friends was killed," Maddie whispered. "Were you talking about Savannah's husband?"

"He died in a roadside bombing two months ago." In Carter's arms.

The color drained from Violet's face. "Savannah must be devastated."

"And she's expecting." Maddie briefly closed her eyes. "I can't imagine what she's going through. Knowing that her husband will never have the chance to hold his child."

The child he hadn't known about.

The thought never made it past Carter's lips. Better to let them think that everything between Rob and Savannah had been fine. Until a week ago, it was what he'd believed, too.

Accepting the alternative was the equivalent of accepting Rob's death all over again…and he wasn't ready to do that. Not yet.

"Does she have any family?"

Carter had wondered the same thing. He'd tried to recall if Rob had mentioned anything about parents. Siblings. "I'm not sure. I don't think so."

"Well, she has us now," Violet said. "I meant what I said when I told Savannah that she is welcome to stay as long as she'd like."

"Thank you." Carter meant it, but suddenly it didn't seem like enough. "And I'm sorry I overstepped my bounds. I should have asked your permission to invite Savannah to the ranch."

Violet acknowledged the statement with a jerky nod, pivoting toward the door as if she couldn't get away from him fast enough now.

"Violet?"

She stopped and reluctantly turned to face him.

"Is something else bothering you?" Carter asked cautiously.

"Yes." Hurt flashed in Violet's eyes. "Your apology."

Apparently he'd somehow messed that up, too. "This is your home and I had no right to invite someone to stay here without asking your permission first—"

"Stop right there."

Carter stopped.

"You don't *have* to apologize at all."

"I don't?"

"I want you to think of the ranch as your home."

Violet's chin lifted and she looked him straight in the eye. "And do you know why?"

She didn't wait for him to answer.

"Because like it or not, Carter, *I'm* your sister, too."

The door closed softly behind her.

* * *

A peaceful silence settled into the corners of the room as Savannah started to unpack her things into a stout antique dresser next to the bed.

The faint scent of lavender from a sachet tucked in the corner stirred the air, soothed the raw edges of her emotions. Already she could feel her heart settling into the beauty of her surroundings.

Framed in the weathered window frame, a star winked against the indigo sky. A sky the same shade of blue as Carter's eyes....

Savannah yanked the unruly thought back in line.

She didn't want to think about Carter. And she certainly didn't want to notice the man's eyes.

Or the emotion she'd seen lingering there, one Savannah recognized all too well in spite of his attempt to hide it.

Pain.

The comment he'd made about his family situation being complicated made sense in light of what she'd just found out.

Identical twins, separated. Why?

Savannah felt a delicate flutter below her rib cage and the rush of love that inevitably followed in its wake. She would do anything to protect her child.

Maybe Carter's parents had felt the same way. Had circumstances forced them to separate their daughters?

The deep affection between Violet and Maddie appeared genuine. Real. But judging from some of the comments Carter had made in the car, he didn't think of the Colby ranch as home. He'd claimed Maddie as his sister, but not Violet. And if Jack Colby was Violet's older brother, didn't that mean he was Carter's brother, too?

Savannah was beginning to believe that Carter hadn't

been exaggerating when he'd described his family situation as "complicated."

But where did he fit in the equation…and in the family?

Not that it was any of her business. Carter had provided Savannah with a place to stay, not given her access to his personal life.

She had her own secrets to keep. Things that Carter wouldn't want to know, considering that he and Rob had been friends.

The less time she spent in his company, the better. Carter Wallace was too observant, attuned to the slightest change in her expression the way he would notice a shift in the wind. Savannah didn't need—or want—that kind of attention. It could only lead to trouble.

He was a soldier. Hardwired to defend. Protect. It would be too easy to rest her head on that broad shoulder. Seek shelter and safety in his arms.

She'd trusted Rob and look what had happened. Now she was determined to make a new start for her and the baby.

Savannah smoothed out a wrinkle in the quilt and straightened one of the decorative pillows, a square of faded pink muslin with a verse from the Bible neatly embroidered inside the hedge of delicate ruffles.

Rejoice always. Pray without ceasing. In everything give thanks.

Her grandmother would have approved, especially the giving thanks part. She could still hear Edith Callahan's lilting voice.

Count to ten, Savannah. Count to ten.

As always, her grandmother had put her own unique spin on the familiar advice. It hadn't been a reminder to hold her tongue or her temper. Her grandmother encouraged Savannah to count her blessings—and not to stop until she got to ten.

Savannah had embraced the words. In elementary school, when she struggled to fit in at her new school after her parents had divorced and left her in the care of her elderly grandmother because neither of them wanted their daughter along the journey to find themselves. During her senior year of high school, when Edith's health started to decline following a stroke that put Savannah in charge of the tiny household. The last few months of Edith's life, when Savannah dropped out of college to take care of her.

There were times in Savannah's life when she'd flown past ten and kept right on going—and times when it took every ounce of strength to reach that particular number.

Like the day Rob had told her that their marriage had been a mistake. The day he'd walked out the door without looking back.

Savannah closed her eyes. Shut out the memories of the past that threatened to drag her down again. Focused on the present.

Tonight it wasn't difficult at all to find things to be thankful for. Her car hadn't broken down on the way to Grasslands. A place to stay. Space to think. Room to breathe. Violet. Maddie…

Savannah stopped, afraid to add the name that hovered at the edges of the prayer. It didn't matter. He appeared in her thoughts, anyway.

The man whose smile threatened to sneak through her defenses when she'd promised herself she would never let her guard down again.

Carter stood on the front porch of the cottage, wondering if he should take his own advice and let Savannah have the rest of the evening to settle in. Alone.

Except that he wanted to be sure her suitcase hadn't found its way back to the trunk of her car again. The way she'd grabbed on to the chair for support continued to bother him, too. Savannah had claimed she was tired—but Carter couldn't shake the feeling there was more to it than that.

He knocked once, lightly, just in case she'd already fallen asleep.

The light flicked on above Carter's head, dousing him with a spray of light. The door opened a crack and a pair of spring green eyes met his.

Carter lifted up the plate of leftovers he'd commandeered from the fridge.

"I thought you might be hungry."

The door opened a little wider and Savannah reached for the plate. A mouthwatering aroma drifted from the foil-covered dish.

"This smells wonderful."

A low rumble of appreciative agreement followed the statement and Savannah pressed one hand against her stomach, clearly mortified.

"I believe that's the typical response to Lupita's cooking." Carter couldn't help but grin. And he took full advantage of the moment and ducked inside the cottage, taking a brief but thorough inventory on his way to the kitchen.

Relief poured through him.

Not a suitcase in sight.

"You didn't have to do this, you know." Savannah followed, a look of consternation on her pretty face.

"I wasn't sure if you'd stopped for something to eat along the way."

The telltale color that bloomed in her cheeks told Carter his hunch had been right.

"I had some fruit," she murmured.

"If you write down a list of your favorite foods, I'm

sure Lupita will add them to the cart the next time she goes shopping."

Savannah looked almost horrified by the suggestion. Not quite the reaction Carter had anticipated.

"I can drive to the grocery store in Grasslands," she protested. "I don't expect special treatment. Just…pretend I'm not here."

Somehow, Carter doubted that was possible. He hadn't been able to stop thinking about Savannah since the day they'd met.

But she'd been wary of his motives then and judging from the expression on her face, those feelings hadn't changed.

Maddie and Violet were right.

He had some explaining to do.

"Thank you for bringing over dinner." Savannah set the plate down on the table and summoned a polite smile.

Carter's cue to leave. Which he ignored.

"Aren't you going to eat?"

"Yes." And then a cautious, "Are you going to stay?"

"Don't mind if I do."

Carter heard a faint but unmistakable chirp of alarm as he pulled a chair away from the table and guided Savannah into it.

He ignored that, too.

"Let's see what we've got here." Carter peeled the foil off the tray even though he already knew what was underneath it. "Baby red potatoes. Clover-leaf rolls. Sweet potato pie. Fried chicken. Ah, and my favorite Texas staple—barbecued ribs."

Savannah stared down at the variety of food mounded together on the platter. Carter didn't know what she liked, so he'd added a little of everything he'd discovered in the refrigerator. A veritable culinary relief map of texture and color.

"Is that a...waffle?" Savannah was pointing to something next to the green beans.

"Uh-huh. There are also bagels and cream cheese if you want to sleep in tomorrow morning and skip breakfast at the main house," Carter added casually.

Savannah's eyes narrowed.

"You wouldn't be trying to keep me away from your family, would you?"

Carter didn't miss a beat.

"Yes, ma'am."

Chapter Eight

❧

"Carter—" Savannah's gurgle of laughter took them both by surprise.

They stared at each other across the table, a fragile silence humming between them, linking them together.

Carter pushed to his feet. The chair scraped against the floor and shattered the moment.

"Better dig in before it gets cold," he said, struggling to regain his equilibrium. "I'll see if there's anything to drink."

He retrieved a bottle of water from the fridge and shut the door just in time to see Savannah bow her head and close her eyes.

Carter felt a strange tightening in his chest as a silky tassel of toffee-colored hair slid forward, outlining the delicate curve of her jaw.

His fingers twitched with the urge to smooth it away from her face. To trace the half smile that touched her lips as her lips moved in silent petition.

A moment later Savannah's head lifted and she looked across the table at him, the smile still there, in her eyes.

"What did you pray for?" Carter couldn't prevent the words from slipping out.

"That I would continue to seek God's guidance," she said softly.

Something Carter had stopped asking long ago.

"And—" Savannah hesitated, stirring his curiosity in spite of the fact that talking about God left Carter feeling uncomfortable. Restless.

Envious.

"And—?" he prompted.

To Carter's absolute amazement, Savannah blushed.

And you.

Savannah wondered what Carter would say if she said the words out loud.

She hadn't meant to pray for him. By all rights, she should still be upset with him.

She *was* still upset with him.

He hadn't even bothered to tell his sisters that he'd offered her one of the cottages, making for an awkward first meeting....

"Yeah, I'm sorry about that."

Savannah blinked, wondering if she'd said the words out loud. Because it was unsettling to think that Carter could read her mind.

"I should have told Violet that I'd invited you to stay here."

Yes, he should have. He should have told her *a lot* of things. Savannah flattened a piece of potato with the back of her fork.

"Ouch."

Savannah glanced up and her heart got tangled in Carter's rueful smile.

"I'm glad you're taking out your frustration on those poor vegetables instead of me."

"I'm not—" Savannah started to deny it, but the proof was there, soaking in a pool of barbecue sauce.

A wave of fatigue swept in, eroding what remained of her energy.

"I don't know how to do this, either."

Savannah's gaze lifted to Carter. "Do what?"

"This." He leaned back in the chair and studied her. Serious. Intent. One hundred percent soldier. "Trying to figure out what to say. What not to say. How *much* to say."

For some reason, the candid admission moved Savannah more than the smile.

She traced a vine embroidered on the tablecloth. "Neither do I."

Savannah didn't know if she could trust him. Wasn't sure she could trust herself anymore.

"Did you ever play the game twenty questions when you were a kid?"

It was the last thing Savannah expected Carter to say.

"Yes," she said cautiously.

"Good. You start. We each get one question."

"I thought it was twenty questions."

"It's late—I'm fast-tracking this." Carter's lips curled at the edges. "You can ask another one tomorrow."

She would never have guessed that the man would have a whimsical bone in his body. His attempt to lighten the moment, put her at ease was charming…and terrifying.

Savannah speared a piece of chicken with her fork, thinking hard. Afraid to delve too deeply into his personal life because he might expect her to do the same.

Some of the names Savannah heard mentioned scrolled through her mind.

Jack Colby. Landon.

Or did she ask about Maddie and Violet, who claimed to have met only five months ago?

Carter's fingers drummed against the edge of the table and he lifted an eyebrow.

Savannah took the hint.

"The woman you said was injured in a riding accident. Belle Colby? Who is she?"

Carter's expression darkened and Savannah immediately wished she could take it back.

"I'm sorry—"

"No, it's a fair question," he interrupted. "You just happened to pick the one question no one knows the answer to." The chair creaked as Carter shifted his weight. "We do know that Belle Colby is Maddie and Violet's biological mother."

But not Carter's, she guessed.

"Maddie and Gray—he's the oldest in my family—grew up thinking that Sharla Wallace was our mother. Our dad never said anything that led us to believe she hadn't given birth to all three of us. Not even after she died in a car accident when I was three."

"I'm so sorry." Savannah found herself mouthing the words that had brought little comfort when she'd learned of Rob's death.

"I don't remember her." The words were spoken matter-of-factly, but the flash of pain in Carter's eyes spoke of a wound that had never completely healed.

"A few months ago, after Belle's accident, Violet went on a search for her biological father in Fort Worth. She found Maddie instead. It turns out that my dad had been married to Belle Colby. No one knows why they divorced."

The edge of bitterness in Carter's voice cut deep; his eyes flashed a silent warning to keep her distance. Savannah laced her fingers together in her lap because her first inclination was to reach for his hand.

To let him know that she understood what it was like

to have your world turned upside down in the blink of an eye. To discover that all the things you'd thought were real had been based on secrets. Lies. But even more difficult to accept when they came from someone you loved.

"A few months ago, Violet's fiancé, Landon Derringer, hired a private investigator to do some digging into Belle's past. He hit a brick wall. There *is* no Belle Colby. Technically, the woman doesn't exist. At some point she took on a new identity. Gray's a cop and he's been using his connections to piece everything together, but so far, he's come up empty-handed."

Savannah tried to come up with reasons why a woman with young children would change her name. Cloak herself in secrecy. None of them were good.

"Even if your parents divorced, your dad must know something," she ventured.

"He might, but no one has been able to question him," Carter said tightly. "Dad's a medical missionary and he went off the grid near the Mexican border last summer. None of us has been able to get in touch with him. As far as I know, he doesn't even realize I'm back in the States. Not that it would have made a difference," he added. "It's not like he put aside his work the last time I was home on leave."

"It must have been difficult, to be so far away when you found out," Savannah said softly.

"I wasn't that far away," Carter said wryly. "Maddie and Gray decided it would be better to tell me in person. I found out about an hour after I stepped off the plane last Saturday."

The day before they'd met.

Savannah pulled in a breath so sharp it felt like a knife sliding between her ribs. Carter had been dealing with all of this and yet he'd sought her out at the diner, to deliver Rob's message.

It revealed the kind of man he was. A man who set aside his feelings to do the right thing.

"The police must be involved if your father is missing."

"He's not considered missing. That's part of the problem. If we had proof of foul play, the authorities would get involved, but unfortunately, this is Dad's MO. He gets completely focused on his work and forgets everything else."

Including his children, Savannah thought.

"He's supposed to be back for Thanksgiving," Carter continued. "That's why Maddie insisted that I stick around for a few weeks. Once he plugs into the outside world again, he'll know we're here, at the ranch, waiting."

"Praying," Savannah murmured.

"I'll leave that to the rest of the family." Bitterness edged into Carter's voice. "No matter what Dad says, nothing will be the same. I mean, maybe we'll finally understand why he and Belle split up, but nothing they say can ever make up for the damage they caused by splitting up two sets of twins."

There was no way—*no way*—Savannah had heard that correctly.

"You mean Violet and Maddie."

"And Gray and Jack Colby. They're identical twins, too."

Carter waited for the gasp of surprise. The expression of disbelief.

Instead, he was blindsided by Savannah's wistful smile.

"You're so lucky."

"Lucky?"

"No, not lucky," Savannah corrected. *Now* she was making some sense. Until she added, "Blessed. To have family. People who…want to be with you."

Carter hadn't considered that. Sure, Violet and Jack were okay but they were Maddie and Gray's identical twins. It was difficult to wrap his mind around the fact that they were his family, too, no matter what Violet had said in the den a little while ago.

"They're my *half* siblings. And Gray—" Carter couldn't even say it out loud. He still couldn't accept that a guy named Joe Earl could be Gray's father, not even if Joe's own wife believed it. Patty Earl had hinted that Belle Colby, at the age of sixteen, had been more attracted to the inheritance Brian Wallace would eventually receive from his grandmother than she was to Joe.

Violet was adamant that her mother wouldn't have married Carter's father for money. It was a touchy subject—one that Maddie had warned him not to bring up when Violet or Jack were around.

People in a small town talked and Belle's reputation had already come under suspicion when James Crawford, the original owner of the spread, had left the ranch to her after he died.

Belle had become a wealthy woman over the years, something that might have prompted Patty Earl's decision to get to know "her" boys.

The thought sickened Carter. It was one thing to maintain a polite distance from Jack Colby, but what would it do to his relationship with Gray if they discovered the only thing they had in common was the fact they'd been lied to all these years?

"What about Gray?"

Compassion shimmered in Savannah's eyes and Carter mentally took a step back. He hadn't meant to go into so much detail. He'd invited her to stay at the Colby Ranch in an attempt to ease her burden, not add to it.

"You only get one question, remember? You can ask another one tomorrow. Now it's my turn."

Savannah's fork clattered onto the plate.

It was clear she assumed that he was going to question her about Rob. What had gone wrong in their marriage? Why he'd left her?

Questions that Carter wanted the answers to—but not if they brought that wary look back into Savannah's eyes.

Maybe someday she would trust him.

Savannah's teeth sank into her lower lip but she lifted her chin to meet his gaze.

"What do you want to know?"

Carter leaned forward, elbows propped on the table. Smiled.

"Are you going to eat that waffle?"

Chapter Nine

"Got a minute?"

Carter took one look at his brother's serious expression and *knew* he should have gone straight to his room instead of taking a detour to the study to check his email.

The conversation with Savannah had left him feeling restless, the words she'd said continuing to play through his mind.

You're so blessed to have family.

Whenever Carter had thought through every scenario, he'd always thought of the outcome in terms of what he could lose, never what he might gain.

Carter shut down the computer so Gray wouldn't see what he'd been up to.

"I was just keeping up with traffic, officer."

"I'm off duty." Gray's lips twitched. "And from what I heard, you already got busted."

"Twice. Or—" Carter tipped his head thoughtfully "—maybe it only counts as once if the women who chewed you out are identical twins?"

"I'll have to look that one up in the statutes." Gray sauntered into the room and pulled up a chair.

Uh-oh.

"Are you sure I don't need a lawyer?"

Carter was only half joking.

"Maddie said you invited a friend to stay at the ranch for a while."

This was about *Savannah?*

Carter immediately bristled. "Is that a problem?"

Gray leaned forward and met his gaze.

"You tell me."

Carter wasn't fooled by the mild response.

"Let me guess. You want her full name and date of birth?"

"Do you know them?"

Carter ignored the question. "Savannah was being evicted from her apartment."

"And she didn't have anywhere else to go?"

The flash of skepticism in Gray's eyes turned up the heat under Carter's temper. "No."

"And you're sure…Savannah…isn't taking advantage of the situation?"

"Moving to the ranch was a last resort. She didn't want to come here." Not only that, Carter had a feeling that Savannah was already working on an exit plan. She'd made it clear she didn't want to be a burden.

"I'm surprised you never mentioned her, that's all."

"You're surprised," Carter repeated. "Really? Because we haven't exactly exchanged diaries over the past few years."

"You keep a diary?"

"You're worse than Maddie," Carter scoffed.

"And you're avoiding the question."

"I didn't realize you'd asked one."

Gray's bark of laughter echoed around the room, defusing the tension in the air. "Sorry. Elise says that sometimes I use that voice on her, too. I sounded like a cop just now, didn't I?"

He sounded like a big brother. Carter wasn't sure quite what to do with that. The changes in their family structure hadn't been the only ones he'd noticed in Gray since he'd arrived at the Colby Ranch. There'd been a few changes on the *inside,* too.

"Savannah isn't going to take advantage of Violet's hospitality. Or steal the silver," he added.

A heartbeat of silence followed.

"After dealing with Patty Earl, I admit I'm a little suspicious of people's motives," Gray finally admitted. "Jack and I suspect the only reason she's been trying to cozy up to us is because she found out the Colby Ranch is a lucrative operation."

Carter didn't want to be reminded of the woman who'd claimed that her husband was Jack and Gray's biological father.

Another secret. One that could have led to his father and Belle Colby's breakup. But if Gray and Jack weren't Brian's sons, why hadn't both boys stayed with Belle?

If these were the questions that Gray had been wrestling with the past few months, no wonder he was tense.

Carter released a slow breath, reminding himself to cut the guy some slack.

"I promised my friend Rob that I would check on Savannah. Make sure she was okay. I'm guessing that meant he didn't want her living on the street."

Instead of taking offense, Gray regarded him thoughtfully, leaving Carter to wonder what else Maddie and Violet had told him.

"You remind me of Dad."

Carter stiffened. "Sorry."

"It was a compliment, Carter. Dad has devoted most of

his life to taking care of people. Making sure they were okay."

Carter couldn't argue with that, but it would have been nice if their father had spent some time with his own family, too. Instead, he'd left them in Rachel's care.

Gray nodded, almost as if he'd read Carter's thoughts. "I always wondered why Dad seemed to think that his patients needed him, but it never seemed to cross his mind that we did, too."

Carter tried not to show how stunned he was by the quiet admission.

He had never considered the possibility that Gray might have felt the same way he did. Guilty for wanting their father's attention. But tossing a football in the backyard had seemed a frivolous thing compared to treating people who were injured. Sick. People who needed Brian Wallace more.

"Dad always told us to trust God—but it would have been nice if he would have trusted us, too." Carter couldn't keep the edge of bitterness from his voice.

"You're talking about Belle."

"Dad shouldn't have kept something like that a secret. Aren't you angry that he kept you from knowing your twin brother all these years?"

"We can't change the past," Gray said evenly. "All we can do, with God's help, is move forward."

"Easier said than done."

"It's occurred to me that Dad might have kept his distance from us for a reason," Gray went on. "No one knows why he and Belle split up—or why they split *us* up—but it must have been pretty big. Maybe his work is his way of trying to make up for something. Something he considered a...personal failure."

Carter wandered over to the window overlooking the courtyard to hide his expression.

He had more in common with his dad than Gray thought.

"For what it's worth, Violet and Maddie agreed that Savannah should stay here, too." His brother rose to his feet. "I guess the majority rules on this one."

"She needs some time."

"Meaning?"

"Meaning you don't get to interrogate her, Office Wallace."

A smile played at the corner of Gray's lips. "Got it. I'll see you in the morning. I'm sticking around until Sunday night."

"Thanks for the warning."

"It's better than a ticket," Gray quipped.

Carter's eyes narrowed. "I don't remember you having a sense of humor."

"You can thank Elise for that, too. The love of a good woman…" Gray began to whistle as he sauntered out the door.

Carter couldn't remember his brother ever whistling, either.

The love of a good woman…

Unbidden, an image of Savannah's face flashed through his mind.

No way. Not going there.

Carter wandered back to the desk and faced the computer again. Belle Colby smiled at him from inside a metal picture frame beside the monitor. Carter couldn't help but stare at the woman who didn't even know she'd turned his life—and several others—upside down. It was a candid shot, taken while Belle was sitting on a hay bale. Ribbons of sunlight winnowed through the cracks in the barn board, illuminating a face that was both familiar and strange at the same time.

Shoulder-length auburn hair. Wide, sparkling brown

eyes. The strong resemblance between her and Maddie was almost eerie, but that wasn't what Carter found the most unsettling.

Who *was* she? Had his dad loved Belle? Had he married Sharla to provide his children with a mother or because he'd fallen in love with her?

Where are you, Dad? We need some answers.

Carter opened up his email account and skimmed through the messages in the in-box.

Nothing new.

Almost of their own volition, his fingers began tapping out a message.

Maddie and Violet said that every letter they'd sent to their father had been ignored, but something pushed Carter to try again.

Dear Dad,
When you get this message, please call me. I'm back from Afghanistan now and staying at the Colby Ranch in Grasslands with Gray and Maddie. We're all worried because we haven't heard from you in a while. Can you take a few minutes to let us know you're okay? There are some things going on that you should know about....

Things he needed to know.

Carter hesitated, unsure how to end it.

He released a slow breath. Wrote his name. Hit Send.

A few seconds later, a new message appeared. Carter's heart buckled.

Message returned. Unable to deliver.

He pushed to his feet, palms flat against the desk. Holding him upright because he didn't trust his knees to do their job.

What had he expected?

Without realizing it, Carter reached for the Bible that lay open on the desk, traced the embossed letters on the cover with the tip of his finger. While he was growing up, Rachel had encouraged him to read a passage every day.

It's a love letter from God, Carter.

A letter he hadn't read for a long time. And right now, God was silent. And as unreachable as his father.

Pressing a hand against the small of her back, Savannah eased into one of the chairs on the porch. In the distance she could see the boxy silhouettes of the Herefords grazing on a hill in the distance. Hear a low whicker from the horses in the corral and the rumble of a utility vehicle.

She hadn't seen anyone since Violet had delivered a basket of warm muffins and a container of fresh fruit right to her door that morning.

Savannah felt a stab of guilt that she'd let Carter's sister think she'd missed breakfast because she'd slept in. The truth was, she'd been avoiding Carter.

It was only a matter of time before he asked the questions she had seen simmering in his eyes the night before.

Questions about Rob.

What was she supposed to say? That the man Carter obviously respected and admired had walked out a week after he'd promised to love and cherish her forever?

Carter hadn't been able to conceal his bitterness over the secrets his father had kept from the family. How would he react if he ever learned the whole truth about Rob?

A flurry of movement caught her eye and someone ducked behind one of the shrubs that formed a hedge between the two cottages.

A very small someone.

Savannah angled her head, trying to get a better look.

"Hello?"

A pair of big brown eyes peeked over the leaves. "Hi."

Savannah lifted one hand and motioned her over. "You can come over, if you'd like."

"I don't want to disturb you."

"You aren't disturbing me. I promise."

There was a rustling sound and a little girl about seven or eight years old inched into view. She wore a denim skirt with an embroidered ruffle around the bottom and a matching vest. Tiny cowboy boots completed the adorable ensemble.

Carter hadn't been kidding when he'd said there were a lot of people coming and going at the ranch. Was she the daughter of the housekeeper? One of the ranch hands?

"I'm Savannah."

"I know that." The child giggled.

Savannah realized that word of her arrival must have gotten out. "And you are—"

"Darcy Garland."

"Do you live around here, Darcy?"

"The white house with the green door." Darcy pointed farther down the row of cottages. "My daddy is the foreman. That means he's the boss," she added proudly.

"I see." Savannah tucked away a smile. "I haven't had a chance to meet him yet. I just got here last night."

"I haven't lived here very long, either," Darcy said. "But you'll like it. I do. It's the best place in the world. I know where all the good hiding spots are." Her voice dropped to a whisper. "And where Lupita keeps the extra cookies."

"Lupita is the cook," Savannah remembered.

"Uh-huh. And she scolds people if they forget to take off their boots."

The cook and the housekeeper. Any ideas Savannah

had entertained about helping out around the house died a quick death.

Savannah patted the wicker chair next to hers. "You're welcome to join me, if you'd like."

"Can't." Darcy wagged her head from side to side, setting the glossy brown ponytail swinging like a pendulum. "Uncle Carter said that no one's s'posed to bother you."

"Your *uncle* Carter said that?" Savannah didn't know whether to be annoyed or grateful to discover that the man had been issuing orders behind her back.

"He's not really my uncle," the girl went on blithely. "He's Maddie's brother, but she said it's okay to call him that. She's going to marry my daddy, and then we'll be a real family."

Savannah had noticed the stunning diamond ring on Maddie's finger but hadn't realized Carter's sister was engaged to the ranch foreman.

"I'm going to be the flower girl and carry a basket of rose petals and wear a new dress and everything."

"That sounds like a very important job."

"Uh-huh. Pastor Jeb said it's the most important one."

Darcy's bright smile proved to be contagious.

"I wouldn't mind a little company if you're not busy right now," Savannah said. "It's been a little lonely around here this afternoon."

"Okay." Darcy was on the porch in an instant. She bounced into the chair and settled in. "Do you like animals?"

"As a matter of fact, I—"

"Good, 'cause there are *tons* of them around here. Goats and pigs and chickens—but you have to be careful because they'll peck your fingers if you try to pet them." Darcy examined the adhesive bandage wrapped around her finger, leaving no doubt in Savannah's mind that she was speaking from experience.

"I'll remember that."

"Daddy has been teaching me how to ride after school. Rambo is the sweetest horse *ever*."

Given the animal's name, Savannah would have to take her word for that.

"I'm going to get a pony for Christmas. It's white with brown spots so I'm going to call him Freckles." Darcy paused long enough to take a breath. "Everyone's going on a trail ride tomorrow morning and then we're going to have a picnic by the lake. Do you want to come with us?"

Savannah was touched by the invitation. "Not this time, I'm afraid. I'll have to wait until after my baby is born."

"When will that be?" Darcy stared at Savannah's belly with wide-eyed curiosity.

"February."

Darcy tapped the fingers on one hand, a look of concentration on her face as she silently added up the months. "That's not *too* far away."

To Savannah, it seemed aeons away...and much too close. Where would she be in three months? In three weeks? Not at the Colby Ranch, even though Savannah didn't have the heart to tell Darcy that. If everything went according to plan, she would be back in Dallas before Thanksgiving.

Spending another holiday alone.

The thought left a familiar ache in her chest.

Maybe staying here wasn't such a good idea. Although she hadn't met Carter's brothers, she'd liked Maddie and Violet immediately. What if being surrounded by Carter's family only made it more difficult to be alone again?

"Do you like kittens?"

"I've never had one." Savannah couldn't help but smile at the abrupt change in subject. Darcy reminded her of one of the songbirds she'd seen flitting from branch to branch outside the kitchen window while she'd brewed a cup of tea.

"Maddie and I found *five* of them living in a shed behind the barn. They get kind of lonely when I'm at school during the day. You can play with them if you want to."

"I just might do that." Savannah laughed.

Nanny to a litter of kittens. Well, she'd told Carter that she wanted to be useful!

"I've got a worksheet to do before supper. *Science.*" Darcy wrinkled her nose as she hopped down from the chair. "I better get home in case Uncle Carter comes back."

A masculine voice suddenly joined the conversation. "Uncle Carter *is* back."

Chapter Ten

Carter caught Darcy as she jumped down from the chair and launched herself into his arms.

"What are you doing here, young lady?"

"I'm not disturbing Savannah, Uncle Carter," she announced solemnly. "She *asked* me to come over 'cause she was lonely."

"We can't have that, now can we?" Carter glanced at Savannah, who quickly averted her eyes.

And blushed.

He *knew* she would blush.

With her toffee-colored hair falling loose around her shoulders and a bright yellow afghan draped over her lap, Savannah looked relaxed. Content.

Beautiful.

Carter had heard her laughing as he walked up to the cottage. The sound had spiraled through him, a melody he had a feeling would stick in a man's mind for a long time.

He'd spent the day following Ricardo, Lupita's husband, around the ranch in order to give Savannah the space he'd told his family she needed.

Who was he kidding? The space *he* needed.

Because knowing a handful of details about Savannah's likes and dislikes…carrying around her photograph… wasn't nearly as dangerous to his peace of mind as having her right there. Close enough to breathe in the delicate floral scent of her perfume. Close enough to see the flecks of emerald-green in her eyes.

Close enough to touch.

"Uncle Carter!" Darcy tugged on his sleeve. "You're not listening."

"Sorry, squirt. One more time?"

Darcy released a patient sigh. "Savannah's going to take care of the kittens while I'm at school."

"That sounds like a lot of responsibility."

Savannah must have sensed he was struggling to keep a straight face because she leveled a stern look in his direction.

"You can show her how, Uncle Carter. You took care of them yesterday."

Apparently, he was going to have to explain to Darcy what the term *classified information* meant.

"That's different," he muttered. "Savannah is a civilian. I'm a marine. We're trained to—"

"Handle all kinds of situations?" Savannah finished.

"Right."

Darcy bobbed her head. "He knows how to put barrettes in. One fell out yesterday right before I got on the bus," she told Savannah.

"Very impressive."

Carter stifled a groan when he saw the twinkle in Savannah's eyes.

He could also fix an armored vehicle, but Carter decided that must not rank high in importance to an eight-year-old girl.

"And he—"

"Darcy?" Fortunately, Carter was spared from further

embarrassment as Maddie's lilting voice drifted across the yard. "Where did you run off to, young lady? You've got some homework to finish before supper."

"Gotta go." With an engaging grin, Darcy scampered away. "I'll see you later, Savannah."

"Bye—"

The word hit the screen door as it slammed shut.

"It looks like you've already made a friend." Carter leaned against the door frame.

"So have you."

"Darcy's a sweet kid." Carter watched the little girl zig-zag across the yard and dive into Maddie's waiting arms, proof of the close bond the two shared.

His sister had mentioned that Darcy hadn't always lived at the ranch. Ty Garland's ex-wife had died in a car accident and he'd become an instant father to a grief-stricken little girl he hadn't even known about before the tragedy. Ty had hired Maddie as a part-time nanny and Darcy had gradually come out of her shell, flourishing in the warmth of Maddie's love and attention.

Of the three of them, his sister's faith had always been the strongest, but she had always been focused on her career. So fiercely independent that Carter had never pictured her in the role of caregiver. But from what he'd seen so far, Maddie was a natural. Babysitting Darcy while Ty put in long hours at the ranch. Pitching in at the farm stand to help out Violet. Sitting by Belle Colby's bedside for hours.

Maddie was also quick to pull Carter into the family circle and ask his opinion on things, something she'd never done before.

You can't change the past. All you can do is move forward, with God's help.

Gray's words cycled through Carter's mind again, churning up the familiar restlessness that had plagued him since he'd arrived at the ranch. Carter seemed to be the only one having a difficult time leaving the past behind. And looking to God for strength.

"Darcy told me that Maddie's engaged to her dad."

Carter turned his attention back to Savannah. "Ty Garland. He hired Maddie to take care of her while he worked during the day. That's how they got to know each other."

Savannah tipped her head to one side. "But you don't approve?"

And here Carter thought he'd become adept at hiding his emotions.

"It's not that," he said slowly. "I hardly know the guy. He and Maddie have only been together a few months. The last I knew, she was supposed to marry Landon Derringer. You'll probably meet him within the next day or two. He travels back and forth between Grasslands and his office in Fort Worth."

"Meet him?" A frown creased Savannah's brow. "You just said that he and Maddie broke up."

"They did." He slid her a sideways glance to gauge her reaction. "Derringer's engaged to Violet now."

Maybe now she would understand why he'd done her a favor when he'd told everyone not to bother her. Savannah had enough on her mind without trying to figure out who was who. Especially with two sets of identical twins.

"*Another* brother." Savannah's wistful sigh stirred the air. "I'm trying really hard not to be envious."

"Future brother-in-law," Carter corrected. "And you're kidding me, right?"

"No." Savannah's eyes sparkled with sudden mischief. "And that, Sergeant Wallace, was *your* question for the day. Now it's my turn."

Carter stared at her in disbelief as she repeated his words from the night before. "The question of the day?"

"You said I could ask another one today, didn't you?"

Yes. Yes, he had.

"Fine." The word sounded grudging even to his own ears.

Savannah had a unique way of turning the tables on him. Making him see things from a different perspective. He just wasn't sure if he liked it or not.

"Don't look so grim," she chided. "I believe you just told Darcy that, and I quote, 'Marines can handle any situation.'"

True, but Carter was beginning to think it meant every situation that *didn't* involve a woman with sparkling green eyes and a smile that melted his defenses.

"What's the question?"

"When do I get to meet the rest of your family?"

Carter was beginning to regret starting this "game." Savannah had a gift for asking the questions he preferred not to answer.

"Tonight."

"Really?"

"Maddie and Violet issued a formal invitation for you to join everyone for supper at the main house," Carter said reluctantly. "But are you sure you want—"

He stopped when Savannah's eyes lit up.

Well, that answered *his* question.

He'd been doing his best to avoid family gatherings for the past few days. The smile on Savannah's face told him that she couldn't wait.

"Are you sure I can't get you anything else, Miss Savannah?"

"I'm sure." Savannah smiled up at Lupita, who was hovering near her shoulder, a platter of homemade rolls balanced in one hand.

"All right." The gray-haired housekeeper looked a little disappointed as she moved to the next person seated at the table. "Elise?"

"No, thank you, Lupita." Elise Lopez had arrived just before dinner with her son Cory, who had peeked up at Savannah below the brim of a pint-size cowboy hat and offered a shy but adorable smile. "Everything was amazing, as usual, but I can't eat another bite."

"Good." With a satisfied smile, the housekeeper swept toward the door. "I will be back with coffee and dessert."

"Just to warn you, Savannah—" Jack Colby lowered his voice to a stage whisper. "When you tell Lupita that you can't eat another bite, she doesn't think dessert counts."

Savannah could smile at the handsome rancher now that the initial shock had begun to fade.

Carter had said that his older brother, Gray, had an identical twin, too, but when the two men had walked into the dining room, side by side, it had taken all the good manners her grandmother had taught her not to stare.

Jack Colby and Gray were the same height and roughly the same build. Both had brown eyes and chestnut hair, although the styles were different. Jack's was on the shaggy side and a day's growth of stubble shaded his jaw, which Savannah thought only added to the man's rugged appeal. Gray was clean shaven, his hair clipped almost military short, like Carter's. Although Gray wore jeans and a flannel shirt, it was easy to tell which twin had grown up on the ranch because Jack's skin was stained a deep bronze from working outdoors.

Savannah's eyes strayed to Maddie and Violet again.

Two sets of identical twins.

It was a little surreal, seeing all four of them together at the table.

No wonder she got the feeling that Carter, with his

wheat-blond hair and deep blue eyes, felt like the odd man out when he was in their company. The bond that had formed was evident in every smile that passed between them.

"I agree with Lupita. I don't think dessert should count, either." Keira Wolfe, Jack's fiancée, winked at Savannah across the table.

The slender blonde had been the last one to arrive, dashing into the dining room with a breathless "sorry I'm late—colicky horse" right before Jack had said a blessing over the food. After the prayer, she'd bounded over to Savannah's side and said hello, the welcome in her vivid hazel eyes as warm as the one Savannah had received from Carter's sisters the day before.

She'd been a little worried that supper at the main house would be a solemn affair, especially in light of what Carter had told her about Belle Colby's precarious condition and their mounting concern about Brian Wallace's whereabouts. Instead, conversation—and laughter—flowed as easily as the pitchers of mint tea that Lupita set at each corner of the mile-long table. Darcy and Cory Lopez sat next to each other, giggling as they tried to make words out of their pasta.

This, Savannah thought, was what a family was supposed to be like. Noisy and affectionate.

But she couldn't help but notice that Carter didn't join in. He didn't engage in the good-natured teasing or the laughter.

Savannah couldn't understand it. As an only child, she would have given anything to be part of a family like this. Before her parents divorced, she remembered silent dinners. And even though her grandmother's tiny home was filled with love, there had only been the two of them.

This was what Savannah had dreamed of.

What Rob had promised.

"Anytime you're ready to leave—" Carter's breath stirred her hair and Savannah suppressed a shiver as that unexpected jolt of electricity momentarily stopped her heart. It started thumping again, so loudly that Savannah was afraid everyone at the table would hear it.

"No." Her voice came out sounding a lot like the squeak in the screen door of the cottage.

"Okay, what are you two whispering about over there?" Maddie teased.

Savannah realized that everyone's attention was focused on them now.

"Is Carter telling stories about us?" Maddie's frown belied the sparkle in her eyes. "Because if he is, Gray and I know a few we could share about *him*."

"True." Gray leaned back in the chair and crossed his arms behind his head. "Like the time Mr. Holbrook hired Carter to cut his grass."

Maddie clapped a hand over her mouth. "I'd forgotten about that."

"What happened?" Violet's eyes glowed with anticipation.

"Here we go," Carter muttered.

"I think he was about eleven—"

"Twelve," Carter said under his breath.

Gray's eyebrow lifted. "Do you want to tell the story?"

"No."

"Then I will." Gray didn't seem the least bit intimidated by Carter's scowl. "Mr. Holbrook hired Carter to do his yard work and then went out of town for the day. Carter was supposed to use his push mower—"

"Mr. Holbrook never actually *said* what I was supposed to use," Carter interjected.

Gray ignored him. "All the kids hated to use it because

it was one of those contraptions invented shortly after the wheel. And Mr. Holbrook had about two acres of lawn to cut." He smirked. "Anyway, when he got home that afternoon, he followed a line of tools up the driveway to the garage. Instead of using the push mower, Carter had souped up—"

"Fixed."

"—a riding lawn mower he had stored in his shed."

"One of the neighbors heard the commotion and almost dialed 911," Maddie added with a laugh.

She and Gray had everyone's attention now, even Darcy and Cory were listening.

"Why?" Keira asked. "Couldn't Carter put it back together?"

"Oh, my little brother got the thing running." Gray chuckled. "But he'd fixed the engine, not the brakes."

"In my defense, I did get around to it the next day."

It was the second time Savannah had seen that elusive dimple appear in Carter's cheek but the result was the same.

Instant tingles.

"After you took out his hedge," Gray pointed out.

"Did you get in trouble?" Cory's worried gaze swung back and forth between Carter and his brother.

"No way." Gray ruffled the boy's dark hair. "Carter was the neighborhood hero. Mr. Holbrook gave the push mower a one-way ticket to the salvage yard and everyone he hired to cut the grass after that got to use the riding mower instead."

"And people started to show up at our door, asking for Carter," Maddie said. "Dad couldn't even pull the car into the garage because it was filled with everything from lawn mowers to toasters."

"It became Carter's personal mission to fix anything that was broken."

Chapter Eleven

"Is everybody awake?"

Darcy burst into the kitchen, almost colliding with Carter as he shuffled toward the coffeepot.

"They are now." Carter scooped the little girl up in his arms and gave her silky ponytail a playful tug. "You're up awfully early on a Saturday morning."

Darcy practically vibrated with excitement as he deposited her on one of the vinyl-covered stools at the end of the breakfast counter. "I couldn't keep my eyes shut anymore."

Funny. Carter had experienced the same problem—but for an entirely different reason. For once, it hadn't been nightmares that kept him awake most of the night.

He wasn't sure which was more dangerous to his peace of mind. The nightmares that continued to plague him... or thoughts of Savannah.

It hadn't escaped Carter's notice that she fit in with his family more than he did. After supper, she'd sat on the floor with a pillow propped behind her back and played a lively game of Chutes and Ladders with Cory and Darcy.

Watching her, Carter was convinced that Savannah was going to be a great mom. Her daughter would blossom the way that Darcy had under Maddie's loving care.

The difference was that Savannah's daughter wouldn't have a father like Ty to protect and cherish her. To slay invisible dragons underneath the bed and intimidate the teenage boys who would eventually ask her out...

The images that tumbled like dominoes through Carter's mind had brought him up short. The chances of Savannah giving him permission to be part of her baby's life were as slim as her letting him become part of *hers*.

Even if he wanted to be.

Carter had been relieved when his cell phone began to ring, providing the opportunity to escape for a few minutes. With everything that had been happening at the ranch the past few days, he hadn't returned his commanding officer's calls.

Sixty seconds later, he'd found himself wishing he hadn't taken that one, either. Carter had assumed the lieutenant would tempt him with another bonus if he agreed to reenlist. Instead, he'd been informed that his name had been officially submitted to receive a Silver Star.

Carter had said the right words and returned to the family room, wondering what he would say if Maddie asked him who had called. And why. The last thing he wanted was for Savannah to find out that he might receive a medal. A medal he might actually deserve if he'd saved her husband that day....

But Savannah had disappeared.

Maddie told him that she was tired and decided to call it a day. That she'd decided to leave before he could walk her home told Carter that she still wasn't completely comfortable in his presence.

Well, that made two of them....

"Are you going on the trail ride with us this morning?"

It took Carter a second to realize that Darcy was talking to him.

"I don't think so, squirt."

"But Lupita packed a lunch for us to take along and we're going to eat around a campfire like real cowboys." Darcy dug into the stack of pancakes Maddie slid on her plate. "It'll be fun."

"She's right, Carter." Violet sauntered into the kitchen, cowboy hat in hand, and made a beeline for the coffeepot. "It'll be good to get outside and clear our heads a little."

Carter was tempted to tell Violet that when he wanted to "clear his head" he chose to go alone, not travel with a herd.

Maddie must have read his mind, because her smile slipped a notch. "Everyone is going, Carter."

"S'vannah can't," Darcy said around a mouthful of sausage. "I asked her but she hasta wait 'til her baby is born."

"I think I'll stick around here this morning." Carter sat down next to Darcy. "I've got a few phone calls to make."

A quick but knowing look passed between Maddie and Violet.

"What?"

"It's just that you can keep Savannah company if you're staying at the ranch," Maddie said casually.

They didn't think…

Carter swallowed a groan. Because the smile Violet aimed at Maddie told him they did.

"You're way off track. Savannah is—"

"Your friend?"

Rob's wife.

"Someone who needs a quiet place to stay." Emphasis on the word *quiet*. "Not a bunch of people getting into her business."

"She's lonely," Darcy said matter-of-factly. "Last night she said that we make her smile."

Insert knife and turn, Carter thought.

Violet brightened. "I've got an idea—" She pretended

not to hear Carter snort. "She might not be able to ride, but the two of you can drive out to the lake and join us for lunch."

Carter didn't know what was worse. Maddie and Violet's matchmaking or their sneaky tactics to get him to be part of the family.

"Double trouble. That's what you two are."

Darcy giggled. Maddie and Violet looked as if he'd just paid them a compliment.

"Savannah might have other plans." Plans that didn't include him.

"She seemed to enjoy herself at dinner last night," Violet said.

Enjoy herself? Savannah's expression had reminded Carter of a kid looking through the window of a candy store.

Someone squeezed his shoulder. He glanced up, expecting to see Maddie, but it was Violet who stood behind him.

"I'm glad you two met and that you brought her here," she said softly. "I'm sure it brings Savannah comfort that she can talk to someone who knew her husband."

That's what Carter had thought—*hoped*—until the first time they'd met. Now he knew better. Memories of Rob weren't going to be a connecting point between him and Savannah. If anything, they were a wedge keeping them apart.

Savannah opened her eyes and blinked at the old-fashioned light fixture on the ceiling until it came into focus.

For the first time in months, she'd slept through the night. No doors slamming. No sirens or horns blaring. No trains rattling down the tracks.

Just the low murmur of cattle and the faint but unmistakable sound of...laughter.

Wrapping herself in the quilt, Savannah padded over to the window and peeked through the curtain to see what was going on.

A group of people had gathered outside the barn and she remembered that Darcy had said something the day before about a trail ride.

Savannah recognized Violet and Maddie immediately, working in tandem as they brushed one of the horses. Gray, who traded his khaki slacks for faded jeans and a long-sleeved T-shirt, stood next to Elise. Darcy and Cory were perched on the top rail of the round pen watching Jack bridle an enormous gray horse. Keira knelt beside the animal, running efficient hands down its length, lifting up the enormous hoof.

Savannah's curiosity piqued as a man led a coal-black horse from the barn. He paused and flicked the brim of his hat back.

Ty Garland.

It looked as if the entire family had set aside their normal activities for the morning in order to spend time together.

Except Carter.

When Carter had left the room to take a phone call after dinner the night before, she'd seen Maddie glance at their older brother. The look of resignation and disappointment on Gray's face spoke volumes.

Savannah wasn't the only one who noticed that Carter held himself apart from the rest of the family. Gray and Maddie had told a humorous story from their childhood, but Savannah had read between the lines. Could see that the boy who'd kept his promises had grown up to be a soldier.

Carter was the kind of man people depended on. Looked up to. It was the reason he'd come to the ranch. He'd set his own feelings aside, his questions and confusion about the secrets his father had kept, because Maddie and Gray had asked him to.

And he'd invited her to stay at the ranch because she'd had nowhere else to go.

Carter's a good man, Lord. Help him see that his brothers and sisters are a gift from You. I pray that You'd bring his father home safely and that Belle recovers from her injuries. Bring healing to this family....

Darcy's squeal of delight brought Savannah's head up. She watched Ty swing his daughter onto the back of a buckskin horse that didn't so much as twitch with all the commotion going on around it.

Even from the distance that separated them, Savannah could see the camera in Lupita's hand as she herded everyone together for a picture. Violet planted a cowboy hat on Gray's head and Jack's shout of laughter scattered the chickens pecking the gravel. Ty's arm came around Maddie as they took their place by Darcy.

It was tempting to join them. Safer to hide behind the curtain.

This was a family it would be all too easy to fall in love with.

And not just the *family,* if Savannah were completely honest with herself.

She let the curtain swing shut and backed away from the window, afraid to let her thoughts continue down that road.

I'll take care of you, Savannah.

Rob had said the words and she believed him.

And even though she was beginning to realize that Carter was a man who could be trusted, she no longer trusted herself.

Carter watched Savannah brace one foot over the rail and lean across the fence to stroke Piper's nose. The mare whickered and nosed the pocket of her jacket, looking for a treat.

He took advantage of the fact she hadn't spotted him yet and took a moment to study her. The loose-fitting dress that was the exact shade of green as her eyes, her hair pulled back in a loose knot at the nape of her neck accentuating her delicate profile. And the pensive look on her face.

Guilt propelled him across the yard.

The group had set out half an hour ago, riding away in single file with Jack in the lead on an enormous gray horse.

Carter had checked his email. Twice. The house was quiet. Too quiet. He thought he would welcome the change, but the silence closed in around him instead. Along with the restless feeling that had become his constant companion since he'd returned to Texas.

"It looks like we're both temporarily sidelined, aren't we, girl?" he heard Savannah say. There was no resentment in her tone, only an undercurrent of laughter, bubbling below the surface like spring water.

"Her name is Piper."

Savannah's gaze lifted, and he saw a flash of disappointment in her eyes. "You didn't go on the trail ride?"

"I had a few things to take care of this morning."

"But what could be more—" Savannah stopped but the words dangled in the air between them, unspoken.

More important than family.

"You do have one question, remember?"

Carter tried to lighten the moment, but Savannah's eyes searched his face.

"That's not the one I want to ask," she said simply.

Carter felt a ripple of relief—and trepidation. It was his fault for bringing up that stupid game. The one *he'd* started.

Savannah seemed to have a gift for asking the one question that Carter didn't know how to answer.

Turning her attention back to the horse, Savannah combed her fingers through the tangled mane. Piper's liquid brown eyes drifted shut in absolute bliss. "I've never gone riding before."

Carter felt a stab of jealousy. For a horse.

No doubt about it, he was in trouble.

"Never?" He pushed the word out.

"City girl." Savannah shrugged. "My grandmother and I lived in an apartment that didn't even allow pets."

Carter filed that bit of information away. Rob had talked about Savannah, but never mentioned her family. Or his own, for that matter.

Why hadn't that occurred to him before?

"Does your grandmother still live in Dallas?"

Savannah shook her head. "She had a stroke two years ago and while she was in the hospital, she contracted pneumonia. The doctors couldn't get it under control with antibiotics and she…she passed away the next day."

"I'm sorry." Carter heard himself say the very words that had brought little comfort to him after Rob died.

"At least we had the opportunity to say goodbye. That made it easier."

Carter felt a strange tightening in his throat. The last time he'd been home on leave, over a year ago, his dad had asked him to hang out for an afternoon but he'd gotten a call just fifteen minutes after Carter had arrived. An emergency. Brian had been apologetic—told Carter that he'd make it up to him the next day—but Carter hadn't answered the phone. He'd grown tired of having his father's work schedule dictate their lives.

What if that had been the last time he'd spoken to his father? The email he'd written a few minutes ago remained in the in-box. Locked in the computer's memory like the emotions Carter didn't want to deal with.

"You must miss the city. It's pretty isolated out here." He steered the conversation to safer ground.

"No." Savannah shook her head. "I love the ranch. It's peaceful. There's room to breathe."

"I've heard Maddie say that, too. Five months ago, you wouldn't have thought she knew the front end of a horse from the back. The next thing I know, Gray will be bringing in cattle instead of criminals. He and Maddie both want to live here permanently."

Now why had he told her that?

Savannah tipped her head to look at him.

"Are *you* planning to stay?"

Chapter Twelve

One look at Carter's face and Savannah knew she should have chosen a different question.

"I'm sorry. It's none of my business." It really wasn't. But the more she got to know Carter Wallace, the more she *wanted* to know.

"You can ask me anything." Carter drove a hand through his hair. "I'm just not sure I'll always have an answer."

Which, Savannah decided, was an answer in itself.

Maddie and Gray were planning to make Grasslands their home and embracing the new members of their family while Carter prowled the perimeter, keeping a protective watch. Keeping his distance.

Well, there might be something she could do about that.

"When will they be back from the trail ride?"

"Not for a while. Maddie mentioned they'll be stopping at the lake for a picnic lunch and campfire. Like real cowboys, according to Darcy."

"She was pretty excited about the trail ride today."

"Darcy gets excited about everything." The affection in Carter's tone affirmed what Savannah already knew. In spite of his feelings for the Colbys, the little girl had won him over.

"How far is the lake from here?"

His cobalt eyes swung back to her. "About a mile or so. You aren't thinking of walking out there, are you?"

"No." Savannah tamped down a sigh. "I doubt my doctor would consider a mile-long hike 'staying off my feet.'"

Savannah regretted the words when Carter's eyes narrowed.

"What do you mean? Are you supposed to be on bed rest or something?"

"Not…exactly."

"Define *exactly*."

"Dr. Yardley suggested that I cut back on my hours at the diner, that's all."

Savannah could almost see him silently connecting the dots.

"Is there something wrong with the baby?"

"The baby is fine."

Another heartbeat of silence followed.

"Are *you* all right?"

Something in Carter's voice suddenly made it difficult for Savannah to breathe.

"I'm fine," she managed to say. "My blood pressure was a little high at my last appointment, that's all."

"That's why you came here, isn't it?" Carter said slowly. "It wasn't just because of the apartment."

Savannah nodded reluctantly. "When I asked my boss if he would reduce my hours, he gave all of them to one of the other waitresses. If my next checkup goes well, I can ask him to put me back on the schedule."

"But won't the same thing happen again?"

"I'll be careful." Savannah rested one hand protectively against her abdomen.

"What caused this? Stress?" Carter obviously wasn't ready to let it go.

"Dr. Yardley said the same thing you did." Savannah summoned a smile. "That a change of scenery would be a good thing right now."

She wished she hadn't brought it up. She didn't want Carter to feel sorry for her.

What do you want him to feel? an inner voice teased.

Savannah elbowed it aside. Those kind of questions only borrowed trouble. Trouble she didn't need. In a week or so, she would be returning to Dallas and Carter would stay at the Colby Ranch with his family to wait for his father's return on Thanksgiving.

What was important now was to somehow help Carter see that he needed his family as much as they needed him.

"A change of scenery," Carter murmured, squinting at the horizon. "I could take you out to the lake to join up with the others. If you want me to."

Savannah struggled to hide her astonishment. And then looked down to hide her smile.

Thank You, Lord.

"I'd love to."

Savannah's initial confidence that she'd done the right thing began to erode with every bump and jolt that brought her into direct contact with Carter.

"Doing all right?" Carter glanced at her as the utility vehicle rolled slowly through the gully.

Define "all right," Savannah wanted to say. Because she was pretty sure that this time, the increase in her blood pressure didn't have anything to do with the fact that she was on her feet too long.

"That's where Jack lives." Carter pointed to an older, two-story home nestled between two mature pecan trees. "He moved in a few months ago and he's been fixing it up. Maddie said that he and Keira plan to live there after they're married."

Another couple who'd decided to make their home on the ranch.

"When will that be?"

"I'm not sure." Carter's expression clouded. "They're… waiting."

Savannah didn't have to ask, she knew what they were waiting for. For Brian Wallace to return. For Belle to wake up.

Carter slowed down as they passed the gate and Savannah saw the neat stack of lumber piled next to the stone foundation.

"It doesn't look like he's finished yet."

His jaw tightened. "From what I hear, Gray's been helping him on the weekends."

Savannah had guessed that he and his older brother had never been close, but that didn't mean it would be easy to accept Jack's presence in his life.

"Look." Carter aimed the vehicle at a wisp of smoke rising in the distance. "I think we found them."

The tiny man-made lake winked like a sapphire, a welcome oasis in the center of the windswept grazing land. Reins dangling, the horses stood, ground-tied shoulder to shoulder under a bouquet of cottonwood trees. A group of people circled a roaring campfire.

As they got closer, Savannah realized that everyone was looking at them, not the flames.

Violet rose to her feet and waved her cowboy hat as Carter stopped several yards away. "Look who's here! You're just in time for hot chocolate."

Savannah started to get down from the vehicle, but Carter was there before her foot touched the ground. His hand on the small of her back, guiding her forward over the uneven ground.

Savannah saw Maddie and Violet exchange a knowing look that she was afraid had nothing to do with some mysterious "twin" connection. It reminded her of the matchmaking gleam in Libby's eye the day Carter had walked into the diner.

Maybe this hadn't been such a good idea. She was glad when Gray immediately intercepted Carter and steered him toward the group of men standing around a portable grill.

"Sit down." Keira scooted down the blanket to make room for her. Elise already had the thermos open and was pouring another cup of hot chocolate.

"Yeah, now we can eat!" Cory pumped the air with one small fist as he and Darcy raced toward the adults.

Savannah glanced at Violet. "What were you waiting for?"

A smile played at the corner of her lips. "You and Carter."

"But…how did you know we'd be here?"

"Because we told Carter that he should bring you out here for lunch," Maddie said. "And no matter how he feels, my brother always does the right thing."

Savannah knew that, but for some reason, a knot formed in her throat. He hadn't run into her at the corral by accident.

This was what you wanted, wasn't it? For Carter to spend time with his family?

What difference did it make what had prompted his change of heart?

Because Savannah didn't want to admit she wanted Carter to seek out her company because he *enjoyed* it, not because his family had suggested it.

Not because he felt sorry for her.

"Did I say something wrong?" Maddie was looking at her closely now.

"No," Savannah said quickly. "It's just that Carter might have had other plans. I didn't come here to be a…burden."

To her astonishment, Violet nodded. "I know what you mean. When Landon showed up at the ranch and tried to help, I didn't want to accept it. I wanted to prove to him that I was capable. Confident. The kind of woman who could stand on her own two feet, like my mom. But you know what I learned? God puts people in our lives for a reason."

"Even when you think you don't want them there," Maddie added with a smile.

That's how Savannah had felt. At first. She hadn't wanted to admit that Carter been part of God's plan. And now she was afraid that he *wasn't*.

Maddie squeezed her hand. "I'm really glad you're here. You're good for my brother, Savannah."

Savannah froze, not sure she'd heard her correctly. "I don't know what you mean."

"Carter has always been a lone wolf. He separated himself from the rest of the family years ago. Dad was gone a lot and all of us dealt with that in different ways." Maddie sighed. "I think that's why Carter joined the marines right out of high school. I see how protective he is around you. It's obvious that he really cares."

"He—" *Cared about Rob.* "He's a good man."

"He's great with the kids, too," Violet said casually.

Too casually.

Savannah couldn't look at them now. It seemed that Violet and Maddie had a plan, too. To get her and Carter to spend time together.

"Is there anything I can do to help with lunch?" she asked.

Fortunately, Violet took the hint. She reached into the

picnic basket. "Let's see what Lupita packed to go with the hamburgers Ty is grilling. She had Ricardo drop the food off before we got here and then they were going to visit Mom at the Ranchland Manor for a few hours."

"How is she doing?" Savannah asked tentatively.

"No change," Violet whispered. "But we're waiting. And praying."

Savannah impulsively reached for her hand. "Sometimes that doesn't seem like enough…but it's everything."

Violet's eyes misted over but strangely enough, she smiled at Maddie.

"Would you like to go to church with us tomorrow morning, Savannah?" Maddie asked unexpectedly. "The service starts at ten."

"I'd like that."

"Great. There's so many of us, we carpool, so meet us in front of the house at eight-thirty."

Savannah's gaze drifted to Carter. He knelt on the ground next to Cory, eye to eye, listening intently to something the little boy was telling him.

He would be a good dad, she thought.

She wanted to ask if Carter would be going with them to church. But Savannah was afraid she already knew the answer to that question.

"Thanks for your help, Carter." Ty wiped the beads of sweat from his brow with the back of his hand. "It's always good to have an extra set of hands."

"No problem." Even though Carter had a hunch that his sister's fiancé could manage just fine on his own. Ty Garland had pulled him aside when they'd returned from the trail ride and asked if he would take a look at one of the four-wheelers that was being, in Ty's words, "a little cranky." All part of a plot designed to make him feel useful.

Not that Carter cared. Because it also kept his thoughts focused on a project and not on Savannah. Kind of.

When she'd admitted that the doctor had some health concerns, Carter had gone cold, struck by a fear that hadn't gripped him since the day he'd run toward the smoking convoy. During lunch, Carter had found himself watching her closely, looking for telltale signs of fatigue.

He couldn't imagine her going back to Dallas alone. Who would watch out for her?

God, please keep Savannah and the baby safe.

The prayer slipped out before Carter even recognized it for what it was. Something that used to come as easily as taking his next breath.

"Here's the wrench you needed." Ty waved it in front of his face.

"Thanks." Carter reached for it and saw Savannah walking back to the cottage from the main house. The women had decided to watch a movie together in the family room, an announcement that sent the men scattering like someone had dropped a stick of dynamite in the chicken coop.

Carter was the first one out the door, although he was glad Maddie and Violet had taken Savannah under their wing. He'd heard the three of them laughing about something right before Ty had pulled him aside.

Ty rocked back on his heels. "I know you're the mechanic, but I think it might work better if you use the wrench to tighten the bolt instead of *staring* it on."

Carter tore his gaze away from Savannah. "I was thinking," he muttered.

"Yeah." Ty's lips twitched. "I could see that."

Carter used the wrench with a little more force than was necessary. "You're good to go."

"I have to go into town and pick up a few things before the feed store closes," Ty was saying. "Want to ride along?"

Carter shot him a wry look. "How much is Maddie paying you to babysit?"

Ty grinned, not even pretending he didn't know what Carter was talking about. "I'm doing it for free, although she might have said something about apple pie."

"That's what I thought. I'll see you later."

"Maddie worries about you."

Carter had started to walk away but Ty's comment stopped him in his tracks.

"I'm a big boy." *A marine,* Carter wanted to add.

"You're also her baby brother."

"*Half* brother." Carter regretted the words as soon as they slipped past his lips. Regretted even more the look of disappointment that flashed across Ty's face.

"Does that change the way you feel about her?" he said evenly.

If they were going to talk about feelings, Carter was out of here.

"I don't know what Maddie's told you about our father, but he raised us to be independent." A quality that had made Brian Wallace's life easier. "The four of us haven't exactly been what you'd call close over the past few years."

"Maddie wants that to change." The look in the ranch foreman's eyes warned Carter to make sure he was willing to do his part to make that happen.

"I'm not used to having her and Gray fuss over me."

"I get that," Ty said. "It took me a while to realize how important family is. I almost lost Darcy because of it."

"I know Maddie wants us to be one big happy family, but it's a little difficult under the circumstances, don't you think?"

"If this isn't the time when you need family, I don't know what is," Ty shot back as he hopped into the cab of his pickup. "I don't want you to make the same mistakes I did. When a man finds something precious, he holds on to it."

An image of Savannah's face rose in Carter's mind.

But she wasn't his to hold on to.

"Where does this go?" Carter hoisted the old metal tool-box up in the air.

"Why don't you put it the shed?"

Carter thought he heard Ty laugh as the window rolled up. Strange, considering how serious the guy had been a minute ago.

What did they want from him?

Grabbing the toolbox, Carter headed toward the storage shed behind the barn.

And almost tripped over the woman sitting cross-legged on the floor.

Chapter Thirteen

Savannah had been so lost in thought she hadn't heard the door open. But light suddenly spilled in and there was Carter, looming above her.

"What are you doing here?"

Savannah could have asked him the same thing. The last she knew, he and Ty had been walking toward the barn.

"Darcy is helping Lupita make cookies so I volunteered to check on the kittens." On cue, a tiny gray-and-white kitten darted from the shadows and attacked the laces on Carter's boot.

"Are you going to adopt one?" He scooped up the ball of fluff, his large hand forming a safe cradle. A moment later, the tiny body began to vibrate with a loud, rumbling purr.

"I can't." Savannah picked up the kitten's littermate as it rubbed against her ankle. "My next apartment might not allow pets."

The reminder that her stay was temporary cast a shadow over Savannah's heart. A sign she was getting too comfortable at the Colby Ranch.

"There's no rush," Carter said quietly.

Maddie and Violet had said the same thing when Savannah had asked if she could use the computer in Belle's office to check for new apartment listings in Dallas.

Savannah didn't have the heart to tell Carter's sisters that the reason they wanted her to stay was the very reason why she had to leave.

"I saw Ty leave a few minutes ago." As soon as Savannah said the words, she hoped the dim light in the shed would conceal her blush. Nothing like telling the man she'd been keeping tabs on him!

"He had to run a few errands after I fixed the four-wheeler."

"Maybe I should talk to Ty," Savannah said darkly. "Your sisters won't let me set foot in the kitchen unless I want something to eat—and then they insist I sit at the table while they make it." Even something as simple as microwave popcorn.

"Mmm." Carter bent down and set the kitten on the floor, his innocent expression instantly setting off an internal alarm.

"Did you have something to do with that?"

"I *might* have said your doctor recommended that you take it easy."

And he didn't look the least bit apologetic.

"I'm not made out of glass."

"You're a guest here, remember?" he murmured.

"How can I forget? You keep reminding me—and now everyone else."

Carter's laughter rolled over her. "Someone has to look out for you."

Savannah felt tears scald the back of her eyes and she buried her face in the kitten's downy fur before Carter could notice.

Rob had said the same thing. Savannah wanted to think she was a different person than she'd been seven months ago. That girl had been naive. Lonely. Susceptible to the charms of a man who'd used her vulnerability to his advantage.

Carter had never been anything other than straightforward with her from the first time they'd met. He'd told her the truth about what had prompted his invitation to stay at the ranch. She knew he was only following through on the promise he'd made to Rob.

She knew that every time Carter looked at her, he saw his best friend's widow.

The growing realization that she wanted him to see her as *more* than that left Savannah reeling. She leaned against the post before her knees gave way.

"It's okay to accept help, you know. You don't have to go through this alone." Carter reached out and tucked a strand of hair behind her ear. His fingertips paused to linger on the sensitive spot below Savannah's jaw, where her pulse had begun to jump in time with the erratic rhythm of her heart.

His cobalt-blue eyes searched her face and a frown settled between his brows, almost as if he were seeing her—really seeing her—for the first time.

"Savannah—"

A low, mournful wail erupted behind them.

Savannah was already following the sound to the back of the shed. "I think one of the kittens got tangled in something."

Carter caught her hand as she reached for the canvas tarp thrown over an old piece of farm equipment.

"What did I just say?" He pulled the cover off and knelt down. Savannah hovered in the wings, watching as he disappeared beneath the tire.

"Are you pulling rank again?"

"Yes," came the muffled response. Carter extracted

the kitten and deposited it next to its brothers and sisters, perched like a row of knickknacks on a low wooden shelf to watch the show.

"I don't believe it," Savannah huffed.

"Neither do I." Carter let out a low whistle. "Do you know what this is?"

Savannah followed his gaze to the vehicle that, like the kitten, had been trapped under the dusty tarp.

"A truck?"

"Not just a truck." Carter prowled around the front, his palm following every curve and line. "It's a '67 Chevy."

"Um, that sounds like a truck to me."

Carter's husky laugh sent the kittens scrambling for cover. If Savannah were smart, she would follow their lead.

"It *is* a truck. A classic." His enthusiasm was so contagious, Savannah couldn't help but smile as she ventured closer for a better look. "Who put you out to pasture?" Carter gave the truck's chrome fender an affectionate pat.

"Someone who wanted to *drive* a truck instead of push it?"

Savannah couldn't believe she was actually teasing him.

Carter flashed a boyish grin and patted the door. "Let's take a look at her."

"How do you know it's a *her*?"

"Too pretty not to be."

Carter threw open the doors to let in more light and the wind snaked inside the shed. Savannah shivered. Without a word, he stripped off his sheepskin-lined coat and dropped it over her shoulders. The heat from his body wrapped around her like an embrace. She caught her breath, trapping the tangy scent of his cologne in her lungs.

Carter slid into the driver's seat. He took a quick inventory of the interior, checking the glove box and running his hand along the underside of the seats.

Savannah spotted a set of keys hanging from a nail near the door. "Here. Try one of these."

The truck shuddered to life. And promptly died.

Which did nothing to dim Carter's enthusiasm.

"What's wrong with it?"

"I'm not sure yet," he murmured.

"Is that easy to fix?"

Carter grinned. "Easy, no. Possible, yes."

"I thought I heard someone in here." Jack's shadow blocked the afternoon sunlight streaming into the shed. "Hey, Savannah...and Carter."

"He was helping Ty. And I was visiting Darcy's kittens," Savannah explained quickly. She didn't want anyone to get the impression that she was looking for anything more than a place to stay for a few weeks.

"Uh-huh." Jack sauntered into the shed to take a closer look at what had caught their attention. "I forgot that thing was here."

Carter twisted around, a look of patent disbelief on his handsome face. "You *forgot?*" he echoed.

"It belonged to James Crawford. I remember he drove it in the Fourth of July parade every summer. It started to have issues so he must have put it out to pasture, so to speak."

"And you left it here."

Jack shrugged. "Ty and I have enough old junk to keep running around this place."

"Old junk?" Carter mouthed the words as if he couldn't bear to say them out loud.

"You're welcome to try—" Carter had the hood up before Jack completed the sentence. He winked at Savannah and dug a light bulb from a drawer in the storage cabinet. "The sun is going down. You might need this if you're out here all night."

Savannah noticed that Carter didn't contradict him.

"What's going on?" Maddie stood in the doorway. She'd changed out of her casual riding clothes into a long skirt, tall boots and a form-fitting suede jacket.

"Carter found a truck to play with," Jack quipped.

Maddie took a step forward, eyed the skeins of cobwebs hanging from the ceiling and stopped just inside the door.

"Violet and I are driving into town for a few hours to visit Belle. Pastor Jeb offered to meet us there so we can all pray for her. Do you want to come along?"

"Sure. 'Where two or more are gathered in my name,'" Jack quoted softly, a verse familiar to Savannah. "I'll meet you out front in a few minutes."

"Great. I'm going to track down Gray and ask him, too." Maddie lingered in the doorway. "Do you want to come with us, Carter?"

Carter's head snapped up. "No, thanks."

An awkward silence descended. Jack looked as if he wanted to say more, but the set of Carter's jaw must have discouraged him.

It discouraged Savannah, too.

Because even though Carter had claimed she didn't have to go through difficult times alone, it was clear he wasn't willing to take his own advice.

The sun had set by the time Carter returned to the house. He'd heard the slam of a car door signifying his siblings return over an hour ago. By now, the family would be through eating supper and lined up on the sofa in the family room, watching football.

He shrugged off his jacket and padded down the hall. An inner voice taunted that it was pointless to check his email again but Carter ignored it.

They needed answers, and with Belle not showing any

signs of regaining consciousness, there was only one person who could answer them. His father.

Now if only he could make it to the office before Darcy spotted him…

Carter's hand froze on the knob as he pushed the door open. Because he hadn't bypassed game time in the family room, he'd stumbled into some kind of family summit.

Which explained why he hadn't been invited.

Guilt reared up to pinch his conscience. Maybe because they'd asked him to accompany them to Ranchland Manor only a few hours ago and he'd turned them down flat?

Maddie and Violet sat in the window seat overlooking the courtyard while Gray and Jack paced the length of the room like a pair of caged mountain lions.

Conversation skidded to a halt when they spotted him.

"Sorry." Carter started to back up. "I didn't mean to intrude."

Gray cast an impatient glance his way. "You aren't intruding. We were waiting for you."

Carter's emotions shifted into high alert, the same way they had in Afghanistan when there'd been an imminent threat to the soldiers on base.

"What's going on?"

"Maybe you should shut the door," Jack suggested, his voice tight.

Carter closed the door and looked at Gray.

"Landon got here about an hour ago. I'd asked him to stop by the apartment and pick up my mail before he left Fort Worth."

For the first time, Carter noticed the envelope in Gray's hand.

"Dad?" Carter felt his lips form the word but he wasn't sure if he'd said it out loud.

"No." Gray hesitated, glanced at Jack. "A few months

ago, Jack and I decided to have our DNA tested, to see if Patty Earl was telling the truth about Joe being our biological father."

Something else no one had bothered to mention until now.

"Was it necessary for both of you to be tested?"

"No, that was our decision," Gray said.

Another indication that the men had not only accepted each other, but were forming the same strong bond that Maddie and Violet had since they'd discovered each other.

"What did you find out?"

The brackets on either side of Jack's mouth deepened. "We haven't opened the results yet."

Carter didn't have to ask why. At no time since his arrival had Jack and Gray looked more alike than they did at this moment, when they had the answer to a pivotal piece of their past literally at their fingertips.

"You should open them when you're ready," Violet finally said.

Maddie rose to her feet and took both men by the hand. "A piece of paper doesn't change anything. It's not going to erase the memories we have of growing up together. Or the ones we've made over the past few months."

Gray stared down at the envelope with the same intensity Carter had seen on a bomb tech's face. Wondering what kind of shape he'd be in if he made the wrong call.

"There's nothing saying you have to open it now," Carter heard himself say. "Why don't you give it a few days?"

"Carter is right," Maddie said, stunning him once again.

Gray looked at Jack. "What do you think?"

"Yeah." Jack plowed his fingers through his hair. "I wasn't expecting the results to come back this soon. I wouldn't mind some more time to think about it."

"And pray about it," Maddie added.

"Why don't we do that right now?" Violet stood up and stretched out a hand to Gray.

Carter felt that familiar tightening in his chest as both sets of twins clasped hands and formed a tight circle. It wasn't just the similarities in their looks that made him feel like an outsider.

For a split second, Gray's eyes met his and Carter saw the question there.

Carter responded with a shake of his head.

And this time when he backed toward the door, no one stopped him.

Chapter Fourteen

"You're going to love Grasslands Community Church!" Maddie linked her arm through Savannah's as they walked to the car. "It's small and everyone knows everyone's name, so don't be surprised if they ask you a million questions. It's not because they're nosy—"

"Sure it is." Ty winked at Savannah as he opened the door of the backseat and waited for her to buckle up next to Darcy.

Savannah glanced out the rear window as Ty's pickup cruised down the driveway, but there was no sign of Carter. When Lupita fussed about him missing breakfast, Maddie and Gray had exchanged a solemn look but didn't comment.

Savannah didn't know if it was because he hadn't accompanied the family to the convalescent center or if something else had happened.

Right before she'd gone to bed, she'd heard a door snap shut. When she'd peeked through the curtain, she'd seen a man sitting on the bench in the courtyard. Even in the dark, she'd recognized Carter's silhouette.

It had taken all Savannah's strength not to join him.

She'd prayed for him instead. Prayed that Carter would

forgive his father for keeping secrets and let God heal whatever had caused the wounds in his soul.

The disappointment on Maddie's face when he'd refused to accompany the family to the convalescent center to visit Belle continued to weigh on Savannah's mind. While Gray and Maddie had made peace with the fact that Belle was their mother, to Carter she was a reminder that Brian Wallace had kept things from his family.

And Savannah knew firsthand just how painful secrets could be....

"That's the Colby farm stand." Maddie pointed to a one-story concrete building on Main Street. "I'm sure Violet would love to give you a tour. I've been helping out behind the counter once in a while."

"I wouldn't mind—"

"We're covered, Savannah." Maddie tossed a smile over her shoulder.

Savannah gave in. For now. But there had to be some way she could feel useful without breaking Dr. Yardley's orders—or Carter's.

They passed a small town green, and Savannah spotted the church up ahead. With its white clapboard siding and slender steeple, it looked like a picture on the front of a postcard. Ty stopped by the doors to let them out.

As Savannah slid out of the backseat, she saw Violet hurrying toward them. The man at her side had no trouble keeping up with her, and Savannah saw a few heads turn in their direction.

She wasn't surprised. Violet and Landon Derringer made a striking couple. She'd met him briefly when he'd arrived the night before, just minutes before the rest of the family returned from visiting Belle Colby.

A reunion where, once again, Carter had been noticeably absent.

"Come on. We'll introduce you to Pastor Jeb." Violet tucked her arm through Savannah's as they reached the white paneled door.

People paused to greet her, and Savannah wondered what it would be like to live in a town like Grasslands. To have people know your name.

This was what she wanted for her child. A place to belong.

Violet waved at a tall, slender man standing just outside the doors leading into the sanctuary.

The minister was younger than Savannah expected, only in his late twenties or early thirties. A shock of russet hair matched the spray of freckles across his nose.

He smiled at Violet and navigated through the clusters of people until he reached their side.

"Pastor Jeb, this is Savannah Blackmore, my brother Carter's friend. She's staying at the ranch for a while."

Savannah hoped the pastor wouldn't read more into the "Carter's friend" description. She didn't want people to get the wrong impression about them.

Behind a pair of horn-rimmed glasses, the pastor's eyes were as welcoming as the church he served. "I'm glad you joined us for worship this morning, Savannah."

Two teen girls rushed over. "Did you bring something for the bake sale, Violet?"

"I brought one of Lupita's confections." Violet grinned. "How are things going in the kitchen? Do you need some help?"

"Yes!"

"I'll meet you in the sanctuary in a few minutes." Laughing, Violet allowed the girls to tow her down the hallway.

"Violet and Landon are really involved in Teen Scene, our youth ministry," Maddie said. "Landon's foundation funded a remodeling project last summer and the number of kids showing up on the weekends has doubled since then."

"That's a good thing, because we're going to need their help for the harvest dinner next weekend." Jeb plucked at his tie in a halfhearted attempt to straighten it that wasn't quite successful.

Savannah glanced at Maddie. "Harvest dinner?"

"Grasslands Community is putting it on, but the whole town is invited. It's a chance to come together and publicly thank God for the blessings He's given us. The whole family will be volunteering in some capacity...." Maddie's smile slipped a notch. "Well, most of us."

With a sinking feeling, Savannah guessed she was talking about Carter. "I'd like to help, too, if you're looking for volunteers."

"Always." Jeb smiled. "I'll introduce you to Sadie Johnson, the church secretary. She knows more about what goes on around here than I—"

A petite woman wearing a shapeless green cardigan and ankle-length khaki skirt suddenly materialized beside them.

"Oh, good, there you are! Sadie, this is Savannah Blackmore." Jeb wrestled his tie into place again. "She's staying at the Colby Ranch and would like to help with the harvest dinner."

A pair of bright green eyes blinked at Savannah behind oversize glasses. "It's nice to meet you," she murmured.

"Sadie's been handling most of the details so she can fill you in after the service," Jeb went on. "I don't know what I did without her."

Savannah was amazed to see twin swatches of color appear in the secretary's cheeks. Jeb Miller, however, seemed oblivious as he nodded at the usher who was waving a bulletin at them.

"I guess that's my cue." The pastor grinned, his tie flapping like a windsock as he loped away.

Savannah realized the prelude had started, beckoning the congregation inside the sanctuary. She followed Maddie down the center aisle to a pew near the front of the church where the rest of the family slid down to make room for them.

A feeling of peace swept over Savannah and she bowed her head.

God, thank You for bringing me here. Thank You for your presence. For the hospitality that Violet and Maddie have shown me…

The pew creaked as someone sat down beside her.

Savannah opened her eyes and slid a sideways glance at the latecomer. "Good morn—"

The whispered greeting died as she found herself staring into a pair of deep blue eyes.

The expression on Savannah's face told Carter that she hadn't expected to see him in church.

Well, he was a little shocked himself. He hadn't planned to attend the service. The last time he'd attended church with his siblings was a Christmas Eve service shortly before he'd joined the marines. Their dad had promised to meet them there, but another emergency had come up and he'd missed it.

"Not everyone wants to be here this morning."

Carter's head jerked up as he heard someone voice his thoughts out loud.

The pastor, Jeb Miller, stood behind a wooden pulpit, Bible in hand.

"Some of you are worn out. Discouraged. Seeking. Maybe you've been running away from God. Maybe you're running to Him. But God brought you here—to this place—for a reason this morning. I trust that He'll reveal it to you."

Carter felt the words pierce his soul. He shifted in his seat, suddenly uncomfortable in a place he had once found comfort.

Savannah paged through the hymnal to the song listed in the bulletin. Her clear alto mingled with the other voices and Carter could tell she'd not only memorized the words, she believed them.

Maddie cleared her throat. The sparkle in her eyes told Carter she knew exactly where his thoughts had drifted.

He *knew* he should have stayed home.

When the song ended, Pastor Jeb tucked his glasses in the front pocket of his shirt and opened up the worn Bible.

"Praise the Lord. Praise God our Savior..." His gaze lifted. Swept over the congregation. "Some of you might be wondering how that's even possible. Maybe you've been experiencing health problems. Maybe you've lost a loved one. Maybe you have to force yourself to get out of bed because even though the sun is shining, life seems...dark. You have doubts. Questions. Circumstances that make you wonder what there is to be thankful for.

"The rest of the verse gives us the answer." Jeb's smile encompassed the people around him. *"He saves us. He carries us.* No matter what we're going through, these are the things we can hold on to. God adopted us into His family—He saved us—and He'll never leave us alone...."

Carter felt beads of sweat pop out on his forehead.

Not here. Not now.

The flashbacks swept in without warning, like a flash flood. Something as ordinary as a word—or a sound—could release the images stored in his memory.

Carter's hands fisted at his sides. This was a part of *his* past he couldn't share with anyone. He swallowed the bile that rose in his throat, ready to bolt.

A hand covered his. Held him in place.

Anchored him.

His heartbeat began to even out and the haze lifted as Savannah's fingers twined with his.

Carter was dimly aware that the message was over and Pastor Jeb was closing in prayer.

He bowed his head, wondering how he'd drifted so far from his faith. Because it hadn't occurred to Carter that when he'd carried the wounded soldiers to safety, one by one, bullets striking the sand all around him, God had been carrying *him*.

Savannah rose to her feet, unable to look at Carter.

What had she been thinking?

He had never given any indication that he wanted her sympathy. Or her friendship.

But something Pastor Jeb said must have struck a nerve. She'd heard the subtle change in his breathing, saw his hands clench at his sides. Sensed he was about to leave.

She hadn't thought—she'd simply…acted. And now that the moment had passed, Savannah was going to have to face Carter again, afraid he would question why she'd taken his hand.

Afraid of what her answer would be.

"Got a second, Carter?" she heard Gray say.

Savannah quickly made her escape. Sadie Johnson was waiting for her in the hallway.

"Do you need to think about it for a few days, or would you like to sign up to help with the harvest dinner now—"

"Now would be *great*."

Sadie gave her a curious look but nodded. "Okay. Follow me."

Savannah was relieved when the secretary bypassed the

crowd of people milling in the hallway and turned down a narrow corridor to a small office tucked in the back of the church. Plants lined the windowsill and a large picture of Jesus, reaching for a lost lamb, hung on the wall.

"Is there a particular area where you'd like to serve?" Sadie handed her a clipboard and pen. "We need people on the setup crew and the hospitality team. I'm in charge of making the meal that night so I'll be doing a lot of the prep work that day."

"I worked at a diner, so I know my way around a kitchen. I'm not supposed to be on my feet for long periods of time, but if you give me a knife and a cutting board, I'm in."

Sadie paused to straighten a stack of papers on the desk. "This is Je—*Pastor Miller's*—way of filing things."

Savannah couldn't help but notice the secretary's tone sounded more affectionate than exasperated. She glanced at Sadie's left hand. No wedding or engagement ring.

"Do you have family in the area? Is that why you moved to Grasslands?"

Savannah had been making conversation, but Sadie shrank back as if she'd aimed a bright light in her eyes.

"Here's the sign-up sheet." She thrust a piece of paper at Savannah. "The youths are sponsoring a bake sale so I better make sure the kitchen is still in one piece."

"Sadie." Savannah took a deep breath. "I'm sorry—I didn't mean to be nosy when I asked about your family."

Sadie's shoulders hunched and her chin disappeared into the collar of her baggy sweater, reminding Savannah of a turtle pulling into its shell.

"It's okay," she murmured. "I don't like to talk about the past, is all. I'm in Grasslands because this is where God wants me to be."

Savannah felt an instant kinship with the woman.

"I understand." She really did. "I'm here to help. With… anything."

For a moment, Sadie didn't respond. And then her lips curved in a shy smile.

"I can give you a quick tour of the kitchen now, if you have a few extra minutes," she offered.

Savannah smiled back. "I'd like that."

A few extra minutes were *exactly* what she needed. To get to know Sadie better.

And to avoid Carter.

Even though something told her it would take a lot more time than that to sort through the feelings he stirred inside her.

Chapter Fifteen

Ten steps away from freedom.

Carter maneuvered around the obstacles in his path—a gray-haired lady holding a plate of brownies, a young mother pushing a stroller roughly the size of an SUV, a teenager holding up a coffee can filled with donations—and kept his gaze trained on the target.

The front door of the church.

"Carter Wallace." Pastor Jeb's lanky frame suddenly blocked his escape route. "I hoped I'd get an opportunity to talk to you after the service. You've been on my prayer list the past few weeks."

"Thank you, Pastor." Carter dug deep and scraped up a smile. The red-haired preacher reminded Carter of one of the young chaplains he'd met overseas. Compassionate. Wise.

Dangerous.

The pastor's message had stripped away Carter's emotional armor, left him feeling vulnerable and exposed. And running for cover.

He took a quick surveillance of his surroundings, searching for the people he'd been trying to get away from five seconds ago. His family.

But now, when he could have used them as a buffer—or a shield—they were nowhere in sight.

"Everyone is checking out the bake sale in the youth wing." Pastor Jeb grinned, as if he'd read Carter's thoughts.

Dangerous, no doubt about it.

Carter weighed his options. Hang out with the preacher or join the people chatting in the fellowship hall.

"I'll wait here." Or outside. In the parking lot.

"Come with me." The pastor came up with another idea. "If you've got a few minutes, I'll show you what your sister's been up to."

"Knowing Maddie, it could be anything," Carter said as he fell into step with Jeb.

The pastor slid a sideways look at him. "I was talking about Violet. She and Landon have been working on Teen Scene, our youth program, for the last few months."

When was he going to start thinking of Violet as family?

It should have been easy, given the fact that she and Maddie were identical twins. There were similarities in their personalities, too. Jack Colby, on the other hand... The guy eyed him like he would a bronco trapped in a chute, as cautious about Carter as Carter was about him.

They turned down a narrow corridor that connected the sanctuary to another building.

"Landon funded the repairs so we could fix up this area for the teenagers after it was vandalized a few months ago. Every Friday and Saturday night, adult volunteers supervise the activities. Game nights. Pizza parties. You name it, we've had it." Jeb opened the door. "The kids congregate here after the Sunday morning services—"

The gym was empty.

"Well, they *usually* congregate here after the Sunday morning service," he said ruefully. "I guess it's a good sign they're all helping with the bake sale."

A door at the far end of the gym swung open and an adolescent boy with a shock of wheat-colored hair slipped inside.

"Tommy?" Jeb waved to get his attention. "Where is everyone?"

"The back parking lot. Jairo can't get his car started."

"Again?" Jeb chuckled. "I think he pushes that thing more than he drives it."

"I can take a look," Carter offered. "No one in my family seems to be in a big hurry to leave."

No one except him, anyway.

Tommy sidled closer. "You fix cars?"

"He can fix anything, kid." Gray had walked up behind them. "Cars. Armored trucks. Tanks."

Tommy's gaze swung back to Carter. *"Tanks?"*

"Sometimes."

"Sometimes." Gray cuffed Carter on the back of the head. "They give you a medal for modesty?" He lowered his voice to a conspiratorial whisper. "My kid brother can get a car without an engine to start."

"Cool!"

Carter rolled his eyes. "He's exaggerating."

"I hope you can fix it. Jairo is supposed to give me a ride home," Tommy added with a mischievous grin.

"You fix Jairo's car and you'll be a hero around these parts," Jeb said.

Carter flinched. There was that word again.

He followed Tommy to the parking lot, where a group of teenage boys circled a rusty pickup like mourners at a graveside service.

"This guy—Carter—he's going to take a look at the engine, Jairo," Tommy informed everyone breathlessly. "He fixes armored trucks. And tanks."

A lanky Hispanic boy stepped away from the vehicle, eyeing Carter with a mixture of skepticism and hope.

"I've got a few things to check on before I head over to Ranchland Manor," Jeb said. "Do you mind—"

"We're good." Carter was already bending down to take a look inside the engine. The boys crowded around him, blocking the light.

Ten minutes later, the engine coughed once and came back to life.

"That should do it." Carter wiped his greasy hands on a bandana one of the kids had tossed at him.

Savannah wouldn't want to hold his hand now....

Carter gritted his teeth in an attempt to channel his thoughts down a safer path.

A futile attempt, it seemed, because questions ricocheted inside his head.

Why *had* Savannah taken his hand? How had she known it was exactly what he'd needed?

"There you are."

Carter stiffened as a familiar face appeared in his line of vision. A familiar face whose brown eyes were shaded by the brim of a cowboy hat.

Jack.

"Maddie and Violet are going to help Sadie clean up from the bake sale and then we decided to stop over to Ranchland Manor."

To see Belle. Fortunately, Jack didn't ask if he wanted to go along.

"Okay. No problem."

"Can you give Savannah a ride back to the ranch?"

The two of them. Alone in the car on the drive back to the ranch.

Now *that* was a problem.

* * *

Savannah crumpled up the empty wrapper and licked a smudge of chocolate frosting from her finger as she left the fellowship hall to look for Maddie and Ty.

She'd stopped by the bake sale for a few minutes and ended up buying a piece of cake from one of the teenagers. Violet had been scurrying around the kitchen, helping Sadie, and Savannah had caught a glimpse of Keira striding down the hall, but at some point she'd lost track of the couple she'd ridden with.

She saw an open door halfway down the hall and slipped inside to look for a wastebasket.

Music drifted from tiny speakers mounted in the corners of the ceiling. Checkered curtains trimmed the windows. A padded rocking chair was stationed at the foot of a rainbow stenciled on one bright yellow wall.

The church nursery.

On their own volition, Savannah's feet carried her forward. She traced a finger along the rail of a wooden crib.

"It's amazing, isn't it? The smaller they are, the more stuff they seem to need."

Savannah turned at the sound of the pastor's voice behind her.

"I guess so." Savannah was three months away from her due date and hadn't set up a nursery yet. She had to find an apartment. Soon. Had to paint the walls and buy a crib. No matter what Maddie and Violet said, she couldn't take advantage of their hospitality much longer.

"We've got a wonderful group of volunteers to staff the nursery," Jeb said. "Your baby will be in good hands."

It was too dangerous to imagine being part of Jeb's congregation. Part of the community.

"I'm not staying in Grasslands very long."

"Oh? Violet made it sound like—" Jeb shook his head. "Never mind."

Savannah could only guess what Violet had made it sound like!

"I don't want to be a burden on the family."

"I know the Colbys pretty well," Jeb said easily. "I doubt they see it that way."

Did Carter?

That's what Savannah wasn't sure about.

Jeb turned off the CD player and for the first time, Savannah noticed the ring of keys dangling from his fingers. It suddenly occurred to her that while she'd been lingering in the nursery, the pastor was ready to leave.

"I'm sorry," Savannah stammered. "I didn't mean to keep you from locking up." Not to mention that Maddie and Ty were probably wondering what had happened to her.

"Don't apologize. I never want to miss out on a divine appointment." Jeb smiled. "God brings people together for a reason."

And hopefully, sometimes He kept them apart, Savannah thought as she made her way back to the foyer.

She pulled up short when she saw Carter prowling back and forth in front of the door as if he were waiting for someone.

The blue eyes drew a bead on her instead.

Heat swept into Savannah's cheeks even though she couldn't tell what he was thinking.

"Have you seen Maddie?"

"They decided to stop at Ranchland Manor and Jack asked if I'd take you back to the ranch. So I guess it's just you and me."

Savannah swallowed hard.

He'd been waiting for someone, all right.

Her.

Savannah kept her head down as Carter escorted her to the car.

It was clear he was going to have to have a little talk with Maddie and Violet. Because this arrangement had their matchmaking fingerprints all over it.

Carter opened the passenger-side door for Savannah and went around to the other side. When he got in, she was trying to wrangle the seat belt into place.

"Need some help?" Carter automatically reached for the buckle and ended up holding Savannah's hand instead.

"Sorry—"

"*—Sorry.*"

The words bumped together and the interior of the vehicle seemed to shrink in size, narrowing his focus to a pair of stunning green eyes.

As far as casual touches went, Carter had had more contact with a woman in the checkout line at the grocery store, but suddenly he found it difficult to breathe.

"Let's try that again." His voice was as uneven as his pulse. "The buckle," he added, just for clarification.

Savannah ducked her head as Carter snapped the metal clip into place but even though she wasn't looking at him, a new awareness shimmered between them, as warm and real as the sunlight streaming through the windshield.

"Thank you." Savannah's sigh fractured the silence. "Some of the little things I've always done without a second thought are getting more complicated."

"I know what you mean." Carter spoke without thinking and then tried to cover the words with a laugh.

"Do they happen…often?" she asked softly.

Carter's gut clenched. No one in his family had questioned him about the flashbacks, although they probably wondered why he sometimes walked out of the room without a word of explanation.

"Often enough," he heard himself say.

"What—" Savannah hesitated "—helps you get through it?"

"If I can get away by myself for a while." Solitude didn't prevent a battering from the internal storm but at least when he was alone, his pride remained intact.

"Oh." Savannah's troubled gaze dropped to his hand and a hint of pink stole into her cheeks.

Carter suddenly had another flashback. Savannah taking his hand during the worship service, holding the darkness at bay.

That wasn't the way it was supposed to work.

He was supposed to be there for her, not the other way around. Keeping the promise he'd made to Rob, not fighting a growing attraction to the woman his friend had left behind.

Maybe a few hours spent tinkering with the engine of the Chevy would put things back in perspective.

He understood the way an engine worked. Knew exactly what to do when it didn't.

It was too bad life wasn't that simple.

He was about to put the car in gear when his cell began to ring. He glanced at the tiny screen and saw Maddie's name and number pop up. Anchoring the phone between his shoulder and his ear, he adjusted the rearview mirror.

"What's up?"

"Are you still at the church?" Maddie said breathlessly.

"Just leaving."

"I left my bag in the sanctuary. Can you check—"

"Sure." Carter swallowed a sigh.

"—and bring it to the convalescent home? We're there now with Belle."

Carter's hands gripped the wheel.

"Carter? Are you still there?"

"Yes."

"Thanks." Maddie seemed to think his response covered all the questions. "Belle is in room one-fourteen. We'll see you in a few minutes. Bye."

Carter heard a click in his ear. "Maddie left her purse."

"I'll get it." Savannah reached for the buckle on her seat belt.

"Don't take this the wrong way—but I can move faster than you."

"Is there a *right* way to take that?" Savannah muttered.

Carter grinned, feeling some of the tension between them ease.

When he entered the church, he saw a slight young woman about Savannah's age sitting in the front pew, her head bowed. He would have tried to sneak in, locate the missing purse and sneak back out, but the floor creaked beneath his foot.

Her entire body jerked at the sound and she twisted around. The church secretary. Sarah? No. Sadie, that was it.

"Sorry." *Whoa.* Carter backed up when he saw the tears rolling down her cheeks. "I didn't mean to startle you. My sister left her purse in here."

"It's on the table."

Carter looked to his left and recognized Maddie's purse. Of course it had to be *pink*. If the guys in his unit saw him now, he'd never hear the end of it.

He stuffed it under his arm, took a step toward the door and hesitated.

"Is something wrong? Do you want me to get Pastor Jeb?"

"No!" The word ricocheted around the room. "I mean, thank you—but that's not necessary. I'm…fine."

Yeah. There seemed to be a lot of that going around,

Carter thought grimly. But he sensed that pushing the issue would only make the woman more uncomfortable.

He retraced his steps back to the car. Fortunately, Ranchland Manor was only a few blocks from the church.

"Maddie should be waiting by the door," Carter said as he pulled into the parking lot.

Except that she wasn't.

Five minutes ticked by and there was no sign of her or anyone else in the family.

Reluctantly, Carter parked the car and turned the key in the ignition, the engine dying along with the hope that Maddie was going to show up.

"I'll go inside and track her down."

To Carter's amazement, Savannah unbuckled her seat belt.

"I'm coming with you."

A nurse's assistant wearing bright yellow scrubs smiled at Savannah as she and Carter walked up to the desk.

"Can I help you?"

"We're waiting for my sister," Carter said.

"She might be in the family lounge. It's the second door on the left."

"Thank you." Carter was already on his way down the hall, obviously in a hurry to complete his mission.

"There's no one here." Frustration leached into his voice.

"Do you know what room they're in?"

He gave a reluctant nod. "One-fourteen."

Savannah didn't have to work to keep up with Carter as they walked down the hall.

"This is it." Carter made no move to go inside.

The door was open a crack but Savannah couldn't hear the sound of voices. She knocked on the door and then gingerly pushed it open.

"They aren't here, either. Maybe they're getting a cup of coffee." Without waiting for permission, Savannah walked into the room.

A moment later, Carter followed. Fresh flowers bloomed in vases on the windowsill and someone had taken the time to fill the bulletin board on the wall with photographs of the family.

Savannah pressed her fingers over her lips when she saw Belle Colby for the first time.

Ribbons of copper hair spilled over the pillow, framing the woman's delicate porcelain features. Belle's eyes were closed, but Savannah just knew they would be the same shade of brown as Maddie's and Violet's.

Carter released a ragged breath. "Maddie… She looks just like her."

Savannah swallowed hard, trying to dislodge the lump that had formed in her throat.

What had Maddie thought the first time she'd seen her biological mother?

Belle moved restlessly and Savannah pulled the blanket up higher, tucking it around her shoulders. When she turned around, Carter was staring at the bulletin board. Someone had tacked a picture of Maddie and Gray alongside photographs of Violet and Jack.

"I don't understand why he did it," he said tightly.

Savannah knew Carter was talking about his father.

A soft moan from the woman in the bed brought both of them back to her side. Belle's forehead was furrowed and she tossed her head back and forth.

"Maybe I should get the nurse," Savannah whispered. "She seems agitated."

"Maddie said they talk to Belle like she can hear them," he said quietly.

Savannah's heart swelled as Carter reached out and took

Belle's hand. An instinctive move meant to comfort the person who had turned his life upside down.

"It's going to be all right," he murmured.

The copper lashes fluttered in response to the husky timbre of Carter's voice. Belle's head rolled toward him. Her shallow breath took the shape of a word.

"Brian."

The color drained from Carter's face. "Did you hear that?" he said hoarsely.

"I...think so." Savannah pressed her fingers against her lips, certain her imagination had been playing tricks on her.

Carter stared up at her, his eyes dark with disbelief.

"She said my dad's name."

Chapter Sixteen

"Mom *spoke?*"

Violet was suddenly there beside them, Maddie, Gray and Jack one step behind her as they rushed into the room.

Carter shook his head. "I'm not sure she—"

"Did she open her eyes?"

"What did she say?"

The questions tumbled over each other. Carter didn't know which one—or who—to answer first. But the commotion caught the attention of one of the nurses in the hallway. She poked her head in, her expression a mixture of concern and disapproval.

"Is everything all right?"

"Mom said something." Tears glistened in Violet's eyes. "Carter and Savannah heard her."

"Can you describe what happened?" The nurse moved toward the bed, her movements brisk and efficient as she began to take Belle's vitals.

Everyone was looking at Carter now, waiting.

"I'm not sure." Carter was already second-guessing what he'd heard.

Jack pinned Carter in place with a look. "What did she say?"

"It sounded like she said…Brian," he admitted.

Violet let out a startled cry and Maddie grabbed the back of the chair for support.

The nurse frowned. "Is that a name you recognize?"

"It's our dad," Violet whispered.

The room was silent as the nurse brought up Belle's chart and tapped something into the computer.

Jack finally voiced the question on everyone's mind. "Does this mean she's waking up?"

"I can't say that for certain," the nurse said cautiously. "But we'll keep a close eye on her today, and I'll bring it to the doctor's attention when he makes his rounds."

"I think I'll stay for a little while." Violet pulled a chair closer to the bed. "But the rest of you can go home if you'd like."

"I'm not going anywhere, either." Maddie brushed a strand of hair off Belle's cheek.

Gray pulled up a chair, and Jack propped a hip against the metal nightstand.

Apparently that meant they were staying, too.

Carter started for the door, prodded on by guilt.

"Are you leaving?" Maddie asked.

"It's pretty crowded in here already."

And he didn't belong. If—*when*—Belle Colby woke up, her family should be the ones at her bedside.

Carter forced himself to match his pace to Savannah's on the way to the parking lot. He opened the door for her and then slid in the driver's side. His fingers trembled as he stuck the key in the ignition.

"You didn't imagine it," Savannah said softly.

Carter's head whipped around. "Belle's own *children*—" he stumbled over the word "—have been talking to her for months. Praying for a sign that she'll come out of this and be all right. Why did it happen when *I* was there?"

"Maybe—" Savannah stopped.

He glanced at her sharply. "Maybe what?"

"You took her hand. Said her name. Maybe Belle heard your voice and thought *you* were Brian and she…responded."

"That's—" *Impossible,* Carter wanted to say. But then he remembered all the times that people had mistaken him for his father when he'd answered the telephone.

Could Savannah be right?

And had anyone else come to the same conclusion?

"She and Dad had been in their teens when they were together. They'd gone on with their lives. Why would Belle say his name?"

"Maybe there wasn't any closure," Savannah said after a moment. "She might…regret…the way things ended between them."

"Regrets." The word left a sour taste in Carter's mouth.

He had plenty of those. But did his dad have some, too? He'd married again. Had another child. Did he wish he'd stayed with Belle? Was that the reason he'd always seemed so distant? Buried himself in his work?

"You said no one knows why they split up. It could be that something forced them apart."

"Something like wondering whether Gray and Jack are really his sons?" The words slipped out before Carter could stop them.

Savannah stared at him. "What are you talking about?"

"Gray and Jack might not be my brothers."

"Of course they are. Look at Maddie and Violet."

"They resemble Belle—not my dad."

Savannah looked shaken. "That doesn't mean anything."

"Apparently Violet and Maddie met a woman in Fort Worth who claimed that her husband fathered the boys. Joe Earl and Belle went to high school together. So when it comes right down to it, they might not even be related to the girls by blood."

"I don't believe that. From everything Violet has said about her mother, Belle doesn't seem like the type of person who would have done something like that."

"It would explain why they split up," he ground out.

"Wouldn't a DNA test rule that out?"

"Gray and Jack took one while I was overseas. The results are back but they aren't ready to look at them yet. I guess they're not ready to deal with the ramifications of it."

"Or they already have," she murmured.

Carter parked the car in front of Savannah's cottage and turned to look at her. "What do you mean?"

"Maybe they decided it doesn't matter."

Savannah stared out the window.

The main house remained dark. Lights blazed from the window of the shed where Carter had discovered the truck.

It had been several hours since he'd dropped her off at the front door and she'd spent a lot of time in prayer.

There were things she might never understand about the past, but she was determined to trust God's plan, for her and her unborn child. She thought she'd lost everything when her husband walked out, but the baby had been a gift from God. An unexpected blessing that had encouraged her to keep going. To keep trusting.

She prayed Carter would begin to trust Him, too. Understand how blessed he was to have a family who loved him.

But right now, he was alone.

Savannah grabbed her jacket and went outside.

The door was closed to hold the chill at bay but a country ballad rattled the walls, trying to escape.

Now that she was here, she was having second thoughts.

Carter hadn't sought out her company, which meant that he preferred to be alone.

Or it had become a habit.

The door opened and Carter stood there, effectively shutting off all thoughts of retreat.

"Come on in. It's cold outside."

"How did you know I was here?"

He raised an eyebrow.

"Marine. Right."

To Savannah's absolute amazement, Carter's elusive dimple surfaced, giving her the courage to venture inside.

"Did you get the truck running yet?"

"Are you familiar with the old saying 'good things come to those who wait'?"

"Uh-huh. So that means it's still broken."

"Not broken." Carter reached into the engine. "A work in progress."

Savannah reached out to pet one of the kittens, who'd commandeered the jacket Carter had tossed on a chair.

"Did you eat supper at the main house?" Carter asked.

"No one's back yet."

Carter went still. "They're still at the convalescent home?"

"I think so."

Carter didn't say anything, but Savannah could see that he blamed himself for that.

"They're where they want to be, Carter."

And if she were completely honest, so was she.

"Can I help?"

Carter looked as surprised by Savannah's impulsive offer as she was to have made it.

"What do you know about trucks?"

"I know when you put the key in the ignition and step on the gas they're supposed to go."

"Then no, you can't help. But you *can* follow your doctor's orders." Carter yanked a chair into the light and swiped at the upholstered seat, an invitation to stay that Savannah didn't hesitate to accept.

For the next half hour, she watched him work, humming along with the radio or muttering under his breath, depending on what was going on underneath the hood.

A slow country song, as much a classic as the truck Carter was trying so hard to resuscitate, drifted from the speakers of the dusty radio parked in a corner of the shed.

The toe of Savannah's shoe tapped the dusty floor, and it caught Carter's attention.

"You're a fan?"

"Uh-huh, but I'm not sure how it happened. At the diner, Bruce either had a country music station blaring from the radio, or a football game. I tried to fight it—"

"And ended up liking both." Carter grinned.

"Exactly." Savannah couldn't resist grinning back.

"In that case—" Carter held out his hand "—would you care to dance, ma'am?"

"I can't…dance."

Savannah backed away from Carter as if he'd offered her a stick of dynamite.

"Everyone can dance." For his own sake, Carter hoped he was right.

"My balance is off. I can hardly walk a straight line anymore."

"Swaying…dancing…they're kind of the same thing, aren't they?" Carter had been teasing—until he saw the wary look return. Carter still didn't know what Rob had done to put that expression there but he wanted to do something to extinguish it. For good.

He drew Savannah into his arms and ignored her chirp

of protest, surprised at how good—how right—it felt to have her there.

The top of her head grazed Carter's chin and the delicate floral scent of her shampoo reminded him of spring.

"See?" he murmured close to her ear.

She promptly stepped on his foot.

"I warned you that would happen."

Carter smiled. "What happened?"

"You'll know when the bruise shows up," she muttered. "I'm not exactly graceful anymore."

"You're beautiful." The words slipped out before Carter could stop them.

Savannah averted her gaze. "You don't have to do this, you know."

"Do what?"

"Tell me what you think I want to hear."

Is that what Rob had done? Just because they'd been good friends didn't mean that Carter was unaware of Rob's weaknesses. The guy could have sold fertilizer to a rancher.

Suddenly, Carter wanted her to see *him,* not Rob.

"I'm telling you the truth." He cupped the delicate curve of her jaw and lifted her face. Pressed a kiss against her forehead.

Savannah stared up at him, her eyes wide with shock. And something else; something that made his heart trip.

Carter's hands settled on Savannah's waist and he dipped his head, capturing her lips in a lingering kiss that she sweetly returned.

Something moved under his palm and Carter jerked back in surprise. *"What—"*

Color flooded Savannah's cheeks. "The baby is pretty active this time of the day. Sometimes I'm convinced that she's going to be a professional soccer player."

If Carter had ever questioned how Maddie and Gray

could feel so…*connected*…to Belle, a woman they'd never met, he understood it now, when he felt another tiny flutter, as delicate as the brush of a butterfly's wing, against his palm.

Carter wanted to take care of *both* of them, and not because of the promise he'd made to a friend. Somewhere along the way, Savannah and the baby had become linked together in Carter's mind. And in his heart.

"Savannah—"

"Uh-oh." A teasing sparkle lit Savannah's eyes. "Why do I get the feeling that you're about to ask your question of the day?"

"What happened between you and Rob?"

Carter felt the tremor that ran through Savannah and she slipped out of his arms. He felt the chill of her retreat the moment she stepped away.

For a moment, he didn't think she was going to respond. And Carter was already regretting that he'd shattered the closeness of the moment by bringing up the past.

"I—I worked the closing shift at the diner and Rob came in one night. The other waitresses actually argued over who would get to wait on him because he was so good-looking.

"I was bussing tables that night, so I stayed out of it. Rob knocked a glass of water over and insisted that I let him help me clean it up. He told me later that he'd done it on purpose in order to meet me."

So far, that sounded like Rob, Carter thought wryly.

"He told me that he was in medical school and needed a quiet place to study."

That didn't. "Medical school?"

"To become a pediatric surgeon."

Carter frowned. "Rob never mentioned that he wanted to be a doctor."

"Because he didn't. He made it up to…impress me. Rob

never even finished high school. When we met, he was working for a cleaning service. He stopped at the diner before his shift started and ordered a cup of coffee because it was all he could afford, not so he could stay awake all night studying."

"Why didn't he just tell you the truth?"

"Believe it or not, I asked Rob the same question. He didn't think I would be interested in a high school dropout so he made up all these stories to win me over." Her voice quivered with emotion. "I didn't ask for details, I just—"

"Trusted him."

Savannah nodded. "My grandmother was gone and I didn't have any family. It was easy to ignore the red flags and let Rob sweep me off my feet. He said if we loved each other, there was no reason to wait to get married." She swallowed hard. "Looking back, I think he was afraid I would find out the truth and leave—but he left *me,* a week after we got married. We had a huge argument. He said that marrying me had been a…mistake."

None of this lined up with the guy Carter had known.

"Is that why you didn't tell Rob about the baby?"

Savannah flinched. "I didn't know I was pregnant right away. I thought the symptoms, what I was feeling, was caused by…stress. When I finally went to the doctor, I was already four months along. I sent Rob an email, asking him to c-call me, but it was too late."

Carter did the math and released a ragged breath.

Would it have made a difference, if his friend had known about the baby? Would Rob have taken steps to reconcile with Savannah?

"I wanted to work things out," Savannah went on in a low voice. "I was hoping that when Rob found out I was pregnant, it might make a difference. That he would give our marriage another chance."

Carter felt as if he'd just been sucker punched.

"You would have taken him back?"

"I may have rushed into getting married, but I took the vows seriously." Savannah searched his face. "You still don't believe me, do you?"

She pivoted away from him and walked out the door.

Carter let her go.

Because he was the one who should have died when the convoy was attacked.

Rob hadn't been given another chance.

But for some reason, *he* had.

If only Carter knew what he was supposed to do with it.

Chapter Seventeen

"Mail call." Violet breezed into the kitchen where Savannah sat at the breakfast counter, frosting a cake for the harvest dinner. With a little coaxing, Lupita had agreed to let her help out and this was the only job the housekeeper decided wouldn't be too taxing.

"The house is pretty quiet today. Where is everyone?" Violet hopped onto the stool next to Savannah and eyed the bowl of cream cheese frosting. "That looks yummy."

"Carrot cake. Lupita made three of them for tonight."

"I suppose Maddie isn't home from work yet, is she?"

"Not yet."

"This one goes to the bottom of the pile then." Violet sifted through the stack of envelopes. "Carter?"

The knife Savannah had been holding almost slipped out of her hand. "N-no."

"He must be helping Ty again today. I know he wants to feel useful, but I'm beginning to think we're taking advantage of him." She furrowed her brow. "I haven't seen much of him the past few days so he must have found something to keep himself busy."

Or else, Savannah thought, Carter was avoiding her.

It was a little hard to tell, given the fact that she'd been avoiding *him*.

But keeping her distance hadn't stopped Savannah from thinking about the kiss they'd shared.

She ducked her head, hoping Violet wouldn't notice the color stealing into her cheeks.

Violet surreptitiously swiped her finger around the rim of the bowl. "Sadie stopped by the produce stand this morning and said you're planning to meet her at the church."

"She has some last-minute prep work for the harvest dinner." And Carter wasn't the only one who wanted to feel useful. "Making the stuffing. Getting the turkeys in the oven—"

"Peeling the hundred pounds of potatoes I donated." Violet grinned. "Keira and I signed on to set up the tables, so we'll swing by later this afternoon. Gray picked up Elise and Cory and they're on the way to Grasslands as we speak."

"What about Landon?" Savannah teased.

"He had a project to finish up, but he'll be here, too."

Savannah wasn't surprised to hear that everyone had adjusted their schedules so they could help with the dinner. Both the community and the congregation had rallied around the family over the past few months and the event provided a way for them to give back.

"Something smells good." Jack wandered into the kitchen, looking every inch the cowboy in a canvas work coat, faded jeans and leather boots.

"Carrot cake." Violet pushed the bowl of frosting toward him.

Jack reached for it, spotted the mail on the counter and flicked a questioning look at his sister.

"Nothing," Violet said gently. "Darcy got a card from her grandparents and there's a letter for Carter. Looks kind of official."

Jack nodded. "Gray mentioned something about him being nominated for a medal."

"A medal?"

Two pairs of brown eyes cut to Savannah and she realized she'd said it out loud.

"The Silver Star. Apparently Carter saved three men during an ambush a few months ago, one of them a high-ranking officer who was visiting the base. He risked his life to get them to safety."

"I can't believe he didn't tell us that," Violet murmured. "That's quite an honor."

"An honor Carter doesn't think he deserves, according to Gray."

"Why—"

Savannah saw Jack shake his head and Violet lapsed into silence.

That's when she knew.

The ambush they were talking about…it had to be the one that claimed Rob's life.

"Excuse me." Savannah slid off the stool and felt her knees wobble. "Sadie's waiting. I should probably go."

Violet caught her hand and squeezed it.

"I'm sorry, Savannah. I wasn't thinking." Violet bit her lip. "I didn't mean to remind you of something so painful."

"I know. And you *should* be proud of Carter. He's a hero."

He always does the right thing, Maddie had said.

Risking his life for a fellow soldier.

Or keeping a promise to the one he hadn't been able to save.

* * *

Sadie was already stationed at the sink when Savannah arrived at the church.

"You should have told me you'd be here early."

"I had some extra time so I thought I might as well get to work." Sadie nodded in the direction of an enormous plastic bucket.

Violet's potatoes.

Savannah grabbed an apron from the hook near the door and tied it around what remained of her waist.

The side door of the kitchen swung open and a teenage boy with shaggy black hair prowled in.

"What do you need, Jairo?" Sadie asked calmly.

"Is there anything to drink?"

"Lemonade in the fridge." Sadie gave him an indulgent smile. "And if you promise not to track in any more dirt, I'll throw in some of these cookies."

"Deal." Jairo flashed a boyish grin at odds with his tough exterior and tiptoed across the kitchen floor.

"How is it going out there?" Sadie began to pile cookies on a plate.

"We're working on the brakes right now. Carter has to order a part, but he thinks it will be here by the end of the week."

The potato Savannah had been peeling slipped out of her hand and landed in the sink with a thud. "Carter *Wallace?*"

"*Sí.* He's helping us." Jairo snagged a cookie from the plate, dodging Sadie's playful slap to the back of his hand. "Gotta go. They're waiting for me."

After Jairo left the kitchen with the refreshments, Savannah tried to wrap her mind around the fact that Carter was here. At the church.

Sadie didn't seem to notice how flustered she was.

"Jeb…" The receptionist caught herself. "*Pastor* Jeb said

that Carter Wallace donated an old truck to Teen Scene so the boys will have something to keep them busy after school."

"An old truck?"

"It's an antique, I guess. I can't remember what he said it was."

"A '67 Chevy."

Sadie's eyes widened. "That's right. Have you seen it?"

Savannah had not only seen it, she'd seen the look on Carter's face when he'd discovered it in the shed. And yet he'd donated it to the church. Volunteered to help the boys fix it up.

"You don't mind running a plate of sandwiches out there, do you? I've seen the way those boys eat and they're going to need more than a handful of cookies to tide them over until the dinner tonight." Sadie handed her a platter.

"I—" Savannah tried to come up with a reasonable excuse to decline.

"Go on." Sadie gave her a gentle nudge. "The setup crew will be here in a few minutes so I have to be here to tell them what to do."

Savannah somehow found herself on the other side of the door.

Her steps slowed as she spotted Carter, surrounded by a pack of boys who appeared to be listening intently to his instructions.

In a camouflage jacket and loose-fitting jeans the faded blue of an April sky, Carter looked confident and in control.

And way too appealing.

Carter handed Jairo a tool and the boy beamed as if he'd been given a medal.

A Silver Star...doesn't think he deserves it.

Jack's words cycled through Savannah's mind again and she suddenly realized why.

Carter blamed himself for Rob's death.

Savannah stumbled, wondering why it hadn't occurred to her before. But she knew without a doubt that Carter would have done everything possible to save Rob. The fact he'd put his own life at risk to save the other soldiers showed the kind of man he was.

The kind of man it would be all too easy to fall in love with.

"Food!"

Carter had just shimmied under the truck when he heard a muffled cheer and the clatter of tools hitting the ground around him.

It appeared he was going to have to lecture the kids on their priorities. Because they'd just abandoned an icon for an afternoon snack.

Sadie must have taken pity on them.

Out of the corner of his eye, he saw a dozen pairs of size eleven tennis shoes...and one pair of dainty blue ones.

Savannah.

Carter jerked. His forehead connected with the undercarriage and he growled.

"Are you all right?" Savannah was on her knees, peering under the vehicle.

"I'm fine." At least he would be. Once the spots in front of his eyes went away.

"I don't believe you. Your face is all scrunched up like you're in pain."

"Marines don't feel pain." He pulled in a breath. "And we don't...*scrunch*."

"You're bleeding."

That got the attention of the boys, who momentarily abandoned their snack and hustled over for a better look.

"Cool!" Tommy breathed.

Carter felt a trickle of *something* run down his cheek.

"I'll get the first-aid kit." Savannah was already pushing to her feet.

"Don't you dare." Carter rolled out from under the vehicle and pressed the hem of his shirt to his temple.

"You might have a concussion."

"I don't have a—" Carter's breath snagged in his throat as Savannah stood on her tiptoes to examine the tiny scratch on his forehead.

"It's not deep," she murmured.

Carter was close enough to see the lavender shadows beneath her eyes.

Close enough to kiss her again.

His gaze dropped to the full curve of her bow-shaped lips and he swayed a little.

Maybe he *did* have a concussion. Or maybe his subconscious was reminding him how right she'd felt in his arms.

Savannah's hands reached out to steady him and the contact sent another jolt of awareness rocketing through his veins.

He took a step backward to put some distance between them.

"You look tired," he said bluntly. "I think you should be on the sofa with your feet up, reading a book."

"Really?" Savannah crossed her arms. "And I think you should be at the clinic. This cut might need stitches."

The boys, who had drifted away, perked up their ears at that.

"I don't need—" Wait a second. "You're doing this on purpose."

"Doing what on purpose?"

"*Fussing* over me."

"Fussing?" Savannah blinked, as innocent as one of Darcy's kittens.

"Giving me a taste of my own medicine, so to speak." Carter's eyes narrowed. "You are under no obligation to worry about me. But I—" He stopped.

"Have an *obligation* to worry about me."

Carter tried not to let Savannah see how the words affected him.

How *she* affected him.

Over the past two weeks, the promise he'd made to Rob had undergone a subtle change. Now, instead of looking out for her, Carter looked forward to spending time *with* her.

Which was why he'd tried to put some distance between them the past few days. A plan that had backfired. Just because he hadn't seen much of Savannah didn't mean he'd stopped thinking about her.

Or the way she'd returned his kiss.

The one he'd had no business initiating. The one he had no business repeating.

"I told you before that I'm not your responsibility," Savannah said slowly. "But here's my promise to you—I'll be leaving soon, and you won't have to worry about me anymore."

Carter didn't miss the irony. The government wanted to give him an award for bravery but he was afraid to tell Savannah the truth.

He wanted her to stay.

Chapter Eighteen

The church kitchen was bustling with activity by the time Savannah returned.

Praise music played in the background, a sweet accompaniment to the chatter of conversation as everyone set to work. Maddie and Violet were working in tandem, chopping up fresh vegetables for the teenage girls who were making up the trays.

The phone began to ring and Elise reached for it. "Grasslands Community Church." She put her hand over the mouthpiece. "Does anyone know where Sadie went?"

Kiera glanced up. "I saw her a few minutes ago. She said she was going to look through the storage closet and round up the centerpieces for the tables."

"Sally has a question about the pies."

"I'll find her," Savannah offered. It would give her a few minutes to collect herself.

The unexpected encounter with Carter had left her shaken.

Savannah didn't like secrets—but realizing she'd fallen in love with a man who only saw her as his best friend's widow wasn't one she could share with the women gathered together in the kitchen.

Savannah heard voices down the hall as she rounded the corner.

Pastor Jeb and Sadie. They stood at the end of the hall and Savannah started in that direction. She saw Jeb touch Sadie's arm. With an anguished cry, Sadie jerked away from him and fled down the hall.

Right toward Savannah.

"Sadie! Wait!"

But the other woman streaked past her, tears streaming down her cheeks.

Jeb started after her but Savannah blocked his path. "What's going on?" In spite of what she'd just witnessed, Savannah couldn't believe that Jeb was capable of a harsh word.

"I didn't mean to upset her." Jeb winced when they heard a door slam. He looked discouraged. Defeated.

Two emotions that Savannah wouldn't have expected him to display, either.

"Was it bad news?" she asked cautiously. She didn't want to pry, but she was concerned about her new friend.

Jeb's lips twisted. "I guess so," he muttered.

Savannah didn't understand the cryptic comment. "I'll find Sadie and make sure she's all right."

Jeb scrubbed a hand across his jaw. "I guess that would be best, under the circumstances."

What circumstances? Savannah wanted to know. But she gave the pastor's arm a reassuring pat. "Can you let Maddie and Violet know I'll be back in a few minutes?"

"Sure." Jeb's gaze strayed to the door again. "Thanks, Savannah."

She had a hunch she knew where Sadie would go. Sure enough, she stepped out the back door of the church and spotted her sitting on a bench under one of the trees in the prayer garden.

"Sadie?"

Sadie's head jerked up and she rose to her feet, poised to flee again. The panic in her eyes subsided a little when she saw Savannah approaching.

"I'm sorry I ignored you." Sadie's voice wobbled. "I just needed...some air."

"No apology's necessary." Savannah drew her back down to the bench. "What did Pastor Jeb say to upset you?"

A sniffle followed the question. Sadie twisted her fingers together in her lap. "The dinner...Pastor Jeb asked me to go."

Savannah frowned. "The harvest dinner?"

Sadie bobbed her head.

"Of course you'll be there. Why would he ask you that?"

"He—" Another sniffle. "Asked me to go *with* him."

"Like a...date?"

"Yes!" Sadie wailed.

It was all Savannah could do to wrestle back a smile, but the anguished look on Sadie's face told her that this wasn't the time to tease.

"He likes you," she said cautiously. "Isn't that a good thing?"

"It's *terrible*." Sadie's shoulders wilted. "I didn't lead Jeb on. I have no idea why he would be—"

"Attracted to you?" Savannah pulled a clean tissue from her apron pocket and handed it to the other woman.

"Yes. I mean, just...*look* at me."

"I am." Savannah smiled now. "You care about people. You're pretty and smart and sweet and kind—"

"I'm none of those things." Sadie's voice barely broke a whisper but the hint of steel beneath the words told Savannah that she believed it. "I've been living a lie. I'm not who people think I am. I don't deserve a man like Jeb." She closed her eyes. "I don't deserve *any* of this."

"Sadie, that's not true. Didn't you tell me that God brought you to Grasslands for a reason?"

"Yes, but not *this* one." Sadie lurched to her feet. "I have to go. Do you mind handling the rest of the dinner preparations without me?"

"Not at all, but—" Savannah didn't have an opportunity to finish the sentence. Sadie was already running toward the parking lot and something told Savannah to let her go this time.

God, I have no idea what's going on with Sadie, but You do. Comfort her. Remind her that You love her.

Keira was just taking a pie out of the oven when Savannah returned. "Did you find Sadie?"

All she could do was nod.

"She left."

"Left?" Maddie echoed.

Savannah wasn't sure how much to say. "Pastor Jeb asked her to go the harvest dinner tonight—as his date."

A chorus of cheers rose from the women gathered around her.

Violet grinned. "It's about time! I knew they were perfect for each other."

"Did she leave early so she could get ready?" Elise asked.

"Maybe she's going to buy a new outfit." Maddie clapped her hands together.

"I think she turned him down," Savannah told them.

Everyone stopped talking and looked at her.

"I don't believe it." Violet smacked a palm against her forehead. "It's taken Jeb months to gather the courage to ask Sadie out."

"We all know she's crazy about him, too," Elise added. "Why would she do that?"

Savannah didn't want to break a confidence, but she was

concerned about Sadie. Briefly, she relayed the conversation they'd had in the prayer garden.

"Why would she think that she doesn't deserve everyone's respect? Or Jeb's attention?" Kiera asked. "Sadie is amazing. Everyone loves her."

"We've been trying to get her to see that for months," Maddie said with a sigh.

Savannah knew it wasn't simply a case of low self-esteem. The pain in Sadie's eyes had been real. Deep. She had the feeling it wasn't that Sadie didn't care about Jeb. For some reason, she didn't want him to care about *her.*

"Did she go home?"

"I'm not sure—but she asked if we could handle the dinner preparations without her."

"That doesn't sound good." Violet reached for her purse. "Sadie has poured her heart and soul into this event the last few weeks. Maybe someone should make sure she's all right."

"I'll tell the kitchen crew to keep working." Maddie disappeared through the doorway.

"I'm coming with you." Violet started after her.

"I can stay here and supervise," Savannah offered. "I know what needs to be done."

Violet cast a grateful look over her shoulder. "We'll be back in a flash."

"With Sadie," Keira added.

Savannah, remembering the tortured expression on Sadie's face, could only pray she was right.

"You're pacing."

"I'm not—" Carter stopped, midpace. "I thought you said that Savannah was going to the harvest dinner. Where is she?"

"Maddie went to the cottage to check on her a few minutes ago." Violet slipped her coat on.

"She seemed quiet when she got back this afternoon." Carter was afraid that was his fault.

"She's probably worried about Sadie." A frown creased Violet's forehead. "We all are. It isn't like her to disappear like that. Especially with the dinner this evening."

Even though Carter didn't know the church secretary very well, from the positive comments he'd heard people make about her, he had to agree.

"Savannah—" Maddie rounded the corner and came up short when she saw Carter.

"What about Savannah?" he demanded when it became clear she wasn't going to finish the sentence.

His sister glanced at Violet. "It's just girl talk."

"But she's all right?" he pressed.

"She's fine."

Carter wasn't convinced. "I need more intel."

Maddie rolled her eyes. "She's fine…physically."

Okay. Carter released the breath he'd been holding. "What else is there?"

"Do we have to spell it out for him?" Violet looked at Maddie.

"It looks that way."

"She doesn't feel attractive," Violet said.

"And she only has one dress."

"Correct me if I'm wrong, but isn't that enough? I mean, you can only wear one at a time, right?"

"It's her little black dress," Maddie said, as if that should mean something.

It didn't. "So?"

"So, Savannah doesn't think she's…little…anymore."

"She doesn't feel like it's festive enough for the dinner

tonight," Violet added. "None of us can lend her anything of ours because she's in maternity clothes."

Carter locked on a single word. "Festive?"

Maddie looked up at the ceiling, as if asking for divine help. "How to explain this in a way that a guy would understand?"

Violet nibbled on her thumbnail.

"I know." She brightened. "Chrome."

"Chrome?" Maddie burst out laughing.

"Chrome," Carter repeated thoughtfully.

"Uh-huh. And...detailing."

Now he got it.

"Give me five minutes."

Savannah heard the honk of a horn in the driveway. A final boarding call that she ignored, hoping that Maddie and Violet would give up and go to the harvest dinner without her.

The knock on the door a moment later told her that they hadn't.

She pushed to her feet and drew the crocheted afghan around her shoulders like a cape. It was the only thing that fit.

"You are in a mood," Savannah muttered on her way to the door.

It swung open before she reached it and Carter stood there, his broad shoulders blocking her view of the driveway. Just the sight of him sent her heart into a freefall.

"Ready to go?"

Maddie and Violet had obviously called for reinforcements.

"I...decided to stay here tonight."

Carter's gaze lit on the afghan and then traveled down

the length of her black dress before pausing to linger on her bare feet.

"Are you feeling all right?"

The genuine concern Savannah saw in his eyes made her feel better. And worse.

He was checking up on her again. Performing the duty he'd been assigned.

Frustration surged through her. She wanted Carter to let her in, to share his thoughts and hopes and fears. To seek out her company and spend time with her, not out of obligation but out of...love.

Because she'd fallen in love with *him*.

How had it happened? *When* had it happened?

And what was she supposed to do now?

"Savannah?"

Carter's husky voice filtered through her panic.

"Sorry. I'm—" *Totally in love with you.* "—just a little tired, I guess."

It was the wrong thing to say.

"Fine. We'll put in a movie."

"What?" The word came out in a squeak.

"If you're not going, neither am I."

He wasn't playing fair, Savannah thought. Carter should be with his family tonight and she didn't want to be the reason he stayed behind.

"Fine. I'll go." The words rolled out on a sigh. "I'm shaped like a pumpkin, so at least I'll blend in with the harvest decorations."

Carter's low laugh rumbled through her.

"That's right—I have something for you." He dipped his hand into his jacket pocket and pulled out a long swatch of green silk.

"It's gorgeous." Savannah touched the shimmering fabric in wonder. Maddie had probably worn it to some fancy event when she'd worked at *Texas Today*. "But I can't—" Her voice cracked as Carter tugged the yellow afghan off her shoulders and replaced it with the scarf, his large hands surprisingly gentle as he looped it around her neck.

"It matches your eyes." He nudged her toward the antique oval mirror hanging on the wall by the door. "Look."

Savannah looked. Not at the scarf or even her own reflection—but at the man standing beside her. Tall. Strong. If she took a half step backward, her head would fit perfectly in the cradle of his shoulder....

Their eyes met in the mirror.

"Did you forget what I told you a few nights ago?" he asked quietly.

Savannah hadn't forgotten anything. Not the way he'd drawn her into his arms for a slow dance. Not the kiss they'd shared.

But she remained silent, afraid that her heart would speak out of turn.

"I said you were beautiful."

"You also said the truck was pretty."

Carter grinned and glanced down, settling his hand on the curve of her waist, in the exact spot where the baby had kicked a moment ago. "Your mama can be a stubborn woman, can't she?"

Carter realized what he'd done when he saw the stunned look in Savannah's eyes.

Great. Now he was blushing like one of the teenage boys who'd been helping him fix the truck. If the guys in his unit could see him now he'd never hear the end of it.

"Don't you ever talk to the baby?" He shoved his hands in his pockets. To keep them out of trouble.

"All the time, but—"

Savannah stopped but the word hung in the air between

them. Reminding Carter that he didn't have the right to touch her. To hold her.

Reminding him that she—and her baby—didn't belong to him.

Chapter Nineteen

"This was a wonderful idea." An elderly gentleman smiled at Savannah as he reached for a glass of apple cider on the buffet table. "I hope the church puts on a dinner like this next year."

"I think we—*they*—will. I already heard people talking about it," Savannah said.

"Turn on the news in the morning and you feel like crawling right back in bed. We need to take some time and remember the good things that God has done." He punctuated the statement with a decisive tap of his walking cane against the floor.

"I love the scarf," Violet whispered as she picked up an empty tray.

"It was sweet of Maddie to let me borrow it tonight."

"It's not Maddie's scarf."

"Then who does it belong to?"

Violet grinned. "Maybe someone who thinks it matches your eyes?"

It matches your eyes.

Savannah sucked in a breath.

"Carter?" She was almost afraid to believe that Violet

was telling her the truth—that the scarf had been a gift from him. Or what it meant.

"We might have mentioned that you were going to skip the harvest dinner tonight because you felt a little blue. Or orange, as the case may be. We weren't sure how to convince you, so Carter took matters into his own hands."

Of course he had. Because Carter *fixed* things.

Discouragement crept in, casting a shadow over the joy that had initially blossomed in her heart.

And it explained why he hadn't spoken to her since he'd arrived at the church. He'd convinced her to attend the dinner.

"I better start washing some of these dishes." Violet darted back into the kitchen.

"Savannah?" Maddie tapped her on the shoulder. "Can you tell Elise it's time to serve the pie?"

"Sure." She wiped her hands on her apron and ducked into the kitchen. Volunteers darted back and forth but there was still no sign of Sadie.

Savannah couldn't believe she hadn't shown up.

Neither, it seemed, could Pastor Jeb. He'd poked his head in the kitchen at least a dozen times in the last hour, his worried gaze scanning the faces of the volunteers.

Elise blew a spiral of dark hair off her forehead. "I heard! We're getting the trays ready now."

Savannah walked out of the kitchen, careful not to let her gaze drift in Carter's direction. He sat at a table with some of the boys who had helped him work on the truck that afternoon. They hadn't spoken, but several times over the course of the evening Savannah had felt him watching her.

"If I could have everyone's attention for a moment, please."

Conversation instantly subsided to a hushed whisper as

Pastor Jeb rose to his feet and faced the people gathered in the fellowship hall.

"I would like to thank everyone for coming to the harvest dinner this evening. I didn't plan on preaching tonight, but with Thanksgiving less than a week away, I would like to take a minute to share some of the things we can be thankful for. I receive dozens of emails and telephone calls asking for prayer, and I think it's important that we take a moment to celebrate the way God answered them."

Savannah didn't recognize many of the names and situations that Jeb talked about, but she saw people nod at each other and smile.

"The entire congregation prayed that God would provide a secretary for the church and He brought Sadie Johnson here." A long pause followed and across the room, Savannah saw Violet look at Maddie and shake her head.

The pastor's gaze shifted to the long table where Jack and Gray had assumed responsibility for Darcy and Cory while the women helped in the kitchen.

"Belle Colby is alive after an accident last summer and is in the care of gifted physicians and her loving family. Ty Garland and his daughter, Darcy, were recently reunited. Keira Wolfe recovered from a car accident and her memory has come back.... Carter Wallace is safely back with us after his tour in Afghanistan.

"I'm sure that each of you can add something of your own to this list tonight." Jeb smiled. "And if you can't think of anything, well, all you have to do is look at the people around you. Will you bow your heads and join me in prayer?"

When Savannah opened her eyes, Carter was gone.

"Do you hear that?"

Savannah glanced up from the stack of thank-you cards

she'd been helping Violet address. She tipped her head. "Darcy...singing?"

"Someone sounds happy to have a few days off from school." Violet sealed an envelope and added it to the growing pile.

Violet had asked for Savannah's help writing thank-you notes that afternoon. Belle not only received get-well cards on a regular basis, but the people in the community and surrounding area often sent flowers or small gifts to Ranchland Manor.

Everyone, Savannah thought wryly, was getting quite creative at finding things that she could do while sitting down!

"I'm hungry!" Darcy's announcement made its way to the kitchen a few seconds before she did.

"Lupita made molasses cookies. Help yourself, sweetie."

"I don't have school until next Monday." Darcy twirled her way to the plate of cookies cooling on a rack near the oven. "That means I can go riding and play with the kittens and feed the chickens every morning."

It also meant that Brian Wallace should be returning in less than forty-eight hours.

"Hi." Maddie trudged into the kitchen.

"What's wrong?" Violet, tuned in to her twin's mood, half rose to her feet.

"Pastor Jeb left another message on my voice mail."

Violet lowered her voice a notch. "Sadie still hasn't shown up for work?"

"No, and I drove by her house after I picked up Darcy from school. The lights were on, so I'm guessing that she's there, but she won't come to the door or answer the phone."

"I know that Gray suggested we give Sadie some space,

but I'm worried about her," Violet murmured. "She hasn't left her house since the harvest dinner."

"That was four days ago." Maddie sank into a chair across the table from Savannah and set the mail down. "You two look busy."

"I got behind on the thank-you notes."

"That reminds me…" Maddie turned to Darcy. "What did you do with the mail, sweetheart?"

"It's in my backpack." Darcy wiggled out of the straps and handed it to Maddie.

"This one is for you, Savannah."

"Me?" Savannah glanced at the return address on the plain manila envelope and felt her heart drop to her toes. Something must have shown on her face because Maddie and Violet were at her side in an instant.

"Take a breath," Violet commanded. "Who is it from?"

Savannah pressed a hand against her stomach but that didn't stop it from churning.

"I'll be back in a few minutes."

"Are you sure?" Maddie's forehead creased. "You don't have a speck of color in your face, Savannah. Maybe you should stay here—"

"I'll be fine," Savannah whispered. She moved toward the door on autopilot. By the time she reached the cottage, her hands were shaking so badly, she could barely tear open the envelope.

Inside the larger envelope, a handwritten note was clipped to a smaller one.

Dear Mrs. Blackmore,
This letter was discovered after your husband's per-
sonal effects were shipped back to Dallas. Please
forgive the delay, but it took some time to find out
where you were living.

The signature was a name Savannah didn't recognize. But she did recognize the handwriting on the outside of the smaller envelope. It was Rob's.

Dear Savannah,

If you are reading this letter, it means I finally got up enough courage to send it. I want you to know how sorry I am for leaving the way I did. It wasn't that I couldn't live with you—it was because I couldn't live with myself. I'd lied to you and destroyed your trust. I was angry with myself and with God and I didn't think I deserved a second chance with either of you.

Dozens of times, I imagined coming home to you— praying that you would forgive me. But lately, I've started to wonder what would happen if I didn't come home. How would you know that I changed? That I recently gave my life to God? I think about you all the time and imagine what our life would look like if I had done things differently. I hope you find it in your heart to forgive me. I've made a lot of mistakes, but asking you to marry me wasn't one of them.

I hope someday I can make up for the pain I caused.

Love,

Rob.

A tear slipped down Savannah's cheek and she dashed it away with the back of her hand as the words sank in.

Everything Rob had told Carter was the way he *wanted* things to be.

She left the letter on the table and went to find him.

Maddie had said he'd been tinkering with some of the farm equipment so she veered toward the barn.

She heard Jack's low familiar drawl through the open door.

"A Lieutenant Mitchell called a little while ago. He said he's been trying to get in touch with you."

"He's been encouraging me to enlist again."

Savannah's breath tangled in her lungs and she stopped just outside the door of the barn.

"I didn't realize it was something that you've been considering. Gray and Maddie never mentioned that you planned to make the military your career."

In the short silence that followed, Savannah realized she was holding her breath.

"I'm thinking about it," Carter said slowly.

"Have you told…the rest of the family?"

"I'm not used to checking in with anyone. But no, I haven't said anything yet. I'm waiting until I know that Dad's okay."

"Ever think of staying here?"

"In Grasslands?"

If Savannah had entertained a crazy notion that Carter was as taken with the area as she was, it died a sudden death when she heard the incredulous note in his voice.

"Hey, I know it's not Fort Worth, but you have to admit, we've got a lot to offer. If a man knows what he wants," Jack added.

"And a man can do a lot of damage if he doesn't," Carter finally said.

Savannah didn't wait to hear Jack's response. It didn't matter. What mattered was that Carter didn't want a ready-made family.

He didn't want *her*.

Carter couldn't believe he was spilling his guts to Jack Colby of all people.

"You're talking about Savannah."

"She's already been hurt enough. I don't have anything to offer her and the baby."

"I guess that depends on what she wants, doesn't it?"

"I want to protect her, not cause any more pain. She's been through enough the past few months."

"Convenient, isn't it?"

"What?"

"When a guy says he wants to protect someone, he's usually protecting himself."

Carter opened his mouth to deny it—

"Don't bother. Been there, done that and I was miserable." Jack tossed the reins at him. "Here."

"You want me to put your horse away?" Carter automatically reached out and caught hold of them.

"I want you to ride him. It'll clear your head."

"There's nothing wrong with my head." It was his heart that was causing the problems.

Jack folded his arms across his chest. "You've been headed for a showdown since you got here. This is probably as good a time as any."

"A showdown?" Carter frowned. "With Savannah?"

"With God," Jack said simply. "I think it's time you stopped avoiding Him and had a long talk. I had to do the same thing a few months ago. Let go of the guilt and the anger. It's like holding on to a hot iron. The longer you do it, the more it changes you."

Carter's gut rolled over. "Guilt?"

"It's eating you up. Believe me, I recognize the symptoms." Jack met his gaze evenly. "I blamed myself for Mom's accident for months. Until Keira made me see things differently. Go on now. I have a feeling that you and God have a lot to get straightened out."

Tiger nickered and Carter scowled at the animal. "You're only on his side because he's the one who gives you oats."

"He also knows I'm right."

Carter set his heel in the stirrup and swung over the stallion's broad back.

"You've got a home here at the Colby Ranch if you want one. As far as I'm concerned, we're family."

Carter's throat tightened and he nodded curtly.

"Come on, Tiger. Let's go for a ride."

The ranch was a speck in the distance when Tiger finally downshifted from a canter to a slow walk, but it wasn't as easy for Carter.

He'd been tied up in knots since he'd returned to Texas.

If he were completely honest with himself, he knew it went farther back than a few weeks. He'd been angry with God…as long as he'd been angry with his father. It had burned deep, like that branding iron Jack had mentioned. Maybe it had already changed him.

I'm sorry, Lord. Sorry for trying to do all this on my own. For not seeking Your will and listening to Your voice. I have no idea what's going to happen in the future, but I know You're with me. I want to stick to Your path now.

And he wanted Savannah by his side.

Carter patted the horse's neck and tugged on the reins, feeling as if a weight had been lifted from his shoulders.

"Come on, Tiger, it's time to go home."

As he bent down to unlatch the gate, he saw Maddie standing by the corral, jumping up and down and waving both arms.

He waved back and loosened the reins, permission for Tiger to break into a canter as they reached the barn.

But one look at his sister's face chilled his blood.

"What's wrong?"

"You have to come to Grasslands Medical with me," Maddie choked out.

"Is Belle all right?" Carter gently took hold of her hands. "Did something happen?"

"It's not Mom." Tears filled Maddie's eyes. "It's Savannah."

Chapter Twenty

"What happened?"

Concern distilled to fear, causing Carter's blood to pump sluggishly through his veins. He was already unbuckling the girth but couldn't get his fingers to work properly.

Ty emerged from one of the outbuildings. "Go on, Carter. I'll take care of him."

Maddie struggled to match Carter's pace as he strode toward the car. "Savannah got a letter in the mail. Violet and I could tell she was upset, but she took it back to the cottage to read. I got worried when she didn't come back and went to check on her.

"She was lying on the sofa and at first I thought she was taking a nap, but she'd fainted or something. Jack and Violet drove her to the clinic to get checked out, but I thought you'd want to be with her."

"What was she doing today?" Gravel sprayed up from the tires as Carter put the truck in gear.

"Helping Violet. Savannah's been kind of quiet the past few days, but we just figured she had a lot on her mind."

Guilt burned its way through Carter. He should have bared his soul to her sooner.

When a guy says he wants to protect someone, he's usually protecting himself, Jack had said.

That's exactly what he'd been doing. He'd tried to convince himself that Savannah wouldn't be able to forgive him if she knew he hadn't been able to save Rob. That he had nothing to offer her...

"We love her, too, you know." Maddie's voice intruded on his thoughts. "She belongs here."

She belonged with him.

Carter nodded, unable to trust his voice.

The short trip into Grasslands seemed to take forever.

"Turn at the next stop sign," Maddie said.

Carter couldn't see anything that remotely resembled a hospital. When they arrived at the clinic, Carter turned to Maddie in disbelief.

"Jack brought her here?"

The clinic didn't resemble the ones he was used to seeing in the city. It looked like someone's home. But sure enough, a sign that said Grasslands Medical Clinic sprouted from the lawn.

"Don't let the outside fool you," Maddie said briskly. "Dr. Garth knows his stuff. He can treat everything from a bee sting to a fractured bone."

The receptionist looked a little surprised when they charged through the front door into the tiny waiting room.

"We're here to see Savannah Blackmore," Carter said without preamble. "My brother Jack brought her in about half an hour ago. Where is she? Is she all right?"

The receptionist frowned. "Under law, I can't release information about a patient. Are you immediate family?"

Carter sensed that the answer to the question would determine what happened next. He glanced at Maddie.

"Close friends," she said firmly. "Savannah lives with us."

"I'll check with Nurse Hamm." The receptionist slid

the glass door shut and punched a number on her phone. A moment later, she turned back to Carter and Maddie. "The nurse is with another patient at the moment. You can take a seat in the waiting room."

Carter didn't budge.

"I want to see the doctor."

"He's also with another patient at the moment—"

"Another patient," Carter interrupted. "Shouldn't he be with Savannah?"

The receptionist gave him a patient look. "I believe they're waiting for some test results at the moment."

"Come on." Maddie tugged on his arm. "I'm sure it won't be long."

Sixty seconds would be too long, but Carter let her drag him to a chair in the waiting room.

"Do you want a cup of coffee?"

"I want you to cause a disturbance while I find Savannah's room."

In spite of her concern for Savannah, Maddie grinned. "I think *you're* the one causing a disturbance," she whispered. "Do you want to see Savannah or get arrested?"

"No one will arrest me." Carter crossed his arms. "Gray won't let them."

Maddie intercepted Jack as he strode into the room with Keira at his side.

"What did the doctor say?"

"They took Savannah away the minute we got here and no one will tell me anything." Jack raked a hand through his hair. "Clinic policy, I guess."

"That's what they told us, too. Family only."

"I'm open to suggestions," Carter said.

Violet and Maddie exchanged a smile and for the first time, it didn't strike fear in Carter's heart.

"Okay, what have you got?"

* * *

Savannah moved restlessly.

Someone should turn off the timer on the oven. It kept beeping....

She opened her eyes and blinked up at the fluorescent light fixture on the ceiling.

Where was she?

The sheets hissed as she struggled to sit up.

"Hey, take it easy."

Carter?

He loomed above her. Stubble shadowed his lower jaw and there were shadows under his eyes.

"You look terrible," Savannah said without thinking. "Are you all right?"

"Am I all right?" Carter tossed the words back. "I'm fine. But you sure gave us a scare."

Savannah pressed a palm against her stomach as the fog parted. The last thing she remembered was stumbling back to the cottage, feeling light-headed. "The baby—"

"Is doing fine." Carter pulled the chair closer to her bedside. "The doctor said that your blood pressure dropped and you had a dizzy spell. Maddie went to check on you and found you unconscious. Don't you remember?"

Savannah remembered reading Rob's letter.

And the conversation she'd overheard between Carter and Jack.

She looked away as a nurse came into the room.

"I'm Nurse Hamm. And you gave everyone quite a scare, young lady." She clucked her tongue. "Especially your fiancé."

Her fiancé?

Savannah looked at Carter and saw a red stain creep up his neck. She waited while Nurse Hamm took her vitals.

When the woman bustled out of the room, she shot Carter a questioning look.

"It was Maddie and Violet's idea," Carter said gruffly. "Doctor Garth would only discuss your condition with a family member."

"Or a fiancé."

Carter nodded.

Savannah drew in a shaky breath. "And you picked the short straw?"

Her weak attempt at humor fell short at the expression on Carter's face. "Savannah—"

A rap on the door cut off the rest of what he'd been about to say. Doc Garth, a prematurely graying gentleman in jeans and cowboy boots, who looked as if he'd be more at home with a lariat in his hands than a stethoscope, ambled in. If the man hadn't been wearing a lab coat over his plaid, Western-style shirt, Savannah would have mistaken him for one of the cowboys that worked the Colby Ranch.

"How are you feeling, my dear?"

"A little better."

The doctor's eyes twinkled. "I'm glad to hear that, but I was asking your fiancé. He looked so pale a little while ago that Nurse Hamm considered assigning him his own room."

Savannah knew better than to take the man's words seriously. Carter was a soldier. Accustomed to remaining calm in stressful situations.

Dr. Garth flipped through the sheets of paper attached to his clipboard. "I spoke with Dr. Yardley, your primary physician, a few minutes ago. She said you're scheduled for an appointment on Monday and she wants to set up an ultrasound. A standard precaution, given the fact that it appears you had some trouble a few weeks ago. Have you been getting the rest she prescribed?"

"No, she hasn't," Carter butted in.

Savannah glared at him. "I get plenty of rest." When she wasn't thinking about Carter…

The doc looked back and forth between them and his lips twitched. "Your color seems to be coming back. That's a good sign."

"Does that mean I'm free to leave now?"

"I don't see why not." Doctor Garth scratched his signature on a piece of paper. "The nurse will be back in a few minutes to give you some instructions. And—" he leveled a finger at her "—I expect you to follow them."

"I will."

"If you're planning to stay in Grasslands, I'd like to see you in a week."

Savannah didn't look at Carter, afraid that he would see the answer in her eyes.

That was one appointment she didn't plan on keeping.

Chapter Twenty-One

Preparations for the family's Thanksgiving dinner were well under way when Carter wandered into the kitchen the following morning.

Maddie and Violet sat at the counter peeling apples while Elise, who'd arrived with Cory the evening before, was rolling out dough for a piecrust. Keira was at the table, chopping up celery and onions for the stuffing.

The room was filled with women. But none of them were the one Carter had been hoping to see.

Violet spotted him in the doorway and grinned. "Looking for someone in particular?"

He had been, but there was no way he was going to admit it. He wrestled down his frustration.

After Dr. Garth had signed the necessary paperwork and released Savannah the day before, Violet and Maddie had taken charge, clucking over her like hens with a brand-new chick.

When Maddie had finally returned to the main house, she'd pulled Carter aside and handed him an envelope.

"Savannah asked me to give this to you," Maddie had said.

Carter recognized Rob's handwriting immediately.

"If you need us, we're here, you know."

Carter had hugged his sister. "I know."

He'd gone into Belle's office and shut the door, almost afraid to read the contents of the letter that had upset Savannah.

But she'd asked Maddie to give it to him.

As Carter skimmed through the words, he understood why. Rob had asked for Savannah's forgiveness because he hadn't trusted her with the truth about his feelings.

Carter was determined not to make the same mistake.

"Hi, Uncle Carter!" Darcy ambled into the kitchen, one of the kittens nestled in the crook of her arm. She made a beeline for the cookie jar.

"I don't know, squirt." Carter shook his head. "Maddie used to scold me about eating cookies right before lunch."

Darcy stood on her tiptoes and reached into the jar. "They're not for me. I told Savannah I'd bring her some."

"You saw Savannah?"

The little girl nodded. "But I wasn't disturbing her. Promise."

Carter tried to keep a straight face. "I'm sure you weren't. Savannah likes your company and it's sweet of you to bring her some cookies. She likes those, too."

"Lupita says she's eating for two an' I don't want her to get hungry on the way home." Darcy carefully deposited several oatmeal raisin cookies in a plastic bag.

Home?

Carter's stomach clenched. "What do you mean?"

"Savannah said she hasta go back to Dallas. That's where she lives."

Everyone in the kitchen had stopped working and was staring at Darcy now.

"Did Savannah tell you that she was leaving?" Maddie shot him a quick look.

"No," Carter said tightly.

But then, he hadn't given her the opportunity. He'd planned to let Savannah rest a few more hours before showing up at her door to deliver the speech he'd been rehearsing all morning.

But if Darcy was right and Savannah *was* planning to leave, it was time to take action instead.

Carter squatted down until he and Darcy were eye to eye. "How about I deliver those cookies to Savannah?"

"You want to say goodbye before she goes home, too?"

"Nope." Carter winked at her. "I want to convince Savannah that she already *is* home."

Savannah zipped the suitcase shut and looked around the room to see if she'd forgotten anything.

The cottage felt so…empty.

But it was time to make a gracious exit. Release Carter from the promise he'd made to Rob once and for all. He needed to be with his family now—not distracted by her problems.

So why did it feel as if she were going to leave a huge chunk of her heart behind when she left?

Savannah shrugged on her jacket and grabbed the suitcase, careful not to let her gaze linger on the bouquet of yellow roses the florist had delivered to her door shortly after breakfast.

Carter's thoughtful gesture had only affirmed Savannah's decision.

Maybe it was cowardly of her to leave a note instead of saying goodbye, but she couldn't run the risk that he would see the truth in her eyes. She didn't *want* to leave.

But Savannah didn't want him to feel obligated to convince her to stay, either.

She left the key on the table and blinked back the tears

that threatened to spill over as she pulled the door shut behind her.

"Going somewhere?"

Savannah's heart missed a beat when she saw Carter leaning against the side of her car.

"Dallas. I have an appointment with my doctor.... What's that?" Savannah was distracted as the sunlight glinted off the object Carter casually tossed into the air and caught again.

"A spark plug."

"I thought you got the truck running."

"I did." Carter looked smug. "This is *your* spark plug."

"My—" Savannah's mouth dropped open. "But my car won't run without that. Will it?" she added.

"No, ma'am."

Carter's lazy drawl—and his equally lazy smile— threatened to sever the last thread of her composure.

"You have to put it back. Right now." Her voice shook. "I have an appointment with Dr. Yardley—"

"Next week."

He wasn't making this any easier. "And I need to find a place to live."

"Why?"

The simple question lodged in her heart. "Tomorrow is Thanksgiving. You need to focus on your family." And she was a distraction that Carter didn't need right now. "Your dad—"

"Would love to meet you," Carter interrupted. "Everyone is expecting you to stay for Thanksgiving dinner. Why don't you stick around for a few days?"

Because it was getting harder and harder to keep her feelings to herself. Not that she could tell Carter that. If he knew how she felt about him, it would only be one more duty tying him down. Holding him back from the future God had planned for him.

"I can't," she stammered.

"Can't? Or won't?"

Savannah stiffened when Carter closed the distance between them.

"Why are you really leaving, sweetheart?"

The soft endearment broke through what was left of her defenses and the truth spilled out before Savannah could stop it.

"Because I don't want to be someone that you feel sorry for. The woman who always needs you to rescue her."

Carter didn't seem to hear her.

"I don't feel sorry for you, Savannah." He hooked a strand of hair behind her ear with a tenderness that made her heart ache. "And I *want* you to stay."

The suitcase hit the ground with a thud.

"Why?"

If Carter hadn't realized how serious the question was, he would have smiled.

"Because *you* rescued *me*," he whispered.

"I don't understand.... I overheard you talking to Jack yesterday." Savannah's cheeks turned pink. "I didn't mean to eavesdrop. I was waiting outside the door for a chance to tell you about the letter I got...from Rob. You said you were thinking about enlisting again. That you didn't know what you...wanted."

Carter sifted through the conversation and tried not to wince.

"You should have stuck around a little longer. You would have heard the rest of the conversation."

"The rest of the conversation?"

"What you overheard...it was never about what I wanted, it was about what I thought *you* needed," Carter said quiately. "I told Jack that you've been through enough the past few months and I didn't want to cause you any more pain.

"I tried to convince myself that you and the baby deserved more than I could offer. That the best thing I could do was stand in the background and keep an eye on you. But the truth is, I'd rather be at your side." He swallowed hard. "I might not know what's going to happen down the road, but I trust that God does. He and I had a long talk and I realized something. The promise I made to Rob didn't bring us together, God did."

Tears shimmered in Savannah's eyes but there was something else there, too. Something that gave Carter the courage to continue.

"I love you, Savannah. That's why I want you to stay."

Carter *loved* her?

Maybe, Savannah thought, she should pinch herself to see if this was real. Or maybe…

She reached out and traced Carter's angular jaw with her fingertips instead. She heard him catch his breath as he drew her into the circle of his arms.

It felt like coming home.

"I love you, too," she murmured. "But I never dreamed—" Her throat swelled shut, making it impossible to continue.

"I think both of us have been afraid to do that." Carter's arms tightened around her. "But you can trust me, Savannah. With today…and whatever happens tomorrow."

Tomorrow suddenly looked a whole lot brighter.

Carter's expression turned serious. "There is one thing we have to talk about, though."

Savannah's heart dipped. "All right."

"You have to let me teach Hope how to throw a football and change a flat tire." Mischief sparked in Carter's eyes.

She couldn't believe that God had brought this amazing man into her life.

"What if she wants to take ballet?" Savannah teased, responding in kind.

"Then I'll be sitting in the bleachers, right next to her beautiful mother, with a bouquet of roses."

Savannah felt as if her heart were going to burst.

"Agreed," she whispered.

Carter bent his head and his lips captured hers. When the kiss ended, Savannah could feel her heart racing in time with his.

"So I have a question," Carter murmured in her ear.

"I believe you only get one," Savannah said promptly.

"Will you go out with me?" Carter looked down at her, his smile a little unsteady. "On a real date?"

"That sounds…wonderful."

"I was thinking…dinner."

"When and where?"

"Tomorrow? Turkey with all the trimmings." Carter pointed to the main house. "Right over there."

"With your family?"

"Yes." Carter tipped his head. "Is that all right?"

"All right?" Savannah closed her eyes and felt the steady drum of Carter's heart against her cheek. "It sounds absolutely perfect to me."

Chapter Twenty-Two

"**Y**ou were up early this morning."

Carter looked up and saw Maddie in the doorway, a cup of coffee in one hand.

"So are you."

"I had a hard time sleeping last night," she admitted. "Did you convince Savannah to spend Thanksgiving with us?"

Carter had a hard time keeping a smile from surfacing. "I think so. She'll be here in a few minutes."

"Good." Maddie released a heartfelt sigh. "We don't want any extra chairs at the table today."

She was still holding out hope their father would return. They all were.

But now, Carter realized it was more important to see his dad's face again than to hear his explanations.

Lord, bring him back safely and we'll go from there.

Moving forward with God's help. Just the way Gray had said.

"Come on, you two." Violet shooed them toward the dining room. "We've got a lot of last-minute things to do."

Things that kept him and Savannah apart.

Carter wanted to be alone with her, but decided he was willing to share her with his family for a few hours.

"Dinner is served!" Maddie called out.

Landon Derringer carried the turkey into the dining room and Violet lit two slim taper candles in the centerpiece.

Jack waited until everyone found a seat at the table.

"Mom started a tradition when Violet and I were young. On Thanksgiving, she would choose a portion of scripture, reminding us how much we have to be thankful for. I took the liberty of carrying on the tradition this year."

Under the table, Carter felt Savannah squeeze his hand.

"'We ought always to thank God for you, brothers, and rightly so, because your faith is growing more and more, and the love every one of you has for each other is increasing.'"

Jack cleared his throat. "I think that's been happening the past five months. Our faith has grown—and so has our love for each other. Mom would say we have a lot to be thankful for today."

A murmured chorus of heartfelt *amens* followed.

"Amen," Cory chimed in. "Can we eat now?"

Gray laughed as Elise tried to shush her son. "We sure can."

Jack began to carve the turkey as the side dishes made their way around the table.

Above the hum of conversation, a car door slammed.

Maddie jumped to her feet and ran to the window, her lips forming a single word.

Dad.

A collective sigh circled the table as Maddie shook her head.

Savannah realized how desperately everyone wanted

Brian Wallace to show up. To keep the promise he'd made to his family.

"Can I have another roll, Savannah?" Darcy pointed to the basket. "Before Uncle Carter eats them all?"

The comment brought a smile to everyone's face and broke through the shadow of silence that had fallen.

"Here you go." Savannah made a point to hold it out of Carter's reach as she passed it to the little girl.

Maddie smiled at her. "I'm glad that Carter talked you into staying, Savannah."

"They're gettin' married," Darcy said matter-of-factly.

Heads swiveled in their direction.

Savannah felt her cheeks begin to glow and she looked helplessly at Carter. "We aren't—"

"What makes you say that, Darcy?" Violet interrupted.

"I saw them kissing yesterday. Can I have some mashed potatoes, please?"

No one, Savannah noted, passed the mashed potatoes. She wanted to slide under the table—except that she wouldn't fit.

"If you marry Savannah, she'll be my aunt, won't she, Uncle Carter?" Darcy had obviously thought this through.

"And mine, right?" Cory wasn't going to be left out.

"That's right." Carter winked at her.

"Oh, don't blush, Savannah." Keira nudged her shoulder. "This family is getting so big, you may as well enjoy the attention while you can."

Carter took pity on her and cleared his throat. "Right now, I think the *turkey* needs some attention."

"Fine—but don't think you're off the hook, little brother," Maddie said. "We expect you to keep us in the loop."

"Whatever you say, sis," Carter muttered under his breath.

Savannah smiled despite herself.

"Not quite what you imagined when you prayed for a family, is it?" Carter murmured in her ear a few moments later.

"No," Savannah whispered back. "It's much, much better."

No one seemed in a hurry to leave the table, lingering over dessert.

Waiting.

Carter caught hold of Savannah's hand underneath the table.

"Would you like to go for a walk?"

There was a look in his eyes that made Savannah's heart skip a beat.

She nodded. "I'll help clear the table first."

"Oh, no, you won't," Violet said cheerfully. "We already assigned a cleanup crew and your name isn't on it."

Maddie made a shooing motion with her hand. "Go on. I'm sure you've got a lot to talk about. After we take care of the dishes, we're going to drive into Grasslands and visit Belle."

Savannah gave Carter a questioning look. She knew his feelings toward Violet and Jack had changed, but she wasn't sure how he felt about Belle.

"Do you mind if we delay our walk for a few hours?"

"I was thinking the same thing."

His smile took her breath away and he turned to Maddie. "We'll come with you."

Carter followed Gray's car as it turned into the parking lot at Ranchland Manor.

The last time he'd been here, he'd heard Belle Colby say his father's name.

Savannah laid her hand on his arm. "We don't have to go inside."

"Yes, we do." Another step forward, with God's help.

Gray would be amazed to know Carter was following his advice.

The young woman at the reception desk, who looked barely out of her teens, greeted them with a bright smile. Her badge was the kind with the adhesive back and the name Taylor, embellished with several curlicues, had been neatly printed in blue marker.

"Can I help you?"

"Must be new here," Maddie murmured.

"I just started yesterday," came the cheerful response. "So far, it's going really well."

"I'm glad to hear that." Violet ducked her head to hide a smile. "We're here to see Belle Colby."

"Colby— *Oh*." The girl's gaze swept over them and she lowered her voice a respectful notch. "You're Mrs. Colby's family?"

"That's right." Gray didn't miss a beat.

For the first time, Carter didn't feel any resentment that Gray considered Belle family.

"She's our most popular patient today."

Jack frowned. "Popular?"

The aide nodded. "She's already had a visitor today."

"Who was it?" Gray demanded. "A woman or a man?"

Taylor bit her lip. "Did I do something wrong?" she stammered. "I didn't see a note that she couldn't have visitors."

"You didn't do anything wrong," Maddie intervened, her smile meant to temper Gray's curt response. "It's just that we're not sure who it could have been, because everyone is…here."

"Not everyone," Jack muttered.

Carter looked at Gray. His dad knew where they were and what had happened to Belle. Was it possible he would have stopped by the convalescent home to see her first?

"Let me see." Taylor checked the sign-in sheet. "I must have been on the phone at the time. She signed in a little after ten.... I can't read the signature."

She.

Carter released the breath he hadn't realized he'd been holding.

"Can I see it?" Gray sounded more in control now but Taylor still looked nervous as she handed him the clipboard.

"I can't make out the name, either." He frowned. "You said it was a woman? What did she look like?"

Taylor took a step back.

"Cop voice," Elise whispered.

"Sorry...Taylor." Gray flashed an apologetic smile. "Habit."

Taylor tipped her head. "She was short. Thin. Glasses."

"That sounds like Sadie," Savannah ventured.

"You know what a sweetheart she is," Violet said. "She was probably visiting some of the residents who don't have family and stopped in to see Mom."

Jack took Keira's hand. "Makes sense."

But it didn't erase the look of disappointment on the faces of the people gathered around the desk. Carter felt Savannah rest her head on his shoulder. Being on the receiving end of comfort was a new experience. One it would take some time to get used to.

A lifetime, if he was lucky.

Violet was peering at the clipboard. "I've seen Sadie's handwriting. It doesn't look anything like this."

"Maybe she was in a hurry," Maddie said.

"Maybe, but—"

"I was hoping to see you before my shift ended." A dark-haired nurse in lime-green scrubs and a colorful bandana emerged from the backroom.

Taylor retreated quickly. No doubt relieved to hand them over to someone else, Carter thought wryly.

"How is Mom doing?" Jack asked.

The nurse hesitated. "Belle seemed a little restless this morning," she admitted. "There've been a lot of people in and out of our facility visiting family over the past few days, so it's possible she's reacting to subtle changes in the environment. I made a note for the doctor to check on her tomorrow when he comes in, but I'm sure there's nothing to worry about."

Then why did she looked worried?

One glance at his siblings told Carter they had the same thought.

"We put out coffee and refreshments in the lounge for family members today in honor of Thanksgiving." The phone rang and the nurse reached for it. "Please help yourself."

The aroma of cinnamon scented the air as everyone made their way to Belle's room at the end of the hall. They could hear murmured conversations and laughter behind the doors.

"It's too gloomy in here." Maddie strode to the window and pulled open the drapes, flooding the room with afternoon sunlight.

"Someone fixed Mom's hair." Violet was staring down at her mother. "Do you think it was Sadie?"

Belle's thick copper hair lay in a neat braid over one shoulder. A vase of bright yellow daisies trimmed with delicate baby's breath graced the nightstand.

Jack bent down and kissed his mother on the forehead. "Hey, Mom. It's Jack. Keira and I stopped by to say hello."

"I'm here, Mom." Violet nudged her brother to the side

and took Belle's hand. "Maddie and Ty and Gray and Carter are here, too."

Carter didn't feel awkward being included anymore. It felt...right.

"When you wake up, you're going to have a lot of weddings to help plan. Me and Landon are first, by the way." Violet cast a teasing glance at Maddie.

Belle's head rolled to the side and a soft moan escaped her lips.

"She seems different today," Violet murmured. "Do you think she's in pain?"

Carter put his arm around Violet's slender shoulders. "The nurse said it was normal, remember?"

She leaned against him. "That's right."

"I think we should pray for her." Jack took hold of Maddie's hand. She, in turn, took hold of Savannah's until the entire family was linked together in a circle around Belle's hospital bed.

"Lord, thank You for bringing us together. We can see that You are at work in our lives. We see Your hand in the things that have happened the past few months and because You love us, we trust You with the future. You've blessed us with so much—how can we doubt Your love?"

Carter didn't. Not anymore. Not in a million years would he have imagined that God would bring a woman like Savannah into his life.

Thank You, Father. I'm going to be the kind of husband Savannah deserves, and I'm going to raise Hope as if she were my own.

"We—" Jack's voice faltered. "Mom?"

Carter heard Savannah gasp and his eyes flew open. Maddie pressed her hand against her lips.

"What—" A second later, he understood why.

Belle's breathing had changed. The sudden silence

more frightening than the soft moans they'd gotten used to hearing.

Gray turned to Elise. "Call the nurse, sweetheart," he said in a hoarse whisper.

"No." Jack's throat convulsed. "Wait."

"What's happening?" Maddie stared down at Belle, her eyes dark with rising panic. "What's wrong with her?"

"Mom?" Jack's hands closed around the metal rail, his gaze riveted on Belle's face. "I think she's…waking up."

Maddie let out a strangled cry and Carter took a step closer to the bed.

Velvet brown eyes blinked at the faces above her.

Maddie and Violet clung to each other, unable to believe that after all these months, Belle was with them again.

"Thank You, God."

Carter wasn't sure who said the words, Gray or Jack, but it didn't matter.

He looked down at Savannah. Tears streamed down her face but she was smiling.

"Carter—"

"I know." He pulled Savannah into his arms.

No matter what happened next, they did have a lot to be thankful for.

* * * * *

Dear Reader,

Some of my favorite books (to read *and* write) are centered around a holiday, so it was a double blessing to be asked to participate in the Texas Twins continuity and have Thanksgiving play a significant role in the story.

While writing Savannah and Carter's story, I was challenged and encouraged to count the blessings in my own life. Sometimes when we experience trials, it's easy to forget just how much there is to be thankful for. Maybe we should all take Savannah's advice and "count to ten" on a regular basis!

I hope you've enjoyed the series so far. Faith. Friendship. Family…and secrets. What could be more exciting?

You won't want to miss *Reunited for the Holidays* by Jillian Hart, book six in the Texas Twins series.

Keep smiling and seeking Him!

Kathryn Springer

Questions for Discussion

1. Have you ever made a promise to a friend? What was it? Did you find it easy or difficult to keep?

2. Do you think Carter's siblings, Maddie and Gray, did the right thing when they waited for him to return from Afghanistan before they told him what had happened in the family? Why or why not?

3. Brian Wallace and Belle Colby kept a secret from their children. Do you think it's ever all right to withhold the truth about something from a family member? In what kinds of situations might it be justified?

4. Both Savannah and Carter had experienced loss, but they handled it in different ways. What were they? Which character could you identify with more?

5. In what ways did the hero and heroine's life experiences impact their faith in a positive way? A negative way?

6. Savannah assumed that Carter was only helping her out of a sense of duty or obligation. Have you ever misunderstood someone's intentions? What was the situation? What was the outcome?

7. What was the turning point in Carter and Savannah's relationship?

8. Can you think of ten things, right now, that the Lord has blessed you with? What are they?

9. Discuss some of the challenges that soldiers might face when they return home from active duty. Which one do you think Carter struggled with the most? Give specific examples from the book to support your answer.

10. How did Carter and Savannah use their talents to serve the church? How have you used your unique gifts and talents in your local community or congregation?

11. Brian Wallace loved his children, but he was an absentee father while they were growing up. Share your views on "quality versus quantity" as it relates to parenting.

12. Carter and his siblings spent a lot of time waiting. For Brian to return and for Belle to show signs of improvement after her accident. Have you ever experienced a "season" of waiting? Describe. Did it strengthen or weaken your faith?

13. What was your favorite scene in the book?

14. Sadie Johnson tells Savannah that she doesn't "deserve" Pastor Jeb's attention—or his affection. What would you tell a friend who feels the same way?

15. Pastor Jeb quotes a verse from the Psalms during his message one Sunday morning. Have there been times you felt that God was "carrying" you? Describe the situation.

A HOPE SPRINGS CHRISTMAS
Brides of Amish Country
Patricia Davids
When Amish buggy maker Levi Beachy turns the tables on matchmaker Sarah Wyse, they just might discover they've already found their perfect match—in each other.

REUNITED FOR THE HOLIDAYS
Texas Twins
Jillian Hart
Separated two decades ago, Brian Wallace and Belle Colby are reunited with their children for Christmas, only to discover that a stronger love is worth waiting for.

YULETIDE PROPOSAL
Healing Hearts
Lois Richer
Single mom Brianna Benson returns home seeking a fresh start, but can she put aside the past and work with former flame Zac Enders for the sake of her troubled son?

HIS MISTLETOE FAMILY
Men of Allegany County
Ruth Logan Herne
Brett Stanton doesn't expect a second chance, but when lovely Haley Jennings storms into his life toting two adorable orphaned boys, he can't resist the tug on his heartstrings!

SNOWFLAKE SWEETHEARTS
Carrie Turansky
When old high school friends Alex Jameson and Annie Romano reconnect at his grandmother's bakery, Annie and her sweet daughter show Alex exactly what's been missing in his life.

A GIFT OF FAMILY
Mia Ross
Starry-eyed waitress Lisa Sawyer and disillusioned soldier Seth Hansen are instantly drawn to one another. Is it simply the spirit of the season, or a love to last long beyond the mistletoe?

REQUEST YOUR FREE BOOKS!

2 FREE INSPIRATIONAL NOVELS
PLUS 2
FREE
MYSTERY GIFTS

YES! Please send me 2 FREE Love Inspired® novels and my 2 FREE mystery gifts (gifts are worth about $10). After receiving them, if I don't wish to receive any more books, I can return the shipping statement marked "cancel." If I don't cancel, I will receive 6 brand-new novels every month and be billed just $4.49 per book in the U.S. or $4.99 per book in Canada. That's a saving of at least 22% off the cover price. It's quite a bargain! Shipping and handling is just 50¢ per book in the U.S. and 75¢ per book in Canada.* I understand that accepting the 2 free books and gifts places me under no obligation to buy anything. I can always return a shipment and cancel at any time. Even if I never buy another book, the two free books and gifts are mine to keep forever.   105/305 IDN FEGR

Name	(PLEASE PRINT)	

Address		Apt. #

City	State/Prov.	Zip/Postal Code

Signature (if under 18, a parent or guardian must sign)

Mail to the **Reader Service:**
IN U.S.A.: P.O. Box 1867, Buffalo, NY 14240-1867
IN CANADA: P.O. Box 609, Fort Erie, Ontario L2A 5X3

Not valid for current subscribers to Love Inspired books.

**Are you a subscriber to Love Inspired books
and want to receive the larger-print edition?
Call 1-800-873-8635 or visit www.ReaderService.com.**

* Terms and prices subject to change without notice. Prices do not include applicable taxes. Sales tax applicable in N.Y. Canadian residents will be charged applicable taxes. Offer not valid in Quebec. This offer is limited to one order per household. All orders subject to credit approval. Credit or debit balances in a customer's account(s) may be offset by any other outstanding balance owed by or to the customer. Please allow 4 to 6 weeks for delivery. Offer available while quantities last.

Your Privacy—The Reader Service is committed to protecting your privacy. Our Privacy Policy is available online at www.ReaderService.com or upon request from the Reader Service.

We make a portion of our mailing list available to reputable third parties that offer products we believe may interest you. If you prefer that we not exchange your name with third parties, or if you wish to clarify or modify your communication preferences, please visit us at www.ReaderService.com/consumerschoice or write to us at Reader Service Preference Service, P.O. Box 9062, Buffalo, NY 14269. Include your complete name and address.

LIREG11B

celebrating 15 YEARS

USA TODAY bestselling author

JILLIAN HART

brings you the final installment of

◄— TEXAS TWINS —►

Twenty-five years ago Dr. Brian Wallace and Belle Colby were married with two sets of twins—toddler boys and infant girls. Then the young family was torn apart. Each took a girl and boy and went their separate ways—never to see one another again. Brian is stunned to return home from a mission to find all the siblings reunited at their mother's Texas ranch. Will unanswered questions stand in the way of this family finding their long-awaited second chance?

Reunited for the Holidays

Available November 13
from Love Inspired Books!

celebrating
15
YEARS

Love Inspired®

Discover a second chance at love with author

Lois Richer

Helping children in her hometown is a dream fulfilled
for single mother Brianna Benson. But being back
in Hope, New Mexico, isn't easy for the medical
clinic's new child psychologist. Ten years ago, Brianna
discovered that her fiancé, Zac Enders, betrayed her—
and she left town in tears. Now a school administrator,
Zac is asking for her help with kids at risk. But how
can she work with the man who broke her heart?
As Christmas approaches, the gift of reunited love is
waiting to be unwrapped.

Yuletide Proposal

Available November 13 from Love Inspired Books.

Dear Reader,

I'm often asked which of my books I like best. It's a question I can only shrug at and reply that's like trying to choose your favorite kid. Each book owns a chunk of me, and I love them all equally.

That's the Scout's honor truth...as far as the big picture goes.

In the narrower scope of things, I usually love the book I've just finished the best—primarily because it *is* finished, because it all came together despite my darkest midbook doubts when I was certain it never would, and because in the end my characters finally settled down long enough to let me write their story my way.

Still, I have a sneaking fondness for this book in particular. I'll even cop to feeling the teensiest sliver of favoritism. John Miglionni has been building in my mind for the past two books, and I truly knew this guy by the time I sat down to write him. He's a former marine with a troubled past and a bad attitude when it comes to relationships. Give them a week, he maintains, and they start to stink.

Oh, boy. That's just *begging* for a comeuppance, don'tcha think? So I gave him his worst nightmare in the form of Victoria Hamilton, the one woman to walk away from him before he was ready to see her go. Being thrown together with her again is blowing his ironclad notions about the interchangeability of women all to you-know-where and gone.

I just adore John and Victoria and their assorted family, friends and foes. And when all is finally said and done, I'm tickled pink with the way their story turned out.

I hope you will be, too.

Susan Anderson

Susan Andersen

hot

& bothered

MIRA®

MIRA®

ISBN 0-7783-2021-9

HOT & BOTHERED

www.MIRABooks.com

Printed in U.S.A.

This is dedicated to that wild and zany,
Whitey's-territory wedding party

To the bride and groom, David and Heather

To John and Sam, Uncle Chuck, Mom
and those dancin' fools, Austin and David

And especially to Colleen and Dave,
for sharing it all with me

It was crazy fun, and I love you all
—Susie

ACKNOWLEDGMENTS

I'd like to acknowledge Marcine Egender, Co-Executive Director of StandUp For Kids in Denver, Colorado. Thank you so much for answering all my questions, and for your insight into life on the streets for today's at-risk youth. I hope my interpretation of the facts you shared is in the ballpark. If not, the inaccuracies are mine alone.

—Susan

Prologue

Ford Evans Hamilton opened his eyes and blinked the blurry room into focus. Pain splintered through his skull and throbbed along his nerve endings, and he lifted a cautious hand to probe the back of his head. It felt like an overripe cantaloupe.

What the hell had happened? Hearing muted voices, the clink of heavy crystal, he drew his eyebrows together. Was there a party going on?

Images flickered and floated on the peripheries of his mind and his brow grew smooth. Ah, yes. That's right. There *was* a party—the one he'd thrown to watch McMurphy squirm. Well, McMurphy and one or two others, but the point was he had guests and he'd come into the library for a box of cigars to go with the after-dinner brandy. And…Jared had been there, right? Ford scowled as bits of their argument came drifting back and he suddenly recalled the shove his son had given him as the boy had stormed for the door. Jared was nothing but a blotch on the Hamilton name. *Both* his children were big disappointments.

The faint swish of fabric brushing against the Aubusson rug snagged his attention. He turned his head, wincing as fresh agony stabbed like a series of ice-pick thrusts from cranium to tailbone. He was going to make Jared rue the day he was born. Peering sourly at the slowly merging double image of the person kneeling by his side, he demanded, "What the hell are *you* doing here?" Then he pushed the question aside with an impatient wave of his fingers. "Never mind that." He extended his arm imperiously, furious that he hurt all over. "Give me a hand."

"Oh, I intend to," the person murmured. "I plan on giving you a helping hand straight to hell."

Then faster than Ford's confused mind could process the facts, the razor-sharp silver-handled letter opener that usually rested on his mahogany desk flashed downward. And his heart exploded.

One

"Come on, darlin'," John Miglionni murmured to the curvy little redhead. "Just let yourself go. You know you wanna—it'll feel so good."

He sucked in a satisfied breath when she did as he urged. "Yes!" he whispered…and zoomed in the lens of his camcorder on the woman across the field as she finally swung herself up onto the back of a quarter horse at least fifteen hands tall. His client, Colorado Insurance, would be ecstatic, as this would go a long way toward putting a serious crimp in the woman's multimillion-dollar disability claim against the company. The injury she had insisted under oath rendered her unable to ride her beloved horse was clearly fraudulent.

He kept his camera trained on her as she took the horse over the paddock fence and galloped across the high plains that spread out east of Denver. Once she was no longer identifiable through the lens, he packed up his equipment and headed down the road to where he'd left the dusty, beat-up old tan pickup truck he was using for this morning's surveillance.

Forty-five minutes later he banged through the front door of Semper Fi Investigations, grinning when his office manager Gert MacDellar jumped and slapped a hand to her bony chest.

"Good Gawd, Almighty," she snapped, glaring at him over the top of her rhinestone-studded cat's-eye glasses. "You scared a dozen years off my life! And at my age, boy, I can't afford to lose a single minute, much less more than a decade."

"As if you aren't gonna outlive us all, Mac." John hooked a leg over the corner of her desk, perching a bun on its solid oak corner. He handed her the camcorder. "Download this for the Colorado Insurance file. Then tally up the final invoice to include three and a half hours for today."

Her faded blue eyes, which were several shades lighter than her rigidly upswept hair, lit up behind the pristine lenses of her glasses. "You got her?"

"Yes, ma'am. Dead to rights."

Gert whooped and plugged the high-tech digital camcorder into its docking station. Downloading its contents with one hand, she used the other to pull a short stack of pink "While You Were Out" slips from beneath a chunk of polished quartz. "Here. You had a few calls."

John read the first slip, then slid it to the back of the stack. He handed the second message back to Gert. "Give this one to Les," he said referring to the engineer he'd recently hired to handle the increased spate of product liability cases that had been coming his way. Scanning the next message, he narrowed his eyes and looked back up, pinning Gert in place as he thrust that one, too, at her.

"You know I don't do domestic cases anymore."

"Well, you oughtta," she said unrepentantly, making no move to take the slip. "They pay very well."

"Yes, they do. They're also chock-full of highly charged emotions and invasion of privacy problems, and frankly I'm not interested in sneaking around taking pictures of people having quickies. Now, if one of the spouses is hiding assets on the other, I'm your man, and I'll be more than happy to ferret them out. But if they just want someone to dig up dirt they can use to bury their partner, refer 'em to the Hayden Agency down in LoDo.'' He dropped the message slip onto the desk.

Gert huffed and gave her lacquered updo a comforting pat, but she argued no further and John looked at the last note.

And smiled. "All right, now this looks much more my thing. Give me a runaway any day of the week." Settling himself more comfortably on the edge of the desk, he gave Gert his full attention. "Tell me about this one."

She perked up, her disgruntlement forgotten. "Have you read about that tycoon down in Colorado Springs who got himself stabbed through the heart with a letter opener?"

"Yeah. Somebody—Somebody Hamilton, wasn't it?"

"Ford Evans Hamilton. His daughter Victoria is our potential client. Well, I actually talked to the lawyer, but you get my drift. Ms. Hamilton's seventeen-year-old half brother Jared disappeared the same day Daddy bought the farm."

"The kid kill him?"

"According to Robert Rutherford, the attorney, Ms. Hamilton, or Evans Hamilton, or whatever she calls herself, swears young Jared isn't capable of that kind of violence. But he's been in trouble before—and he's definitely a person of interest to the police, so she'd like to locate him before they do. Apparently he has a tendency to give a lot of attitude when he's cornered or scared and she knows that lipping off to the cops won't improve his situation.''

Having suffered similar tendencies as a youth, John could readily identify with the teenager and he flashed his office manager a big, feral smile. ''Then isn't it lucky for her that her lawyer called in the best.'' It wasn't couched as a question.

''Lord, you are the cocky one.'' Gert bared her own bright white dentures. ''It's one of the things I've always liked best about you.''

He laughed. ''Aw, Mac, admit it, you like everything about me. We're so compatible, in fact, I'm surprised we haven't run off and gotten hitched by now.''

Her puckered mouth looked as if she'd sucked a lemon, but John knew the flush tinting her cheeks stemmed from pleasure, not disapproval. She loved being teased, but he was more likely to see her update her stuck-in-the-fifties look sometime in the new millennium than ever hear her admit it.

As if reading his mind, she gave him a stern look over the top of her glasses. ''I swear you could go to a wake and end up flirting with the corpse.''

He slapped a hand to his heart. ''Why, Gert Mac-Dellar, I'm crushed you'd think so. You *know* I'd only do that if the corpse were female.''

Her lips quirked, which was no doubt what prompted the impatient flip of her fingers that waved him off. ''Get out of here, you fool. Go call that lawyer back and make us some money.''

''Yes, ma'am.'' He snapped off a smart salute. ''I know how you love those billable hours.'' Then he rose from the desk and headed for his office to talk to a man about a case.

* * *

Victoria knew she had to get a grip. Sometimes, though, that was a lot easier said than done and, pacing the parlor of her late father's mansion, she freely admitted her emotions were in chaos.

At the small, quiet core of her, she was simply glad to be back. As much as she loved the hustle and bustle and history-soaked atmosphere of London, it wasn't home, and she'd never quite gotten past feeling like a dispossessed expatriate while living there. She'd only gone in the first place because her aunt Fiona was there and, more importantly, because she'd needed to get Esme out of Father's range before he could screw up her daughter the way he'd screwed up her and Jared.

But as glad as she was to finally be home, the circumstances gave her no peace at all. Her father was dead. And not merely gone forever—which heaven knew would have been traumatic enough, given all her unresolved feelings for him—but *murdered.*

Damn him. Half the time he'd been such a bastard. Most of the time, really. But he'd still been her father, and no one deserved to die the way he had.

Yet, wasn't it just typical of him to go out in a blaze of notoriety? He'd never minded that for himself, with his increasingly younger wives and his cutthroat business practices. But when she or Jared made even a *fraction* of the waves Ford Evans Hamilton had, he'd given them no end of grief. The two of them had been expected to be good little Hamilton clones always, and there was a part of her that was steamed her father had died on her before she could unload just *once* her opinion of his parenting skills.

Which of course made her feel guilty, which in turn rendered her so twitchy she could barely sit still for more than twenty seconds running. So here she was, waiting for her lawyer to show up with a private eye in tow. Dear Lord. Whoever would have guessed she'd live to see the day *The Maltese Falcon* intersected the life of an Evans Hamilton? Old film noir images of men in fedoras who referred to women as dames and legs as gams kept flicking through her mind.

A bark of laughter that sounded dangerously close to hysteria escaped Victoria and she slapped a hand over her mouth to contain it. Carefully, she regulated her breathing.

Okay, let's try not to lose it here. She focused on a priceless piece of art showcased on one of the sitting room's pale yellow, watered-silk-covered walls. *Just don't think about any of this too closely. Take it minute by minute, and let the details blur.* And if that smacked suspiciously of The Ostrich School of Coping Skills, so be it. The only way she knew how to deal with this mess was one problem at a time. Anything else was too overwhelming.

The telephone rang and she started. Then, fed up with her raw, edgy nerves, she crossed to the small credenza and picked up the receiver. "Hamilton residence."

"Victoria, dear, is that you?"

The voice hiccuped in and out in the telltale manner of a cellular phone about to leave its service range, but she was pretty sure it was her lawyer's. "Robert? Is that you?"

His voice faded out.

"I'm sorry, I can barely hear you."

"Oh. Hold on." Then suddenly his voice came through with crystalline clarity. "There, I switched to a new channel. Is that any better?"

"Much."

"I'm calling to let you know I won't be able to make our appointment with the Semper Fi investigator. I've been called into court. I apologize Victoria, but I want to assure you that I've talked extensively with Mr. Miglionni and everything is in order. To get him started, you merely need to meet with him, tell him about Jared and answer any questions he may have. You do have the number for my cell phone, don't you?"

"Yes."

"Excellent. If you think I might be able to answer any of the questions you can't, give me a call."

"I will. Thank—" the call abruptly disconnected "—you." She blew out a breath and set down the receiver. "*O*-kay. Looks like I'm on my own."

Nothing new there. She'd been on her own most of her life.

It was about time, however, to be a little less reactive and get a lot more proactive. God knew she owed Jared that much, since she'd always felt that by leaving she'd sacrificed him to save Esme.

She took a firm grip on her emotions and walked to the sitting-room desk where she forced herself to sit. She began sorting condolence cards into one stack that could be answered by her father's secretary and into another requiring a more personal touch. By the time she heard the doorbell ring a short while later, she felt far more composed. Heading for the front entry, she smiled back at the housekeeper when she heard the woman bustling down the hallway from the kitchen. "It's all right, Mary, I'll get it." Reaching the immense mahogany door, Victoria pulled it open.

Bright afternoon sunlight poured into the foyer, blinding her and backlighting the man standing on the brick steps. The only thing she could tell for sure was that he was tall and lean. Not that seeing his features was necessary in order to give him her best social smile—she'd attended far too many upscale girls' schools for manners not to be second nature by now. "Mr. Miglionni?" she inquired softly. "Please, won't you come in?" Stepping back to allow him entrance, she extended her hand. "I'm—"

"Tori," he acknowledged in a husky tone that feathered down her spine. Her hand remained suspended between them for a moment when he made no move to take it.

Then she dropped it to her side, but it was the use of her nickname that knit her eyebrows together. Only a few of her closest friends, Jared and Aunt Fiona ever called her that. Robert Rutherford must have somehow let it slip, however, so she smoothed her brow and gave the private investigator another polite curl of her lips. "Actually, I go by Victoria."

"Un-frigging-believable," he said hoarsely.

She didn't see why and surely the vulgarity wasn't necessary. Nevertheless, she needed this man's help if she were to have any chance of finding Jared, she reminded herself. She took refuge once more in the lessons learned from years of etiquette. "I'm sorry—what must you think of me to keep you standing on the doorstep. Please, do come in."

He stepped forward and bent to set something on the floor. The strong lines of a tanned throat flashed briefly into sharp focus and sunlight caught a sleek, black ponytail that unfurled over his shoulder with his movement. The thick rope of hair was so shiny it shimmered with blue highlights. Then he straightened and once again turned into an impenetrable shadow limned by the blinding sun…all except for the olive-skinned, long-fingered hand that he extended toward her. Just as she accepted the belatedly offered handshake, he took a forward step that rendered his features a bit less obscure.

And Victoria's stomach dropped with a sickening swoop. Flabbergasted, she stared up into the coal-black eyes of the one man she'd never thought to see again. She snatched her hand from his warm grasp. *"Rocket?"*

Hearing herself say the only name she'd ever known him by, realizing the consequences that his presence could have for her, a lifetime's worth of composure vanished. Oh, God, oh, God, this was the *last* thing she needed. She had to get him out of here. She had to get rid of him before—

He swung the door shut behind him and for the first time jumped sharply into focus, all wide shoulders, dark skin and flashing white teeth. She'd barely begun even the quickest of inventories, however, before he reached out to pull her into his arms for a quick, hard hug that lifted her Ferragamos clear up off the floor. Setting her back on her feet, he gripped her shoulders and stared down into her face.

Youhavetogo, youhavetogo, youhaveto—

"Damn, girl," he said, "it's good to see you again."

Two

John couldn't seem to stop smiling. It wasn't often anything caught him by surprise, but when the door opened and he'd seen Tori standing on the other side, she could have knocked him on his butt with a nudge from one well-manicured fingertip. For an instant he hadn't been able to believe his eyes.

But a guy didn't forget the woman responsible for making him take a good, hard look at the identity he'd chosen for himself as a boy and question if it were still valid for the man he'd become. So although the always laughing, sun-streaked brunette he remembered was now cool-eyed, sober and remote, it only took a moment for him to logically accept what he'd known without question on a deeper, more visceral level. His new client was indeed the beach-scented woman with whom he'd once spent the better part of a never-to-be-forgotten week.

Sliding his hands from Victoria's shoulders down to her wrists, he noted that her skin was every bit as silky as he recalled. It was amazing, in fact, the way his body seemed to remember every single detail about her. Feeling incredibly pleased, he smiled down into her moss-green eyes. "I waited for you to come back, you know."

She stood very still within his grasp. "Excuse me?"

"When you took off. The note you left only said that a family emergency had come up, so I waited to see if you'd be able to get back."

"You were the one who set the ground rules of no last names and 'this week only.'"

Because until I met you that sort of arrangement suited me fine. "I know." But his brows furrowed slightly, for while her voice had been perfectly polite, there'd been something beneath the surface that he couldn't quite identify. Accusation, maybe? Regret?

Whatever it had been was gone when she inquired coolly, "So what made you think I would have come back even if I could?"

"Wishful thinking, I suppose." He ran his hands up and down her arms. "I guess I just hoped you'd resolve whatever the problem was and come back, so I stayed on a couple of extra days, just in case."

"You can't seriously have expected me to return, though. Not when we only had two days left and you'd never said a word to indicate you had any desire to change the status quo."

Before he could respond, she dismissed the subject with an abrupt wave of her hand. "That's ancient history, however," she said in the same reserved voice she'd used earlier. "So while it's been very nice seeing you again, I'm afraid I'm going to have to ask you to leave. I'm in the middle of yet another family crisis and I have an appointment with someone I'm expecting at any moment."

She was perfectly polite, but the message couldn't be clearer, and this time he didn't have the sun shining in her eyes to blame it on. *What did you expect, Ace— that she'd offer to take up where the two of you left off? Get a clue. She hasn't smiled once and if she were*

any stiffer beneath your hands, she'd be a surfboard.
It didn't say a hell of a lot for his detecting skills that
he just now was getting around to noticing that little
fact. His only excuse was that he'd been happy to see
her.

Clearly, she was not as pleased to see him. He
dropped his hands to his sides and stepped back. The
barefoot twenty-five-year-old of his memory now wore
mango-colored linen and a long strand of knotted
pearls, and her wild, streaky-brown, waist-length hair
was subdued in a cut that curved sleekly just above her
shoulders. This was plainly no new transformation, either. It was much more likely that the Tori of his memory, the woman with the sandy feet, frayed cutoffs and
tropical-print bikini tops, had been the real aberration.

For the first time since stepping through the door, he
took his eyes off her and glanced around the foyer,
taking in its sweeping staircase, black-and-white marble
tiles and the opulent art on the walls. Then he turned
back to give Tor—no, *Victoria*—a slow appraisal and
his eyes narrowed at the sudden suspicion that popped
into his head. "So, tell me. You and me that week—
were you just slumming?"

"Please. It was a long time ago and I truly don't
have time for this right now. My appointment—"

"Is here." Screw it. She was right; it was a long
time ago and some things simply couldn't and
shouldn't be resurrected. Not to mention that she had
some heavy emotional shit going on in her life at the
moment and he was here to do a job. Pushing every
other consideration from his mind, telling himself she
was simply another new client, he thrust out his hand.
"John Miglionni, at your service."

"*No.*" Horrified, Victoria simply stared at the extended hand. No way was she touching those long, lean fingers again—the sensory impressions from the first time were still too fresh. "You can't be." Shooting a glance at the mostly red tattoo beneath the silky black hair on his forearm, she shoved down the memory of tracing it with her fingertips and instead studied it just long enough to assure herself that the words *Swift, Silent* and *Deadly* still surrounded the white skull and crossbones on three sides. Then she looked back up into his dark eyes and, even as she recalled the name of his agency, said insistently, "You're a *marine*."

"Former marine. And as you said, ma'am, it's been a long time. I mustered out of the service over five years ago."

Ma'am? Victoria watched him bend down and pick up a computer case off the floor. Sure, he was here in a professional capacity—and she most emphatically did not desire to start up anything with him again. But, please. *Ma'am?*

He straightened again and regarded her without expression. "If you'll lead me somewhere I can set up my laptop, we can get started."

She should have been glad that he was suddenly all business. She *was* glad. The only reason she hesitated at all, she told herself, was because she wanted the man she knew as Rocket *gone*.

Unfortunately, she feared she had dire need of John Miglionni's services if she wanted to locate Jared any time soon. Recalling that his was the name that had repeatedly popped up as their best chance of locating a missing teenager when Robert checked around, she blew out a long, resigned breath. "Please. Come into Father's office." It was better to get this over with. The sooner she did, the sooner Rocket-slash-John Miglionni

would be on his way. Then any future dealings with
him could be handled by Robert.

They settled into facing leather chairs a few moments
later, and as he booted up his computer and pulled up
a file, Victoria subjected him to a covert inspection. The
only obvious difference that jumped out at her was the
length of his hair, which was completely opposite to the
military buzz cut he'd worn when she'd known him.
It was longer than her own now, which should have
lent his face a feminine aspect. Instead it managed to
do just the reverse and accentuated his high cheekbones, hawklike nose and the spare angularity of his
face.

A cell phone rang into the silence of the dark-
paneled office. With a rumbled apology, he twisted
with supple grace to paw through the leather laptop
case he'd set on the small table next to his chair. Bringing the phone to his ear, he punched the talk button.
"Miglionni."

Watching him from beneath her lashes as he asked
an occasional question, said several *uh-huhs* and scribbled notes on a legal pad, she concluded he was still
as long and lanky as ever. Except for his wide shoulders, he had the type of body that looked deceptively
skinny in clothing. She knew for a fact, however, that
beneath the black silk T-shirt and immaculately pressed
black slacks, were muscles hard as tungsten.

Her gaze skittered back to his slacks and lingered a
moment on another long and lanky shape forming an
impressive bulge to the right of his fly. She tore her
eyes away. Damned if she'd let herself be dragged back
into *those* memories.

More insidious and harder to ignore, though, was the
recollection of how he'd made her feel. Good about

herself. Safe. Free to explore her sexuality. He might have had a butterfly's commitment to relationships, but she'd sensed a rock-solid core to him, and he'd treated her so *nice*. After a lifetime spent dodging Father's verbal slings and arrows, she'd found Rocket's rough-edged sweetness even more seductive than his sexual expertise.

Involuntarily, her lips curled up. Well, that might be stretching it a bit, since the two were so closely entwined in her memories. God knew she'd been a fool for his way of making her feel like the funniest, smartest, sexiest woman in the universe. Another female might have questioned how many other women he'd made feel the same way. Victoria hadn't cared—at least at first. More accustomed to bracing herself for a caustic remark than fielding compliments, she'd discovered protectiveness and sweet-talking attentiveness to be her personal version of Spanish Fly.

"Rocket!" Surprised laughter exploded out of her when sun, surf and sand suddenly whirled in a kaleidoscope of colors as he snatched her up off her feet and swung her in a half circle. She was vaguely aware of something whizzing past, but paid it no heed as she stared, mesmerized, up at the man holding her in his arms. She was five-ten, and hardly a fragile flower, but he was forever handling her with an ease that made her feel daintier than Tinkerbell.

"Sorry," called out a voice and Victoria blinked when Rocket set her back on her feet as abruptly as he'd swept her off them. He bent to retrieve a volleyball off the sand. Her heart thudded in slow, thick beats as she watched the fluid slide of his muscles when he tossed the ball up and, with one powerful swing of his

fist, sent it winging back toward the game they'd just passed.

That's when her head quit whirling long enough to realize he'd just saved her from being knocked on her face by a serve ball. "You must have the reflexes of a cat." She felt warm and secure, which in turn started nerves deep in her body to humming and she stepped close. *"You couldn't possibly have seen that coming."*

He shrugged as if it were no big deal. *"I sensed it— felt it displacing the air, probably."*

She stroked her hands down the hair-roughed skin of his forearms. *"That was just so…heroic."*

He made a rude noise, but it died in his throat and he went very still as she leaned her weight against him and pressed a soft, openmouthed kiss against his neck.

"I think an action so heroic deserves to be rewarded," she murmured, pressing a second kiss a bit south of the first, humming in appreciation as her lips picked up a hint of salt from his skin. She settled her breasts more firmly against his chest and his arms wrapped around her to pull her closer yet. Feeling him begin to grow hard against her stomach, she smiled, wiggled subtly, and tilted her head back to look up at him. *"Don't you?"*

His dark eyes were heavy-lidded as he stared down at her. *"Damn, Tori,"* he said hoarsely, and his hands clenched on her back. *"When you do stuff like that, I just want to tear your clothes off and take you where you stand."*

She licked the little hollow at the base of his throat, feeling powerful when it made her tall, tough marine shiver. *"In front of all these people?"*

"And their little dogs, too," he agreed, regarding her with hot, reckless eyes. *"So, darlin', unless you're*

*prepared to let 'em watch, I suggest you take a quick,
large step back and give me a minute to regain a little
control.''*

"I'm sorry, I didn't mean to keep you waiting."

Victoria couldn't have started more violently if
someone had goosed her with a cattle prod. Feeling her
face flame, she was relieved to see that Rocket had
turned away once again as he returned his cell phone
to the computer case. Taking a few quick breaths, she
attempted to collect herself before he focused the force
of those dark eyes on her.

"That's quite all—" her voice sounded like Froggy
and his magic twanger, and she cleared her throat
"—right. May I offer you something to drink before
we get started?" What on earth had she been *thinking*
to let her mind go back there?

"No, thanks. I'm set." Sitting back, he opened the
thin computer on his lap and looked up at her. "Why
don't you tell me about your brother."

"Oh. Yes. Jared. Of course." She was mortified that
for one brief instant she'd forgotten all about him.

Annoyance straightened her spine. She'd forgotten a
lot of things and that was dangerous. Forcing herself to
focus, she met John's gaze head-on. "First of all, he
didn't kill my father. I want that understood."

"All right. Can you tell me why you're so certain of
this?"

She leaned forward, but before she could say a word,
the office door opened and her father's fifth wife
strolled in.

The busty blonde stopped when she saw them. Her
gaze skimmed past Victoria with supreme disinterest,
but John was apparently a different matter for she sub-

jected him to a lengthy once-over. "Sorry," she finally said. "I didn't realize anyone was in here."

Tori suppressed a sigh. "Mr. Miglionni, this is my father's widow DeeDee Hamilton. DeeDee, this is John Miglionni, the private investigator Father's attorney helped me hire."

DeeDee's big blue eyes grew even bigger and bluer. "Why the hell would *you* need a P.I.? As far as I can tell, the only even halfway interesting thing you've ever done is piss off your daddy by having Es—"

"Mr. Miglionni has a reputation as the man to call when a teenager is missing. He's going to find Jared."

"No shit? Aren't you worried the cops'll slap him in irons the minute you bring him home?"

Fury flared in Victoria's chest. "Jared didn't kill Father!"

The lush blonde simply shrugged.

"He did *not*."

DeeDee looked bored. "Okay, fine. So why did he run, then?"

"Well, let me think. Could it be that he stumbled across his father's dead body, and that he's seventeen years old and it probably scared him to death? Or for all we know, he could have walked in *while* Father was being killed. Am I the only one worried that he might not have left voluntarily?"

"Yes."

"For heaven's sake, DeeDee, if you've spent any time with him at all, you must know he hasn't got a violent bone in his body."

"Yeah? So how the hell would *you* know? Except for the odd holiday or flying visit, it's not like you've been around much during the two years I've been here."

"You're right, I haven't. And I have to live with the fact that I left him to Father's less-than-tender mercies. But that doesn't keep me from knowing that a person's basic nature doesn't change. And Jared wouldn't hurt a flea."

"Maybe not." DeeDee shrugged once again. "But who else had any reason to kill Ford?"

"My God, are you serious?" The laugh that escaped Victoria went a little wild, and ruthlessly she slammed a lid on the urge to give in to unchecked hysteria. "Considering Father's personality, and the fact that he was killed in the middle of a dinner party he was giving to rub salt in the wound of a CEO whose company he'd just acquired in a hostile takeover, I'd have to say darn near everyone."

She turned to include Rocket. "I realize it's unkind to speak ill of the dead, but you might as well know up front that my father wasn't a nice man. He liked nothing more than to toy with people, and from what I've gathered, none of the guests attending his little soiree the night he was killed had a clue if they'd still have a job come Monday morning. I'm not just talking about the employees of the company he'd taken over, either. *No* one could afford to relax around him. He was just as apt to can his own people as the ones from his new acquisition, if for no other reason than to provide himself a moment's entertainment."

"And here I thought my old man was the daddy of dysfunction." John had been watching the interaction between the two women with fascination, knowing they had no idea how revealing it was. But it was time for a more straightforward approach. He needed to start directing the conversation to where he wanted it to go.

It was clear the women weren't overly fond of each

other, and turning to DeeDee, he decided she couldn't be more than a year or two older than Victoria—who, if he remembered correctly, would be about thirty-one now. As Victoria's new stepmama, that had to make for some friction. He'd bet the main source of dissension, though, was the fact that you'd have to search hard to find two more dissimilar women. Even way back when, he'd understood that Tori wasn't one of the party girls he was accustomed to picking up in bars. So when she'd allowed him to do exactly that, he'd noted her relative inexperience, then simply felt grateful to whatever karma had thrown him in her path at the exact moment she'd decided to cut loose.

DeeDee, on the other hand, had the look of a woman who knew her way around a wet T-shirt contest. Not that you could always go by appearances, he admitted, remembering when his friend Zach had first met the woman who'd become his wife. Still, there was an indefinable aura about DeeDee that said she knew the score, and at the very least, she struck him as the quintessential trophy wife.

He favored her with his most charming grin. "You have a point," he said. "A homicide detective will always look first within the family for his suspect. Hell, any cop will be happy to tell you that nine times out of ten the victim is killed by someone he knew."

Something about the smug look she shot Victoria rubbed him the wrong way, but he wasn't stepping into the middle of *that* brouhaha. As a man, he knew better than to get between two women with opposing points of view. As a professional, he didn't get involved in his clients' lives, period, or anyone else's who might be connected to a case. As far as he was concerned, in fact, the two of them could dive right into a knock-down drag-out fight, and he'd simply pull up a chair and enjoy the show. Especially if the ripping of clothing was involved.

He glanced at Tori's svelte little sheath, then at her patrician nose poking ceiling-ward, and swallowed a snort. *Sure, Ace, that's likely to happen.* Turning his attention back to DeeDee, he added, "Of course they generally look at the spouse first, since that's who most often inherits the lion's share of money."

She curled her lip at him. "Lets me out, then. I signed a prenup that said if Ford divorced me or died for any reason during the first three years, I'd get bupkis—or next to it, at any rate. He was my golden goose, pal—it was in my best interests to keep him healthy."

John glanced at Tori, who nodded. "He had all his wives sign the same prenuptial agreement, and it was set up in such a way that they only received a truly generous bequest if they lasted ten years." She shrugged. "The only one who ever came close to lasting that long was my mother, but she died just before my eighth birthday."

A shaft of light found its way through the shutters and shone directly in her eyes. It highlighted the gold flecks around her pupils, and he was irritated that seeing them gave him the urge to cut her a little slack and not pursue the next logical line of questioning. He gave her a flat stare to compensate. "So I'm guessing you and your brother inherited the bulk of Daddy's fortune then."

When she narrowed her eyes, he had a feeling it wasn't against the light. But she said without inflection, "Yes. And before you ask, I was living in London when he died, and I've already told you that Jared couldn't have done it."

Hit men could be hired as easily from London as anywhere else, and John never trusted in the goodness of young men he hadn't met. Since he had a hankering for this case, however, he knew better than to say so. He might be one of the best at locating missing teens, but he was by no means the only investigator qualified for the job, and his prior relationship with Tori was more likely a strike against him than anything that would work to his benefit.

But what the hell—when in doubt, project confidence, he always said. Besides, it wasn't as if he actually believed she'd put a contract out on her old man. No, the woman he'd met this afternoon was more likely to freeze a man to death.

Seeing DeeDee watching the two of them as if this were improvisational theater, he leveled a look on her. "Would you excuse us, Mrs. Hamilton? My client's paying by the hour and I'd like to get down to business with her."

"I just bet you would," she murmured, but then spun on her stiletto heels and sashayed out as blithely as she'd entered.

The moment the door shut behind her, he pinned his best no-nonsense look on Victoria. "Okay, look, I plan to look for your brother regardless, but I'd still like to know why you believe he's incapable of violence. There's probably not a person in the world who doesn't have the capacity for it, given the right circumstances."

"I simply can't visualize what those circumstances would ever be in Jared's case," she said. "He's scared to death of spiders, for heaven's sake, yet he's *still* the type of guy who'd perform a catch and release if one got in the house. Now, me, I'd rather see the damn thing dead."

He remembered. She'd climbed up his back once, screaming *Kill it! Kill it!* in his ear when a hapless daddy longlegs had shown the poor judgement to venture across their bedroom floor in Pensacola. Irritably shoving the memory away, he focused on the facts. "Yet he's been in quite a bit of trouble, if I understand correctly."

"It's true he's been expelled from several schools. But always for things like drinking, or smoking or not knowing when to stow his attitude." She leaned forward in her chair as if she could compel his understanding through sheer physical intensity. "When he was little, he was always running up to Father saying 'Watch this! Watch this!' All he ever wanted was the tiniest bit of his daddy's attention, and his expulsions were just a continuation of the same. They were a way to get Father to pay him a little regard, if only in a negative way."

"Tell me who his friends are."

Victoria sat back. "That's one of those good news/ bad news things," she said. "He has a habit of falling in with the malcontents, which as you can probably imagine contributes considerably to his problems. The good news is, he didn't do that this time. Since there were only a few months remaining in the semester when he was bounced from his last school, Father decided to enroll him locally to finish out the year. Jared joined a baseball team, discovered he really liked the sport, and actually met a couple of nice kids on the team. The bad news, though, is that whenever he told me anything about them, he only referred to them as Dan and Dave."

"That's okay, just give me the name of the school." He'd contact the coach and go from there.

She told him, and he was keying the information into her file when the office door opened once again. Brows furrowing, he glanced up. Now what?

A little girl with a long, wild, tangle of baby-fine brown hair that was held off her face by sparkling butterfly barrettes stood in the doorway. Casting him an intrigued glance, she ran over to Victoria. "Hullo, Mummy," she said in a clear British accent, leaning into her. "Nanny Helen told me a 'tective was here to find Uncle Jared."

Mummy? John felt his jaw drop as he watched Victoria wrap an arm around the little girl and hug her close. She was a *mother?*

"Yes, that's true," Victoria said. "So you really should run along, sweetie, and I'll come see you just as soon as we're finished."

That "something" he'd heard earlier was back in her voice and he narrowed his eyes on Victoria. What the hell was it? Alarm? Wariness? He couldn't quite pin it down.

"But, Mummy, I want to say hello."

There was an instant of dead silence. Then Victoria succumbed to her manners. "Very well. Sweetheart, this is Mr. Miglionni. He's the private detective Nanny Helen was telling you about. John, this is my daughter Esme."

His experience with little girls—or any kids her age, for that matter—was nil. But what the hell, a female was a female and John bestowed his warmest smile upon the little girl. "Nice to meet you, Esme. Love your butterflies."

Her little hand went up to touch one of her barrettes in an ageless feminine gesture. "Thank you. My mummy bought them at Harrods." A pleased smile curved her rosebud mouth and she stared at him with big eyes as dark as his own.

His stomach began to churn as a sudden suspicion splintered through him. Holy shit. Oh, holy, fuckin' shit. It couldn't be. Could it?

Hell, no. They'd used protection.

Which any fool knows is never one hundred percent fail-safe. He took a deep breath and got an iron grip on his emotions. "Harrods, huh? That's a department store in London, right?"

"Uh-huh."

"You look like you're nearly grown up. Got your driver's license yet?"

She giggled. "No, silly. I'm only five and a quarter years old."

"Ah. I guess that *is* a little young." The hot roil in his gut had turned to ice. He might not be the world's greatest mathematician, but he could sure as hell add two plus two and arrive at the right answer. Especially when you factored in the kid's eyes. Although it took every ounce of his self-control, he managed to keep the easy smile plastered on his kisser until the little girl skipped out of the room. But it dropped the instant the door closed behind her, and he swung to pin Victoria in place with furious eyes.

"You've got some explaining to do, lady."

Three

Damn! Victoria's heart pounded in her chest, and to her disgust every last drop of moisture in her mouth had turned to dust. Damn, damn, *damn!* She'd feared this exact situation ever since discovering her private investigator's identity, and for a moment all she could do was stare at Rocket while a pool of churning acid tried to eat a hole in her stomach. But drawing on a lifetime of displaying composure even when it was the last thing she felt, she sucked in a quiet breath and leveled a gaze on him. "For what exactly do you believe I owe you an explanation?"

"Don't pull that ice princess crap on me, Tori. You know damn well what this is about." He took a step that left him towering over her and Victoria swallowed dryly at the banked rage she saw burning in his eyes. "Esme. I want to know who that little girl belongs to and I want to know now."

"Me." A healthy surge of anger roared through her and her back snapped straighter than a yardstick even as her heart settled down to a more manageable tempo. Tilting her chin up at him, she met his furious gaze head-on. "Esme belongs to *me*. She's my daughter."

"And *mine*," he snarled. "A not-so-minor little detail I never would have known about if I hadn't come here today."

She might have categorically denied his parentage if she'd just had a moment to think things through. After all, they'd religiously used condoms that week. But over the course of the current past two weeks, her father had been murdered, her brother had disappeared and she'd packed up and moved everything she owned from one side of the world to the other. Add to that the father of her child dropping into her life from out of the blue and her mind had turned to chop suey. Besides, what was the point? She had a feeling he knew that her fling with him had been unusual enough. She'd sustained too many shocks and was worn to a nub—she simply didn't have the wherewithal to pull off the pretense that she'd gone straight from his bed to someone else's.

Still, his gall made her gape and she had to snap her sagging jaw shut. "You'll have to excuse me, Rocket, or John, or whatever you're calling yourself these days, if I find your self-righteousness just a little hard to swallow. How do you suggest I *should* have informed you—sent a letter to the U.S. Marine Corps addressed to Rocket, last name unknown? And tell me—during the two months it took me to see beyond the fact we'd used protection to realize my flu-that-wouldn't-go-away was actually the first stages of pregnancy, where were you? Sleeping with *other* women you knew only by their first names? Regaling your buddies with all the details of our time together?"

"*No.* Dammit, Tori, I never said a word to anyone."

Ignoring the little surge of satisfaction she got from hearing him deny the charge, she clung grimly to her indignation. "Why not—that was your usual MO, wasn't it? The night we met, one of your buddies made a point of warning me you liked to kiss and tell. That you were real big on sharing the particulars with your friends, right down to the last moan.'' And the thought of him sharing the specifics of *their* time together had chewed on her for months after she'd cut and run.

"Oh, let me guess—Bantam, right? The same guy who tried everything in his arsenal to get you to leave with him instead?'' Hands thrust in his pockets, Rocket stared at her for a moment before essaying a curt shrug. "Still, it's true enough. That was my MO...until you.''

"Uh-huh.'' Skepticism permeated the erstwhile agreement. "Because I was so *special,* I suppose. Just what kind of fool do you take me for?'' She threw up a hand even as he opened his mouth to speak. "Don't answer that. The fact that I left with you despite the warning makes me too many kinds of an idiot to list.'' She could still recall the heart-pounding excitement of his company, though—remembered too clearly that feverish and dangerous feeling of being swept away by something beyond her control.

It had seemed particularly delicious because she'd come so close to passing on the Pensacola trip. Her accommodations were at the type of swinging singles resort she'd been raised to shun, so when the architectural firm she worked for presented her with a gift certificate as a thank-you for creating the design that had won them a lucrative new account, she'd fully intended to let it quietly expire. But, God, she'd been proud—not only of her work, but of the appreciation her bosses had shown her. And she'd been eager to share it with her father.

She should have known he'd blow her off. At the very least, she shouldn't have been surprised—nothing she'd done was ever good enough for him. Once again, however, he'd managed to stagger her with his lack of affection. But this time, when he'd skipped right over her accomplishment to arrogantly proclaim that *of course* she wouldn't step foot in a resort that had no more taste than to bill itself as Club Paradise, she'd rebelled.

However much the vacation may have started out as a screw-you to her dad, though, it had changed into something else entirely the minute she'd met Rocket. She'd found being with him a thrill a minute, arousing and terrifying and increasingly addictive. He'd made her feel so—

Stiffening her backbone against memories that managed to grab her by the throat even now, she pinned him with a stern look. "Don't think my being a fool means you get to take the high road. You never made the least effort to contact me and you sure as heck never gave me any personal information when we were together that would make finding you feasible. I didn't even know what part of the *country* you were stationed in. So *I* made the decision to keep my baby, and *I* battled my father's demands that I rid myself of it before it could reflect badly on him."

He stilled. "Your father wanted you to have an abortion?"

"Either that or marry the investment banker of his choice."

Something savage flashed in his eyes, but just as quickly it vanished, and his expression grew remote. "Okay, so we've established you had no expectation of being able to contact me when you discovered you were pregnant." His tone contained the same cool politeness he'd used to call her ma'am earlier, but his eyes burned with the devil's own fire, holding not the tiniest vestige of polite objectivity as they drilled into hers.

"That doesn't begin to address your failure to mention Esme or her relationship to me since I arrived."

"Are you serious?" Staring at him, she could see that he was. "Well, what can I say, Rocket? Coming face-to-face with a man I haven't seen in six years took me a bit by surprise." The edge of bitterness in her own voice shocked her. Reminding herself she was an adult, she drew a deep breath, grabbed hold of her manners before they could slip-slide their way right into oblivion and exhaled quietly. "I apologize. That wasn't civil."

His mouth twisted. "God-frigging-forbid we should be uncivilized."

Yes, well, not all of us have the luxury of verbalizing every thought that pops into our head. Unclenching her teeth, Victoria inquired with hard-won equanimity, "Then how about this? I have a well-adjusted little girl, and for all that I remember you as a very nice guy, I also recall that long-lasting relationships weren't exactly your forte. I have no reason to assume that's changed." An edge of hardness crept into her voice and she didn't attempt to soften it. "Frankly, I don't care how nice you may or may not be. I will fight to the death before I'll allow Esme to be exposed to a father who flits in and out of her life like Peter Pan."

His eyes grew fiercer yet. "I have news for you, honey—I was never the Peter Pan type. I might have been a partier when we met, but not wanting to grow up was never the problem. Set aside the fact that I was first and foremost a marine, which by definition is a person of credibility. I grew up rough and I grew up fast, at an age, by God, younger than most. You want to exchange resumes on responsibility? I was out dodging bullets and eating mud while you were still attending your posh little schools for pampered princesses.''

"So what is it that you want, Rocket?" For a moment, watching his grim face, she could see the warrior in him and she couldn't keep the sarcasm from her voice to save her soul. "Visitation rights? Custody every other weekend and two weeks every summer?" That was the *last* thing the man she'd known would want.

And perhaps he hadn't changed all that much, because the question seemed to stop him in his tracks. He simply stared at her while a look that in any other man she might have construed as panic crossed his face. Then he blinked, and his expression resumed that noncommittal blankness at which he was so adept. But his voice was wary when he said, "Visitation rights?"

"I assume that's where all this indignation is leading." And she didn't even want to consider the idea. When she'd found out she was pregnant, she'd been perhaps the tiniest bit relieved that she didn't know how to locate him. The *last* thing she'd wanted to do was force a guy who'd made such a point of their fling being just that into instant fatherhood. *She'd* had a father who wasn't interested in the job—there was no way in hell she'd intended to subject her child to that sort of unrelenting rejection.

Yet if Rocket truly wanted to be a part of Es's life— well, maybe this wasn't about *her* wants and desires. Maybe it was about doing what was best for her child. And, God help her, as much as the idea pained her, maybe she had no real moral or legal right to keep the faithless bastard rat from his daughter. Not if he was willing to devote himself to being a caring father.

He gave her a wary look. ''What exactly does she know about me?''

''Nothing.''

''What do you mean, nothing? Didn't she ever ask why other kids have a daddy and she doesn't?''

''Of course she asked. But what was I supposed to tell her, that she was the result of a slam-bam-thank-you-ma'am fling with a marine who didn't even want to know my last name?''

''So…what? You told her that I'm dead, instead?''

''Certainly not!'' Insulted right down to the ground, she glared at him. ''I don't lie to my daughter, Miglionni. And I plan on telling her the truth when she's old enough to understand. Until that day, I'll keep reiterating what I've told her so far.''

He looked at her with unfriendly eyes. ''Which is?''

''That while her papa couldn't be with her, God wanted me to have a special little girl, so He sent her to me. I've told her that I love her enough for two parents, and that we don't need a da—'' She cut herself off, recognizing a don't-go-there situation when she blundered into it.

But it was too late, and his eyes narrowed. ''Don't need what, Victoria? A daddy? You might not, lady, but I bet that little girl could use one.''

''So I ask you again. What do you want?''

Plowing his fingers through his hair until they ran into the rubber band clubbing it back, he stared at her in frustration. ''I don't know.''

''Well, know this. I would have given the world for a loving and attentive father. Instead I learned firsthand the damage a neglectful parent can do. If my baby girl can't have the former, I *will* see to it that she never has to know the pain of the latter.'' She looked him straight in his pretty black eyes. "I'm trying extremely hard to be reasonable and see your side of the situation. But unless you're fully prepared to be the kind of papa Esme deserves, Rocket, don't even *think* of informing her that you're her father."

"Fine."

He stared at her for several silent moments and Victoria had the feeling that nothing would ever be fine again. She was actually relieved when he finally broke eye contact and reached for his laptop. Before she could ease out so much as a single thankful breath, however, he turned back and pinned her in his sights once again.

"Have a room prepared," he said, and although his voice was low and reasonable on the surface, it had a demanding undertone that was unmistakable. "I'm moving in."

"*Excuse* me?"

"The fact of my paternity may be six years old to you, Tori, but as far as I'm concerned, I've been a daddy for exactly ten minutes. I admit I don't have a clue how I feel about my newfound status. But I sure as hell deserve the chance to get to know my daughter while I figure it out."

"Yes, you do." Her heart was trying to beat itself through the wall of her chest again. "So get yourself a hotel room and stop by daily to see her."

"And give you the opportunity to pack her up and beat feet for places unknown? Not a chance, lady."

"I wouldn't do that!" She stared at him, appalled that he'd believe her capable of such a thing.

"You forget, baby, I was the one left behind when you did it before."

Yes, but that was because I was in over my head with you and getting way too involved after giving you my word I wouldn't. Her heart, her skin, the very core of her throbbed at memories that had a habit of surging to the fore without a hint of encouragement from her. Six long years ago, she'd sneaked out as dawn crept over the Pensacola beach because she'd found herself falling too hard and too fast for a man whose rugged sexuality was far removed from the sanitized men in her world. She'd initially assumed sticking to his rules to enjoy their time together with no strings attached would be easy as pie. But when every day spent in his company sucked her deeper under his spell instead, it had scared her silly. To preserve her heart before she ended up with something a great deal worse than its already growing ache, she'd slipped away with the sunrise.

She wasn't crazy enough to admit that to the hard-eyed man standing in front of her, however. He bore little resemblance to the charmer she remembered, and she didn't doubt for a moment that he would take full advantage of any weakness she displayed. She met his gaze with faux composure and lied without a qualm. "I told you before, a family emergency called me away."

"And I plan to be right here should another one suddenly crop up to call you away again."

Even though there was neither skepticism nor so much as a hint of sarcasm in his voice, she felt mocked—and somehow threatened. It was those eyes, she decided, and longed desperately to defy him.

But Rocket looked at her as if he were prepared to make things truly nasty if she fought him on this. And the fact was, Tori knew, someone had killed her father and it wasn't her brother. So perhaps it wouldn't hurt to have a man in the house who was capable of protecting Esme if the real killer decided to pay them a return visit because this hadn't been a grudge against her father after all.

Unsatisfied with the decision but too tired to figure out what else to do, she said stiffly, "*I* plan to stay exactly where I am until Jared is found. Nevertheless, I will inform Mary to prepare a room for you."

"Good." His look said there'd never been any doubt. "Then if you'll supply me with a photograph, I'll get to work locating your brother." And he thrust out his hand as if closing the most mundane of business deals.

To refuse his handshake would have been rude, but the minute she accepted it, Victoria knew she'd made a mistake. The chemistry that had existed since she'd first laid eyes on him in a resort bar all those years ago—and had been doing funny things to her pulse as recently as a few minutes ago—was still at work. Her skin heated where it touched the hard brown hand wrapped around her own and nerve endings deep inside sizzled and seethed, dispatching urgent messages to every erogenous zone she possessed.

She broke the contact the instant she could do so without giving away its effect on her. *It'll be okay,* she assured herself. *If you try hard enough, you can make this work, and Esme will emerge the winner.* Victoria would put up with anything to see that happen.

So why, then, couldn't she shake the feeling that she'd just sealed a deal with the devil?

John was pissed. *Seriously* steamed. "I apologize," he snarled in a high-pitched falsetto. "That wasn't *civil.*" He climbed into his car, fired it up and reversed in a hard, tight U out of his parking spot. Well, screw

Tori's weak foray into sarcasm. Slamming the gearshift into First, he aimed the car down the drive. Not telling him he had a kid the minute he walked through the door was *uncivil*.

Fury and frustration boiled in his gut, enticing him to strike out. He wanted to hit someone, to feel the satisfaction of flesh giving way beneath his pounding fists. And, frankly, right this minute he wasn't particular about whose flesh it was.

That was just too freaking reminiscent of his old man in one of his drunken rages, though, so John sucked it up and contented himself with punching the accelerator instead to send the car shooting through the closing estate gates with barely an inch of clearance on either side. His car fishtailed onto the road before he straightened it out and laid rubber down the highway. He was damned if he'd allow Tori's betrayal to flush years of hard-earned self-discipline down the toilet.

Still. He had to do something or he'd explode. Letting up on the gas until he had the speed down to a more reasonable level, he reached for his cell phone and punched an auto-number.

He was grateful when Zach answered so he didn't have to go through his friend's wife. John adored Lily, but small talk was simply beyond him at the moment, and without any preliminaries, he snarled, "Pass out the cigars. I'm a daddy."

There was a brief hesitation, then Zach said, "Rocket?"

"Yeah. Hang on a sec. I want to see if I can get Coop, too. I have a real need to vent, but I'm afraid blood's gonna flow if I have to explain this twice."

"Take your time, buddy. I'll be right here."

That cooled John's temper by several degrees and he

turned his attention to reaching the other number. Within moments he had a three-way connection going with Cooper Blackstock and Zach Taylor, former team members from his reconnaissance days in the marines and his two closest friends. As succinctly and unemotionally as he could manage, he told them he had a daughter, then laid out the details of how he'd come to learn of her existence.

There was a moment of silence when he concluded his story. Then Zach breathed, "Holy shit," at the same time Coop said, "I don't believe it. The Muzzler finally has a real name."

"Victoria," Zach concurred. "The timing fits."

"Huh?" Brow furrowing, John lifted his foot off the gas pedal. "What the hell are you two babbling about?"

"Marines don't babble, chief," Zach said. "Did you think it somehow skipped our attention that six years ago you suddenly embraced total discretion after more than a decade spent regaling us in pornographic detail about whatever girl had ridden the rocket the night before?"

"Give us some credit," Coop agreed. "The transition was too abrupt not to note."

"I don't recall either of you ever asking me why."

"We might have, but you were so damn close-mouthed about it we didn't feel we could. It was so out of character for you to keep time spent with a woman under wraps."

"Gotta admit, we would have appreciated just a *couple* of details, though," Zach added. "Ice and I spent a lot of time speculating on who could have taken the bite out of the dog."

"Great." The car drifted to a stop on the shoulder

of the road, and he slapped the gearshift into Neutral, then yanked on the brake. "That's fucking swell. A pivotal moment in my life and the two of you were giving it a funky label and yukking it up."

"No," Coop said flatly. "We weren't. Your silence told us it must be important, so we never laughed, John. But we were curious and we needed to call your sudden change of heart or epiphany or whatever the hell you want to call it *something,* so The Muzzler was born. It seemed appropriate."

"Yeah." Burying his frustration with the adeptness of lifelong habit, he looked at it from their point of view. "I guess it was. Something about Tori made me realize there was more to my identity than being good in the sack."

"Hell, man, I never realized you assumed there wasn't," Coop said. "You were one of the few, the proud."

A bitter bark of laughter escaped John. "You met my old man—you didn't think growing up with him might have tilted my thinking a little left of center?" He could still vividly remember his father showing up at Camp LeJuene, drunk on his ass and belligerently vocal about his son's decision to join the corps. "Before I discovered my ability with the ladies, I was just the pitiable kid of that crazy non-com who was always being busted back to seaman first class."

"Navy asshole," Coop said scornfully.

"Fuckin' A," Zach agreed. "The navy is for pussies who can't get into the corps."

Tactfully neither of his friends mentioned the vitriol his old man had spewed at him that night, or how John had allowed the elder Miglionni to shove him around until he'd finally lost his temper and flattened him. But the truth was, it wasn't the marines he'd glommed onto to validate his sense of self-worth. He'd liked knowing he had something in his pants that most guys would kill for.

"So now it turns out you've got a kid, too," Zach said. "Aside from being hacked off over the way you found out about her, how do you feel about that? You always swore you'd never have one."

"Yeah, but now that the choice has been taken out of my hands, I don't know—I feel like I've gotta get to know her. At the same time, I'm scared shitless to get too close. Jesus, Midnight, she's got a British accent. She sounds like the frigging queen of England!"

"Yeah, I can see where that would unnerve a guy."

"Is your Victoria a Brit, then?" Coop asked.

"She is not *my* anyth—" He cut himself off, knowing how merciless his friends would be if he protested too much. "No. Tori's not a Brit. She took Esme there to get her away from her father's influence."

"That's your daughter's name? Esme?"

"Yeah."

"Pretty," Coop said. "What's she look like?"

"Little. Sweet. A real girly-girl. She has this wild head of hair like her mother used to have back when I knew her before." *She's got my eyes.* That just blew him away every time he thought of it.

"Sounds like a cutie to me. Little girls are awesome. I never realized just how cool until I met my niece Lizzy. Get your hands on a camera, pal, and send me a picture."

They talked a while longer without saying anything of real consequence. John felt better, though, and more in control when he finally disconnected. But as he sat in his car on the side of the road, staring out at the trees, he admitted he was still as confused as ever about his new status as a parent.

Luckily, he had a job to do. When things were out of whack, it was comforting to have something to do that you did well. Figuring out puzzles was something he did very well. So he took off the brake and put the car in gear.

Then he headed down the road to talk to Jared's high-school coach.

Four

"I was informed your team lost its game."

Jared Hamilton looked up to see his father in the library doorway. The great Ford Hamilton didn't usually instigate a conversation with him unless it was to catalog his faults, but he appeared almost...interested. He must be to have pulled himself away from the dinner party that Jared could hear going on in the dining room. Stealthily sliding the brandy bottle from which he'd been sipping behind his backpack, he straightened from his dejected slouch, an optimistic kernel of hope unfurling in his chest. Maybe he didn't have to drown his sorrows after all. *"Yeah."*

"And I understand it was you striking out that ended the game."

The hope shriveled and Jared's stomach began to churn, but he rose to his feet and gave his father the bored, insolent sneer he'd perfected years ago. *"Yeah, well, what can I say? Shit happens."*

Ford gave him a look of disgust. *"Shit does not just 'happen,' young man. It's a result of sloppy preparation."*

He shrugged, but his gut roiled harder and fiercer. Wouldn't it be something if just once his father didn't take the opportunity to tell him what a huge disappointment he'd turned out to be? Other guys had dads who *actually tossed balls around with them. He had Ford Evans Hamilton, who tossed his son's every mistake in his face. His chin jutted out. "And who do you see giving me a hand with these preparations? You?"*

"Don't be ridiculous." Exuding polish from his expensively barbered hair to his gleaming loafers, the older man strode across the room until he loomed over Jared. "You're seventeen years old—call a baseball camp or hire yourself a coach. Exert yourself for once in your life. A Hamilton strives to excel."

"Maybe I am striving! How would you know? You've never even seen me play."

Ford shot his cuffs impatiently. "Is this going to be another whine because I didn't attend your little game? How many times do I have to tell you that business—"

"Takes precedence over sports." Jared completed the familiar litany in unison with his father's cultured tones. "Yeah, yeah, yeah." A thought popped into his head and left his mouth before he had time to censor it. "Man, you are such a hypocrite."

Ford stilled. "What did you say?"

The fury in his father's eyes made Jared's heart pound so hard he could barely breathe, but he didn't back down. "I didn't want to join the stinking team in the first place, but you insisted it would build character and turn me into a team player." And as it turned out, he'd discovered baseball was something he was pretty good at and had ended up loving the sport. But everyone else had family at the games to cheer them on. With Tori and the pip-squeak in London the past couple of years, his own cheering section was diddly-squat. Thrusting his chin a notch higher, he put forth his best I-could-give-a-rip curled lip. "Team player, my ass." His voice cracked embarrassingly on the last word and he played with the sleeve of his jersey, uncovering the bottom half of his tattoo to distract the old man's attention from that sign of weakness. "You talk the talk," he sneered. *"But what you really mean is that everyone else oughtta be a team player. Not you, though. You're the frickin' owner of the franchise, always too damn important to waste your time doing anything nice for anyone else."*

"I can't believe I sired you." Ford's voice neither raised in volume nor exhibited anger. Yet like an arctic wind, it sliced an icy swath through Jared's self-esteem. *"You look like some punk off the street, with your tattoo and your earrings, and you've disgraced our good name by being tossed out of three schools."*

"Four," Jared said, clenching every muscle in his body to prevent his father from seeing the way they'd started to tremble. *"You always forget Chilton. And hey. At least I don't keep marrying women young enough to be my daughters."*

Ford's eyes turned more frigid yet. Leaning down, he murmured conversationally into Jared's ear, *"I really should have insisted your mother have an abortion. Things would have been so much better all the way around."*

Pain sliced deep and scalding tears rose in an unstoppable tide in Jared's eyes. Feeling as if he were suffocating and would die if his father saw how powerfully the words had wounded, he reached out blindly with both hands to thrust Ford out of his way. He had to get out of there. Please. Just let him get out with a shred of pride left intact. Pushing past, his shoulder bumped the old man's chest.

With an undignified yelp, Ford stumbled back. He bumped a table, scattering its contents across the Au-

*busson rug and his arms windmilled before he finally
caught his balance. Yet even as he straightened, he took
a step back with his left foot and rolled the heel of his
tasseled loafer over a corner of the first edition leather-
bound, gilt-edged classic that had tumbled to the floor.
He pitched backward.*

*"Dad!" Jared leapt to catch him, but his fingers slid
along the smooth, pampered length of his father's hand,
and he watched helplessly as Ford crashed onto his
back on the floor. There was a sickening thud as the
older man's head came into contact with the marble
hearth before he lay still.*

*"Oh, God, oh, man." Jared squatted down. "Dad?
I'm sorry, I'm sorry—I never meant to hurt you."*

*His father didn't move and Jared reached out. Ford's
head canted awkwardly against the edge of the pale
veined marble. "Are you all right? Come on, Dad,
wake up!" He felt for injury, but there was no blood
from the contact site at the back of his father's head,
no soft spot that he could discern. But...that angle
couldn't be normal, could it? Bringing his fingers
around to the front of his father's neck, he pressed
against the artery.*

*No pulse beat beneath the pounding blood in his own
fingertips.*

Jared snapped awake, sick horror pumping through
his veins. He blinked in confusion at the rows of flowers that hovered overhead on either side of his prone
body. Then he blew out a breath. Okay. All right. He
knew where he was now: in the gardens of the Civic
Center park in Denver.

Swearing under his breath, he sat up. Since hitting
town, he'd slept in fits and starts, and then only during
the day because he was scared to sleep at night. He

lived in constant fear of getting rousted by the cops or—worse—by someone who'd just as soon slit his throat as look at him. The sun had definitely gone down, though, and not only had he dozed off, he'd had the damn dream again. It seemed like every time he closed his eyes, he relived those awful ten minutes that he wished more than anything he could take back and do over.

But, oh, God, he couldn't, and no spin in the universe could get around the fact he'd killed his own father. Nauseated, he hugged his knees to his chest and buried his face in the notch between his kneecaps, rocking in abject misery.

Almost worse was the way he'd run afterward without even stopping to call 911. It probably would have been too late to save his dad anyway, but he'd never know that for certain because he'd panicked, showing only enough foresight to grab the brandy bottle and his backpack before hauling ass for the front door. He'd had it in his mind that his father's guests were about to walk out of the dining room at any minute. The thought of one or two or maybe even the whole frickin' lot of them staring at him with knowing eyes as they pointed accusing fingers and called him *murderer* had filled him with so much terror there hadn't been room left for anything else.

For a second he desperately wished for his mother, but the desire passed as quickly as it had come upon him. The truth was he'd been so young when she died that all he really knew of her were the stories Tori had told him in an attempt to keep her memory alive.

What he really wanted was Tori. God, he wished he could call her, but not only did he hate the thought of making her an—what?—accomplice or witness or whatever in his crime, he didn't have her number with him and doubted he could get a London number by calling 411.

Besides, what would he say—Sorry, but I offed Dad?

Snatching up his backpack, he leapt to his feet. He had to get out of the park, had to go someplace where other people hung out, even if he didn't talk to anyone. He needed noise to drown out the voices in his head. Exiting onto Colfax Avenue, he headed for the 16th Street Mall.

Lost in misery, he failed to pay attention to the slight figure that detached itself from the shadow of the Greek amphitheater and followed him.

Victoria paused in the doorway of Ford's second office the next afternoon and watched John as he sat with the telephone receiver clasped between his ear and a hunched-up shoulder, scribbling furiously on a legal pad that sat at an angle on the desk in front of him. She didn't understand why her father had felt the need for two offices, but the south wing that housed this one had been added while she was abroad, so perhaps he'd had plans to turn his old office into something else. That wasn't really important, anyway. She only knew she'd chosen this room for Rocket's use because it was farther away from the heart of the house than Father's original study.

Which hardly explained why she was standing there staring at John's muscular shoulders and the bunch and release of the sinews in his forearm as he wrote with the twisted, upside-down awkwardness of a leftie. You'd think she'd never seen silky black hair feathering a guy's arms before. Shaking off a niggle of unease that whispered she'd never found *any* features on another man quite so virile as this one's, she stepped into the room.

And heard him murmur, "You're the woman, Mac. You sure you won't change your mind about running away with me?"

Well, there's a reality check for you. The guy was a lady-killer and she'd be wise to keep that in mind. Composing her features to reveal nothing beyond polite disinterest, she waited until he'd hung up the phone before saying, "You wanted to see me?"

His head jerked up and she froze as something hot and dangerous flashed in his eyes. Then his face went neutral and, setting down his pen, he reached for his coffee cup. Bringing it to his lips, he took a sip, and looked at her over its rim. "I thought you might like a progress report."

She took an eager step toward the desk, her momentary discomfort forgotten in a wash of anticipation. "Have you found Jared, then?"

"No, not yet. But I will."

Swamped with disappointment, she nevertheless gave him an apologetic grimace as she pulled out the chair across from him and sank onto its edge. "I guess it was naive to jump to that conclusion in the first place. I know it's too soon to get my hopes up."

"It's too soon for me to have much to report, as well, but I've found that most clients appreciate being kept up to date. So if you're interested...?"

"Yes. Please. My imagination has conjured up some truly horrendous scenarios, so to have something—*anything*—else to think about would be helpful."

"I talked to Jared's friends Dan Coulter and Dave Hemsley. Unfortunately he hasn't contacted them."

Her disappointment deepened. "Could they be lying? Perhaps they think they're protecting him, or that telling you where he is would break that unwritten adolescent code not to rat out your fellow teen.''

''It's possible, Tori, but I've interviewed a lot of teenagers over the years, and it's taught me to pay attention to their body language and the nuance in their conversations. Kids are my specialty and these two struck me as a couple of straight shooters whose biggest secret was having attended a rave and a few beer blasts.''

She wanted to be stoic. She *meant* to be stoic. But she couldn't prevent the low moan that slipped past her compressed lips.

''Heeey,'' he crooned, leaning forward. ''This is not the end of the world. It eliminates the easiest possibility, but it also gives us more eyes and ears around town. I stressed the seriousness of Jared's situation to his friends, as well as the danger he could be in, and asked them to put out the word. Jared doesn't have a girlfriend, which is unfortunate, since teenage boys often tell their girls things they'd never say to their buddies. But kids talk, and Dan and Dave swore they'd call me if he gets in touch with anyone they know.''

''So if he isn't hiding out at a friend's house here in town, what now?''

''I go talk to the cops. I generally do that right off the bat, but decided to talk to his friends first this time instead.''

''The police seemed pretty determined to make Jared their prime suspect when I talked to them.'' Her stomach flip-flopped at the memory of that conversation.

John merely shrugged. ''If they don't feel like sharing, I'll go talk to the cab companies and see if any fares were picked up in this neighborhood on the night of your father's death. If I get a hit, I'll talk to the cab driver and show him Jared's picture. And if that doesn't produce anything, I'll take his photo to the airport and bus station to see if anyone remembers selling him a ticket.'' He reached across and stroked gentle fingertips atop the hands she hadn't even realized she'd clasped tightly on the smooth cherrywood surface of the desk in front of her. ''I will find him, Victoria.''

She appreciated the reassurance, but his touch registered clear down to her toes, and she sat back in her chair, easing her hands out from beneath his long fingers. Looking around the office to avoid meeting his eyes, she found the distraction she sought and frowned in puzzlement. ''There's something wrong with this room. I can't quite put my finger on it—whether it's a dimension or a spatial aberration, or maybe it's just the color scheme, which isn't my cup of tea. But *something* about the office is off. It bugs me that I can't figure out what.''

He leaned back, his dark eyes bright with interest. ''That's right—you're an architect. As I recall, you were on the fast track at some hotshot firm when I knew you. You were in line to become…an associate, wasn't it? Did that happen for you?''

''No. Well, they offered me the position, but I had to turn it down.''

''You're kidding me!'' Straightening, he stared at her. ''I remember you being totally psyched about that promotion—wasn't it your design or something that landed a big contract?''

''Yes.'' She smiled at the memory.

''So, why the hell would you turn down something you'd been working so hard to attain?''

''Esme.''

"You walked away because you had a kid? That's kind of a fifties attitude, don't you think? News flash, darlin', lots of women actually handle both."

"Well, thank you for the tip, Miglionni." Anger erupted and for once it didn't occur to her to try to contain it. "You think it was an easy decision? I *loved* that job and I was damn proud of my work. But it also required putting in more than sixty hours a week and I've got a little news flash of my own, *darlin'.* I know what it's like to have a parent whose work is more important than his kids. I wanted better for my child."

Feeling agitated and restless, she climbed to her feet. She had to get out of here. Somehow Rocket pulled a multitude of feelings and sensations out of her without even trying, and she wanted no part of them. The last time she'd felt this way had also been with him, and in the end it had nearly broken her heart. So she was *so* gone. But first…

She stared down the length of her nose at him. "I have a suggestion for you. Go talk to those women who do it all. Ask them if they'd stay home with their children if they could afford it. You might be surprised at how many would leap at the chance. I know I'm fortunate to have the resources that gave me a choice, so guess just how much your input means to me? You're the *last* person I'd ever solicit an opinion from on parenting. My God, you bullied your way into moving in here with unfounded accusations that I never in a million years would have thought to do. Not to mention that subtle threat to make things ugly for everyone involved if you weren't given the opportunity to get to know your daughter." She ignored the fact that she was using him in return for protection.

"*What* subtle threat? I haven't said one freaking word that could remotely be construed as a threa—"

"But now that you've gotten what you wanted," she said right over the top of him, surprised to find she was all but quivering with fury, "funny thing. I haven't seen you make any effort to spend so much as *five minutes* with Esme since I introduced the two of you."

John stared at the passion in Victoria's face and felt his heart pound in his chest. This was the woman he remembered, with her electric eyes and intense fervency. The cool and reserved socialite he'd been dealing with since entering the Hamilton mansion annoyed the hell out of him, but he almost wished she'd come back. At least she didn't confuse him so much, and God knew she was a whole lot easier to hold at arm's length. This woman he wanted to throw down on the desk and have the kind of red-hot head-banging sex he remembered from six years ago.

She made a sound of disgust deep in her throat and he realized he'd been staring at her too long without responding to her accusation. Before he could say a word she'd whipped around on her expensively shod heels and he watched her hair bell out then settle back into place as she stalked from the room. The door closed behind her and he threw himself back into his chair. Swearing, he rammed his fingers through his hair and ground the heels of both hands into his scorched eyes.

What the hell was he doing here? He knew nothing about being a parent. *Less* than nothing. The truth was, just the thought of it scared the bejesus out of him.

And wasn't that one for the books? In the ordinary run of events he wasn't a man prone to fears. The day after graduating high school he'd forged his old man's signature so he could join the marines and he'd spent the next fifteen years in every hellhole and hot spot in the world. It wasn't that he'd never been afraid, of course—only a fool went up against trigger-happy terrorists armed with the latest in automatic weaponry without a healthy dose of fear to keep him cautious. But he'd learned to take in stride the kind of things that would probably start the average guy's bowels to churning.

Wasn't it a hell of a note, then, that a tiny peanut of a girl with a mess of hair and big dark eyes should be the one to strike terror in his soul?

He'd deliberately stayed out late last night and had left before breakfast this morning in order to avoid running into Esme. Not that curiosity wasn't gnawing at him like a rat on cheese. He wanted to know everything about her—what kind of toys did she like, which vegetables did she hate, did she like to be read to? Or maybe five-year-olds read for themselves—what did he know about such matters? He'd like to discover the answer to that, too. But the voice in his head that had kept him one step ahead of his father's fists, one dodge away from bullets sprayed by captors of the political hostages he'd been sent to retrieve over the years whispered warnings to keep his distance.

He should probably head back to Denver and let Victoria get back to her well-structured life. Hell, let her raise little Esme any way she saw fit; she was obviously an excellent mother.

He, on the other hand, knew bugger-all about being a father.

But much as the idea appealed to him, he knew he wasn't going to do it. Not yet at any rate. Gert had the office running with the precision of a German-made engine, and he'd caught up on all of the cases requiring his attention in Denver. Then, too, he still had a number of people to contact here.

Besides—his jaw stiffened—there wasn't a female born who could make him tuck tail and run. Not some little bit of a thing less than three feet tall and not her leggy mother, either.

Tori probably hadn't meant it as such, but she'd issued him a challenge. She'd all but accused him of being too chickenshit to get to know his daughter. And, fine; he'd admit it—that was exactly how he'd behaved. Didn't mean he couldn't do better, though.

It might take a little time for him to gird his loins. But John Miglionni didn't run from any challenge.

Five

"Here, sweetheart." Victoria stooped to untuck a
narrow ruffle that had bunched beneath the strap of
Esme's backpack. Glancing into her daughter's dark
eyes, she smiled at the excitement shining there. She
smoothed the hem of the little retro flower-power tank
top over Esme's cotton shorts, then brushed back a
stray tendril of baby-fine hair that had escaped the little
girl's fat braids. "Do you have everything you need?"

"Uh-huh." Esme fidgeted away from her mother's
fussing fingers. "I'm tidy, Mummy," she said impatiently. "When's Rebecca gonna be here? I been waiting for*ever*."

"Or at least five minutes, anyhow." Victoria struggled to keep her amusement to herself. She heard foot-
steps coming up the steps of the portico and patted
Esme's arm. "There. That's probably Rebecca and her
mum now."

Instead of the expected knock, however, the big mahogany door simply opened, bringing a wash of sunlight into the house. Then the door clicked closed and
there stood John. A fierce scowl marred his brow, but
the instant he saw Tori and Esme in the foyer, it disappeared. His eyes were slow to lose their storminess
and remained watchful, but the glower was immediately replaced by a courteous curve of his lips.

The insincerity of that smile irritated Victoria no end. Good Lord, he seemed more like a soldier to her now than he had six years ago when he'd still actually been one. Back then, at least, he'd never hesitated to exhibit emotion, and his expression had always been open. These days she couldn't tell what he was thinking.

"Hullo, Mr. Miglondoanni!"

Victoria's heart clutched at the bright expectancy in her daughter's face as she stared up all unknowing at the man who'd fathered her. But she managed to say calmly, "It's Miglionni, sweetie."

"It's a mouthful either way, especially when the mouth trying to pronounce it belongs to such a dainty little thing." He smiled down at Esme, and this time genuine humor warmed his eyes. "Instead of trying to wrap your lips around all those syllables, why don't you just call me—" with a quick glance at Victoria, he cleared his throat "—John. That would probably be simplest."

"'Kay."

He dropped to a crouch in front of her and reached out long, tanned fingers to the braided and bespeckled doll that peeked over Esme's shoulder from her backpack. "Who is this? Your sister?"

"No, silly. That's my American Girl doll. Her name is Molly Mack-'n-tire."

"She's very cute." He hesitated, clearing his throat again as patent uncertainty dimmed the usual lady-killer wattage of his charm. "Nearly as cute as you," he added and gave her a small, crooked grin so diffidently sweet it made Victoria blink.

"Oh, you." Esme giggled in delight and gave him a flirtatious poke with one soft little finger. It didn't cause so much as a dimple in the soft cloth stretched across his hard chest. "Do you like her Route 66 frock?"

"Yeah, sure. It's very, uh…blue."

"Yes, lovely, isn't it? It's new. Mummy sent away for it on the inner net."

"Internet, Esme."

"Uh-huh." The little girl didn't spare her so much as a glance. Her bright-eyed gaze was locked firmly on Rocket. "I have a play date with Rebecca Chilworth. She and her mummy are s'posed to pick me up, but they're late. Rebecca's my best friend, you know. Fiona Smyth was my best friend, but now that I live in the States, Rebecca is. Her and *my* mummies usta know each other a long time ago. Do you have a best friend?"

"Yes, I have two." He looked a little dazed, but added gamely, "Their names are Cooper and Zach. We were in the marines together."

Her brow puckered in confusion. "What's that?"

"They're soldiers, Es," Victoria interjected. "Like the Queen's Guards at home."

"Only better," John added. "A marine wouldn't be caught dead in one of those tall-ass furry hats."

None of which appeared to enlighten Esme, so Victoria added, "You know, sweetie. Like what Mr. Mc-Intire is in."

Her daughter's whole face lit up and the look she flashed John couldn't have been more awed if a superhero had suddenly sprung to life. "You been over the seas, then?" she demanded.

"Yes. I've spent quite a bit of time in other countries."

"Molly's papa is over the seas, and she has to make sack fries."

John's expression not only lacked comprehension, he looked downright stupefied. Esme's gregarious chatter could do that to a person, so Victoria decided to take pity on him. But she didn't bother to swallow the little smile that quirked her lips. It was refreshing to see him at sea in his dealings with a female.

"Glad to see you're having a good time," he growled and her smile grew.

"Oh, I am." But she saw Esme's baffled expression and straightened her face. "Each of the American Girl dolls are set in a different era," she informed him. "And part of their appeal lies in the books that come with them, with settings in the doll's specific period in history. Molly's stories describe life on the home front during World War II, from the challenge of having a father who's overseas, to the sacrifices her family makes to help their country win the war."

Esme beamed at the dark-haired man in front of her. "Sack fries," she agreed. "Mummy says that's part of what makes Molly a hair win."

"Heroine, sweetie."

"Ah." Then John, too, grinned, a slash of white so reminiscent of the carefree, I-can-charm-your-pants-off, you-gotta-love-me smile that had first sucked Victoria into his orbit all those years ago she felt her knees grow weak and her thighs clamp tight.

She unlocked the latter and took a hasty step away to give herself some distance before she did something foolish like reach out and run her fingers over the same hard surface her daughter had poked. Hot awareness surged so fast and furiously through her system that blisters were no doubt popping up in its wake, and she gave silent thanks when the doorbell rang. She crossed the entryway and opened the door, greeting Rebecca and her mother with even more warmth than usual.

With the arrival of her friend, Esme lost interest in John so fast and completely it made his head swim. He'd been doing okay there for a while, but apparently she had bigger fish to fry now, and there was a lesson to be learned from thinking he'd been making some kind of headway. He watched as she threw her arms around Tori's neck, pursed her little rosebud lips for an enthusiastic smooch, then tore away and clattered out the door, exchanging machine-gun-rapid patter with a little curly-haired dishwater blonde he could only assume was the aforementioned best friend Rebecca. Being able to charm a little girl for five minutes didn't mean he knew squat about kids in the long term, he reminded himself.

"I'm sorry we're late," a more mature version of the little blonde said breathlessly to Victoria, pulling his attention away from the children who were climbing into a minivan parked on the circular drive. "I overestimated how quickly I could run a few errands. And Lord knows—"

"*Ma*-mmmm!"

With a shrug and an assessing, curious glance at him, Rebecca's mother moved toward the door. "The natives are definitely restless. I'll have Esme back by six."

"Thanks, Pam."

Victoria walked the woman out and John listened to a flurry of farewells and slamming car doors. Then between one moment and the next she was back, closing the front door behind her as silence settled over the entryway. Blowing a strand of hair out of eyes that were alight with humor, she grinned at him. "Whew."

She was mussed and flushed, and looked so much like the Tori he remembered that he experienced a sudden sharp desire to pin her against the door at her back and rock his mouth over hers. Man, just one little kiss, that was all he asked. Just to see if the new, uptight Victoria had the same addictive flavor that had lived on in his mind all these years. Heartbeat picking up tempo, he took a determined step forward.

She scooped her hair back. "So, tell me. Why were you in a bad mood when you came in?"

He halted, jerked back to the present. "What?"

"When you let yourself in a while ago, you looked furious. Then you saw Es and me and slapped on your company face. Which was pretty smarmy, by the way."

O-kay. He took a large step back. That wasn't the brightest plan he'd ever had. Hell, he had professional standards to maintain here. But still... "What do you mean, smarmy?"

"Come on. The way you went from being clearly out of sorts to that phony hail-fellows-well-met smile? Smarmy with a capital smar, Miglionni. I thought for a minute there you were going to try to sell us a used car."

"Yeah?" He stepped forward again. "So what about you, then?"

She, too, took a step forward, her chin angling up at him. "What *about* me?"

"You've been giving me that little society-princess smile since I first landed on your doorstep, when both of us know damn that well if you had your way I'd be six states away. What's that all about?"

"Good manners."

"Uh-huh. So let me get this straight. When you do

it, you're Little Ellie Etiquette, but when I do it I'm a used-car salesman?" He shrugged. "That's fair."

The last thing he expected to see was the wide, amused grin she flashed him. "No, it's not, but somehow it seems different when I'm the one doing it. I suppose, though, that it's just as much a way for you to keep your feelings to yourself as it is for me."

Damn. He started measuring the distance between them and the door again, deciding that pressing her up against an unyielding surface was a mighty fine idea after all. Screw professionalism. Stacked up against the thought of getting his hands in that hair, kissing those lips, it was highly overrated.

And if *that* wasn't dangerous thinking, he didn't know what was. Stuffing his hands into his slacks pockets, he took a large step back, feeling like he was performing some spastic do-si-do but determined to put distance between them. "You wanna know what was bugging me?"

"Yes. If you'd like to tell me."

Sunshine from the leaded-glass entry sidelights shone in her eyes, picking out the gold flecks in her moss-green irises. Feeling a sudden need for an emotional, as well as physical distance if he wanted to keep himself from doing something they'd both regret, he said flatly, "It was the conversation I had with the police about Jared. I was thinking about the lead detective, who's a donut-eating lard-ass too lazy to look at anyone else when he's got a nice, convenient scapegoat in your brother."

That gave him the distance he wanted, but seeing the humor wiped from her face gave him no satisfaction. On the contrary, the strained worry he was responsible for putting in its place made him feel like a schoolyard bully. Pulling his hands from his pockets, he leaned toward her.

Only to watch her back snap poker-straight and her expression smooth out into the bland aloofness he hated. It should have put his back up. Instead her words played back in his head. *I suppose, though, that it's just as much a way for you to keep your feelings to yourself as it is for me.*

Shit.

He reached for her hand. "Come on." Tugging it gently, he led her down the hallway toward the office she'd assigned for his use. "Let's go sit down and talk about it."

A moment later he seated her in the chair facing his desk, then circled it to take his own. "Can I have Mary bring you anything? Some iced tea, maybe? Something stronger?" He wasn't exactly accustomed to summoning servants, but he'd been the housekeeper's golden boy since he'd questioned her and the rest of the help yesterday, so what the hell. Might as well take advantage. No one understood better that he was likely to drop out of favor just as quickly as he'd come into it.

Victoria merely shook her head, however.

"She agrees with you, by the way."

She blinked at him. "Mary does? About what?"

"Jared's innocence."

That got her attention and John saw with satisfaction a spark of anger igniting in her eyes. He considered that a big improvement over the defeat that had dulled them.

She straightened in her chair. "You questioned Mary?"

"Yes, ma'am. And the cook and the two girls who come in once a week to clean, as well. Oh, and the gardener." He gave her a smile he knew would aggravate the hell out of her. "And except for the gardener, who's still hacked off at Jared for running over his dahlias with the car, they all agree the kid couldn't have killed your father. Swore that he wouldn't hurt a fly."

"*I* told you that!"

"Yes, you did. But I take nothing on faith and no one's word is good enough for me. I'm not satisfied I'm even getting in the vicinity of the truth, in fact, until I've double—and preferably triple or quadruple—checked every statement I take, every assertion I hear. That, darlin', is what you're paying me for."

"To be a cynic?"

"Damn straight. You want someone to hold your hand, agreeing with every word you speak and 'poor-babying' you about your murdered dad and missing brother, go talk to one of your country-club boys. You want Jared found, you got me. And that means poking my nose in every corner of his life, finding out things the help might know, discovering the stuff he'd never in a million years confide in his sister."

He waited for her to ask what kind of stuff, but instead she straightened in her seat and eyed him with speculative consideration. "The police aren't going to look any further than Jared, are they?"

"Not if the conversation I had with Detective Simpson was any indication." Anger burned in his gut all over again at the thought of the cop's incompetence. It wasn't something he was accustomed to running into with most law-enforcement personnel.

"Then I'd like to expand your job."

He stared at her. "In what way?"

"I don't understand the detective's attitude, given that there are literally dozens of people who might have

wanted my father dead. So *you* look into them. Heck,
I can give you ten names off the top of my head just
to get you started.''

"That's probably not a great way to spend your
money. It's likely to cost you a fortune and still not net
you the results you're looking for.''

"I don't care about the money. The police aren't
doing their job, so I want you to do it for them.''

"You do understand, don't you, that I have no authority to compel anyone to answer my questions? If
people don't want to talk to me there's not a helluva
lot I can do to make them. It's why private detectives
rarely get involved in murder cases. We have neither
the jurisdiction nor the contacts the cops do.''

She met his eyes and her lips curled up in a faint
smile. "Yet you'll do it anyway, won't you?''

He hesitated, then shrugged. "If that's what you
want. What the hell, I enjoy a good challenge.'' Leaning back in his chair, he studied her. "It's your money,
of course, but if you don't want to find all your resources going into my pockets, you might consider acting as my entree to the folks in your world. I'm not
exactly the country-club type.''

She considered him for a moment. "No, you aren't.
Does it really matter?''

"Only in that water finding its own level kind of
way. Chances are better than decent that without an
introduction from you, most of that crowd will be leery
about talking to me.'' *Or, more likely, flat-out refuse.*

"All right.''

"All right they'll be leery or all right you'll—''

"I'll perform the introductions.''

"Don't agree without giving it some thought,'' he
warned. "It could turn out to be time-consuming.''

She shrugged. "I don't care how time-consuming it is." She rose to her feet and looked down at him. "If that's what it takes to clear Jared and get on with our lives, then that's what I'll do. Just let me know what you need."

He thought about that as he watched her walk from the office—about letting her know what he needed. Oh, Mama. Then he thought about getting on with his life, and a less-than-amused laugh escaped him. Shit. He would've been all over that concept two days ago. Now he found himself with a daughter he hadn't known existed and didn't have a clue what to do with. Not to mention a persistent lech for a woman who only wanted him to untangle her brother's problem, then disappear. Get on with his life, his ass.

He didn't even know what the hell that meant anymore.

Six

Jared stood outside The Spot, silently reciting a variation of the pep talk his baseball coach always gave the team before a game. He'd heard about the drop-in recreational center when he'd eavesdropped on a conversation between a couple of kids hustling for change on the 16th Street Mall. His ears had perked up when he'd heard one of them claim it was possible to hang out there from five in the evening until ten. The prospect of having a solid five hours before he had to move on made him feel almost giddy. He couldn't remember the last time he'd had a solid block of time to simply sit in one place, never mind sleep. He didn't even care about the activities the rec center might offer. All he wanted was somewhere he could stay put for a while. It seemed like every time he got halfway comfortable, he had to pick up and move.

He stood to the side of the door for several minutes and watched some Hispanic guys horse around inside the center. Then, drawing a deep breath, he took a step toward the opening.

"You don't wanna go in there," a husky voice said from behind him and Jared jerked to a stop, looking over his shoulder. A kid, so slight of build he looked as if a stiff breeze might blow him away, detached himself from the shadows cast by the side of the building.

Thrusting his hands into the pockets of his baggy jeans, he jerked his pointed chin toward the group of boys inside the rec hall. "That's one of the local gangs," he told Jared. "They have a tendency to run off anyone not one of their homeboys."

"Shit." Disappointment was a massive stone around his neck. God, he was tired. He was so freaking tired and he just wished he could go home.

Tears burned behind his eyelids, prickled his nasal passage and he turned his back so the kid with the funny, raspy voice wouldn't catch sight of them and think he was a damn baby. "Thanks for the heads up," he said gruffly. Blowing out a weary breath, he trudged away from the place that for one brief, shining moment he'd believed might actually provide a few hours of sanctuary.

"Hey, wait up!" The kid caught up and gave him a friendly nudge. "What's your name? I seen you around, here and there. I'm P.J." He dug a grimy hand into his pocket and pulled out a candy bar. "You want half?"

Jared surreptitiously knuckled away a couple of tears that managed to leak past his guard. Glancing at the kid from the corner of his eye, he saw him studiously looking the other way and thought maybe he wasn't the only one who succumbed to the occasional overwhelming bout of helplessness. For some reason, the realization made a difference, and after a swipe of his nose with his shirttail, he squared his shoulders. "Yeah. Sure." He was careful when he reached out to accept the portion of candy bar P.J. offered, because what he really wanted to do was snatch it out of the little guy's hand. He couldn't quite remember when he'd last eaten. He'd killed off the brandy last night, but hadn't had any solid food since long before then. Resisting the urge to stuff the entire candy bar in his mouth, he took a small bite. "Thanks."

"No problem. So, you never told me your name."

"Jared."

"That's prett—uh, a good name." He cleared his throat, but his voice was even raspier than before when he said, "What were you hoping to get outta The Spot, Jared?"

"Hell, I don't know. Someplace to just…be, I guess. Do you know what I mean? I just wanted somewhere I didn't have to leave the minute I got settled." He noticed the griminess of his own hand as he brought up the candy for another bite. "And I'd sure like a shower. Maybe I oughtta go to the Salvation Army, after all." He'd been avoiding those kind of shelters, for fear someone might recognize his face. The truth was, though, he didn't even know if he'd been on the news here. What was hot news in Colorado Springs might not be worth mentioning in Denver. And he was rapidly reaching the point where he could hardly stand his own smell.

"Trust me," P.J. interrupted his thoughts, "you wanna steer clear of the S.A. Way too many mean sumbitches there."

"The *Salvation Army* isn't safe?" Jared stared at P.J. in shock. "Aren't those the people who ring bells and say 'God bless' when you drop money in their collection pots outside the stores at Christmas time?"

"Yeah, we ain't in Kansas anymore, Toto." P.J. shrugged. "It's not the people running the place who are gonna hurtcha—they're all pretty nice. But a lot of the homeless grown-ups using the joint?" Blowing out a tuneless, expressive whistle, he shook his head.

''They'd just as soon punch you in the face as give you the time of day.'' Then he brightened. ''We could head on over to Sock's Place, though.''

''What's that?''

''It's another drop-in center. Well, it's really kind of a church, but it's tight. You can get a meal and shower there and catch a few hours sleep. Whaddya say?''

''Sounds good.'' It sounded *great.* Like a little piece of heaven. He wasn't about to say that aloud, though. Playing it cool was difficult, but he sure as hell didn't have to come off sounding like a hick.

It also felt really nice, he admitted a few minutes later as he and P.J. set off for the new place, to have someone to hang out with. Right up there near the top of the Horrendo-meter was how alone he'd felt in this ongoing nightmare. It was good to have someone to talk to.

Not that he did much of the talking. P.J. seemed to be a jawer by nature; he had an opinion on everything under the sun and didn't hesitate to state it. That was fine with Jared. The smaller boy had obviously been on the streets longer than he had and he was a font of good information that most likely would have taken Jared weeks to learn for himself.

Studying the other youth as P.J. skipped backward in front of him, telling him ways to blend in around the Auraria College campus in order to catch some rest during the days, he thought the two of them probably looked like Mutt and Jeff. He possessed the Hamilton genes, which meant he was tall and rangy, all long arms and legs. To his disgust, he wasn't the least bit buff, but Cook said that was because he was still growing into his bones. She insisted he'd be buff enough before he knew it.

He wasn't exactly holding his breath waiting for that to happen, but compared to P.J. he could have been a fricking graduate of the Charles Atlas school of bodybuilding. The other boy was nearly a foot shorter than he and so fine-boned that he appeared almost girlishly delicate. To be fair, that impression was gained mostly by what was on view: the little dude's big-eyed face and stick-thin arms. The rest of him was buried beneath a T-shirt about three sizes too large and a pair of wide-legged jeans that sagged off his skinny hips and pooled their frayed hems around sneakers that had seen better days. Somehow Jared doubted that the rest of P.J. was any more filled-out, though. Hell, his face didn't even exhibit a trace of fuzz yet.

"How old are you, anyway?" he demanded.

"Gonna be fifteen in a few months."

"Yeah?" Jared studied him skeptically. "How many months do you consider a few?"

"'Bout twenty." P.J. grinned unrepentantly. "How about you? I bet you must be around eighteen, huh?"

"Not until November."

"I was close."

Jared snorted. "Closer than thirteen is to fifteen, anyhow." But his disdain was all for show, and they both knew it. "So, what does P.J. stand for?"

"Priscilla Jayne."

Jared stopped dead. "You're a *girl?*" His voice cracked on the last word, but he was too busy staring and reassessing to care.

"Of course I'm a girl! Jeez! Why does everybody think I'm not?" Looking down at her chest, she plucked the cloth away from its flat planes. "It's because I ain't got no boobies, isn't it? Well, I'm gonna have 'em someday, you know. I'm just a late bloomer."

Her little triangular face went forlorn. "I'd sure have a lot less money troubles if I had 'em now, though."

"How's that?" Now that he knew she was a girl, he was amazed he hadn't tumbled to it the second he'd clapped eyes on her. Shit. In hindsight, it seemed so obvious.

"If I had a nice rack—or, okay, any boobs at all—I could turn tricks and my money problems would be yesterday's news." But she made a sour face. "All right, the truth is, part of me is just as glad that's not an option, but if you tell anybody I said so, I'll deny it. Don'tcha think, though, that the whole sex thing seems really…icky?"

"Well, *yeah.*" He looked at her and thought she didn't look all that much older than his niece Esme. His stomach rolled at the thought of some sweaty old man rolling around on top of her and he reached out to rap his knuckles against the top of her backward-facing baseball cap. "Hel-lo! Letting fat old guys do whatever they want to you with their pudgy damp hands? Be glad you don't have the stuff."

"Yeah, well, easy for you to say. I bet *you* could make a bundle." She gave him a jaundiced once-over. "It must be nice to be gorgeous."

He made a face at the latter comment, but warmed inside all the same at the thought of someone thinking he was good-looking. He also perked up at the idea of making some money. He was down to his last twelve dollars. "Women will pay for sex?" That didn't sound like such a bad deal. He'd only had sex twice, but he'd liked it.

A lot.

P.J. made a rude sound. "Not women, you dumb-shit. Men."

"No fucking way!" He jumped back, as if the very notion were contagious. "That's *sick.*"

"Yeah," she agreed glumly. "Like I said, the whole deal is really icky."

"It's not the sex that sucks, P.J. I'm no big expert, but I'd rank getting laid right up there with hot-fudge sundaes. That's with *girls,* though. I'm not into the guy-guy thing." The mere thought made him queasy.

"Hot-fudge sundaes, huh?" She regarded him with some interest. "I like those. Whaddya wanna bet, though, that only boys get that out of sex? Girls probably end up with mud pies that only look like sundaes."

"Hey!" He felt vaguely insulted by her assertion until he thought of Beth Chamberlain, with whom he'd shared his first sexual experience. "Well, maybe it is better for guys the first few times." Then Vanessa Spaulding, an older woman of nineteen who'd taught him a thing or two, popped into his mind. "But if a guy knows what he's doing, it gets way better."

"That's good to know." P.J. shrugged. "Still, if it's all the same to you, I'd just as soon skip the sweaty groping and go straight to the chocolate-covered ice cream."

He laughed. It was the first thing he'd found re-motely amusing since tearing out of the Colorado Springs mansion, and suddenly things didn't seem quite as scary now that he had someone to hang out with. He gave the young girl a friendly shove to the shoulder. "You're all right, you know that? I'm glad we met."

Seven

John climbed the exterior staircase of the six-car garage behind the mansion. Reaching the top, he glanced back over his shoulder toward the kitchen door, which he could just see from his vantage point. Then he turned back and gave the antique brass door knocker several authoritative, decisive raps. Mary, the housekeeper, had told him he'd find Victoria there, and he had no legitimate reason to doubt her. But what would Tori be doing in an apartment over the garage—having a hot and heavy affair with the chauffeur?

Jesus, Ace. Okay, so it didn't strike him as particularly funny. It should have—considering how much she'd changed over the years, the very notion should have been ironic, or at least marginally amusing. Instead, the mere idea of her getting down and dirty with some faceless man irritated the hell out of him. Which made no sense at all. It wasn't as if he expected she'd been celibate for the past six years.

All right, that was exactly what he expected. So sue him.

It didn't help the nascent case of jealousy swirling in his gut that the woman who yanked the door open hardly looked as if getting down and dirty were outside the realm of possibility. Gone was the sheath-and-pearls-attired socialite. In her place stood a familiar barefoot woman clad in a threadbare pair of cutoffs and an oversized white shirt, the tails of which had been knotted at her waist over a lipstick-red sports bra. The shirt looked as if it might have belonged to her father, so long were its tails and so bulky its rolled-back cuffs that ended just below her elbows. And her hair was a wild, sun-streaked, flyaway nimbus floating out from beneath the little red triangular bandana she'd tied behind her head. But it was the ragged threads straggling against her firm, freckled thighs that riveted his attention.

"Can I do something for you, Miglionni, or did you just come up here to stare at my legs?"

He tore his gaze away from the long, smooth, bare expanse. "You gotta admit, they're ogle-worthy," he said, meeting her eyes. "Believe it or not, though, I actually did have something to tell you—those beauties just drove whatever it was clean out of my head." He didn't plan the grin he flashed her; as with damn near every other time he'd ever been in her company, she drew a reaction from him that was purely spontaneous. "Man, Tori. I'd forgotten how pretty your legs are. You oughtta wear short shorts more often." He couldn't stop himself from giving them a final once-over before he made a conscious effort to look elsewhere. No sense giving her any more opportunities to accuse him of sexual harassment.

He glanced past her into the depths of the big open room. A huge worktable, littered with mechanical pencils and blueprints, wood scraps and piles of fabric, stood down near the end of the room. In the midst of the chaos stood two little houses about three feet tall. One was made of balsa wood and was fairly plain, but the other looked very elaborate. Deep shelves behind the table held several other balsa models and one stone one, each in a different style. "Whoa. Are those yours?"

"Yes."

She relinquished her position blocking the door when he stepped forward and he strode past her, crossing to the table. He saw that the models on the table had an open back and, bending down, he checked out the interior of the ornate one before glancing up at her. "What is this, a dollhouse?"

"Yes."

He indicated the other. "And this one?"

"It's the prototype."

"And you made both of them?" He tipped his chin to include the other prototypes on the shelves. "You made all of these?"

"Yes."

"Wow." He gave the one still in progress a more thorough inspection. "I can't believe the attention to detail. It's perfect." It had gingerbread shingles on the roof, a wraparound porch with spindle railings, two balconies and a bay window. Each room was fully realized, from window seats and the tiny oak paneling forming the wainscoting in the parlor, to the old-fashioned wallpaper and white porcelain pedestal sink in the upstairs bathroom. He flipped a switch on a little metal box he saw sitting on the table next to the dollhouse, and minuscule lights within the model came on. Laughter rolled out of his chest. "This is so cool."

Victoria blinked as she watched Rocket circle the table to investigate the other models on the shelves. He possessed such bedrock masculinity that she would have thought he'd find her dollhouses too sissy for his consideration—or at least dismiss them with no more

than a cursory glance. Instead he seemed fascinated.
When he came to the stone castle and glanced over his
shoulder at her, his dark eyes all but shot sparks of
pure, engaged interest.

"This one's different. It's more like a *guy's* dollhouse."

A laugh escaped her. "Good call. I made it for a boy
with an extensive collection of metal toy soldiers, most
of which are knights, kings, horses and other assorted
medieval warriors. It was my first experience with ma-
sonry and I'm pretty proud of the way it turned out."
Coming around the worktable to stand next to him, she
hauled the castle off the shelf and placed it on the table.
"Look." She reached across his arm and past the tur-
rets into the castle's open top. "It has a working draw-
bridge and portcullis and if you move this stone just
so—" she demonstrated with a fingertip "—and then
the one next to it like this—shazam!" The interior wall
swivelled to expose a secret room that had walls bristling with sketches of medieval weaponry.

John laughed. "Excellent! I would have beefed up
the back wall here for a better defense, but it looks as
if you've got the firepower and that's half the battle. A
couple vats of boiling oil, enough supplies to hold off
a siege and you've got yourself a good chance of holding the fort." He turned his head to look at her. "Do
you make these for a living?"

"Yes." Finding his face suddenly much too close,
his enthusiastic curiosity much too compelling, Victoria
eased back a step, trying to ignore the smooth, hot-
skinned drag of his inner forearm against her own. "I
sort of fell into it by default. I made one for Es and a
couple of her friends fell in love with it and wanted
one for themselves. Their respective parents commis-

sioned me to make them and from there word of mouth just started to build. It was confined mostly to the May-fair area of London until last year, when I set up a Web page on the net. Now I've got all the work I can handle. More, really. I've had to turn commissions away.''

"Have you ever considered mass producing?"

"For about five minutes." She met his gaze. "But then I rejected the idea. Not only would mass produc-tion put me right back in the very situation I was trying to avoid when I left Kimball and Jones—devoting more time to my business than to Esme—it would strip all the individuality out of the process…and probably most the fun, as well. I need to keep it small. That way I can build each house to suit the little girl—or in the castle's case, boy—for whom it's meant. Each child gets a quality, almost-one-of-a-kind dollhouse and I get a creative outlet…not to mention steady employment that's fairly lucrative for being so selective." Much too aware of his shoulder bumping up against hers as he leaned down to test the castle's various working parts, she moved away, going to the shelves and finding make-work straightening the remaining models. "Which reminds me, I should get back to it. You said you had a reason for coming up here?"

When she turned back, she found him checking out her legs once again, but he immediately pulled his gaze up to meet hers. "Yeah. The probability that Jared left town just got a lot stronger. I tracked down the cab driver who picked him up the night your father was murdered.''

"Oh, God." Feeling her legs go weak, Victoria reached for the stool she used when working at the table and pulled it beneath her hips. "What did he say? Where did he take him?"

"He said the kid was extremely quiet and seemed stunned. Maybe in shock. That when he asked if he was all right, Jared laughed hysterically, but calmed down enough to insist on being taken to the bus station."

"Did you find out where he went from there?"

"No. I couldn't find anyone at the station who remembers selling him a ticket. But most teens on the run head for a city and since Denver's the nearest one to Colorado Springs, odds are better than even that's where your brother went."

She pushed to her feet. "I can be ready to leave in ten minutes."

"Whoa, whoa, whoa, there. Slow down." He grabbed hold of her shoulders and leveled a no-nonsense, let's-not-get-ahead-of-ourselves look on her. "We're not going anywhere."

"But if that's where you think he is…"

"Think being the operative word here. Running around like a couple of chickens with their heads cut off won't gain us anything. We do this the smart way, which means I tap into my resources. First and foremost among those is Stand Up For Kids in Denver."

"What's that?"

"An organization that gives aid to runaways and street kids. I'll give them a call and fax them Jared's photograph so they can be on the lookout for him when they do their outreach in Skyline Park Sundays and Tuesdays. Kids learn quickly where they can score a free meal and some toiletries, so if Jared's in Denver, he'll likely show up at Skyline sooner or later. I've worked with this organization before and they know they can trust me not to return a kid to an abusive situation. And in return, I can trust the Stand Up counselors to give me a call as soon as they spot him.''

"*Then* we go to Denver?"

"Then I do, anyway."

"If you think I'm sending you off to collect him all by yourself, John, think again. Jared's bound to be scared to death, and he doesn't know you from Adam."

He gave her shoulders a tiny squeeze. "What do you say we wait until we actually have a useable lead before we argue this to a standstill?"

The common-sense suggestion made her realize the silliness of standing here arguing about it now and she couldn't help but smile. She gave him a poke. "Deal."

Surprisingly, instead of treating her overture as the tension breaker she'd intended and returning a smile of his own, John frowned. "Dammit, Tori, I wish you hadn't done that," he growled. "Now I've got no choice but to get an answer to the question that's been driving me nuts ever since I landed on your doorstep."

"What question is tha—?" The query hadn't fully left her mouth before she was caught against his long, hard body. One strong arm slipped down to wrap around her waist and his free hand tunneled beneath her hair to grasp the back of her neck.

She stared up at him in surprised disbelief as his body heat began to permeate every inch of her he touched. "What the hell do you think you're doing, Miglio—?"

John's mouth, firm, hot, and confident, covered hers, cutting off her demand.

For a moment, sheer astonishment held her immobile. Then she absorbed the taste of him, felt the slide of his tongue and with her heart thundering in the outraged fear that she'd never be able to hold herself aloof from this man, she slapped her hands against the solid wall of his chest and gave it a firm shove.

He didn't even budge and she suddenly recalled his strength, remembered the way it used to intrigue her, titillate her. She remembered, too, the way it had once fulfilled the until-then-unacknowledged little girl inside of her who'd always longed for someone to stand between her and the world. Somebody to keep her safe.

Well, she'd buried that child the day she'd learned to accept once and for all that the only person she could depend on protecting her was herself. And assembling all the resistance at her disposal, she once again flattened her hands, which within seconds of her reintroduction to the warm, wet silk of Rocket's persuasive kisses, had softened from a shove to a caress against the rigid muscles of his chest.

Even with steady pushing on her part, though, he held her with ease. He displayed not the slightest hint of roughness, yet his determination to hold on to her was unmistakable. And he kissed her with an expertise that sent her resistance down the drain. His mouth was talented and his kisses were sultry. Forceful.

Familiar. God, so familiar. She knew these lips. She'd kissed them before, studied them as they'd shaped words, slipped bites of food between them with her fingers. It had been six years, but some things a woman never forgot.

Every last defense disappeared and she felt herself start to melt at the knees. For one wild, reckless minute, suffused with a blistering pleasure she'd only known once before in her life, she kissed him back fiercely. She reveled in his hot, rich taste, in the slick inner lining of his mouth that she lapped with her tongue, in the tensile strength that supported her weight so effectively as she plastered herself against him in a futile bid to climb right inside his body.

Then before it even occurred to her to muster the will to pull away, John jerked up his head, released her, and took a giant step back.

"Damn." He brushed the back of his hand against his bottom lip. Then, dropping his hand to his side, he dabbed his tongue against the lip he'd just touched and eyed her sourly. "It's still there, isn't it? I'd hoped it was gone, or at least one of those memories I'd blown all out of proportion over the years. But you're still every bit as addictive as you used to be." His hot-eyed regard slid over her from the top of her head to her crimson-polished toes. "Christ. You're like cocaine in a red bra."

It didn't exactly thrill her that her first reaction was a sheer, fierce pleasure in knowing he'd been as affected as she. But she'd put sex behind her over the years, had assured herself that she was beyond all that—at least for the time being. The few times she'd actually stopped and thought about it long enough to realize she didn't even particularly miss it, she'd simply assumed it was because she was too busy with motherhood and making a living. Somewhere in the back of her mind, though, she'd always believed she'd one day introduce it back into her life. Only she never had, and it horrified her to realize now that the reason she'd rarely been tempted by the men she'd dated was because none of them had been *him*.

Considering she had serious doubts he'd been similarly celibate, his admitting she'd left an impression seemed the *least* he could do.

She pushed his unexpected revelation aside until she could analyze it more closely at a later, less befuddled time. Giving the shirttails knotted at her waist a tug, she cleared her throat. "We seem to have retained the chemistry, all right," she agreed, pleased to hear her voice emerge with commendable coolness, considering she felt like one huge, hot, frazzled nerve ending. The only sign she could see that he might feel the same was the hot color burning high on his cheekbones. "So where do you propose we go from here?"

"To our respective corners, where we keep it nice and professional."

Victoria wondered how that would work with Esme part of the equation, but she gave him a curt nod. Because he was right. Sex was the *last* thing they needed clouding an already volatile and confusing situation. Keep the physicality out of the picture and they could figure out the rest as they went along. "Great," she said with frigid composure. "Fine. Works for me."

She caught him eyeing her legs again, but he yanked his gaze up and lanced her with the blank-eyed military stare. "Yeah. Dandy," he agreed. "That's what we'll do then."

Good going there, Ace. John stalked back toward the house with angry, long-legged strides. *What are you, a fucking moron?*

Tori had always been different from any other woman he'd ever known. Right from the beginning she'd been different, and he should have known better than to get within kissing range of her again.

Most people had a milestone or two in their lives, he imagined. One of his had been the day he'd discovered his dick was more generously proportioned than the average guy's. Up until then, he'd merely been that skin-and-bones sorry-ass kid of Frank Miglionni, the

U.S. Navy's biggest screw-up. Life with the old man after his mom died in a boating accident had been a series of fleabag apartments outside one base or another, because decent housing on base simply offered too many opportunities for Frank to start feuds with the neighbors. It had been living alone when Frank was in the brig, and being waled on when the old man was home and there wasn't anyone else around to afford him a more interesting challenge.

Then one day shortly after puberty's onset, John had started yet another new school in yet another new town. And when he'd dropped his pants in the locker room after gym class, half the guys there had stopped what they were doing to offer up variations of the universally deferential *holy shit, dude.* It was his first taste of respect, and had made him hunger for more. In that moment, he'd grabbed hold of the new identity they offered as if it were a lifeline.

Then he'd learned there were females out there just waiting for a guy with the kind of equipment he possessed, and that was all she wrote. No one had to tell him twice that his cock size *was* his identity. First girls and then women admitted him into a whole new world of sex, one involving so much more than just his own fist and a raft of sweaty fantasies. It was the closest thing he'd ever found to a religious experience, and once discovered, he was its most faithful disciple. His new goal became pleasuring as many women as he could lay his hands on, and regaling his buddies afterward was just part and parcel of the process. One it never occurred to him to question.

Until he met Tori.

He'd known the moment they met that she was totally different from the marine groupies he usually encountered. But he sure as hell hadn't anticipated the way she would affect him. He'd just blithely laid down the same rules and set the same parameters he always had, never dreaming she'd effect the biggest change in his life since that first milestone. But something about her made him realize he was more than the missile behind his fly that had garnered him the handle Rocket by his marine buddies. And the sick feeling in the pit of his stomach when he thought of anyone discussing her the way he had discussed so many others altered forever his ability to share the details of his sexual encounters with his friends.

"Hello, Mr. M."

The soft-voiced greeting jerked him out of remembrances of sun-drenched days and hot steamy nights. Brought him back from a time when killer sex shouldn't have seemed brand-new, yet somehow had—mixed up as it had been with emotions he'd never before experienced. He had to blink before he could focus on the housekeeper and was startled to realize she was only a foot or two shy of crossing his path as she headed for the staircase, carrying a stack of fluffy bath sheets in her arms.

Jesus. If those had been weapons, he'd be a dead man. He jerked his mind back to the here and now. *See, that's the problem with Tori, pal. She's bad for your health.* Needing to get back to a place that didn't leave him screwed up and confused, he concentrated his attention on the housekeeper, flashing her the oughtta-be-patented Miglionni lady-killer smile. "Hey there, Mary. My apologies. I was deep in thought and didn't see you."

"Oh, my, yes, I can only imagine." She gave him an understanding smile. "You must feel like you've got the weight of the world on your shoulders sometimes, what with all your responsibilities.''

Responsibilities. Right. He cleared his throat and thought it was a good thing she couldn't read minds. ''Yeah, I've been, uh, talking to Ms. Hamilton and I'm just heading back to my office to get to work.'' He nodded at the towels in her arms. ''How about you? Are you restocking the rooms? You sure keep things nice. The way you anticipate every need, I feel like I'm in a four-star hotel.''

A blush of pleasure colored her cheeks. ''Thank you! I'm so glad you've been pleased.'' She ran her hand up the stack of towels, flipping the folded edges. ''I'm not changing out all of the bathrooms right now, though. I'm just taking these up to Mrs. Hamilton. She rang down for more.''

''How's she doing? I haven't seen much of her in the past couple of days.''

''Yes, well, that's probably because she hasn't been around very much. She's been spending a lot of time at the country club. Taking tennis lessons, you know.''

''Has a real passion for the game, huh?''

''Or for the tennis pro at least,'' John thought he heard her mutter, but it was said in a low murmur and she gave him such a perfectly polite smile as she headed up the staircase that he might have misunderstood. Making a mental note to look into it, he continued on to the office.

His mind kept trying to return to that all-too-brief kiss up in the workroom above the garage, but he slammed the brakes on, determined not to go there. He had to stay away from Victoria, that was all there was to it. There was just something about her and he didn't try to fool himself into thinking otherwise. One kiss would never be enough with her. Hell, almost a *week* of screwing like minks hadn't be enough, so it wasn't as if there were a hope in hell he was going to work her out of his system that way. He'd learned during their first go-around that one session of lovemaking merely made him crave more.

Crap. He'd said it before and he'd say it again: the woman was crack cocaine and he was a stone junkie. But from now on, no more sampling—cold turkey was clearly the only way he could hope to stay sane around her.

To facilitate that, work was the key. He threw himself down in the chair behind his desk and reached for his Palm Pilot. Then, pulling up the number of Stand Up For Kids, he picked up the phone, punched out the numbers and settled down to do what Victoria Hamilton was paying him to do.

Eight

Jared felt almost…content. For the second time that week he and P.J. had hit Sock's Place—he had a full stomach, was freshly showered and had even caught a few hours of uninterrupted sleep. He refused to wreck his decent mood that evening by worrying about his dwindling money supply and concentrated instead on the last of the sun shining on P.J.'s hair as she danced around him, talking ninety miles an hour as they headed for the 16th Street Mall. Like the last time she'd washed her hair, she'd left off the baseball cap she usually wore and red highlights sparked threads of fire in her short, chestnut curls.

He found it hard to believe he'd ever thought she was a boy.

She stopped suddenly, favoring him with a brilliant smile. "You know what?" she demanded in her funny, raspy voice. "I think I'm gonna give my mom a call."

Panic clawed at his gut, but he swallowed drily in an attempt to push it aside. It wasn't as if he wanted her to remain on the streets. He knew her mother had thrown her out of her house following a big argument and that P.J. wanted desperately to make up so she could go home again—even if home wasn't the most ideal place in the world. God knew he could appreciate the contrariness of that wish.

But what the hell would *he* do if she went? He didn't think he could stand going back to being all alone and the temptation to talk her out of making the call rode him with acid-tipped spurs.

He shoved aside the little voice that told him not to be selfish. Why shouldn't he talk her out of it? It wasn't as if it would take all that much—he knew damn well she was scared to death of being rejected. And with good reason, if half the stuff she'd told him about her mother was true. So, hey, discouraging her would probably be doing her a big ol' favor in the long run.

Just thinking of her, huh? What a guy. He shifted uneasily and looked at her face, alive and shining with hope. Slanting rays of the setting sun picked out the feathery thickness of her eyelashes, highlighted the clear honey-brown of her eyes. He'd never realized it before, but if she ever got enough to eat and wasn't wracked by the worry that was part and parcel of being homeless, she'd probably be pretty—or at least she'd have the potential to be when she was a little older. "So." Rolling his shoulders, he cleared his throat. "You need some change, or what?"

"Nah." But her obvious pleasure in his offer made her smile grow even wider. "I'll call collect."

He tried not to cringe. She'd attempted calling collect the other day and her mother had refused to accept the charges—she'd just flat-out said "no" and hung up. Stuffing his hands in his pockets, he followed P.J. to the nearest phone booth, then stood back far enough to afford her a measure of privacy while she placed the call. But watching her from the corner of his eye, he saw the exact moment all hope drained from her expression and realized her mother must have refused this call, too.

She dragged herself over to him a moment later and he could barely stand it. All her bounce was gone and her face was pinched and almost old-looking. "Here." He thrust a handful of change at her. "You said money was tight at your house. Maybe she just couldn't afford to accept a collect call."

Tears swam in the eyes she raised to his. "She told the operator to tell me to stop calling. Said that I'd made my bed and could just l-l-lie in it." Her face crumpled.

"Aw, fuck." He reached out to give her shoulder a sympathetic pat, but she jerked away.

"Well, the hell with her!" she snarled as if he wasn't even there. "Who needs the old bag, anyway?" But the tears overflowed, streaming down her cheeks.

Jared looked away to show the same respect for her feelings that she'd offered when he'd blubbered. And when she whirled around and stalked off toward the 16th Street Mall, dashing tears from her eyes with jerky movements, he trailed a short distance behind, his stomach churning in miserable empathy.

They were nearly to 16th Street when a newer model silver Toyota pulled over to the curb close to P.J. and slowed down to keep pace with her. A dark tinted window silently rolled down and Jared watched the driver lean over to eye her as he drove slowly alongside.

Still about fifty feet away and not liking the looks of this situation at all, he picked up his pace. Jeez, this was what they needed. When it rained, it just fricking poured, didn't it? One measly half block and they would've been safely on the Mall, a strip of seventeen or eighteen blocks that was closed to all traffic except the free trolley. But that half block might as well have been a hundred miles.

"Hey, little girl," the man said, eyeing P.J. up and down, his gaze lingering on her flat chest. "What are you, honey, about ten?"

P.J. stopped and stared at the man in the car. "Is that what you'd like me to be?"

He licked his lips and nodded.

"Then, yes sir, I'm ten." She stuck her index finger in her mouth and reached up with her free hand to twirl a dark brown curl with her fingers. "But just barely," she added. "My birthday was last week."

His eyes went avid. "You wanna make twenty bucks?"

"No." She waited a few beats, then said, "But I'd like to make fifty."

"Deal." He pushed open the passenger door.

Jared watched in horror as she walked toward it. "What are you, *crazy?*" He rushed to catch up, pushing in front of her and slamming the door shut again. Leaning into the window, he glared at the driver, who had jerked back into his seat. "Get the hell out of here!"

The man looked him over and visibly relaxed. "Get lost, junior. This is between me and the girl."

He was beefier than he'd appeared from a distance, but Jared stood his ground and kept a struggling P.J. behind him. "Bugger off, you fucking perv, or it'll be between you and the police." To demonstrate he meant business, he looked the man in the eye and recited the Toyota's license plate number. "I wonder how many cops have their eye on you already, just waiting to catch you propositioning some little kid?"

Swearing, the man slammed the car into gear. A second later, the only thing left as a reminder that he'd been there at all was a black patch on the pavement where the car had laid rubber.

P.J. jerked out of Jared's hold and he waited with hunched shoulders for her to lay into him.

But when she stepped around to face him, she merely inspected his face curiously for a silent moment. Finally she asked, "Would you really have called the cops?"

"Yes." He thrust his fingers through his hair, staring at her helplessly. "Look, I'm not stupid—I know that one of these days you might have to sell your body to get by. God, much as the idea gags me to even think about, we both might. But neither of us has reached that point yet and I'll be damned if I'll watch you let your anger with your old lady shove you into—"

He staggered back with a grunt, the wind knocked out of him more by surprise than P.J.'s slight weight when she hurled herself against his chest. She wrapped her arms around his neck and climbed him like a monkey. Disoriented, it took him a moment to realize that, contrary to his expectation that she intended to try beating the crap out of him, she was actually hugging him. Gingerly, he wrapped his arms around her and gave her back an awkward pat, tucking his chin in to look down at her. "What's this for?"

"You would've called the cops," she murmured into his chest. "You would have called them to save me— even though it means you'd probably go to jail for that thing with your dad."

He dropped her faster than a bucket of toxic waste, ripping her arms from around his neck and depositing her back on her feet with enough force to click her teeth together. He took a large step back. "What the hell do you know about my dad?"

"I know he was murdered. And that you're wanted for questioning."

Sickness crawled in Jared's gut and he stared at her in horror. "How?" he whispered.

P.J. shrugged her narrow shoulders. "I followed you for a couple days before I ever approached you."

"Why? What the frickin' hell would make you do that? And why *me?*"

"I guess because you were so—I don't know—so preppy, rich-kid looking, except for your earrings and tattoo. And, God, Jared, *so* not like anyone else I've met on the streets."

"But how did you find out about my father?"

"The day before I approached you, I saw you outside the doorway of the bar in that hotel over on Court Place. You were standing there staring into the place, looking like someone had just shot you, so I got close enough to see what had grabbed your attention. And I saw your picture on the TV above the bar—yours and another man's. After you took off, I heard the news guy say your dad had been murdered and that you were wanted for questioning."

"And after hearing that," he sneered, "approaching a killer didn't scare the crap outta you?"

"Nah." But she couldn't quite hold his gaze when it engaged hers. Then, straightening her shoulders, she met his skeptical look head-on. "Okay, it made me wonder how smart I'd be to talk to you and I thought I probably oughtta leave well enough alone. But then, when I thought about it some more, I figured the man you wacked musta deserved it. That he was probably the world's biggest A-hole."

Jared laughed without humor. "He was that, all right. But he was still my dad, you know?"

"Oh, yeah," she agreed glumly. "Do I ever."

"Yeah, I imagine you probably do. And honest to God, P.J., I never meant to kill him."

It was her turn to look skeptical. "So what did you think would happen when you st—"

"I don't want to talk about this, okay?" It just brought too many memories of that awful night roaring back, and he turned away.

"Yeah, okay. Whatever. But Jared?" She touched soft fingertips to his back.

"What?"

"I'm still grateful you told that pervert you'd call the cops if he didn't go away. You really put yourself out for me and I won't forget it. I owe you."

He made a rude noise. "You owe me nothing. The whole idea just creeped me out."

"Tell me about it," she agreed, falling into step as they headed down 16th Street. "I don't know what I was thinking. But what are we gonna do, Jared? We've still got the same problem."

"Yeah, I know. Our money's running out." He didn't mention that neither of them had been overly worried about it until her mom had gone and screwed up their night. Sometimes you just had to take the care-free moments where you found them. Giving the problem some thought now, he finally said, "I've got a couple of baseball cards in my pack. I don't know if they're worth much, but maybe tomorrow we can find a place to sell 'em."

"Hey, that's good." She brightened immediately. "And we're both lookin' real fine tonight."

"We are," he agreed, but eyed her suspiciously. "So?"

"So, we oughtta take advantage of it to spange some money from the tourists."

He stopped in the middle of the sidewalk. "Okay, I'll bite. What the hell is 'spange'?"

"You know—*spange*—spare change. Cover up your tattoo and try to look clean-cut and hungry. I'll look cute and hungry." Skipping around him once again, she elbowed him in the ribs and flashed a cocky smile. "Between the two of us, whaddya wanna bet we blow the frigging competition clean out of the water?"

Nine

"I don't like this," Victoria said under her breath the next afternoon as the church began to fill up for her father's memorial. "We should have waited until Jared was home and could attend."

"No, you shouldn't have," John said firmly. "How many people have started calling or dropping by to ask when it would be?" He gave her shoulder a consoling pat. "You fought the good fight, darlin', but once the coroner's office released your father's body, you could only put it off so long."

"And once again dinked up the only thing Jared's mother ever requested of me."

He stared at her. "She asked you to put off Ford's memorial?"

"Don't be absurd. She asked me to look after Jared." A bitter laugh escaped her. "Fat lot of good it ever did him."

His dark brows puckered. "When did she ask you to do that?"

"When I was sixteen."

"Well, Christ, that's a lousy burden to dump on a teenage girl. Why the hell didn't she look after him herself?"

Victoria turned on him. "She would have if she could," she said hotly for all that she kept her voice low. "But she'd contracted Lou Gehrig's disease and knew she was dying."

"Then I apologize for the crack." John also kept his volume barely above audible as he shifted to face her. "But I still think her request bites. Tell me where she figured into the lineup of your father's wives."

"Elizabeth was his third. My mom was his first and the one after her was Joan." She glanced around, then indicated with the slightest lift of her little finger a woman seated in the back of the church. "That's her in the red dress. She hated kids. I was a clumsy child and her snapping all the time only served to make me klutzier. I always seemed to be toppling things around her. After I broke both her bottle of thousand-dollar-an-ounce perfume and her favorite piece of art glass in the same day, she talked Ford into shipping me off to boarding school."

"Jesus," he breathed, staring with hard eyes at the woman in question. "What a couple of sweethearts. How old were you?"

"Nine." She shrugged as if it didn't matter, but she could still remember how frightening it had been to lose her mother, gain Cinderella's stepmother's wicked twin sister in exchange and be exiled from the only home she'd ever known, all within the space of eighteen months. But she brightened at the thought of Ford's third wife. "Elizabeth brought me home again."

"Jared's mom."

"Yes. She married Ford when I was thirteen. When she learned he had a daughter who was virtually living year-round at school, she threw a fit that made even Father back down, and I got to come home. I loved her." Which made the guilt of her failure to keep her promise bite even deeper. Acid began to churn in her stomach and she twisted around to face the front again, staring straight ahead.

As if reading her mind, John said brusquely, "Quit beating yourself up about it—it's pointless. You were sixteen, for crissake, and Jared was—what?—three?"

"Not quite."

"Not quite," he repeated flatly. "So what the hell were you supposed to do? What kind of power does *any* teenager have at that age, particularly if you're talking about arguing with a baby's legal guardian over the way his kid should be raised?"

Victoria opened her mouth to say she should have done something—*anything*—even if she couldn't define exactly what, but Rocket changed the subject.

"What about wife number four? Point her out to me."

"She isn't here. That marriage lasted less than six months and Cynthia moved away after the divorce. As far as I know, no one in Father's crowd has seen her since."

"Then coming back to Ford's memorial, you have to admit DeeDee had a point when she insisted it was growing too awkward to put it off any longer." The corner of his mouth ticked up. "Speak of the devil," he murmured in Victoria's ear, laying his arm along the back of her chair and raising his chin slightly toward the side door. "There she is now. Interesting duds."

She glanced toward the chapel door. "Oh, for heaven's sake."

Her father's fifth wife wore black from the tip of her dramatic wide-brimmed, veiled hat to her sheer, patterned stockings and satin, needle-toed Jimmy Choo sling-backs. She leaned heavily on the arm of a handsome young man.

Victoria shook her head. "Would it kill her to resist being the center of attention for the length of her husband's memorial?" Feeling John's gaze slide over her own restrained black sheath and the long string of knotted pearls she'd inherited from her mother, she raised her chin and turned her head to meet his eyes. "What?"

"What do you mean, what? I didn't say anything."

"You think I look like a schoolmarm in comparison, though, right?"

He laughed. "Honey, if I'd ever had a teacher who looked anything like you, I probably would've done a whole lot better in school. I was actually thinking you seem to have a knack for knowing exactly the right thing to wear for every occasion."

"Oh." She would not squirm with pleasure as if she were Esme's age; she *wouldn't*. But neither would she try to convince herself his compliment didn't make her feel warm and flushed all over. "Thank you. That's a very nice thing to say."

He shrugged and she examined his own impeccably tailored suit, snow-white shirt and subtly-patterned tie. "You're a very snappy dresser yourself. I remember that from before—how everyone else ran around the beach in ragged cutoffs, but you always wore nice shorts and tanks and tees that were mostly silk." Promptly regretting bringing up a time she was desperately trying to forget, she sat straighter. "Come to think of it, you've worn quite a selection of nice clothing since you arrived on my doorstep. What do you do, keep a suitcase in your car in case you get an invitation to stay somewhere a while?" The question led to unfortunate thoughts of how easily she'd allowed him to move in on her six years ago, which led to thoughts of other women, which didn't serve to improve her mood.

He merely gave her a crooked smile, however. "You must have me confused with the Boy Scouts—I've never been that prepared. I ran up to Denver the other day to touch base with some of my contacts, is all— and while I was there I gathered up everything I thought I might need for a prolonged stay."

His attention suddenly shifted beyond her. "Who's that guy over there?" Nodding toward one of the pews, he added dryly, "The one who looks like he's running for office."

She followed the direction of his gaze to a silver-haired man nodding and shaking hands as he made his way down a pew past averted knees.

"I hate to say it, but he doesn't look especially broken up by your father's passing."

Victoria gave a little shrug. "I told you before, Father didn't have a lot of friends." She thought about it for a moment, then admitted, "I'm not certain he had any, in fact. He had literally dozens of acquaintances, but I can't think of a single person with whom he was especially close." And wasn't that the saddest commentary of all?

"So why is everyone here then?"

"Probably to make sure he's truly dead." Guilt over her flippancy immediately stabbed her, but at the same time she had to admit it likely wasn't all that far from the truth.

Brushing a discreet thumb down her jawline, he favored her with another one-sided smile. "I'd tell you to play nice, except my own old man was a lot like yours."

"Was he?" She turned to him, her interest sparked.

They hadn't talked about their families when they'd known each other before, and having just spilled her guts about some of her own background, she'd enjoy nothing better than to learn something of his. "He didn't have any friends, either?"

"No. Still doesn't, as far as I know."

"Except you, huh?"

He laughed harshly. "Least of all me." He hesitated a moment, then said with patent reluctance, "He's a drunk. A mean drunk."

She wondered exactly what being a mean drunk entailed, but before she could ask, John, in a none-too-subtle bid to change the subject, nodded his head toward the man he'd previously indicated and said, "So, who did you say he is?"

"I didn't." She'd forgotten about this. But Rocket had been the same way in Pensacola—let the conversation grow even the slightest bit personal and he found a way to divert it in another direction. Only the method had changed, although that was something she'd rather not think about too closely. Unfortunately, it was like trying to ignore the elephant in the room and she squirmed a little recalling the physicality he'd used then.

Dammit, it wasn't fair. He shouldn't be all ears taking in her history when he clearly had no intention of sharing his own. Irritated, she nonetheless glanced once again at the subject of his inquiry, and essayed the slightest of shrugs. "I think that might be Jim Mc-Murphy."

He sat a fraction taller. "Why does that name sound familiar?"

"I believe I mentioned him as the CEO of the company Father recently acquired in a hostile takeover."

''One of the people who was at your house the night your dad died?''

She nodded.

''Introduce us at the reception.''

''Sure.''

The memorial started a few moments later, but Victoria quickly found her mind floating away from the eulogy. It was delivered by a minister who'd never known Ford Evans Hamilton and she wondered if anyone ever truly had, a question that seemed validated when the pastor invited the congregation to come to the podium to share a memory of her father and not a soul stirred.

Then DeeDee rose from the front pew and made her way to the lectern with mincing steps hampered by the slimness of her skirt and the height of her heels. Upon arrival, she grasped the minister's hand, dabbed a lace handkerchief beneath her veil with her free hand, then turned and simply stood for a moment, looking out over the gathering. Finally she sighed, a tremulous little exhalation that the built-in microphone picked up and projected to the farthermost pew.

''This is such an overwhelming day,'' she said sadly and patted a beautifully manicured hand against the cleavage exposed by her V-neckline. Lights sparkled off the five-carat diamond of her wedding set. ''I simply can't thank all of you enough for coming.''

Victoria felt guilty about her urge to roll her eyes at the melodramatic tragedy queen pose.

''Ford could be a difficult man and he wasn't always easily understood.'' Another sigh trembled out of DeeDee's throat. ''But I like to think that was because of his passion for the corporate world. He was such an intense visionary that he didn't always take time for the niceties with his family, friends and business associates.''

Tori straightened. That was very…insightful—much more so than she ever would have given DeeDee credit for. She'd always assumed the other woman was as bubbleheaded and shallow as they came. Perhaps, however, that was an unfair assessment that had more to do with her own hatred of the mindless, social maneuvering DeeDee thrived on than—

''But, he gave such marvelous presents, and no one threw a better party. And behind closed doors…well, let me just say that there were a *few* things he took time for. And, *oh,* I'm going to miss him!''

Good grief. Okay, the shallowness was real. Still, DeeDee was the only one to have stood up for Ford today. Perhaps she truly had cared for him in her own limited way.

Following the service, a convoy of cars followed them out to the house. This was yet another battle Victoria had lost. She'd argued in favor of the reception being held elsewhere. The venerable old Broadmoor Hotel or the country club would have been perfectly appropriate, but DeeDee had insisted it must be held at the house. It didn't take more than ten minutes of dealing with the crush of people milling about the walnut-floored parlor and spilling out onto the terrace for Victoria to wish she'd stuck to her guns. Since she hadn't, however, she organized the servers, instigated a few simple changes to help make the traffic flow more smoothly and thought longingly all the while of her quiet suite of rooms upstairs.

But escaping to them was not to be and unluckily that was far from the worst of it. DeeDee corralled her moments later for the receiving line. *That* was a blast to the past not designed with Victoria's comfort in mind. Just like way back when, minutes took on dog years when they were spent hosting an interminable line while standing in the shadow of a more outgoing personality. Ten minutes into it and the line hadn't progressed beyond the crowd bunched around the widow.

"My God," Victoria murmured to herself. "It's my teenage years all over again."

"What's that?" John tugged at his tie. "How the hell did I end up as part of this line anyway?" Then he rolled his wide shoulders in a *forget-that* gesture and bent his head to hers. "Sorry. What's your teen years all over again?"

"This. Standing in yet another reception line, wondering if I've turned invisible." God, how many parties had she been forced to endure where her attendance had been mandatory, even though no one ever seemed to know she was there? Or worse, where she had been noticed, only to have unfortunate comparisons drawn between her awkward, too-tall, too-gangly self and the always urbane Ford and his current hot young trophy wife?

Too many. And she'd blown her single excuse for slipping away from this one by already making sure the servers had everything they needed to make the reception run smoothly. *Crap.*

"Yeah," John agreed dryly. "Clearly the word hasn't gotten out yet that DeeDee didn't inherit a bundle." His expression was unreadable as they both watched a couple fawn over Victoria's youngest-ever stepmother.

Moments later, however, Tori found herself thinking sardonically that she ought to be a little more careful about the things she let bug her. The bottleneck at

DeeDee suddenly broke free and the line poured toward her and John. *Invisible's not the worst state to be in.*

Many of the faces were unfamiliar, but several others she remembered from those awkward days of her youth. The intense scrutiny, which the latter group subjected her to even as they paid lip service to expressing condolences, threatened to plunge her back into old, familiar feelings of inadequacy. And that she refused to let happen. She'd worked too hard over the years banishing those feelings to allow them to gain a new toehold now.

For all that no one seemed to miss Ford very much, curiosity apparently still ran rampant about how *she* was handling his loss. Vivien Boswell, who back in the bad old days used to murmur, "And what size shoes do you wear *now,* darling?" instead of just coming out and saying, 'My, what big feet you have," eyed Victoria's stylish Manolo Blahniks a moment before raising her gaze to ask how long she intended to stay in Colorado Springs.

Roger Hamlin, who had once rushed to console Ford in the wake of her father's public lament that he simply couldn't fathom how two such graceful people as he and Victoria's mother had ended up with a daughter so gawky, reminded her of the incident, then jovially commented that Ford must have been pleased she'd finally grown into her arms and legs. His gaze lingered on the latter several seconds longer than it should have.

Perhaps in retaliation, *Mrs.* Roger Hamlin informed her sharply that having Esme out of wedlock had broken her father's heart. Then she demanded, "Now, who was the child's father again, dear?"

Old Mrs. Beck merely gave Victoria's hands a there-there-you-poor-thing pat and leaned forward to whisper, ''My dear! DeeDee's behavior! What *do* you plan on doing about it?''

Victoria presented the unflappable manners that had been drummed into her since childhood and walked a fine line by responding to rudeness with courtesy while not actually divulging any real information. But she was relieved when Pam Chilworth appeared in front of her.

''Fun crowd,'' her friend murmured. ''And rough day. Anything I can do to help?''

''No, but bless you for offering.''

''If you think of anything, just let me know.''

''I will.'' Victoria gave her a fierce hug. ''*Thank* you.''

She had ignored the others' curiosity about John and merely introduced him by name. But Pam gave him a glance and then pinned Victoria with a look that made her realize she'd be hearing from her friend soon and she'd better be ready to supply details. The corners of Tori's lips curled up as she gave Pam a slight nod of acknowledgment. She knew she could trust her old confidant not to spread tales.

She was still smiling when her hand was taken by yet another person, and she pulled her attention back to her duties. But when she turned and saw who held her fingers, she froze.

But only for a moment. Gathering her composure, she forced one more impersonal smile to her lips and slid her hand free of the two smooth ones sandwiching it at the same time she gazed coolly at the elegantly attired, outrageously handsome man standing in front of her. As usual, he hadn't so much as a single gleaming blond hair out of place. Once upon a time, such uncanny ability to remain untouched by the same elements that inevitably ravaged *her* had charmed her silly.

But that was long ago. She offered him a clipped nod. "Miles."

"Victoria." Where her voice had been brisk, his dripped intimacy and he reached out a beautifully manicured hand. Ignoring her slight recoil, he walked his fingers up her bare arm with ridiculous familiarity, strolling a path from her wrist to the crest of her shoulder. "It's been too long."

Oh, no; she begged to differ. It hadn't been nearly long enough. But before she could say anything she might regret when she regained a grip on her manners, John's arm snaked around her waist and jerked her firmly against him. His body heat, radiating all along her left side, melted a portion of the old feeling of betrayal that swamped her and she turned into him slightly, smiling gratefully up into his dark, expressionless eyes. "John, this is Miles…" She turned back to the other man. "I'm sorry, I fear I've forgotten your last name."

Anger flared in his eyes, but he said smoothly, "Wentworth."

"Of course. How remiss of me. Miles Wentworth, let me present John Miglionni."

The other man tried to look down his aquiline nose at John, but as the two of them were about the same height, he simply couldn't pull it off. Instead he demanded icily, "And your relationship to Victoria is—?"

"Her fiancé," John said.

Victoria jerked in shock and gaped up at him. But he smoothly absorbed the slight movement by tightening his arm around her and disguising it as a hug, while bending his head to press a quick kiss upon her lips. When he lifted it again, his eyes held a warning even as he stroked residual moisture from her bottom lip with a tender thumb. Then he turned his attention back to Miles.

"Sorry. I can't seem to keep my hands off of her."

Miles's lip curled and he gave the sleek black ponytail that fell down Rocket's back a disdainful glance. But he merely nodded at Victoria before turning on his heel and walking away.

Tori promptly forgot all about him as she tipped her head back to stare up at John. For just an instant she thought she saw some unfathomable, male satisfaction deep in his eyes. But his arm giving her waist a squeeze and his long hand splayed out on her hip divided her attention.

He flashed her his most charming smile. "Well, that went pretty well, don't you think?"

"Are you out of your mind?" She rammed an elbow in his side and jerked away from his loosened grip. "Fiancé?" she demanded with lethal, low-voiced frigidity. "What the hell are you *thinking?*" It took every ounce of control at her disposal to resist drilling a furious finger into his chest.

"Hey, this is actually an excellent idea."

"Really?" She folded her arms over her chest. "So dazzle me with your reasoning."

"I will," he assured her with a bland smile, taking her elbow as the next person in line arrived in front of them. "Later."

People passed by in a blur, and as Victoria dealt with each of them with automatic courtesy, she slowly began to relax. *Okay, so he said something in haste. But it was to one person and considering who that person is,*

*it's not likely to go any further than that. You can put
a stop to whatever wild scheme Rocket's hatched before
the rumor—*

"Engaged?"

—has a chance to spread. Damn! The word could be
heard moving faster than a speeding bullet down the
receiving line and Victoria's heart sank right down to
her toes. She looked up at John in horror. "My God.
What have you done?"

His face, as usual, displayed no overt expression, but
his voice was authoritative when he commanded, "Play
along. I do have a good reason for this and I'll be happy
to explain it to you later."

What else could she do? She feared, however, that
when he splayed his long fingers around her hip again
and turned her to face the crowd, the smile she pasted
on her lips looked every bit as phony as it felt. And
when the assembly spontaneously broke into applause,
her only thought was, *I'll kill him.*

Feverishly seeking a Band-Aid to slap on the situation until she could find a more permanent remedy, she
held up a hand and waited for the applause and mur-
muring to die down. "Please," she began softly, only
to be cut off by John.

"We meant to keep this to ourselves for today," he
said coolly.

Implying there was something *to* keep secret. She
could have smacked him. But she forced her stiff lips
to keep smiling and contented herself with raising the
spiked heel of her left shoe, swivelling it a fraction of
an inch, and bringing it down on his toe. She shifted
all her weight onto that leg. "What he means is, today
is intended strictly for memories of my father. John and

I insist that nothing interfere with that. Right?'' she demanded, staring up at him.

"Oh, absolutely." He bumped his kneecap into the hollow behind her knee, buckling her leg and causing her foot to drop away from where she was furiously attempting to drill a hole through his dress shoe.

Smiling through gritted teeth, she reached across her body, slid her hand over the one he had wrapped around her hip, and sank her fingernails into his wrist just beneath his crisp white cuff. "I beg of you," she said to the enthralled audience, "pretend you didn't hear a thing. I'd never *forgive* myself—not to mention John—if this day became about us." Several people nodded approvingly and she exhaled a small sigh of relief.

Then DeeDee stepped forward, tapping her silver teaspoon against the side of the delicate china cup she held in her other hand.

Damn. DeeDee knew exactly who John was and here was the perfect opportunity to put herself squarely back in the limelight, while at the same time making Victoria look, at best, like a fool, and at worst like a conscience-less liar. She shot a glance at Rocket's calm face. *I'm going to wrap my hands around your throat and squeeze and squeeeeeeze until your pretty black eyes bug out of your—*

"Victoria is right," DeeDee said. "This is Ford's day. But just let me be the first to extend to all of you, my dear, dear friends, an invitation to her and John's engagement ball. I'll furnish you with all the details. at a later date."

For the second time in too short a space of time, shock ran up Victoria's spine. She didn't have a clue why DeeDee had deigned to play along with the counterfeit engagement, but it couldn't be for any reason she was bound to like. Tori smiled weakly at the inquisitive crowd, then gazed up at Rocket with limpid eyes. "You're a dead man," she murmured.

She watched in frustration as he slipped away just before the reception line broke up a short while later. But learning the futility of anyone actually respecting her wish for a moratorium on questions, she became much too busy fending off avid inquiries about the two of them to warm herself with thoughts of Rocket's slow and painful dismemberment. Feeling a definite kinship toward the fox at a hunt, she was soon harried almost beyond bearing.

But when she glanced away from yet another of the women-who-lunched set to see Esme hesitating in the doorway, holding the hand of her nanny, Helen, it was as if a breath of fresh air had blown through her world. And just like that, her slipping composure settled back into place.

Her daughter stood with one small patent-leather Mary-Jane stacked upon the other while she searched the crowd. Tori smiled to see Esme's eyes light up the moment she spotted her and watched as her child broke away from Helen to make a beeline across the room.

"Hullo, Mummy!" The little girl flung herself against Victoria and gave her a big hug. "I missed you. Was the memorable terribly sad?"

"Memorial, sweetie. And yes, it was quite gloomy." She kept the details to herself and simply squeezed her daughter the way Esme's ebullience always squeezed her own heart. Observing Es's high-spirited openness never failed to thrill her. She was everything Tori hadn't been allowed to be as a child and she reveled in her child's exuberance.

Esme planted her chin against Victoria's diaphragm and stared up at her. "You should have let me come with you, Mummy—then you wouldn't have been so sad."

"But then *you* would have been." Tori gently pried Esme from her front and stooped to straighten her daughter's little black sundress with its oversize hot-pink flower appliqué. Tenderly, she brushed a loose tendril of hair away from Esme's soft cheek and looked into the child's big, dark eyes. "And that would have been much worse."

"Still, I should prob'ly stay for the rest of the afternoon so you don't get sad again."

"Well, aren't you a dear," said the woman with whom Victoria had been conversing.

"Yes, she is," Victoria agreed, even though she recognized Esme's statement for the sly attempt it was to gain a concession on an already agreed-upon negotiation point. She bit back a smile. *Must come from her father's side of the family.* "But I'll be fine, sweetie. And you already know my feelings about little girls being subjected to funerals or wakes." Not that this was the former nor even a proper latter, as that implied bonhomie, drinks and affectionate stories of the deceased. Not to mention how Father would turn in his grave to hear it described as such. But that was semantics. "Look around you, Es. Do you see any other children?"

"Noooo."

"There's a reason for that, and if you recall we discussed it at length both last night and this morning. So you may say hello to Rebecca's mother before we fix you a plate at the buffet. Then you and Helen may have a picnic lunch on the grounds, just as I promised you."

Esme studied her for a moment, then blew out a gusty sigh. "'Kay."

Victoria smiled at the wealth of weary disgust she managed to pack into that single syllable, but took Esme's hand and turned her toward the woman with whom she'd been speaking before her daughter's arrival. "Say hello to Mrs. Bell, sweetheart. Bettie, this is my daughter, Esme."

The little girl immediately brightened. "Hullo, Mrs. Bell."

"Hello, dear. You're quite a self-possessed little thing, aren't you?"

Esme clearly didn't have a clue what that meant, but she nodded enthusiastically just the same. "Uh-huh. Mummy says I'm very bright."

Tori saw a glimmer of genuine humor in Bettie Bell's eyes as she smiled down at Esme.

"I can see why." The older woman turned to Victoria. "I can also see you're trying to juggle a lot of responsibilities at once, so I'll let you go. I am sorry about your father, dear. He wasn't much of a man, but he was your dad and I imagine you're finding it quite difficult adjusting to his loss."

"Thank you." Then excusing herself before Bettie could add something about her so-called engagement, she turned Esme toward Pam Chilworth, who stood with a group down by the fireplace.

As she passed a small knot of people near the buffet tables she heard one of them murmur, "This is one of the last great estates left in the Broadmoor area. I wonder if the heirs will parcel it out now that the old bastard's kicked the bucket? Wouldn't that be ironic, considering how hard he fought to keep development here to a minimum?"

She glanced toward John, who was carrying on a low-voiced conversation with Jim McMurphy in the corner nearest the French doors. Despite her wrath, she made a mental note to pass on the overheard snippet of information. She recalled her father's fury over the development of the resort community some years back. Considering how unsuccessful his attempt to stop it had been, the conversation she'd heard probably meant nothing.

Yet she wouldn't dismiss it out of hand, for it was also possible it was worth further study.

She overheard several other less-than-flattering assessments of her father's character as Esme spoke to Rebecca's mother and again as Victoria escorted her daughter through the buffet. She was anxious to get the little girl out of here before she, too, overheard something that made her realize the lack of affection in which her grandfather was held. While it was true Ford had never been a very attentive grandparent, Victoria didn't see the point in inflicting the nasty reality of his personality upon her daughter. Neither did she care to have Esme overhear the news of her mother's faux engagement before she could find a way to explain it to her.

She quickly dished up two plates and turned them over, along with her child, to Helen's affectionate care. Then, with a sigh, she went back to her role as cohostess.

It was shaping up to be a long afternoon.

Ten

"**W**ell, so much for your big 'Going to our respective corners, where we keep things nice and professional' speech."

John looked up from the notes he'd been writing to see Victoria stride into his office. Although she softly clicked the door closed behind her, she somehow managed to give the impression that she'd slammed it with all her might. Coming to stand over his desk, she crossed her arms beneath her breasts and glared down at him, her eyes flashing a truer green than usual, her cheeks hotly colored. He clicked his pen shut, rocked back on his chair, and gave her his undivided attention. The woman was clearly pissed.

Big news flash, Ace. He spared the ruddy crescent-shaped grooves that indented his wrist a quick glance before looking back up at her. "We are going to keep things professional." *Somehow.*

"By pretending to be *engaged?*"

The incredulity in her voice that all but added "to *you?*" lashed at a secret little insecurity he hated to even acknowledge existed and he tossed the pen and notepad filled with his impressions of the various people he'd met this afternoon onto his desk. Sliding his feet off the desktop where he'd had them propped, he dropped them to the floor and sat up. "I don't suppose it occurred to you that I might actually have a good reason for suggesting it.''

''Well, certainly. That was the *first* thing to pop into my head. And you know what I came up with? Because you saw another dog showing interest in a bone you used to find attractive.''

She had a point. He'd seen that clown Wentworth finger-walking her arm and some primal, territorial gene had kicked in, making him leap to mark his claim first and think second. ''There's no 'used to' about it. You know damn well I'm having a hard time keeping my hands to myself. But the truth is, babe, I don't do that possessive, branding-what's-mine-against-all-comers crap.'' Or he hadn't until he'd met her, anyway. He'd never understood that sort of behavior, didn't like it, and he sure as hell didn't trust it.

What he *did* trust was his ability to snatch an excellent idea out of thin air and run with it. He had great instincts and he'd learned long ago to follow where they led.

It just so happened that this time they'd led to him announcing his engagement to Tori. If it had given him a great deal of satisfaction to wipe the supercilious smirk off Wentworth's pompous face in the process, well, that was a bonus, to be sure, but secondary to his primary objective. The important thing was the soundness of the plan. And this was a good one—addressing as it did a number of the problems that had been plaguing him about how he'd induce anyone in Victoria's world to give him the time of day, never mind information that might help clear her brother's name.

Instead of telling Tori any of that, however, he heard himself demanding, ''Just who the hell is that joker to you anyway?''

She stiffened. ''What makes you assume he's anything to me?''

''Please— 'I fear I've forgotten your last name?''' he mimicked in a falsetto voice, then let it drop back into its normal register. ''I doubt you've ever forgotten anyone's name in your life. Particularly not someone who acted as familiar with you as that guy did. So, who is he?''

She looked him up and down. ''What did you mean when you said your father was a mean drunk?''

Like a sniper's bullet, he never saw the question coming and it was a direct hit—it took everything he had not to jerk beneath its impact. He faced her without so much as blinking, but ice lined his gut at the thought of how differently she'd look at him if she ever learned of the violence that had marred his childhood. ''What the hell does that have to do with anything?''

''Tit for tat, Miglionni. You seem to think you have a perfect right to my personal information, but you're certainly reluctant to share any of your own.''

''Because there's nothing of interest *to* share. Now, you wanna get back to business or not?''

He should have been pleased to see her face lose all animation and turn smoothly impersonal. It bothered him just how much he minded instead.

''By all means,'' she agreed with the same distant courtesy he'd watched her employ all afternoon. ''Let's do that. You can begin by explaining how on earth posing as my fiancé will possibly benefit my brother.''

Her cool formality belatedly brought him to his feet to indicate the chair across the desk from him. ''Have a seat.''

She did so, her back princess straight, ankles primly crossed and hands folded with ladylike stillness in her lap. For a moment he simply stood there and silently dealt with the discovery that he much preferred her denting his wrist with her nails or trying to grind his toes into paste to the way she managed to look through him now as though he were some presumptuous street tough trying to pass himself off as a man of quality. Then with a shrug, he took his own seat once again. But for an additional second he simply observed her.

She looked tired and frustrated and…sad. Guilt twisted inside him. For a short while today they'd actually conversed with some of the ease they'd once known, and he understood on a gut level that the memorial and reception had been emotional wringers for her. If her father hadn't literally been consigned to his grave this day, at a minimum they'd held what amounted to his funeral. And even if, from all accounts, the guy had been a sorry son of a bitch, he'd still been her father. John admitted—if only to himself—that his own bald announcement to Wentworth hadn't made things any easier for her.

So maybe he ought to give her a break and put this discussion off until tomorrow. The only time he'd seen her look the least bit happy today was when Esme had shown up for a brief period during the reception.

But he didn't want to remember the little girl hanging from Victoria's waist as she'd beamed up at her mama and he squared his shoulders, shoving the memory aside. *Hell, get real, pal.* Victoria would be the first to agree he was a conscienceless sinner. Just look at his failure to do anything about getting to know his own daughter. *So why do you wanna confuse things by developing a conscience at this late date? Stifle that crazy-ass urge to give her a breather.*

But he kept picturing a little sweet-faced, dark-eyed

girl, until, as if in answer to an unstated prayer, the memory of DeeDee giving her eulogy popped up to replace the image. With silent thanks and renewed determination he leaned forward. "Listen, if you want to present the cops with another suspect, I'm going to need access to all the country-club types who had contact with your father."

"So you've said before. And I believe I already agreed to introduce them to you."

"Yes, you did. But I also recall mentioning that private detectives rarely get involved in murder cases, both because cops tend to frown upon their participation and because they have no real authority to compel people to talk to them. I can't make anyone tell me what they don't want revealed. And why do you imagine anyone *would* want to talk to me, Tori? To satisfy some burning desire for truth, justice and the American way?"

Seeing her open her mouth to retort, he rode right over whatever rebuttal she might have made. "As your fiancé, though, I'd have an entrée that few would bother to question. People are less on guard in social situations and I can take advantage of that to work conversations around to the things I want to know. I'd be free to talk to bartenders and caddies and the like without them having to worry that the members they depend on for tips are wondering what secrets they're telling me."

"So you're saying that in order to do your job you'd *lie?*"

"In a heartbeat, darlin'. What'd you think, that a killer would just stand up and confess his crime because he likes my pretty face? Role playing is part and parcel of being a detective."

"You always struck me as more straightforward than that."

"And so I am…if it'll get me the facts I need to close a case. But I've also been known to set up a sting, pretend to be someone I'm not and flat-out lie through my pearly white teeth."

She looked as if she were severely disappointed in him, but didn't comment as she crossed one long leg over the other. "What good does talking to the help do?"

He pulled his gaze away from the slice of thigh revealed by the slide of her skirt up her nylon-encased legs. "For the most part, like servants, they're treated as if they're invisible. And the unnoticed are the very people who tend to observe stuff themselves. To *hear* stuff. For example, DeeDee eulogized your father today as dear, dear Ford, but rumor has it she might be messing around with the tennis pro at the club. The kid who picks up balls and dispenses towels could probably tell me faster than anyone else if that's actually true or not."

"How on earth did you hear that?" Then she shook her head. "Never mind—I don't even want to know. Besides even if it's true, haven't we already established she had no motive for Father's death?"

"That's simply the quickest example that came to mind." Glancing at her legs again, he tugged his tie loose. Then, impatient with himself and feeling a little pissed at her as well for distracting him from the matter at hand, he drilled her with a hard gaze. "Do you see what I'm saying, though, or are you being deliberately obtuse?"

Jesus, Ace, get a grip. He gathered himself, not needing to see her offended expression to know he was out of line. He'd been trained to be more diplomatic than this. "Look, murder isn't my area of expertise, so the whole engagement gig is a long shot at best. But I'm telling you straight out, I've got a much stronger chance of succeeding with that as a cover story than if I simply go in and start asking questions because you hired me to."

She jiggled her foot in its sleek, spike-heeled shoe. "In other words, you want to throw me back in the middle of that phony social scene," she said crankily. "The one I swore I'd never get involved in again."

"Hey, it's your call." But what was with her wasp-ishness all of a sudden? It wasn't like Victoria at all. She was usually much too mannerly to show her temper. Although, come to think of it, that was generally with everyone except him. Still, he studied her with unwelcome concern. "Did you get anything to eat today?"

"What do you care?" She scowled at him. "And have you bothered to give one moment's thought to what Esme might think to find her mother suddenly engaged?"

Oh, shit. The truth was, he hadn't. Dammit, he *wanted* to do right by that little girl. He'd like nothing better than to do right by her…if only he knew what the hell that might be. Was it trying to further his acquaintance with her, or was it keeping his distance?

And his face must have said it all, because the look Tori shot him was pure disgust. "You're a real prince, Miglionni. Even leaving Es out of the equation—and trust me that's highly unlikely—what makes you assume you can pull this off? That damn club is all about golf and tennis and status. And you—" she eyed him critically, her gazing lingering for a moment on his hair

"—well, you're hardly the country-club type, are you."

It wasn't a question and he shoved his chair back with a screech and rose to his feet. "What—you afraid I'll pick my teeth with my pocket knife in the exalted club dining room?" Anger and an edge of something else he didn't care to examine too closely surged through his veins. "You know what? Forget it. We'll spread the word that I'm just another rejected suitor who was jerking your chain at the reception this afternoon and go back to plan A. Having met and talked to several of the club's members this afternoon, I'm guessing it probably won't work. But I'll give it my best shot. Because I sure as hell wouldn't want to embarrass you in front of your tony friends." He headed for the door but stopped with his hand on the knob to look back at her. "I realized you'd changed quite a bit since the good old days," he said flatly, running his gaze over her expensive little outfit before meeting her startled gray-green eyes as she revolved in her seat to stare at him. "But, darlin', I never would have pegged you for a snob."

And ripping open the door, he strode from the room, making a beeline for the front entrance.

"I'm *not* a snob," Victoria said to the empty room. Untwisting from her awkward position watching Rocket's abrupt exit, she slowly settled back into her chair, then simply stared blankly at the bookcase behind the desk for a moment. She *wasn't*, dammit. He'd pointed out himself the other day that he wasn't country-club material. Besides, her comment had actually been a backhanded compliment, since the last thing she could envision John having the slightest interest in was trying to out-Jones the Joneses.

But a tiny interior voice snorted and she sat a little straighter. All right, perhaps her approach hadn't been exactly diplomatic. In her own defense, though, she honestly couldn't envision him caring for or knowing the first thing about golf—and it was a fact the male members of this club tended to be rabid about their game. And realistically, what could a guy with a tattoo of a skull and crossbones that were bracketed by his battalion designation and the words *Swift, Silent* and *Deadly* have in common with the country-club set?

Aside from the fact that he's every bit as athletic and dresses as beautifully as any club member, you mean? Or that you've never once known him to be at a loss for words or out of his element with anyone? Her face burned. Because God only knew, her impressions of people weren't always the most reliable in the world, and as she'd noted earlier, she and Rocket had never gotten around to discussing their backgrounds with each other. For all she knew to the contrary, he could be the product of a family that was every bit as entrenched in their local society as her own was—and his tattoo be damned.

Dear God. She was a snob.

But still. Angry, confused and nearly faint with a hunger she hadn't identified until John's inquiry, she shoved to her feet and headed blindly for the door. Pretending to be engaged was asinine. Who in their right mind would ever believe the two of them were a couple? Well, sure, she had, once upon a time. But that felt like a lifetime ago and even then she'd been smart enough to run as fast as she could in the opposite direction the instant she'd realized her heart was getting much too involved with a man who'd set rules for the end of their affair before it had even begun. Damned if she intended to stick her head back into *that* noose. It was too dangerous.

The truth of the last thought brought her up short in her headlong trek toward the kitchen to grab something to eat before seeking the haven of her rooms. It *was* dangerous—to her peace of mind, if nothing else. She wasn't afraid to admit it: she was much too susceptible where Rocket was concerned. And she sure as hell wasn't inclined to have her willpower tested by being thrust headlong into the forced intimacy of a fake betrothal—not when John hadn't done one damn thing to address his relationship with his daughter, which was his so-called reason for moving into the mansion in the first place!

Besides, as reasonable as his explanation may have sounded, surely he'd exaggerated when he claimed a social connection was the best way to discover information to clear Jared's name. His attitude had struck her as suspiciously testosterone-fueled. Maybe he was embarrassed to be caught out in that inexplicable pissing contest with Miles and thought he had to defend an impulsive declaration.

She snorted. Right. Like she could visualize Rocket being embarrassed by anything.

Still, he certainly hadn't stated his objections in such strong terms when she'd first broached the idea of him searching for another suspect in Ford's murder. If she correctly recalled, in fact, he'd flat-out said he enjoyed a challenge.

So, no. For all that her method may have been ungracious and heavy-handed, she'd done the right thing. Clearly it was far wiser to call a halt to the bogus engagement before matters truly got out of hand than to find herself once again tangled in the snare of this treacherous attraction John Miglionni posed for her.

It was amazing what solid food, a good night's sleep and a morning spent playing with a little girl possessed of a penchant for warm, powdery-smelling hugs could do for a woman's state of mind. Victoria didn't feel nearly as crazed as she had last night and she smiled to herself as she made her way down to lunch. Rebecca had just arrived and she'd left the two girls in Helen's care in the sitting room. They were settled in for an afternoon of pizza and playing with dolls and she was determined to tackle John and DeeDee about putting a stop to this engagement nonsense before it got completely out of hand.

Only this time she intended to keep the discussion courteous. Nonconfrontational. Impersonal.

The two she sought had reached the dining room ahead of her and they both looked up from the table when she walked in a few moments later. John had his neutral parade ground face on, but DeeDee flashed her a big smile.

"*There's* the bride-to-be," she said with such pleased warmth that Victoria paused on her way to the table.

But only for a moment. Crossing the room, she pulled out the chair next to John's and took her seat. Baldly suspicious of DeeDee's sudden friendliness, however, she leveled a look at her. "About that—"

"Yeah, *how* about that?" DeeDee waved her hand at John. "The big guy here is sure as hell a fast worker! Of course, I saw the chemistry between you two right from the very beginning."

Now I know you're yanking my chain. But when Victoria looked closely at the other woman, she wasn't actually certain. The truth was, DeeDee didn't particularly like her and they both knew it, so Victoria fully expected to see satisfaction for her predicament written all over her erstwhile stepmother's face. Instead all she saw was a hint of smugness that could just as easily be the result of having been proved right. On the off chance that was the case, she leaned forward and said earnestly, "Listen, about the announcement yesterday—"

"If you're going to apologize for its lack of formality, don't worry about it. I took care of that." She gave the couple a dry smile. "John's not the only one who can work fast."

Tori's stomach took a spiraling nosedive to her knees. From the corner of her eye, she saw John slowly straightening from his indolent slouch next to her and without thinking she reached over to grasp his hand. "What do you mean?"

"One of my very favorite things about living with Ford was getting to meet all the movers and shakers. I don't know if you recall, what with the heart-warming size of yesterday's turnout, but the publisher of the *Gazette* was here. Well, what good is knowing every power broker in the state if you can't beg one teensy-weensy favor from one of them? So I took Henry aside and look!" She whipped out a copy of the paper, folded to the lifestyles section. "Ta da! Don't you just love how fast you can get things done when you know the right people?"

Victoria leaned forward to read the newspaper DeeDee slid across the table. As her mind assimilated the words, she froze.

Oh.

My.

God.

There it was in black and white. Her mouth gone arid and her heart beginning to pound in her chest, she swallowed dryly, then read aloud, "Victoria Evans Hamilton to wed John Miglionni Saturday, October—" She jerked her head up to stare at her stepmother in disbelief. "You gave them a *date?*"

"Well, I had to. Henry said the *Gazette*'s acceptance policy is for no later than six weeks before the wedding date. But it's not like you're locked into it. You'll probably want to submit a photograph of the two of you for the formal ad anyway, so you can give them the real date then. Or we can always announce it at the engagement ball. This is strictly bare bones, more in the nature of a little prenuptial kickoff than anything. And speaking of prenups," she turned to John with bright-eyed interest, "is she making you sign one?"

"*What* engagement ball?" Victoria demanded and her voice went so high she was amazed the crystal wineglasses on the table didn't shatter.

"Why, the one I promised everyone yesterday." DeeDee whipped a folder up off the floor next to her chair and pushed aside her china and cutlery to make room. Flipping the folder open, she sorted through what looked like a ream of notes before looking at Victoria. "Since the wedding date I gave Henry is only six weeks away, I felt we really had no choice but to have the party right away. So how does next Sunday grab you?"

"By the throat," John murmured and Victoria snapped, "Are you out of your *mind?*"

"I know, I know." DeeDee nodded in understanding. "Sunday is hardly the most chi-chi night for a ball, and all the best places are booked months in advance. Not to mention that not everyone will be able to attend on such short notice. Sometimes, though, things are just meant to be, you know? The club was booked solid, of course, but the Broadmoor actually had a cancellation for one of their ballrooms. So I reserved it. I also personally called the very *crème de la crème* of society and guess what?" She leaned forward in a flashy display of cleavage. "Every single one of them said they'd be delighted to come! Isn't that the greatest?"

Forgetting every rule of behavior ever drummed into her head, Victoria lunged. But John thwarted her desire to climb over the table and wrap her hands around DeeDee's throat by quickly wrapping his arm around Victoria's shoulders and clamping her to his side.

"Yeah, that's damn swell," he agreed easily, but his eyes were cool and watchful. "Excuse us now, though, wont'cha? You sort of sprung this out of the blue and I think Tori and I need a little privacy to discuss it."

DeeDee blinked. "But there's a hundred details to discuss. And what about lunch?"

"Ask Cook to slap warming lids on our plates. We'll get to them later."

"Speak for yourself," Victoria muttered. "I may have lost my appetite for life." But a feeling of fatalism was settling over her as she weighed John's chances of getting answers from her father's crowd now that personal calls and announcements in the newspaper had been thrown into the mix. What were the odds of seeing any cooperation if she turned around and admitted not only that the engagement was a farce, but that Rocket was a private detective she'd hired?

Not good. She tilted her head back and stared up at

John as he rose to his feet. "Is this still what you want to do?"

He froze with his hand on the back of her chair. Then he nodded. "Absolutely."

"For the same reasons you gave me before?"

"Yes."

She hesitated five seconds, ten. Finally she blew out a long sigh. "All right then," she said. She leveled a look on DeeDee. "But I'm certainly not happy with you. This is nothing short of presumptuous. It's not up to you to—"

"Plan a party when I don't actually have the money to pay for it," DeeDee finished, and nodded. "I know. It's 'not done,' as Ford liked to say, to plan an event when you know damn well the one you're planning it for will end up footing the bill."

Victoria stared at her. She hadn't even considered that aspect of it. Until a short while ago DeeDee had been free to give as many lavish parties as she desired. That was no longer an option for her.

"Still," the other woman continued, "you gotta admit it's been like a morgue around here—you'll pardon the choice of words—since Ford died."

"It hasn't even been three weeks!"

"True, but this is the perfect excuse for a bash. Besides, engagements really shouldn't go uncelebrated."

"Perhaps not, but I'd just as soon have celebrated privately."

DeeDee blew out a disgusted breath. "Jeez, you're boring."

"Yes, I am. I'm also busy. I don't have time—" or the inclination "—to handle a hundred party details."

"Of course you don't." Crossing her arms on the table in front on her, DeeDee leaned so far forward it pushed her abundant cleavage up to her collarbones. "I, on the other hand, have nothing *but* time. So, let me do it. You won't have to worry about a thing except showing up next Sunday night suitably attired. I'll take care of all the rest."

Victoria wasn't disposed to be gracious. DeeDee had painted her and John into a corner and she wasn't a hundred percent convinced it was strictly for the opportunity to throw a party. And even if it was, the last thing she was inclined to do was reward the woman for her machinations.

But still…

It looked as though this phony engagement was on whether she liked the idea or not, and as long as it was, she might as well go the whole course and provide John the opportunity to talk to as many people as possible. She could put up with the stifling society milieu for a short while.

She certainly didn't want to spend her time arranging the details of an engagement she knew to be false, though, so she took a restorative breath, silently blew it out and looked at DeeDee across the table. "Fine," she said through stiff lips. "Thank you. That's very kind."

And may God not strike me dead for a liar.

Eleven

It was a déjà vu moment when some sixth sense made John look up from his desk later that evening to see Victoria standing in the doorway. Or close enough to one, anyhow, he decided wryly when she didn't duplicate her slamming-the-door-without-actually-doing-so routine. In fact, this time she didn't even close the door. She simply leaned into the room and said autocratically, "Come with me."

"Where?" he asked but climbed obligingly to his feet without awaiting an answer. Good thing, too, since she promptly turned on her heel and stalked with long-legged strides down the hallway. Tucking his hands into his slack's pockets, he ambled along in her wake and tried not to stare at the beguiling twitch of her hips and the roundness of her ass.

Without a whole lot of success.

"So where did you say we're going?" he asked a few moments later as they reached the top of the stairs and started down the second-floor hallway. His willingness to chase after her had been a problem for him since the first night they'd met, he thought a touch irritably.. He rolled his shoulders. "I suppose it's too much to hope we're headed to your room for a bout of tear-the-sheets-up, hot, sweaty sex."

"Actually, this may be your lucky day." She shot

him a cool look over her shoulder. "You get the first part of your wish, anyhow."

"Yeah?" Intrigued, he caught up. "We're headed for your room?"

"Rooms. And yes."

"Not for sex, though, huh?"

"How do you military types say it—that's an affirmative? No sex."

He knew he should leave well enough alone, but a little devil was riding him and he snaked his arm around her waist, tugged her to his side and bent his head to hers. "No need to be old-fashioned, darlin'," he murmured into her hair. "After all, we're engaged." He inhaled a deep breath. Man, she smelled good.

"Yes, so everyone seems to assume. Which brings us to the reason we're here." Slipping free, she stopped in front of a closed door and turned to look at him.

Something in her expression knocked the desire to tease right out of John's head. "Tori…?"

"This is where we get the fun job of explaining our so-called betrothal to Esme."

He couldn't believe how close to panicking that statement managed to shove him. He who had never panicked in his life, who not only relished an adrenaline rush but once upon a time had actually sought them out on a regular basis, didn't have the first idea what to do with the one roaring through his system now. He broke out in a cold sweat. "Why the hell did you let me waste time when we could have used the walk up here to figure out what we're going to tell her?"

Victoria made a disparaging noise. "This isn't nuclear fusion, John. We'll tell her the truth." She reached for the doorknob.

He whipped out a hand to stop her. "Are you *crazy?*"

"Depends on how you define the word, I imagine. I'm a parent—some would say that's pretty much one and the same." Then the flare of ironic humor disappeared from her eyes. "You've paid lip service to wanting to get to know your daughter," she said in a low, intense voice. "Well, here's your opportunity to actually do something about it. But we are *not* going to lie to her, Miglionni."

"She's five years old! She'll blow the whole deal."

"You think?" She thrust a stubborn chin up at him. "And what's the alternative? You believe letting her fall in love with you and thinking she's finally going to score herself a daddy is a big improvement? That might be swell for *your* purposes, but what happens to Es when you pack up your bags and go back to Denver?"

He didn't have the vaguest idea what state his relationship with Esme would be in when this was all over. And even if he'd put prodigious amounts of thought into the long term potential for a father/daughter connection, it probably wouldn't have mattered.

Because Tori was on a roll, fierce as a mother bear standing between her cub and anything that threatened it. The look she gave him was pure protective indignation. "You don't get to break my baby's heart for the sake of some role you've got a wild hair to play."

It was just another in a long line of the hits his pride had taken since landing on Victoria's doorstep and he retaliated by eyeing her up and down. "You think I'm dying to do this for the pleasure of *your* company? Don't flatter yourself, sweetheart. This *role,* as you put it, just might save your brother's ass!"

''So far, hotshot, you haven't even *found* my brother's ass!''

He watched fire spark from her eyes like lightning from a witch's fingertips and for a millisecond caught a glimpse of the pure outrage and anger she'd been suppressing ever since she'd agreed to go along with their phony engagement. It was immature of him to be pleased as punch that she was pissed, but she'd sure as hell pulled no punches making sure *he* understood he was the dead last man her social circle would ever buy her marrying. Hell, they both knew she'd never had any intention of getting sucked into this arrangement. It would have come to nothing if DeeDee's machinations and the social niceties that formed the basis of Victoria's upbringing hadn't neatly caged her in.

But just as quickly as the crack in her facade had appeared, she paved it over. Her expression shuttered again and the brief peep he'd gotten into her turbulent emotions disappeared. Once again she faced him squarely and said with the studied courtesy that drove him up the wall, ''Much as it pains me to admit this, if I'm forced to decide between protecting Jared or Esme, I'm gonna choose Es.'' Then she drew herself to her full height and stared him down. ''So let's get moving. You and I are going in there to tell Esme what's going on, before she hears it from someone else and starts building expectations we have no intention of filling.''

For all that he grasped what she was saying—and even agreed with it on a strictly logical plane—his gut-level resistance must have shown on his face, for she grew somehow taller yet and her voice developed a snap many of his old drill instructors would have envied when she rapped out, "Now, Miglionni! We *will* do what's right. Understand?"

He understood all right, but he discovered he'd rather face a secret cell of holed-up terrorists with unlimited doomsday weaponry than one little girl packing nothing scarier than his genes. Still he gave a curt nod, but this time when he followed Victoria through the door, he was too preoccupied and jumpy to check out her butt. He got a quick impression of a sitting room decorated in the same icy elegance as the rest of the mansion. But here the barely-lived-in perfection was broken up by books and magazines scattered across the scaled-down coffee table and sofa, a pair of bright, multicolored sandals jumbled in one corner with a more somberly hued pair of pointy-toed stilettos and a miniature pair of sunglasses studded with plastic jewels hanging from the shade of the end-table lamp.

The warm, homey clutter had scarcely registered, when Victoria's soft voice calling their daughter's name jerked his attention back to the matter at hand. He heard the sound of a toilet flushing and Esme's voice calling back that she was coming.

He couldn't *believe* the way his heart began to thump in his chest as he listened to the water turn on and as quickly off in the bathroom. He was a former marine, for crissake, and she was just a kid. Yet he was still working to convince himself that made a lick of difference to his shredded nerves when the door that separated the bedroom from the sitting room was flung open. Esme burst out, still yanking up one side of her little navy patterned pajamas.

"Hullo, Mummy—*hi,* Mr. John!" She verged off course from the beeline she'd been making toward her mother to head straight for him.

Damn. It was like every other time he'd entered her sphere. She was a magnetic force drawing his fascinated attention despite his reservations and the firmness of his intentions to keep his distance.

"Hey, there, Esme." He watched her jerk to such an abrupt stop in front of him that she rocked up onto her toes and his hand reached out as if it possessed a life of its own to touch her hair. Pleasure splintered through him because for all the wavy mass looked almost electrified, it felt incredibly soft beneath his fingertips. "How you doin'?"

"Good! How *you* doing? Did you come to read me a bedtime story?"

"Uh…" He shot a helpless look at Tori.

"No, sweetie," she said soberly. "Take a seat. John and I have something to tell you."

"Uh-oh." Her wattage dimming a little, the child grabbed his hand and tugged him with her toward the silk upholstered sofa.

He allowed himself to be towed across the room, but studied his daughter curiously. "Why uh-oh?"

"Mummy always says sumpin-to-tell-you and take-a-seat when it's serus."

"Serious, Es," Tori said.

"See?" Esme let go of his hand to bounce up onto the couch, then trained her big-eyed gaze on him again as soon as she'd settled herself. "Toldja."

"And you're right, sweetie," Victoria agreed, perching on the edge of the spindle-legged chair facing the sofa. "It is serious. But not anything to make you feel bad. Do you remember why John came here?"

"Uh-huh." But the little girl looked less than sure.

"Remember the first day when you came down to meet him because Nanny told you he was…?"

Esme drummed her bare heels against the couch for a moment. Then her face lit up. "A 'tective! He's gonna bring Uncle Jared home." And wiggling with pleasure, she turned to him, nudged her little shoulder into his side and tilted her head back to flash him a blinding, don't-you-just-think-I'm-brilliant? smile.

Catching him off guard, John's heart clenched so hard and fast it literally hurt.

"That's right," Victoria said. "And in order for John to talk to people who might be able to help him, he and I are going to play a little game of pretend."

Esme quit knocking her heels together and all but went on point like a hunting hound after a fallen bird. "You are?" She straightened from her relaxed slouch against him and focused in on her mother. "I like pretend."

"I know you do, sweetie. Unfortunately it's not my favorite thing, so I'm not as good at playing it as you are. But we're hoping it will help Jared, so I'm going to give it my very best shot." She spared Rocket a brief glance in which he read her reservations, but they were erased from her expression when she turned her attention back to her daughter. Inhaling a deep breath, she quietly blew it out. "Starting tonight, John and I are going to make-believe we're engaged."

"Lovely." Esme nodded in happy agreement. Then she asked, "What's engaged?"

John laughed and Victoria explained, "It's when a man and a woman agree to get married."

Esme stilled, gave John a glance, then stared at her mother once again, her delicate eyebrows furrowed. "Like Rebecca's mummy and daddy?"

"Yes, like that. Except they truly are married and

this is only pretend. But you can't *tell* anyone it's not real.''

"'Cept Rebecca.''

"No, sweetie, not even her.''

"Uh-huh! She's my best friend.''

"I know. But if she should forget and tell someone, and then they tell someone else, pretty soon everyone will know it's only make-believe and John won't be able to talk to the people he needs to.'' Tori scooted to the very edge of her seat. Reaching out, she grasped Esme's big toe between her finger and thumb and gently wiggled it before wrapping her entire hand around the child's instep. "I know secrets can be hard to keep, honey, but it probably won't be for very long. If you really need to talk to someone about it, though, and I'm not around, Nanny Helen knows the truth. And I doubt very much that Cook and Mary will be fooled by our story.'' She hesitated, then said, "Just don't mention anything about this to DeeDee, okay?''

Esme blew out an *As if* breath. "DeeDee's dumb,'' she muttered.

To John's surprise, Victoria said, "No she's not, sweetheart. She simply doesn't know how to talk to little girls.''

Esme looked at her mother for a moment, rocking her bare foot back and forth beneath Victoria's grasp. After a glance at Rocket from the corner of her eye, she once again stared at Victoria. It seemed to John that the silence stretched on forever before she finally said, "Can I still get in bed with you sometimes?''

"Darling, of course you can! Why would you think otherwise?''

"Won't Mr. John be sleeping in your bed?''

Letting loose of the little girl's foot, Victoria snapped

back upright on the edge of her seat. "No," she said in a neutral voice, "he won't. What made you ask that?"

Esme shrugged. "Rebecca's daddy sleeps in her mummy's bed."

"Yes, but this is just pretend, sweetheart, remember?"

"Uh-huh."

"And we aren't pretending we are married, just that we're going to *get* married. You see?" The little girl nodded uncertainly and Victoria added, "Like when the Prince gave Cinderella the shoe."

"'Kay." But John saw the little V of confusion still puckering Esme's brows and doubted she truly did understand. Visions of the already fragile pretense collapsing around them like a house of cards floated before his mind's eye. He understood Tori's point about the consequences if they didn't tell the kid and she found out from someone else. At the same time, though, he didn't want to watch the opportunity to do his job and get the hell back to the real world go down the crapper.

His mind began working fast and furiously to figure a way to control the situation. *Come on, chief, you know women.* Sure, Esme was hardly a woman. But even if she was a tinier person than he was accustomed to dealing with, she was still a female. And the trick with females was to figure out what they wanted and then give it to them. He turned to her.

"You want to play, too?" Ignoring Victoria's jerk of protest, he watched as the little girl's big dark eyes lit up and knew he'd latched onto the right approach.

She nodded eagerly.

"You know what would help make people believe our little game of pretend?" Suddenly finding himself the recipient of her complete focus, he had to suppress the urge to shift uncomfortably. But, God, she had a gaze that was amazingly compelling for a kid her age and it took a genuine effort to pull himself back to his agenda. ''If you were to drop the mister and just call me John.''

''I can do that!'' Plainly taken by the idea, she beamed up at him. ''I'll pretend you're gonna be my daddy.''

''As long as you remember it *is* make-believe, Esme,'' Victoria said firmly.

John had to suppress a spurt of irritation. But how many times did she intend to sing that refrain? They *got* it, already!

Even Esme seemed a little less enamored with her mother than usual. ''And now I can tell Rebecca that he's gonna be my daddy.'' She stared at Victoria challengingly, then added before her mom could launch into a new chorus, ''But not my *pretend* daddy.''

Tori looked hunted for an instant, but then she expelled a quiet sigh. ''Yes, I suppose you can. Right now, though, it's time for you to go to bed. So say good-night to John and I'll tuck you in.''

''He can come, too,'' Esme said. ''''Cause from now on we're gonna play mummy, daddy and me. You said so.''

John saw his own proclivity for playing all the angles in those five-year-old eyes and it frankly scared the shit out of him. He watched as she hopped off the couch and turned to thrust her soft little hand out at him.

''Come,'' she commanded every bit as dictatorially as her mother. ''You can read me my good-night book after Mummy tucks me in.''

Twelve

Dark, heavy-bellied clouds started rolling in over Denver the following Saturday evening as Jared and P.J. struck out for a place to spend the night. By the time they reached the locked cyclone fence that circled the construction site they'd checked out earlier in the day, the sky had turned an inky, premature black.

"I hope we don't get lightning," P.J. muttered as they scrambled up the wire fence. Swinging a leg over the top, she scowled up at the sky. "I hate lightning."

"You do?" Jared spared her a brief glance as he started descending the other side. "I think there's something awesome about it, myself."

"Well, okay, maybe it's not the lightning I hate so much as the—"

A blue-white bolt suddenly cracked across the sky as if summoned by their conversation, sending forked tongues of pure energy snaking toward the Rockies. P.J. screamed.

"Shhh!" Jared hissed, disgusted by her girly reaction. "Jeez, will you keep it down? If the joint's got a security guard, we sure as hell don't want to alert him."

"Well, *excuuuse* the bejeebers out of me," she whispered back fiercely. "But I take it back—I *do* hate lightning." Clinging to the fence, she twisted to peer through the darkness at him as he dropped to the ground and turned to look up at her, his hands fisted on his hips. "But not half as much as I hate—"

Thunder boomed and she lost her grip on the fence, tumbling to the ground. Jared leapt to catch her, but he was a second too late. All he could do was extend a hand to haul her to her feet. "You okay?"

"Freaking dandy," she snarled and jerked her hand free. Breath wheezed in her chest as she struggled to recover the wind that had been knocked out of her. But when he reached out to steady her she summoned enough air to snap, "Get your hands off of me," and bat aside the limbs under discussion. "Go away!"

"Hey, whatever! Works for me." He turned on his heel and headed into the interior of the three-quarters-completed building. The land-use sign they'd read earlier said the finished product would be a multiunit condo with retail space on the bottom floor. Jared didn't give a rip. All that mattered to him was that it provided shelter and that no one else was using it tonight.

Dry shelter, he amended a second later when the skies suddenly opened up. Rain poured down so hard and fast the churned-up earth surrounding the building turned into a quagmire of thick, suck-your-shoes-right-off-your-feet mud. Peering out a hole that would eventually be a window in the exterior wall, his gut clenched. It wasn't even truly cold yet and still the damp permeating the air and the concrete floors and walls created a chill that went nearly to the bone. What would it be like come fall? Or worse yet, during a full-blown Colorado winter?

P.J. trudged in an instant later, a tiny, indistinct shadow swearing a blue streak that concluded with, "Stupid, sonovabitchin' night." Another flash of lightning illuminated the area Jared had chosen for them and, hugging herself, she looked around. Then, her pointed chin thrust ceilingward, she made a production of stalking toward the opposite side of the room from where he'd dropped his pack.

He was hungry, damp and down to his last dollar. He was also so homesick he could die. What he was *not*, was in the mood to placate a thirteen-year-old's temper tantrum. "What the hell is your problem?"

"I ain't got no problem, bub."

"Aside from your grasp of the English language, you mean? Then why are you acting like you've got a big, hairy bug up your butt?"

"I'm *not*," she screeched and indignation made her voice sound even raspier than usual. "I already told you—I *hate* this weather. It sucks."

"Yeah, it bites," he agreed, scooping up his backpack and crossing the room to join her. "But look on the bright side. At least we're dry. And we've got this whole place to ourselves. How often have we been able to say that lately?"

Thunder boomed again, although Jared hadn't seen the lightning that usually preceded it. Feeling P.J. flinch, he slid his arm around her.

She immediately stiffened. "I don't need babying!"

"Good, because I'm in no mood to do that. Jesus, do you think you could quit acting like Princess Pain-In-The-Ass for five fricking minutes? The temperature must have dropped thirty degrees since we got here. Did it ever occur to you that maybe *I'd* like a little body heat?"

"Oh," she said in a little voice and quit straining against his hold. "Okay, then."

He nearly smiled. God, she was independent. And

stubborn as the proverbial mule. It was one of the things he liked best but drove him craziest about her.

They sat quietly in the dark for a while, with nothing but the sound of the pounding rain on the roof three floors overhead to break the silence. It didn't surprise Jared to discover the heat and feel of P.J. pressed up against his side comforted him. The trickle of sexual awareness that also made itself known did, however, and jerking his arm away he scooted several inches across the floor from her.

He tried not to feel guilty about the thoughts that had flashed across his mind faster than tonight's lightning. Hell, they probably had more to do with the simple fact she was female anyway—not to mention that it was dark and they were squeezed close together. No doubt any girl's company would have given him the same reaction. Still, it bugged him that he'd gotten a boner over P.J., of all people, because she was sure as shit too young for him to do anything about it. And even if she hadn't been, even if, despite everything he knew regarding her feelings about sex, she'd been willing and raring to go, she was still skinny, titless, mouthy—and more like his frigging sister than the type of chick he thought of as girlfriend material.

But she was probably a better friend than any other he'd ever had in his life, and when lightning lit up the room again and he caught sight of the tears dribbling silver tracks down her cheeks, he felt as if he'd been kicked in the chest.

"Heyyyy," he said softly, scooching back closer even as he maintained enough distance to be sure they didn't quite touch. "How come you're crying?"

The room was once again hellhole dark, but Jared heard the quick rustle of her movements and didn't need light to know she was adopting the belligerent, get-outta-my-face pose that seemed to be her standard default posture when anyone dared suggest she might be less than superhuman.

"What are you talking about, crying? Whatever gave you a dumb-ass idea like that?"

Aw, to hell with it. "These." Closing the gap that separated them, he slid his arm back around her and reached over with his free hand to brush away the steady trickle of tears with his fingertips. "C'mon, Peej. Don't cry." It simply made it too damn tempting to give in to the urge to do a little howling of his own.

"Yeah, well, so, big deal, maybe I cried a coupla tears." She slapped his hand away. "What do you care? You're just gonna leave me like everyone else has."

"Say what?" He tried to see her through the dark, but light was a meager commodity that shed less illumination than it seemed to begrudgingly provide the occasional patch of less dense shadow. "Where the hell did *that* come from?"

"You know."

"Don't tell me what I know and don't know. If I fricking well knew, I wouldn't be asking."

"You think I'm *stupid* because I'm afraid of th-th-thunder." Her voice caught on the last word, and—no doubt to cover up any sign of weakness—she poked him hard in the side.

"Ow! Stop that." He caught her finger in his fist. "Being afraid of thunder *is* stupid. Hell, it's just noise." But feeling her shoulders quake with silent sobs, he released her finger and tightened his hold around her. Sissy as he found that particular fear, he still wished he had the power to control the weather so she wouldn't be scared. The devil knew there was already enough crap in their lives to trip them up and freak them out without throwing weather into the mix.

"Yeah, well, you're a crummy friend. You just walked away and left me when I fell off the fence!"

"What are you, nuts? You wouldn't *let* me help you!" But that was because she'd been embarrassed, he suddenly realized, and his indignation faded.

As if reading his thoughts and interpreting them as pity, she stiffened, drew in a deep breath and knuckled her eyes. "Bull! I let you pull me up, didn't I? And I let you put your stinking arm around me when you were cold. Not that you weren't in a big, fat hurry to take it back again. But, hey, big deal. I don't need to see the writing on the wall to know you're tired of me and wanna get away. And we both know I'm talking about farther than moving a couple of feet away in this dump!"

"Both know, hell—I don't know *dick* about what you're talking about. God, you babble!"

"I do *not* babble, you stupid, preppy, sonovabi—"

"Then don't be such an idiot. I moved away because I got hot, uh, warmed up, that is *overheated* for a minute." He didn't even want to have to explain that instant of lunacy if she hadn't already figured it out for herself, so he ordered gruffly, "Look, don't cry, okay? I don't plan on going anywhere without you. Jesus, Peej, you're the only thing that's kept me sane since I hit this crappy town."

Her head tilted against his chest and even through the dark Jared could feel her gaze. "Yeah?" she said in an insecure little voice.

"Oh, yeah. Absolutely." He gave her a squeeze and felt more relief than the moment seemed to warrant when she returned a tiny squeeze of her own. Then he felt her rub her face against his chest. "Aw, man! Don't be wiping your snot on my shirt!"

A watery giggle escaped her. "Sorry. I don't have a Kleenex."

"I've got that roll of toilet paper I lifted from Wolfgang Puck's in my pack." He pulled the backpack to him and rummaged one-handed through it until he found the tissue. "Here."

She sat up and unwound several squares, tore them off, then handed the roll back to him, blowing her nose while he put the roll back into the bag. When he turned back to his place against the wall, she immediately reclaimed her position curled up against him. He slipped his arm around her again and tried to ignore the growling of his stomach. "So, what do you want to do tomorrow?"

"What is it, Sunday?"

"Yeah."

"Well, Stand Up for Kids will be at Skyline. We can get something to eat from them."

The thought of food made saliva pool in his mouth. "That's in the afternoon, right?"

"Uh-huh." She yawned. "Maybe we can get a new tube of toothpaste from them, too."

"That would be nice. Except…" He hesitated, then asked, "How are you set for funds?"

His fear that he already knew the answer was justified when she replied, "Pretty much tapped out."

"Crap. Me, too." He blew out a breath. "Well, what the hell. At least we're dry. And we've got the rest of the night to figure a way to scrape together enough change to eat in the morning."

Thirteen

A jazz quartet played softly at the end of the hotel ballroom where John and Victoria stood, but the woman draped in diamonds had no problem making herself heard as she leaned forward to peer at Victoria's naked hand. "Why aren't you wearing an engagement ring, dear?"

As soon as he realized Victoria's response wasn't likely to progress beyond a blank stare, John slipped his arm around her waist. "She didn't want one, ma'am," he said. "We plan on going the wedding band route." He stroked his thumb up and down Victoria's side as he flashed the woman his most charming, just-between-you-and-me smile. "Tori wants simple, but me, I'd like to see her in something with a lot of flash— something that any idiot can see from a football field away means she's taken. I'm trying to talk her into one of those three-diamond numbers."

The woman stared at him in fascination and for all that John was accustomed to getting what he wanted by charming the pants off women, her intense interest gave him an actual moment of discomfort.

Then she blinked. "An excellent choice." Pulling her gaze away from him, she leveled a look at Victoria. "You'd be wise to listen to him, dear. One can never go wrong with diamonds." With a final speculative glance at John, she excused herself and set off after a passing waiter circulating through the crowd with champagne.

Silence fell between John and Victoria, filled only by the music and lighthearted chatter of the guests gathered to celebrate their engagement. Pasting on a smile, he tipped up Tori's chin with a gentle fingertip and gazed into her eyes. He was conscious of appearing the besotted groom-to-be to the casual observer, but his voice was anything but smitten when he murmured, "You're going to have to do a whole lot better than this if you expect anyone to actually believe we're getting married."

To his surprise, she nodded. "I know. I'm sorry. She caught me off guard, and I'm not much of an improviser, I'm afraid." A garbled laugh escaped her. "Oh, hell, who am I fooling? I'm not any kind of actor at all—let alone a natural like you and Esme."

His smile grew genuine at the thought of his daughter. God, that kid. Spending time with her this past week had been a lot like recon missions used to be back in his Corps days—the rush of adrenaline, the didn't-make-a-lick-of-sense combination of terror and happiness at thrusting himself in the face of danger. Each time he'd walked away from one of his sessions with her, he'd been so jazzed he'd barely known up from down. And if *that* wasn't uncharacteristic he didn't know what was. Once or twice he'd even questioned all his reservations about trying to be a real dad. But who knew? Where was it written that he'd turn out to be a chip off the old block? Hell, maybe he wouldn't be the complete bust at parenting he'd always assumed he'd be. Esme seemed to enjoy his company well enough.

Of course that could be nothing more than like calling to like. Because he was discovering that his daughter was similar to him in a lot of ways. And it did something to him that he couldn't deny. Every time he spied one of his own qualities in the little girl—even those not-so-bragworthy ones like his flair for the clandestine or his way of manipulating a situation for his own benefit—it elicited just one more thrills-n-chills mix of panic and pride. Right this moment, though, all he could feel was the pride and he grinned at Victoria. "She's something, isn't she?"

A return smile curved her lips and the tense set of her shoulders relaxed. "Yes, she is. I'm glad you've been spending some time with her."

"So am I. She's a pistol. It's hard to believe the kid's only five, because she's sure as hell an operator." He laughed. "I wonder if she'd be interested in a career in the marines? Or, hey, I could always use her at Semper Fi. If I start her off now, in fact, she'll probably be running the joint by the time she turns ten."

Victoria threw back her head and laughed, and it was a deep, infectious, genuine belly laugh that struck John like a karate chop to the solar plexus. He stilled, staring down at her.

This was the second time tonight she'd managed to knock the breath right out of his chest. The first had been when he'd seen her sweep down the open staircase of the Hamilton mansion before the party began. Her hair was swept up in one of those styles that seemed to challenge the laws of physics. The whole heavy mass appeared mere seconds away from tumbling down around her shoulders, yet somehow it defied gravity and stayed in place. She looked both classy and sexy in the floor-length bronze gown that skimmed her figure and bared her smooth shoulders and creamy cleavage.

It was the dichotomy between her cool classiness and hot sexuality that had been driving him crazy ever since he'd found himself sucked back into her orbit—despite his fierce determination to resist. He didn't know how to reconcile the bright-eyed woman he'd once watched eat lobster with her bare hands and laugh as butter dripped down her sun-kissed chest with the elegant society princess she appeared to be now.

But for tonight, for this brief evening out of time, he didn't feel like worrying it to death. "Hoo-yah," he breathed. "Excuse me while I roll my tongue back into my head." He shook his head with self-deprecating humor. "You know, in certain circles I actually have something of a reputation as a silver-tongued devil." Then, shrugging aside the ineptitude he seemed to display only with her, he reached out to finger a loose tendril of hair near her temple. "Did I tell you how beautiful you look tonight? You do, you know. You're an absolute knockout."

Flashing him a demure smile, she touched the back of her hair with the same feminine gesture he'd seen Esme use. "Thank you. You did mention that, but it's always lovely to hear again. You look very handsome yourself." She gave him a thorough once-over. "That's no rented tux," she finally stated and raised a sardonic eyebrow. "Don't tell me black tie is one of the things you tossed into your bag on that trip you mentioned taking up to Denver?"

"All right, I won't tell you." He treated her to his finest smile—the one his friend Cooper dubbed the Miglionni Special. But when the slender brow remained elevated, he dropped the attempt to charm. Hell, it wasn't as if it had ever worked on her, anyhow, except when he wasn't consciously trying. "You want full disclosure? I needed to check in at the office to sign the payroll checks and see how a couple of cases were going, so I made another trip up there on Friday."

"Pretty soon you'll have more stuff down here than you do in your own place." She gave him a cool-eyed look. "And interesting how you always manage to avoid mentioning these little trips until well after the fact—or perhaps more to the point, until I pin you down about them. You're not a real forthcoming guy when it comes to divulging personal information, are you, Rock—"

"*Here's* the happy couple!"

Made edgy by the direction the conversation was heading, John was pleased by the interruption...until he saw who it was. Great. Miles Wentworth. *Just* the guy he wanted to see at his engagement party. He didn't care that the engagement wasn't real—he still could have gone all night without running into this joker. Especially when he felt Victoria stiffen beside him.

He eyed Miles from the top of the man's gleaming blond hair to his impeccably polished dress shoes and gave him a curt nod. "Wentworth."

Wentworth mispronounced Miglionni twice before waving a grandly dismissive hand. He promptly staggered in the wake of the motion and had to catch himself. "Whatever. Tricky business, those ethnic names." Turning to Victoria, he flashed a loose smile and reached for her hand. "You look ravishing, darling. Dump this bum and marry me instead." Although his diction was precise, he lurched slightly when he bent to press his lips against Tori's knuckles and John's eyes narrowed, much too familiar with the signs of inebriation to ever mistake them for anything but what they were.

It was Victoria, however, who said in a low, cool voice, ''You're drunk.'' She extracted her fingers from the other man's grasp.

Frowning, Wentworth straightened. ''Of course I'm drunk. You would be, too, if you'd been promised—'' Snapping his mouth shut, he smoothed his hand over his hair.

Rocket went on red alert, but again Victoria beat him to the punch. ''If you'd been promised what, Miles?'' she demanded, her moss-green eyes going frigid. ''Did Father promise you something?''

''Certainly not.'' A look of cunning crossed his face, but it vanished in almost the same instant, to be replaced by a mournful puppy-dog expression. ''I'm simply bereft that the woman I adore is marrying a man clearly not good enough for her.''

John was getting tired of the bum/wrong-side-of-the-tracks references. But even as he contemplated showing the stupid fuck exactly how uncivilized a guy trained in all manner of covert warfare could get, Victoria raised her chin and met Wentworth's gaze with her frostiest *You're-the-Peon-and-I'm-the-Queen* look.

''As opposed to someone like you, you mean? Please. You seem to forget I've experienced your brand of 'undying' love.'' Arching the same cynical brow she'd used on Rocket earlier, she demanded, ''So what did Father promise you this time to court my favor?''

Rocket stared at her. *This* time?

''It didn't have a damn thing to do with you,'' Wentworth snapped. Clearly recalling his agenda, however, he quickly replaced both the combative tone and sour look with silky inflections and an adoring gaze. "Seeing you again is a separate issue entirely. It simply brings back a host of feelings both wonderful and... painfully embarrassing."

She nodded as if understanding implicitly. "Of course it does. It's been more than a decade, but I have no trouble at *all* believing you're awash in unrequited love." In spite of her coolly mocking tone, however, a flash of pain crossed her face.

Responding to it, John reached out for her, warming when she promptly slipped her arm through his and hugged it to her side. He treated the other man to a smile that was all teeth and territoriality as he absorbed the warm, plush textures of her breast against his biceps. But his smile softened when he looked down into Tori's face and without another glance in Wentworth's direction he said, "Hey, excuse us, won't you, mate? I believe they're playing our song." He turned her away.

"If this is such a world-class love match," Miles raised his voice to demand stiffly of their backs, "why isn't she wearing your ring?"

Victoria whipped back. "Because we're still arguing which band to get, the plain one I'm leaning toward or the three-stone one Rocket wants for me. Pass that along, will you? I'm growing a bit weary of answering the question, and as we so recently discovered, you're very prompt at dishing the latest dirt."

Tickled to death with the way she'd snapped up and utilized his earlier fabrication, John threw back his head and laughed. Giving her a squeeze, he ushered her onto the postage-stamp-size dance floor and turned her into his arms. "That's my *girl!*"

Victoria, however, felt a great deal less amused. Her satisfaction at having the lie roll like honey off her tongue faded and, feeling faintly heartsick, she merely rested her head against John's solid chest.

As if he somehow understood her feelings, he tipped his chin down to peer at her. "So who the hell is that clown to you, anyway?"

"Her first love."

She jerked her head up to see that Miles had followed them onto the dance floor, where he stood practically on top of them, looking unbearably smug. Complete and utter rage tore a vicious swath through the shock that had momentarily frozen her in place, and damned if she'd allow his slant on their prior relationship to go unchallenged, she transferred her attention back to Rocket. "What he means, John, is that he pretended for a short while to care about me in order to secure my father's influence."

She raked Miles with a contemptuous look. "You were my first infatuation, Slick. My love I saved for someone who actually wanted more from me than my usefulness on his climb up the corporate ladder. Valuing me somewhere along the lines of an expendable pawn wasn't the way to steal my heart."

"Your feelings for me were deeper than infatuation and you know it! I realize I treated you badly, and I've regretted it ever since. But you loved me." Raking her with his gaze, he raised an ash-blond eyebrow. "Otherwise you never would have given me your virginity."

"A very big mistake as it turned out." *But how perfectly lovely of you to bring it up.* John's arm had tightened around her at Miles's revelation and, glancing back up at him, she shrugged as if she weren't mortified right down to her tensely curled toes that her sexual history was being aired on a hotel dance floor. "I was seventeen," she explained, "and it took me a while to comprehend he was playing a game. By the end of the summer, however, I'd learned enough to understand the only result Miles desired from his big seduction was to gain an internship in one of my father's companies.''

''That's not true,'' Miles protested. ''I was crazy about you.''

''You were crazy about what Daddy could do for you. I was little more than a means to an end.'' And, God, it had hurt. He'd rot in hell before she'd ever admit as much, but she *had* believed herself in love with him that summer and discovering he'd only been using her in return had broken her heart. That she felt even an echo of that old pain infuriated her and, for an instant, temptation sang a seductive little siren song, beckoning and cajoling and urging her to lean forward and whisper into Miles's ear that the lawyers said she was worth simply millions and *millions* of dollars now…and hell would indeed freeze over before he'd ever get his hands on one of them.

But bandying about one's financial worth was crass—not to mention that her newly improved assets were undoubtedly what had prompted his sudden renewed interest in her in the first place. She hadn't thought they were popular knowledge in the country-club set yet, but she wouldn't put it past Miles to have somehow seduced the information out of Robert Rutherford's secretary…even if the woman was sixty if she was a day. Drawing a quiet breath, she pinned him with a gaze of studied indifference.

Rocket, however, gave him a big feral smile. ''There's first, Wentworth…and then there's forever. Lots of guys are fast off the mark. It doesn't mean squat if they don't stay the course after they've crossed the finish line.'' Then his eyes went flat. ''You've outstayed your welcome, chief. It's time to show yourself out."

Mile's chest rose and fell beneath his tux for a moment as he stared at them. Then he turned on his heel and stalked away. Victoria watched until he disappeared through one of the ballroom doors, then laid her head back down on John's hard chest. "Interesting little speech," she murmured. "Considering."

"Yeah, I know. Like I've got room to talk." His arms tightened around her. "Still. I may be a bum, darlin', but that idiot is definitely no gentleman." He swayed them in time to the bluesy tune for a few moments. Then he bent his head and rubbed his jaw back and forth against her temple. "I'm sorry," he said softly. "The guy's a jerk, but I imagine you probably cared for him at one time, huh?"

She thought about it and realized her pride was more bruised than anything. For, as desperately painful as the end of that long-ago affair had been, what she'd felt for Miles truly hadn't amounted to more than being in love with the idea of love. "I thought at the time it was an undying, transcend-death-into-eternity kind of passion," she murmured into his lapels. "But it turns out it was only puppy love."

"Still hurts when the puppy gets kicked, though."

"Yes. It does." She became aware that they were still pressed tightly together, swaying in place, even though the song had ended. Before self-consciousness could kick in, however, the quartet began another slow, torchy number. She tipped back her head to gaze up at Rocket as they continued to move. "I'd hardly classify you as a bum."

He shrugged. "I lived in my share of dives growing up, but never in what anyone would call the ghettos.

Still, I imagine my upbringing was a far cry from the guys you usually date.''

"You just met a representative of the type of guy I've been known to date. I doubt I need to tell you you're ten times the man he is.''

He laughed and tightened his hold. "There is that.''

"So what do we do now?'' she asked. "Do you go around questioning people?''

The corner of his mouth quirked up. "Nope. We act like we're crazy in love, and you introduce me to a few folks.''

"Oh.'' Having envisioned something a little more Maltese Falcon–like, she blinked. "That seems easy enough.''

"That's the general idea,'' he agreed and executed a step that rubbed their torsos together. Neurons deep inside of Victoria started snapping and her eyes went heavy.

He gazed down at her with a half smile. "Why don't we start with your friend and her husband?'' His hard thigh slipped between hers as he spun them a half turn, then slid away, and her cognitive processes fried.

"My friend?''

"You know—Esme's little buddy's mom?''

That jerked her out of the sensual haze that being this close to his body produced and she gaped up at him in alarm. "You don't think *Pam* had anything to do with my father's murder?''

"No. And a good thing, too, since you've told her the truth about us.'' He drilled her with the intensity of his dark eyes. "Haven't you?''

Guilty heat throbbed in her cheeks, but she met his gaze squarely. "I knew I'd never get an out-of-the-blue engagement to fly past her. You've been around Esme long enough to know that within five minutes of seeing Rebecca after your arrival she told her all about Mr. Miglionni, the private detective come to find and bring home her Uncle Jared.'' He didn't utter a condemning word, but still she raised her chin defiantly. ''Look, I already told you I'm not much of an actress. And rather than have Pam demanding to know why I'm marrying the private eye in the middle of our engagement party, I told her the truth.''

''Okay,'' he said mildly.

''Besides, she's my frien—'' It sank in that he hadn't disagreed, and she swallowed the rest of the argument she'd been prepared to make. ''How did you know, anyway?''

''I'm a detective, darlin', it's what I do.''

She considered pursuing a less flip answer, but decided it didn't really matter and laid her head on his chest once again. Being in his arms like this took her back and she decided it was probably a good thing that the song ended a moment later because it was foolish, if not outright dangerous, to enjoy his strength, his heat, his scent, this much.

He took her hand as they left the dance floor but allowed her to lead the way as they wove through elegantly set tables to where her friends stood near the bar. They were stopped several times by well-wishers, but although Victoria smiled and chatted easily, she kept a determined forward momentum going until they reached their destination.

''Here comes the blushing bride.'' Frank, Pam's stocky, redheaded husband, stepped forward to greet them, a warm grin lighting his florid face. ''Tori, you look beautiful.''

''Aw, you sweet talker, you.'' She indicated the

men's flawless tuxedos and Pam's strapless cream-colored gown. "Although I must say we're all looking extremely pretty tonight."

"Yes, we are." Then he sobered and reached for her free hand, giving it a gentle squeeze before releasing it. "I'm sorry I missed your dad's memorial."

"I know. Pam told me you were on a business trip."

"I was in Nova Scotia, but I regret not being here to lend you my support. Pammy tells me the service was…memorable."

"Which part?" John asked drily. "DeeDee's eulogy or the surprise announcement at the reception?"

Frank met his gaze. "Both."

Recalling her manners, Victoria squeezed John's hand and slipped her fingers free. "I'm sorry, you haven't been officially introduced to my friends, have you? Frank, Pam, this is my—" she cleared her throat "—fiancé, John Miglionni. John, meet Pam and Frank Chilworth."

He shook hands with the couple and the four of them talked easily for several moments. As a waiter passed, Frank plucked flutes of champagne off his tray. Passing them around, he then raised his own in a toast.

"To Tori and John and a long and success-ful…alliance." After everyone took a sip in ac-knowledgment, he turned to John. "Do you play golf?"

"Sure." Rocket shrugged. "In a hack-divots-from-the-grass, spend-most-my-time-in-the-sand-trap kind of way."

"We'll definitely have to play for money then."

John grinned over the top of the flute he'd raised to his lips. "Why do I get the feeling I have Easy Mark written all over me?"

"Oh, I doubt there's many who'd mistake you for a

mark—easy or otherwise. But that just makes the prospect of taking you to the cleaners all the sweeter." Frank flashed a smile and shrugged. "What can I say? You gotta love easy money. Seriously, though, we'll have to work up a foursome one day soon with Frederick Olson and Haviland Carter."

John straightened. "Weren't both of them—"

"At the infamous last supper, yes," Frank said, then shot a chagrined glance at Victoria. "Sorry, sweetheart."

She smiled as if it didn't matter, but inside she felt a twinge of pain in the region of her heart.

As if possessing X-ray vision into Victoria's emotions, Pam touched her arm. "Well, that was amazingly thoughtless," she said softly beneath the men's conversation. "But he wouldn't hurt you for the world, Tori."

"I know. I also know that Father's soul was probably blacker than the devil's pockets. Only…"

"He was still your dad."

"Yeah." She sighed. "And only I get to badmouth him."

"That seems to be the way of families, all right," Pam agreed. "So what was going on between you and John and Miles Wentworth earlier?"

"I wish I knew. He's tanked and thought he should share with John that he was my first lover."

Pam grimaced. "Classy guy."

"Isn't he? He claims to be carrying a torch for me."

"Since when?"

"I can only assume since Father died and I inherited a chunk of the estate. I don't know, Pam, I have this awful feeling that Father may have promised him something."

"Like what?"

"I haven't a clue, but I'm pretty sure it's not a good thing."

An arm snaked around her waist. "Forget Wentworth," John said, tugging her against him. "The guy's an ass and this is our party. Why don't you introduce me to more of your friends?"

"Frank and Pam are the only real friends I have here," she said dryly, "but I'll introduce you to more of my acquaintances."

For the next hour, she did just that. She led him from one group to the next, introducing him to the people who'd orbited within her father's sphere. But as she stood within the drape of Rocket's arm, she found herself concentrating less and less on their conversations with others and more and more on the warmth and hardness of his body. When he abruptly led her back onto the dance floor and pulled her into his arms for a slow dance, she laid her head back on its custom-made spot, wrapped her arms around his neck, and allowed herself to be sucked back into feelings she'd convinced herself had been resolved and forgotten long ago.

He snuggled her closer, and his breath was warm against her ear when he breathed, "God, this is familiar. Like I've got the memory of dancing with you burned in my cells."

Pure, unadulterated lust, both remembered and brand-new, clenched hot and deep inside her. "You, too? I thought it was only m—"

"Shit," John said at the same moment she became aware of a vibration against her chest. "Hold that thought." He grimaced apologetically. "It's my cell phone." He looked undecided for a moment, then shrugged. "I've gotta get it."

"Of course." She loosened her hold from around his neck, but when she would have stepped back, he held her in place with the arm around her waist.

Reaching inside his tux jacket with his free hand, he pulled out the phone and flipped it open. "Miglionni," he said a trace impatiently. Then the sweet-talking, slow-dancing man abruptly disappeared and "Expressionless John" reemerged. "When?" Listening to the answer he set Victoria loose. "And why am I just hearing about this now?" There was another pause, then his voice softened. "No, *I'm* sorry, Mac. I'm frustrated, but I had no right to take it out on you. What? No, you stay home. I'm on my way."

Mac. Victoria barely heard the rest of his conversation. She remembered that name; it was the woman he'd talked to on the phone one of the first days he was at the estate—the one she'd overheard him inviting to run away with him. Lifting her chin, setting her shoulders, she cloaked herself in composure. But really, how often did she have to be hit over the head with Rocket's lady-killer tendencies before she got the point?

He flipped the cell closed and returned it to his pocket. Grasping Victoria's arm without ceremony, he steered her toward the ballroom entrance. "If there's anybody we should be saying our good-nights to, tell me now," he said in a low voice. "Because that was my business manager. Jared's been spotted."

Fourteen

Back straight, shoulders tense, Victoria sat stiffly upright in the front seat of John's car as they headed back to her father's house. She was still attempting to wrap her mind around the fact that Jared had finally been found—or at least spotted—when they pulled up in front of the mansion.

John turned to face her, his face unreadable in the light of the drive. "Will you be okay if I don't walk you to the door? I'll call as soon as I have something concrete to report."

"What do you mean, report? I'm going with you. It'll just take me a minute to change my clothes."

His dark eyes held none of the teasing warmth that had filled them such a short time ago. "That's not a great idea."

"I'm *going,* John."

He studied her for a moment, then hitched one of his muscular shoulders. "You're paying the tab. But let's get something straight up front. In this I'm the boss and if you want to tag along, be prepared to do things my way."

She nodded and a short while later they were roaring up I-25. She was left with only fuzzy memories of having climbed out of the car, changing her clothes and making arrangements with Helen for Esme's care. Her recollection of kissing her sleeping baby good-night, however, was much clearer. Now she was back in Rocket's vehicle, with her suitcase in the trunk, and as she glanced over at him, she marveled in a muzzy sort of way that apparently he *did* own a pair of jeans.

Then, in a time lapse she would have sworn was no more than five or ten minutes but which she knew logically had to be much longer, John was putting his blinker on for the Colorado Boulevard exit in Denver. Pulling her fragmented thoughts together, she looked over at him. "Will we find Jared tonight, do you think?"

He spared her a glance as he changed lanes in order to be in the right one at the fork in the ramp, but turned his attention back to traffic as they merged onto South Colorado. "Probably not. I plan to hit the streets as soon as I drop you off, though, and if that doesn't produce anything, you and I can try some other places tomorrow. But the odds of stumbling across him aren't in our favor, so prepare yourself for the likelihood of not locating him until Tuesday when Stand Up For Kids offers another free meal." He shot her another glance and this one held a warning. "And even that's not guaranteed."

"I'm going with you tonight."

"Tori, let me check you into a hotel and do my job."

His tone was perfectly civil and patient, but he might as well have snapped her head off or suggested she strip naked and dance down the middle of the street. "Do you honestly think I'll get a wink of sleep worrying about my brother out on these streets all alone?" she demanded incredulously. "Besides, it's not as if you've ever met him and he certainly doesn't know you. I'm much more likely to recognize him—not to mention calm his fears—than you, and I *am* coming along!''

''Jesus, you're stubborn.''

''Oh, trust me, you haven't seen a fraction of how stubborn I can be.''

He shrugged. ''Suit yourself.'' He turned onto Mississippi and within moments was pulling into the valet area of a Tuscan-styled hotel in the upscale Cherry Creek district.

Twisting in her seat, she stared at him in outrage. ''Dammit, Miglionni, I just got done *telling* you—''

''I have no idea what time we'll quit for the night,'' he interrupted. ''But if you want a place to crash when we do, I suggest you go check in and drop off your luggage.''

''Oh, right—so you can drive off the minute I clear the door? Forget i—''

The anger that flared in his eyes chopped her off midword and when he leaned over the console to thrust his face close to hers she drew back until her head pressed the leather of the seat rest. ''You want to name *one* time I've ever lied to you?'' he demanded.

She hesitated, but then admitted, ''Never,'' and felt like a bitch. ''I'm sorry.'' She didn't hear him sigh so much as felt it wash across her lips and she tried to lick away the sensitivity it left behind as she watched him straighten back into his seat.

On his own side of the car once again, thank God.

''Go check in, Tori,'' he said with neutral-voiced courtesy. ''Chances are, you'll be grateful for a place to rest your head before the night is through.''

Without another word, she climbed out of the car, retrieved her bag from the back and went to do as he bid. But she barely glanced around the hotel's elegant lobby with its marble fireplace and columns as she walked up to the desk. And refusing to waste time with anything as unnecessary as having the amenities of her room pointed out to her, she pocketed the room key, tipped the bellboy to take her suitcase to her room, and strode straight back out to the car, where she yanked the door open and climbed in. "Let's go."

She'd thought she was so prepared, but it took Victoria less than an hour to admit, if only to herself, that she hadn't had the first idea what she was getting into. It was after midnight, but she and John had searched dark, smelly alley after dark, smelly alley, starting with those off the 16th Street Mall and working their way toward Colfax. Although they didn't find Jared in any of the flimsily constructed lean-tos that John called squats or behind any of the Dumpsters they checked, to Victoria's complete and utter horror they invariably found some other hollow-eyed teen.

John talked quietly to each one they came across and Victoria noted how careful he was, after the initial sweep of his flashlight, to keep the beam out of the youths' faces and trained on the snapshot of Jared as he inquired whether anyone had seen him. One after another, however, each teenager he asked shook his or her head.

Victoria blew out a frustrated breath as they emerged from yet another garbage-strewn, malodorous alleyway where they'd had to leave another disposable child. "Dear God," she said hoarsely. "I never dreamed anything this awful existed." She looked at Rocket. "Aren't there any *shelters* in this town?"

"None that most of these kids can go to. The homeless tend to fight over resources, and unfortunately the kids are usually the losers.'' He hesitated, then added in a businesslike tone, ''It's often safer for them on the streets. The adults at the shelters can be pretty abusive.''

''Dear God,'' she repeated.

''Yeah, it sucks,'' he agreed. ''But that's the reality of life on the streets for most runaways.''

They were making their cautious way down yet another alleyway about forty-five minutes later when a dark shadow suddenly flew out from the lee of a Dumpster, landing in a crouch in front of them. Victoria screamed and Rocket's arm whipped out to jerk her behind him. She had no shame at all about taking advantage of the shield his back provided and made herself as small a target as possible behind it.

''Gimme your money and nobody'll get hurt!''

The voice was young and male. John slid his hand from where it rested on her hip. She could feel the tension radiating from his hard body, yet his stance as he faced the boy was deceptively casual. After several seconds, when she couldn't stand not seeing what was going on a second longer, she peered around John's side, bending slightly to see beneath his armpit.

Their mugger appeared even younger than he'd sounded. But in the meager moonlight that managed to weave its way down through the buildings hemming them in, he also looked fairly wild-eyed. He had spiked hair that she was pretty sure would be pink in daylight, multitudinous facial piercings and—oh, my God, she felt her own eyes grow wide—a *knife* with the wickedest-looking blade she'd ever seen held thrust out in front of him.

''Hand over your money, I said!'' His voice cracked on the last word, and he slashed his knife with a side-to-side motion that held such turbulent, ego-driven menace it made her draw back behind John again.

He, on the other hand, didn't budge. "Can't do that, kid," he said. "But I can let you walk away."

A crack of laughter echoed in the otherwise silent alley. "Whaddya, *blind* mister? I'm the one with the knife here."

"And a very nice one it is," John said easily.

Then, between one heartbeat and the next, the solid presence protecting Tori was no longer pressed against her front, and almost quicker than she could comprehend let alone track, he'd eliminated the space that separated him from the teen. Snapping out a hand, he locked his long fingers around the boy's wrist, where he must have exerted some kind of pressure, because the kid immediately began to sag at the knees. The knife dropped into John's outstretched palm.

Setting the youth free, he inspected the knife. "Very nice, indeed. Of course, a weapon is only as effective as the skill of the one who wields it." He folded the blade in and pocketed it, then pulled out the snapshot of Jared. Holding it out to the boy, he illuminated it with his flash. "Ever seen this guy?"

Rubbing his wrist, the teen didn't even pretend to give the photograph a cursory glance. "No."

"And you wouldn't tell me if you had, would you?" When the boy merely shot him a sullen glance, he smiled easily. "Fair enough. I embarrassed you in front of the lady and you're gonna thwart me in return by not giving me the information I want. Did I mention there's a reward for information?" He started to put the picture away.

The kid looked torn for about three seconds. Then he thrust his hand out. "Lemme see that again."

"Sure." Without a trace of triumph in his voice, John handed it over and directed the beam of his flashlight on it.

"Yeah, okay, I seen him around. He hangs with a girl called PeeWee, or P.G. or something like that."

Tori's heart began to pound. It was true, then. Jared *was* somewhere in Denver. Not that she'd really doubted it, of course. Only…hearing someone actually say he'd *seen* her brother somehow gave it a more immediate validation.

When she glanced at John, however, he was Mr. Expressionless, looking about as excited as if he'd heard a weather report. "You know where we can find them?"

"Nope. I saw 'em at Skyline earlier, but I wasn't payin' no attention to which way they was headed when they left." He knuckled his nose and looked at John without expectation. "So I guess I don't get no reward, huh?"

John reached into his hip pocket for his wallet and withdrew a twenty. "Tell us about this girl."

"She's, I dunno, just a kid. Younger'n me and sure as shit younger'n that guy." He indicated the photo John still held. "Brown hair, I think. Talks a lot." He stared at the twenty in John's hand and swallowed hard. "Funny voice."

"Funny how?"

"Dunno. Like she's 'bout a minute away from getting a case of that—whatchamacallit—laren crud. Y'know, in your throat?"

"Laryngitis?"

"Yeah. That one."

Rocket handed the twenty over along with his business card. "If you spot them, call me—there's several more where that came from. In the meantime, kid, do us both a favor and leave mugging to the pros. And for crissake, stay away from knives before you end up getting yourself killed.''

The boy shrugged and, pocketing his money, shuffled back to the far side of the Dumpster.

John didn't speak until they reached the street again. Then he stopped Victoria with a hand on her arm when she started down the block. "Let's call it a night. We can pick this up again in the morning.''

Her momentary high had crashed, leaving her discouraged through and through. The thought of Jared out here in as desperate straits as the boy they'd just left shook her to the bone. She wanted in the worst way to find him right this moment. But the emotional ups and downs of the night had taken their toll, and she couldn't summon a single argument for continuing the search. So she nodded.

They walked without speaking back to where John had parked the car. But once on their way back to her hotel, she wondered if she should have come. If she hadn't been so damn insistent on participating, John would probably still be looking for her brother now.

And if that wasn't enough to eat a hole through the lining of her stomach, there was plenty of backup guilt to provide additional acid for the job. She knew moving to England had been the right choice and she'd had to put Esme first. But she should have fought her father harder to send Jared over to her for more visits than the few he'd allowed. Perhaps if she'd put a little more effort into it, Jared would have felt free to come to her when he ran into trouble, instead of taking to the streets. Silent tears began to pour down her cheeks.

John glanced over. "Aw, fuck." He reached across

the console and squeezed her knee. "Aw, fuck, darlin'. Don't cry."

"All right," she agreed and cried even harder.

Whispering curses beneath his breath he hit the gas and raced down the boulevard. Shortly thereafter, they pulled into the parking garage of her hotel, and John pulled into a vacant slot, killed the lights and climbed out, closing the door firmly behind him.

She didn't stir from her own seat and a second later the passenger door opened and John's tan-skinned, clean-nailed hand came into view.

"Come on," he said gruffly.

It never occurred to her to argue. Blinking rapidly in a weak and not very effective attempt to stem the still falling tears and feeling like an idiot, she wiped her cheeks with her wrists. Then she grasped his hand, which immediately closed warm and strong around hers. Reaching a foot out to the concrete floor, she started to scoot forward to allow him to assist her from the car.

Only to be jerked back in her seat by the seat belt that still held her fast.

"Oh, perfect. Poetry in motion." Blowing out a disgusted breath, she popped the buckle free and allowed Rocket to pull her to her feet. But as if to crown her demoralized state with a fricking wreath of thorns, her nose began to run. She sniffed—quietly she hoped, but fearing, as she rummaged through her purse in search of a Kleenex, that she sounded like some forlorn three-year-old in need of a hug instead. And just where *was* her freaking pack of Kleenex, anyway? God in heaven, was it too much to ask that she locate one lousy tissue? Giving up stealth for the lost cause it was, she sniffed loudly.

"Poor baby," John murmured, slipping an arm around her shoulders and guiding her across the echoing cement floor of the garage to the elevators. "Give me your key card and we'll have you settled in your room in no time." He gave her a squeeze. "Once you've had a few hours sleep, I guarantee things won't look so grim."

Okay, what's that old saying? She dug the folder with the room card out of her purse and handed it over as they boarded the elevator. *What doesn't kill you makes you strong?* Probably no one had ever died from mortification. It might even have a plus side—when it came to stopping her tears it was sure more effectual than blinking. Her weeping was down to a few vagrant trickles by the time John stopped in front of a room a few minutes later. He compared its number to that written in the key folder, then quickly opened and held the door for her with one hand while he reached past her to flip on the entrance light with the other.

She walked straight into the bathroom, where she grabbed a tissue from a built-in dispenser and blew her nose. Only then did she shut the door, flip on the light, and take a look at herself in the mirror.

Hoh, boy. That was not an attractive sight. She never had been one of those women who cried prettily. Turning on the tap, she splashed cool water on her face in hopes of reducing the red blotches from her skin and the puffiness from around her eyes. Since the knowledge of having to walk out into the bedroom, face Rocket, and pretend she hadn't just fallen to pieces like a big blubbering baby hung over her head, she took her time blotting the moisture from her face with a towel. She couldn't put it off forever, however, and finally she meticulously folded the towel and hung it just so over the bar.

Then she squared her shoulders and, lifting her chin, marched out of the bathroom.

John stood with his hands thrust in his jeans pockets, staring out the window—although she wasn't sure what he hoped to see beyond his own reflection since he'd flipped on one of the lamps over the bed and another on the desk. He immediately turned to look at her as she entered the main room. "You okay?"

"Yes. I'm sorry. I didn't mean to fall apart on you."

"Hey." He shrugged. "You're entitled. It's been a helluva night and you were a trouper."

It was somehow immensely comforting to hear him say that. But it also served to remind her why she'd sneaked out on him before their allotted week was up six years ago. He'd been dangerous to her peace of mind then and apparently he was equally so now—and in ways that had little to do with the physical. Their encounter with the knife-wielding boy had reminded her of something she tended to forget—that Rocket was trained in covert warfare. But that neither bothered nor intimidated her. Quite the contrary, his competence actually gave her a feeling of safety.

It was realizing—again—that he was a man she could easily fall in love with that scared her silly, and she came to a stop by the desk, determined to be smarter this time around by keeping her distance.

"There's a minibar," John said, indicating the armoire at her back. "You want a glass of wine to help you relax? Or maybe a cup of tea?"

Stop being so damn considerate. Shoveling her fingers through her hair, she held it off her forehead as she shook her head. "No. Thanks. I'm beat. I think I'll just go to bed."

"Oh. Sure, okay. I'll get out of here then."

He started toward her and she stepped back, turning sideways to allow him to pass without touching. Fragile as her control felt at the moment she didn't plan to risk having so much as their clothing brush. But as she walked with him to the door she breathed a little easier. It could be a lot worse. At least the awareness seemed to be all hers.

No doubt from all that slow dancing earlier.

He pulled the door open, but paused with his hand on the knob. "I'll pick you up tomorrow morning and we'll check out some of the daytime places the kids use. What time do you want me here?"

"Whenever you say. Is it better to get an early start?"

"Not necessarily." He looped a long finger beneath a hank of hair that had fallen over her left eye and gently returned it to the mass she'd finger-combed away from her face. Suddenly he was pumping out a raft of pheromones and all the lust that had hummed through her blood earlier this evening came roaring back in full voice. She inched closer.

Then she caught herself and stepped back. "So—" she cleared her throat "—ten then, you think? Or eleven?"

"Let's compromise and say ten-thirty." He stared at her mouth, then jerked his gaze back to her eyes. "Okay?"

"Yes. I'll be ready."

"Excellent." He, too, cleared his throat. "Well. I'd better get out of here so you can get some sleep." His

Fifteen

John didn't need to list why getting involved again with Tori was a bad idea; he'd been categorizing the reasons daily since fate had dumped him on her doorstep. Even so, he was finding the job of resisting the soft, suctioning temptation of her lips rough going.

The discovery was not a reassuring one. But, hey, how hard could it be to resist one woman's kiss? He was Love-'em-and-Leave-'em Miglionni—with more sexual experience than a port full of sailors on shore leave.

The timely reminder kicked some much needed reinforcement around his determination to display a little control. For about fifteen seconds.

Then he caved like a cheap paper plate. Lust roaring through his veins, he bumped the door closed with his hip, thrust his hands into Victoria's hair, and opened his mouth over hers. Licking his tongue over her lower lip, he plunged it into the sweet, slick depths of her mouth. Tongue slid against tongue, and hearing the sharp catch of her breath, he felt like a conquering invader.

But apparently Tori didn't get that she was supposed to be the sexually enslaved one here, and before he could even begin to feel cocky she sent him sucking for a breath of his own by tangling her tongue with his.

She loosened her hold on his shirt and reached up to twine her arms around his neck. Feeling her sweet curves pressed against his body from chest to knees, John lost the last minuscule shred of self-restraint he'd been clinging to.

Whirling them half a step, he slammed her up against the nearest wall, only his hands gripping the back of her head offering some meager protection against its hard surface, and he opened his mouth wider over her lips as his tongue reached deeper. God, he knew these flavors, had never been able to completely erase them from his mind. He knew *her*. And he wanted more of her—*now*. Had to have more.

He leaned into her, pressing her even harder to the wall, and her small grunt of discomfort went through him like a stake. *Jesus, Ace.* He ripped his mouth free and, breathing raggedly, stared down at her. What was wrong with him? He was Mr. Smooth, Mr. I-don't-get-mine-until-I've-made-damn-sure-you've-gotten-yours— and preferably several times. He wasn't some Junior-high Johnny to act like this was the first pair of panties he'd gotten his hands into. He rolled his forehead against hers. "Damn. How suave is this?" Slowly, his heart pounding with disquiet, confusion and unslaked hunger, he straightened to stare down at her.

Victoria blinked at him until her eyes began to clear…only to promptly narrow them at him. "You know what?" she said in a husky voice. "*Bite* suave." Gripping his ponytail at the band with one hand and wrapping her free palm around the back of his neck, she gave a tug, bringing his face closer to hers. "I like you *real*," she said fiercely and launched the full force of her weight against him.

Caught by surprise, he staggered backward several

steps, and this time it was his back that slapped against a wall. Shaking his head, achingly aware he'd never been caught off guard like this with anyone else, he was blown away anew when she plastered herself against him, rose up onto her toes and rocked her mouth over his. She kissed him with a wild, I'd-kill-to-climb-your-body lack of control that he never in his lifetime would have associated with Victoria—but which hurled him back into memories of that long-ago, too-short week with Tori.

And he was toast.

He wrapped his arms around her and kissed her back with the same feverish desperation. The more she clung to him the more avid his mouth grew, until he felt like a case of spontaneous combustion waiting to happen. Bending his knees, he brought them closer in height and groaned low in his throat when she promptly stepped between his spread thighs, fitting herself to his erection like a lock to a key…if the keyhole happened to come outfitted with a chastity belt courtesy of Levi Strauss.

Reaching for the waistband of her jeans, he surged away from the wall and backed her several steps toward the bedroom while he wrestled with the button. They bumped off the opposite wall and ricocheted off the desk, sending a lamp rocking.

The room seemed to take on the dimensions of a damn football field before he finally felt the mattress stop Victoria's backward progress. She tumbled backward onto the bed, and breathing heavily, he stared down at her. At her streaky brown hair tumbled wildly around her face. At her cheeks flushed with color, and her lips red and swollen from his kisses.

"God, you're pretty," he said hoarsely.

"Um-hmm." Stretching her arms above her head with a carnal voluptuousness that caused her entire body to slither against the comforter, she gave him a lopsided smile. "It's the cry-puffy eyes. They're all the craze in the beauty industry."

Since swallowing his tongue was hardly the image he wanted to project, he forced the corner of his mouth to crook up in a sardonic smile. "Yeah, cutting edge would be the *first* thing to come to mind to describe you."

She let loose a deep belly laugh that made his heart clutch and he yanked off her shoes and tossed them over his shoulder. Tugging down the jeans he'd only managed to unbutton and unzip on their samba across the room, he pulled them over her heels and dropped them to the floor. Then he just stared at the tiny, black-lace-over-blond-silk panties he uncovered.

He tore his gaze away to meet her eyes. "Damn, Tori. I want you so bad I can barely walk."

"Yeah?" Her eyes flared hotly before lowering to his fly. "Lucky for you, there's no need to be ambulatory." With a sultry little cat-in-the-creamery smile, she pushed up on one elbow and reached for his waistband. Curling her fingers beneath it, she gave a yank.

He went with the flow, laughing as he tumbled down on top of her. Linking their fingers, he swept her arms up over her head and, bodies touching from head to toe, kissed her again, promptly falling beneath the spell she seemed to weave around his senses whenever he got anywhere near those sweet, sweet lips.

He couldn't get enough of her and soon all he could hear was their ragged, accelerated breathing and the sound of his own heartbeat pounding in his eardrums. He stroked his chest against her breasts, loving the feel of them flattening and shifting beneath him. A high-pitched little moan purled out of her throat and it was like an incendiary device to the dry tinder that was his control. He could feel his need spike at every luxuriant wiggle she gave, every breathy sound she made, and he had to force himself to slap a lid on it before he embarrassed himself.

Then she tugged his shirt from his waistband and the lid threatened to blow clean off. Growling deep in his throat, his kisses grew wilder as he felt her hands slide beneath the fabric, bare skin to bare skin. Her spread fingers stroked up his back and his silk T-shirt followed in their wake, bunching up beneath his armpits and in a band around his chest and back. When Victoria made a soft sound of frustration because the material had gone as far as it could go without a little help on his part, he pushed up on his palms.

She jerked on the shirt, and he ripped his mouth free only long enough to let her pull it off over his head. The moment it cleared, he dropped down atop her again and went back to kissing her. But now the fabric stretching from biceps to biceps was the Great Wall of China, keeping him on one side and her on the other, preventing him from touching her as fully as he needed. So when she gave it a tug, he cooperated by raising his right hand off the mattress and allowing her to strip the shirt down his arm.

She left the garment to dangle from his left arm and he shook it free impatiently, sending it winging toward the nightstand. Tori kneaded his shoulders, scratched her nails down the hollow of his spine and around his ribs, before walking her fingers up his sides to his armpits. He shivered beneath her touch and suddenly desperate to feel her hands on his front, as well, he raised up slightly so she could get her hands between them.

She wasn't shy about obliging, promptly threading her fingers through the hair on his chest, where she found his nipples with her fingertips. She flicked them with her nails.

That wasn't a particularly sensitive spot on his body, but it wasn't long before he started thinking about her nipples. Because he remembered them, hadn't forgotten a thing about them. Not their color nor their shape, aroused or otherwise. Most of all, though, he remembered their hair-trigger sensitivity. Fantasies of her bare breasts with their hard, erect little tips pressed against his chest, caught between his fingers or in his mouth began to crowd out every other consideration. He pushed back to kneel astride her.

"You've got on way too many clothes," he said, reaching for the buttons on her stretchy little cotton blouse.

"Amazing timing. I was just thinking the same thing about you," she agreed and got in his way reaching for the tab of his fly.

By the time he got her blouse unfastened and pulled off, her fingers had managed to brush his erection through the worn denim fly several times without actually unhooking or unzipping anything. Gritting his teeth against the hot urge to just arrange her where his body insisted she belonged—flat on her back with her legs in the air—he grabbed her hands and leaned to pin them to the mattress on either side of her head.

She looked up into his eyes, which his position had placed right above hers, then lifted her head to nip his lower lip. Licking away the slight sting, she dropped her head back to the mattress and raised a brow at him. "Now what, Einstein? You just tied up our hands."

Gaze locked on her face, he rocked back, lowered his head...and used his teeth.

She inhaled sharply and gave him the supreme pleasure of watching her eyes darken from gray-green to olive. "Okay," she breathed. "That works."

He peeled both bra straps from her shoulders, then worked one cup with his teeth until an erect rosy brown nipple popped free. Nearly humming with delight, he lapped his tongue over it, pulled back to study the result, blew on it, then studied it some more. When he could have sworn it had grown another quarter inch, he sucked it into his mouth.

She made a strangled sound and arched her back, shoving her breast closer and working the nipple deeper between his lips. "Oh, please, Rocket, please."

He let her wrists go and pulled her bra free, staring at the offering she thrust up at him. Her breasts were average in size, neither especially tiny nor particularly large. But those puffy little areolae and long, stiff nipples made him crazy. He licked the one he'd just released and plucked the other between his fingers. "Please what, darlin'? Do this?" He pinched his fingers together.

A high-pitched moan sounded in her throat and John grinned. "Oh, man. I could get so used to this."

She arched beneath his hands. "What?" she asked with breathy inattention. "What could you get used to?"

"You. All naked and hot and at my mercy."

She stilled midarch and narrowed her eyes at him. "Excuse me? At your mercy?" She uncurled her arms from above her head, blinking with the realization that

her hands were free and then laughed in his face. "I
know you're a big, strong former marine and everything, but you aren't even holding me down anymore.
So tell me—in what dreamland does that put me at your
mercy?"

"That would be the one where I've got my hands
on these." He gave her left nipple a hard suck and
lightly tugged on the one between his fingers. Continuing to manipulate it, he lifted his head and grinned at
her. "And he who's in possession of these pretty babies
rules, darlin'." He gently squeezed both nipples and
pulled.

Her eyelids drooped heavily and with a long atten-
uated moan, she rocked her hips up, contracted them
deeply back into the coverlet, then thrust them up
again.

The cocky smile dropped from John's face.
"Damn," he whispered and let go of one breast to slide
his hand between her legs. The crotch of her tiny black
and blond panties was creamy with her arousal and it
was all he could do not to grab the fragile material in
both hands and rip it in two. Instead he slicked a finger
down her damp cleft. She gasped and pushed her hips
up, but before he had a chance to make more than a
single pass, she rallied.

Scissoring her legs, she knocked his hand away and
rolled to her knees. "This is getting a little too one-
sided." Her voice was still breathy but her hands, giving his chest a shove, were steady.

John feared "two-sided" might very well be the
death of him, but he flopped over onto his back anyway
because his curiosity was stronger than any concern
about losing control. What the hell. If he came too
soon, he'd simply get it up again and finish the job. It

wasn't as if rebuilding a hard-on had ever been a problem around her. Folding his hands behind his head, he crooked an eyebrow at her. "John Miglionni, at your service, ma'am."

"Ooh." Straddling his thighs, she settled her butt and wiggled. "I like the sound of that." Leaning forward, she spread all ten fingers over his pecs, staring down at him. "I love your body."

"I'm pretty damn wild about yours, too."

"Mine's got flaws, though. But yours…" Dipping down, she kissed the angle where his neck flowed into his shoulder and he clenched his teeth at the feel of her bare breasts, warm and diamond-tipped, rubbing against his diaphragm. He didn't have the opportunity to do more than stroke his hands down her back before she pushed back up to perch upon his thighs once again.

She trailed her fingers over his collarbones. "You can't pinch an inch on your body. No cellulite, no saddlebags, no tummy. Lucky for you I'm so enamored of it, or I'd have to hate your guts." She scooted down his legs several inches and leaned forward to press a kiss on his chest. Her gaze lifted to meet his and nose wrinkling, she smiled against the mat of hair on his chest. "Tickles."

"God, Tori." Her body looked pretty damn perfect to him, spread out over his, but he was too riveted with the wonder of what she might do next to drag out the words to tell her so.

And wasn't that a kick in the ass? Charm-their-pants-off Miglionni, official silver-tongued devil of Company C's 2nd Recon Battalion, tongue-tied. Needing to get back on a more even keel he reached up to tweak her nipples the instant she sat up.

She closed her eyes, arched her back and made a sound deep in her chest. But she also wrapped her hands around his wrists and leaning forward again, she stretched to press his hands down onto the comforter on either side of his head. "Be a good boy," she whispered in his ear. "Don't force me to bring out the belts and scarves and tie you to the bed." Blinking, she rocked her stomach against his erection, which had just given a major twitch. "Oh! You like that idea, don't you?"

"I like any idea that ends with my cock inside of you."

"Ooh, God. Me, too." And right before his eyes, her nipples grew longer yet as she sat back upright. Before he could reach for them again, however, she'd scooted back and leaned to press her lips against his diaphragm. Then she feathered kisses down the thin stripe of hair that ran from the thatch on his chest to his pubic hair. He forgot to breathe about the time she got to the waistband of his jeans.

She glanced up at him then back down at the rampant hard-on making its presence known behind the fly. "I'd forgotten how…impressive…you are," she said and for a second consternation furrowed her delicate brows. Then she shrugged and lowered her head, pressing a kiss on his dick through the denim fly.

He slid his fingers into her hair and gripped two fistfuls of the soft, unruly mass, but even in his own mind he wasn't sure if it was with the intention of pulling her away or holding her in place to make sure she didn't *get* away. He hadn't reached any conclusion when she abruptly gave his cock a gentle bite.

"Jesus, tease us!" He jerked in reaction.

She merely smiled at him and turned her head so her

lips were parallel with his shaft and opened her mouth to delicately grip it between her teeth, widening her jaw in her effort to encompass as much of its circumference as she could through the worn denim. Scraping her teeth delicately across its width, she brought her lips together, kissed the spot she'd just toyed with, then pressed her cheek against it and gave him a satisfied little smile.

John's fingers tightened against her skull, providing the answer to his question. Saving her from herself hadn't been a top priority when he'd initially buried his hand in her hair. And now...

Victoria unbuttoned his waistband and eased his zipper down. She reached inside and wrapped her hand around his penis.

That's when she faltered. She'd been enjoying herself immensely, knowing how hot and bothered she was getting him, but now all her big-shot confidence started to wilt.

God, it had been so long—what if she no longer knew how to do this? "I haven't seen one of these bad boys in a long time," she murmured and glanced up at his face. "I'm not sure I remember what to do with one."

"Hey, it's just like riding a bike," he assured her. "You never really forget how."

The strain in his voice and the sight of his lips pulled back from his teeth as he stared down to where her hand disappeared into his Levi's restored her sexual surety. She gave an experimental squeeze and felt Rocket's...rocket...pulse in her hand. Confidence on the upswing, she fished his sex free of his pants and stared down at what she'd uncovered.

"Oh," she breathed. "I remember you."

He changed in front of her eyes from a sexual sup-
plicant to the man she'd first clapped eyes on in a resort
bar—all confidence and lady-killer smile as he focused
those heavily lashed ebony eyes on her. And for a moment she fell right into his hot, bottomless gaze.

"It never forgot you, either, darlin'." He rolled them
both over in a flurry of long arms and longer legs until
she was flat on her back with him propped up over her.
Brushing a strand of hair off her face, he smiled gently
and lowered his head.

He kissed her with such hot, drugging intensity the
last of her good sense simply dissolved. And by the
time he raised his head again she was once more a mass
of seething, throbbing nerve endings. That's when she
realized he'd begun to work his way inside her. She
sighed and widened her thighs.

Heaping whispered words of praise upon her for everything from the softness of her lips to the freckles on
her chest, he kissed his way down one side of her throat
and up the other. Reaching her ear, he sucked lightly
on its lobe, then flicked his tongue against its sensitive
whorls. She moaned and shifted beneath him. When he
switched ears, she found herself raising her hips in restless yearning.

And the next thing she knew he was all the way
home, as deep inside of her as a man could go. She
felt stretched, and filled, and...*good.* Oh. My. Very
good.

Until a realization struck her. "Condom!" She
pushed at his shoulders. "No condom!"

"Shit!" He pulled out and fumbled with the back
pocket of the jeans that were still pooled around his
ankles. Swearing to himself, he yanked out his wallet
and fished through it as he kicked free of his pants.

"Hoo!" His breath exploded from his chest. "Got one." He pulled out a foil packet and looked down at her. "How about you?" he asked, ripping the package open and rolling the protection down, down, *down* the intimidating length of his erection. "I suppose it's too much to hope that you might have some, too?"

"Yes. No. That is, I don't have any." And regret over her woeful lack of foresight filled her, because she had a strong suspicion that one time with John simply wouldn't be enough to scratch an itch this persistent and deep.

As if reading her mind, he said, "Not to worry," and dropped back over her, catching himself on his forearms. He pressed his hips forward and her legs fell open as if all her nerves remembered the tune they'd been taught and were gearing up to sing the entire "Hallelujah Chorus." John kissed her softly and she blinked up at him when he raised his head and said, "We'll just have to make this time count." He slowly sank back into her.

"Oh, God." She'd almost forgotten this feeling, this chock-full sensation of having him deep inside, encroaching upon every nerve-enriched centimeter of the sheath hugging him. She clamped down to feel even more.

He hissed. For a second he simply breathed in and out, then he whispered, "Oh, man." His eyelids, which had closed, slowly reopened, and he stared down at her as he eased his hips back.

Feeling the tender drag against tissues desperate for more aggressive friction, she grabbed his rear, sank her nails into his hard cheeks and yanked him back.

"You want it faster?" John's hips picked up their tempo and he pushed up on his palms to look down at her, watching her face as he pulled nearly out of her, spread his thighs to widen her legs, then slammed back in. "I can do that."

He bumped a rich bundle of nerves with each inward stroke and she couldn't prevent the needy little sounds emerging from her throat to save her soul. She stared up at him, arching her back as her climax started to build.

"Oh, Jesus." He hunched his back to reach her thrusting breasts. Sucking a nipple into his mouth, he worked it with his tongue for an instant, then let it pop free. Sweat trickled down his tan throat and his ponytail slid over one hard shoulder, tickling the damp tip of her left breast. He looked down at her, but his eyes were unfocused and she wasn't certain how much he actually saw.

"I don't think I can hold on much longer," he said hoarsely, the rhythm of his driving hips picking up speed and force with every thrust. "I'm sorry, darlin'. I really wanted to make this last for you, to give you a couple real good O's before I came…but I don't…oh, fuck, Tori—I just don't think I can hang—"

The desperation in his voice thrust her straight into the middle of a blazing conflagration. Nerve endings deep inside sizzled and popped and strong, long, contractions exploded inside of her, bearing down on the source of all that pleasure. Body afire, mind fried, she heard herself panting, "Oh, God, John, oh, *God!*"

In an endless litany as her orgasm went on and on. And on.

His breath exploded from his chest in a sharp, wordless exclamation, and he shoved himself deep and held there. A long, deep groan climbed from his throat as his own climax erupted.

With another groan he collapsed atop her a moment later and Victoria wrapped her arms around him, holding him tightly as her heart continued its demented beat. Oh, boy. She was in big, big trouble here. She'd known from the first night they'd met that Rocket was experienced in ways beyond her ken, and she'd be a liar if she tried to claim she hadn't taken full advantage of that expertise. His practiced charm, however, she'd found resistible.

It was his honest confusion over his inability to stay in control whenever they made love that had grabbed her right where she lived. Being wanted as strongly as he'd constantly shown her he wanted her had made her feel like the most desirable woman in the world. And she'd felt herself falling deeper and deeper under his spell. It was the main reason she'd run. Having accepted the rules he'd laid down, she'd felt a burning need to get out before she found herself hurt beyond repair.

So what now? It wasn't as if she weren't in every bit as much danger of falling in love with him now as she'd been six years ago. Chances were, she was in even *more* danger, for she was beginning to know him. Not inside and out, of course—at least not in the intellectual sense, her conscience amended wickedly— but certainly so much more than she'd managed to do the first time around.

John's lips pressed the side of her neck and she felt his voice rumble in his chest when he said, "You okay?"

She realized she was. Okay and then some. She needed to put some serious thought into the viability of jumping headlong into another relationship with him, but it had been a long, eventful night, and right this moment she wasn't in the mood. The whole idea of soul-searching, in fact, felt a bit like the old locking-the-barn-door-after-the-horse-has-flown thing. They'd taken a major step tonight, but she was too tired to hash over what it might mean to them.

The heck with it. It would still be there in the morning.

So she said, "More than fine," and turned her head to catch his mouth. Within moments she was sinking into a sensual haze and only one thought filtered its way through the red-hot haze. *I'll figure it out. I will.*

Tomorrow.

Sixteen

John let himself back into the hotel room a little before seven the next morning. Moving quietly, he walked over to the bed to stare down at Tori as she lay sleeping. After making love to her in the wee hours, he'd gone the extra mile to see that she got a little additional satisfaction. Not because his rep as a hotshot lover was on the line, but because he'd wanted to. Almost *had* to.

Of course, being the type of woman she was, she'd then insisted on reciprocating. And what the hell—it had seemed like an excellent idea at the time. He'd been so hot for her and it was just a little oral sex. He was experienced enough that getting a blow job hardly qualified as a novelty, so he'd assumed he was prepared. After all, how different could one woman's technique be?

Mind-bendingly different, as it turned out. Tori might not be the most proficient woman he'd ever been with, but she sure as hell was the most lethal to his peace of mind. Her enthusiasm had damn near been the death of him.

That was the thing that kept grabbing him by the balls—or another organ that he didn't even know what to name—her enthusiastic willingness to try anything. It had been that way during their week together and apparently nothing had changed. She was so genuinely passionate about everything she did that he could never quite get enough of her.

And hadn't he seen *that* coming a mile away? This persistent, constant hunger for her was the reason he'd tried so damn hard not to start things up with her again—because he'd known at a gut level it would only make him want her more and more and frigging *more*.

He shook off a little niggle of unease. Hell, he didn't have a clue what was going to happen between them in the long run. But—he tossed up the box in his hand and grinned crookedly as he snatched it out of the air— luckily for the short run they were in a first-class hotel. And in a good hotel, a guy could get anything.

When he'd explained his problem to the concierge, the man had opened up the gift shop for him. And here he was, with a decent supply of condoms so they wouldn't have to confine themselves to one measly bout of lovemaking if they felt like two. Or three or four or five.

Except…he was beginning to get to know Tori in more ways than merely the biblical sense. And he had a feeling that when she woke up, screwing his brains out wasn't going to be tops on her list of to-dos. He knew how worried she was about her brother and he'd lay money down she'd wake up with a humongous guilt-on because she'd forgotten the kid for a brief time. But a guy could dream and at least he was prepared if it turned out he hadn't read her as well as he thought.

Dropping the box onto the nightstand, he kicked free of his clothing and slid back into bed beside her.

Victoria hadn't been conscious five seconds when a load of guilt dropped out of the sky and landed squarely on her chest. The warm contentment with which she'd awakened curdled and she was left with an uncomfortably speedy heartbeat, tight shoulders and tense limbs. How on earth could she have seen what she had out on the streets last night, then just turn around and blithely blow it off to satisfy some selfish yen to jump Rocket's bones? Good God. What kind of sister was she?

"Don't do that to yourself," John said softly from behind her.

She jerked and only then did she become aware of his warmth curled around her back, his muscular arm draped over her waist. His erection pressed against her bottom.

She ought to move. She knew she should. But to her shame she didn't budge an inch. Her voice sounded weak and little when she inquired, "Do what?"

"Beat yourself up for blowing off a little steam with me last night. You didn't take anything away from your brother."

What was he, a mind reader? Yet against all good sense, her tension faded a little. She gave her head an impatient shake and glanced at him over her shoulder. "Then why does it feel as if I did?"

"Because you care so much? I don't know, darlin', and I don't care. The truth is, we'd finished looking for the night, and the only thing you stole from anyone was a little of your own sleep time."

She rolled over to face him. "We're going to look for him again today, though, aren't we?"

"Sure. We'll hit the 16th Street Mall again and go check out the Auraria College campus. It's a good place for street kids trying to blend in. Then tonight we'll hit the streets again."

"Good, let's go." She started kicking back the blankets.

His long fingers, which had been splayed over her hip, tightened, staying her. "As soon as you've had some breakfast."

Shaking her head, she scooted away from his warm body and eased toward the periphery of the mattress. "I'm not hungry."

"No?" He propped his head on his hand and made no move to leave the bed. "You're going to eat anyhow."

"John—"

"It's fuel. You remember how tough last night was?" He obviously took her involuntary shudder as an answer. "Well, you've got today, tonight and a good part of tomorrow to get through before Stand Up sets up for the kids and it's unlikely to be a helluva lot easier. You want to keep up, you'll eat. Otherwise, plan on staying here while I go out by myself."

"No!" The word came out much louder than she intended, but just the thought of prowling this room like a caged animal all day, instead of being out looking for Jared, made her crazy. "I'll eat."

"Good girl." He threw back the sheet and climbed to his feet, supremely unconcerned with his nudity.

Victoria noticed he was still half tumescent and couldn't seem to stop herself from staring. There was just something so primal and compelling about him in that state.

"You prefer to call room service or go down to the dining room?"

She blinked as she watched him grow fully erect. "What?" Excitement thrummed through her when he suddenly strode across the floor, walking right up to her.

He tapped a finger under her chin and her gaze snapped up. "You gotta keep your eyes up here, dar-lin'," he said in a voice that sounded rusty and hoarse. "You can only expect me to be so good now that I've had a taste of you again—and I'm depending on you to help me out here."

Her cheeks burned like a three-alarm fire. "I'm sorry. You must think I'm such a lousy sister."

"I don't think anything of the kind."

"A slut, then."

Wrapping his hands around her shoulders, he jerked her against him. "No," he said flatly. "I've been with my share of sluts and you're not even a runner-up in that arena."

"No?" The thought of all the women he'd been with in his life shouldn't have the power to annoy her—but somehow it still scratched at her temper. "So what's the difference? I fell into bed with you the night we met, same as them."

"Fell?" He laughed and shook his head. "You have no idea how hard I worked to make that happen. And I wasn't used to that, you know." He flashed her a lopsided, confident smile. "I'd never run up against the need to put so much effort into a seduction before."

It bugged her to know that he probably hadn't and she stuck her nose in the air. "You being so drop-dead gorgeous and all?"

"Honey, just being a marine and having a big dick is like holding the winning ticket to the daily double at most of the bars I used to hang out in. Good looks would've just made it a ticket for the trifecta."

She felt her mouth drop open and snapped it shut so

hard her teeth clicked. "And next I suppose you'll be telling me that women need only take one look at you to know you have a big penis."

"If they're looking in the right place they do."

"My God. Does your ego know no bounds?"

He shrugged. "Not when it comes to this. I'm hung, okay? Word gets around—or it used to, anyhow."

"Like some big Hollywood stud?" A sound suspiciously close to a snort escaped her. "That's ridiculous. I certainly didn't know anything about it."

"Yeah." He grinned. "I know. It was pretty refreshing." She must have looked as irate as she was beginning to feel because he hastened to add, "Look, every branch of the service has its groupies. For my friends and me that meant women who slept with marines simply because we were marines. And a subculture of that were the women who only slept with guys who were particularly well-endowed. Part of the rush for them, apparently, is providing details of whatever guy they bang to their sister size-bunnies. So—like I said—the information got around."

He rubbed his hands up and down her arms and for the first time she realized she was every bit as naked as he was. She started to pull back, but his fingers tightened.

"My point, though," he said, "is that from the moment you walked into that bar I knew you weren't like anyone I'd ever met. And if you think I didn't work like a maniac for your attention, you're crazy. Before that night women had always seemed pretty interchangeable to me. Lose one and there'd be another along to take her place. But I didn't want just anybody else that night—I wanted you."

"Why? Because I was a challenge?"

"No! Maybe. I don't know." He shook his head impatiently. "The only thing I knew was that you were worth any effort it took. Or maybe it was because talking to you *wasn't* an effort. You made me hot, but you also made me laugh and think about things. You made me be…I don't know—just me. That's a person I very rarely was around women, but I knew I was willing to be the real deal if it meant making you stick around. So don't go calling yourself a slut. I don't like it." He set her loose and turned toward the other end of the room. "Why don't you order us room service?" he said over his shoulder. "I'm gonna take a quick shower."

She was still standing there slack-jawed when he disappeared around the corner. A second later she heard the bathroom door click shut.

She walked over to her suitcase and opened it. For a moment, however, she simply stood and stared blindly at the contents while her mind went back in time.

Yesterday she would have sworn up, down and sideways that she remembered every detail about the night she'd met Rocket. Yet here she was, realizing that in the emotional upheaval following her time with him, she'd somehow managed to shove aside the fact that she *had* made him work to catch her. She'd buried that memory in the farthest recesses of her mind where it had languished until it was forgotten.

She'd been attracted to him from the minute he'd slid into a chair next to her at the table where she'd been sitting with two women she'd met earlier that day in the check-in line. He'd struck her as a little too cocky, though—his charm a bit too practiced. So she'd divided her time between him, her new acquaintances, and the man who'd come to the table with him. What had the guy's name been? Rooster? No, that wasn't right. Something like it, though. Oh, wait—Bantam! That was it.

As if it mattered. The other marine hadn't stood a chance with her. Not when Rocket had crowded close, making her feel warm and bursty tight, as if her skin were a size too small. Not when he'd gotten her jokes, laughing as though she were the funniest thing to sashay down the pike since…she-couldn't-think-who. And certainly not after he'd left off consciously milking the Mr. Charm role. The real Rocket had blown away every last inhibition she'd ever possessed.

And the rest, as they said, was history.

She reached into the suitcase, grabbed the first thing her hand came into contact with and carried her selection over to the bed. But she stopped dead before she reached it and stared down at the box of condoms that sat on the nightstand. Where had that come from?

Well, okay, Rocket had obviously gone out and gotten it while she slept. But why hadn't he mentioned them? Or…used one? He could have had her—he had to have known that.

Damn it! She rubbed her forehead. Every time she thought she had him nailed down as this kind of guy or *that* kind of guy, he went and did or said something that messed with all her neat preconceptions. She wanted to believe he was all about sex, because that kind of guy would be so much easier to ignore, since she was pretty sure she'd never fall in love with a man that shallow.

But John *wasn't* merely about sex.

And she had gone and fallen in love with him.

She sucked in a breath. She'd been denying it for a long time now, but she could no longer hide from the truth. The process had begun long before today. She'd had strong feelings for him six years ago—it wasn't as if she'd reneged on their arrangement and slunk off into the sunrise because she'd been *bored* and had felt it was time to move on. She'd left because she'd known she was in imminent danger of developing feelings far deeper than their short-term, open-ended agreement had been designed to bear.

Slowly she set her clothing down on the unmade bed and tugged her mental shields back in place. Okay. She was a strong woman. She hadn't caved under the relentless pressure her father applied when he'd discovered she was pregnant and thought it was his God-given right to know who the father was, and she didn't intend to turn into a hearts-and-flowers type dreamer now. Admitting her newly realized feelings wasn't the same as expecting some fairy-tale kind of relationship to come from them. And everything else aside, she had Esme to consider. She planned to study her options very, very carefully.

But for today... She glanced toward the common wall the room shared with the bathroom and listened to the sound of running water. Well, today she was away from home. Without her child.

She picked up the phone and called room service, where she ordered enough food for a small army. Then she plucked a condom out of the box and strolled down the hall toward the bathroom.

She bet John wouldn't mind washing her back.

By Monday afternoon Jared was so hungry he could feel his belly button kissing his backbone. It amazed him to recall that there had been times back in his former life when he'd thought he was starved. What that had actually meant was that there hadn't been any junk food around—that there'd been nothing in the house to eat except eggs and meat and vegetables and who the hell wanted any of that when it meant having to prepare it for yourself?

Man, what he wouldn't give for just one of those things now. But he and P.J. hadn't had anything to eat in almost twenty-four hours and his stomach stridently protested its lack of sustenance.

He'd spent his last dollar today calling home in the hope that Tori might be there. Surely she'd come over from London for Father's funeral. His empty stomach cramped painfully at the thought and he had to blink furiously against the sudden burning pressure at the back of his eyes. *Don't think about it, don't think about it.*

Think instead about the fact that she would have sent him money if they'd connected. He knew it without a doubt and for a moment her image swam across his mental screen, warming him.

But it didn't take long for heaviness to resettle in his gut. Because in the end he'd thrown away his money. DeeDee had answered the phone and he'd immediately slammed it down in a panic.

"Hey!" P.J. dug her sharp elbow into his side. "Smile pretty for the tourist. That lady over there has been eyeing you." Then her mouth twisted and she pointed in a different direction. "Course, so has that man."

Involuntarily, Jared's glance followed the trajectory of her finger, but he jerked his gaze away when a pudgy older man wearing an expensive-looking suit raised an eyebrow and gave him a·hopeful smile. Ice crawled through his bowels. For the pinch of desperation he was beginning to feel. For the fear that all his choices would soon be used up if his and P.J.'s circumstances didn't improve pretty damn quick.

He honest-to-God didn't know if he could live with himself if it came down to having to do *that* in order to survive.

As if he'd voiced the fear aloud, P.J. said fiercely, "We aren't there yet, bud," and jerked him around so he could no longer see the man. "And you're smart. You'll figure out something before we get to that point."

She tugged him over to the curb where they waited for the trolley to rock past before stepping into the street, which was closed to all other traffic. She nudged him around to face a middle-aged woman waiting for the northwest-bound car and with a final squeeze of his arm, she gave him a little shove. "Now go make nice with the lady. She looks like someone who'd love to part with a bit of change."

Jared dug his feet in. "How about we try something different?"

She quit shoving to stare up at him. "Okay," she said slowly. "Like what?"

He hitched his thumb at his backpack and leaned down to murmur instructions in her ear.

Her big golden brown eyes lit up. "Oh, too good."

He kept walking toward their mark as Peej danced around behind him. A second later he felt the flap of his pack lift and her beginning to rummage through it. When she made a sound of distress and started yanking things out, he nearly smiled. Damn, she was good.

"Wait a minute," she said. She smacked the pack when he kept strolling toward the woman at the trolley stop. "J, wouldja stop? It's not in here."

He craned around to stare at her. "What do you

mean it's not there? It has to be. You just missed it, is all.''

"No, I'm telling you—it's not there."

He yanked the straps of the pack down and swung the satchel off his back, dropping it to the ground practically at the feet of the woman they hoped to con out of a few dollars. Forcing himself not to look her way, he began pawing through the backpack, pulling out items with increasing speed and dropping them on the ground next to the pack. "Oh, God," he said and found it wasn't difficult at all to sound desperate. Because he was—desperate to know he and P.J. would have at least one meal to eat tomorrow. "What are we going to do, Peej?"

"Mom's gonna kill us," she wailed.

"Excuse me," said a gentle voice, and they both looked up at the woman. "Are you kids all right?"

"Yes, we're fine ma'am," Jared said at the same time P.J. wailed, "Nooooo."

"Did you lose something?"

He looked at her kind eyes and worn shoes and realized she wasn't a tourist at all. Jeez, she didn't look much better off than the two of them and he felt lower than a cockroach because he knew he was going to rook her anyhow. Gathering up the stuff he'd dropped out of the pack, he slowly rose to his feet. "It's nothing."

P.J. smacked him. "Yeah, if you don't mind the fact that we now have no money to get *home,* and Mom'll never let us forget that she *told* us we couldn't be trusted to come to town by ourselves."

The woman dug through a purse that had seen better days and pulled out three wrinkled dollar bills. Catching a glimpse into her wallet over her shoulder, Jared saw it only left her with two dollars for herself.

She held the bills out to him. "Maybe this will help."

His growling stomach reminded him just how much it would help, yet he couldn't seem to raise his hand to take the money. P.J. suffered no such qualms and plucked them from the woman's fingers.

"Thank you, ma'am. You just saved our lives!"

"It's my pleasure." She bestowed a gentle smile on both of them. "Your brother reminds me of my son."

"Oh, hey, that's too bad. He's ugly, too, huh?"

A shadow passed over the woman's eyes. "No, he was quite handsome."

P.J.'s incessant movement stilled. "Was?"

"He died in Operation Iraqi Freedom."

"Oh, man, lady. I'm sorry."

"Yes. So am I." She turned toward the trolley that was rattling down the tracks toward them.

Jared dug through his pack and pulled out a pen and a scrap of paper. He thrust it out to the woman. "Will you write down your address?" he asked. "We'll repay your loan as soon as we can."

"That's not necessary, dear."

"Please!"

She looked into his eyes for a moment, then reached for the pen and paper and scribbled on it. The trolley arrived as she was handing them back. "Good luck, kids," she said and climbed aboard.

They stood watching the car depart down the track. Then P.J. turned to him. "Well, that worked like a dream and was a real hoot at first." She stared at him despondently. "So why do I feel like crap?"

"Same reason I do, I guess." Jared carefully tucked the scrap of paper in the pack's front pocket, even though he knew he didn't have a prayer of repaying the woman's generosity. "Okay with you if we save her money for tomorrow?"

"Yeah. It's time to head over to Skyline anyway." Giving him a doubtful look, she said without much conviction. "We'll prob'ly feel better after we get something in our stomachs. Don'tcha think?"

"Sure," he lied. "We'll probably feel a lot better."

Seventeen

"Oh, my God, John. There he is!"

Rocket looked down as Victoria clamped her hand tightly around his wrist. She glanced up at him, her face alight, but promptly swung back to stare across the urban park.

"You were right," she breathed, "Jared *is* here!"

Following her gaze through the concrete canyon that was Skyline Park, he zeroed in on a tall, slim boy with the same thick, streaky brown hair as hers. The kid was wolfing down a sandwich as he listened to a girl who kept flitting around him, darting and dodging like a hummingbird.

John turned his attention back to Tori. He could understand her disbelief. After combing the city yesterday, most of last night and earlier this afternoon without catching a single glimpse of the boy, it was a bit unreal to finally see him. It made John doubly glad the tip he'd received had panned out, but he also felt they'd better discuss the manner in which they approached him. Making contact after a kid had been on the street a while often required delicate, cautious handling.

Unfortunately, the need to warn her had no sooner entered his mind than she dropped his arm and started across the park.

"Victoria, wait!"

But it was clear that she'd worked up a full head of
steam—not to mention an acute case of excitement
deafness—and she took off like a thoroughbred out of
the gate, weaving with long-legged grace through the
throng of kids milling around in groups or lounging on
the cement steps that surrounded a red rock fountain.
He picked up his own pace behind her, but even as he
caught hold of her elbow to halt her, she called out her
brother's name.

Shit. But she'd warned him now and it couldn't be
taken back. He dropped her arm and moved forward,
balancing on the balls of his feet as he prepared to run
Jared to ground if necessary.

The boy merely blinked once or twice, however, as
if he couldn't believe his eyes. Then his lips moved,
shaping Tori's name. He said something to the hummingbird girl, grabbed her by the hand, and just as John
feared, took off at a dead run.

Only…the kid didn't run in the direction he'd expected. Instead, his somber face suddenly alight with a
huge grin, Jared made a beeline straight for his sister.

For once, Victoria wasn't the least bit attuned to
John. He might not have existed at all, in fact, so keenly
was her focus locked on Jared. She raced to meet her
brother halfway, her arms opened wide, and within seconds, she was embracing him. Terrified he'd vanish
again, she wrapped her arms tightly around him, backpack and all, anchoring her fingers in the pack's water-
resistant fabric to keep him close. To keep him *safe.* A
distant corner of her mind registered his slightly ripe
smell, but she didn't care. The only thing that had any
meaning was the knowledge he was here. In one piece.
The rest was merely details.

She felt him begin to tremble and tightened her hold

on him, rocking them from side to side. He responded by hugging her harder and pressing his cheek against the top of her head. A second later she felt him wipe his eyes against her hair, and of all the things she could have, and probably should have, been thinking, her only clear thought was, *When did he get so tall?*

Then he raised his head to look down at her. "I'm sorry, Tor," he said hoarsely. "I'd give anything to go back and do that night over again. But you gotta believe I didn't mean to kill Dad."

Her heart sank right down to her toes and only then did she realize how much she'd been counting on having him clear up what she'd believed in her heart of hearts must surely be a misunderstanding. She'd been so *sure* he couldn't have killed their father. But his tortured expression said even louder than his damning words had that she'd been wrong and her stomach was suddenly full of frozen knots.

She forced herself to shove the discomfort aside, however, and think. He was still her little brother, and given Father's less than warm and cozy personality, she didn't doubt there were mitigating circumstances. Reaching up to trace the light stubble on his cheek with her fingertips, she said softly, "I know you didn't. Can you tell me what happened?"

He let her go and stepped back, thrusting his long fingers through his hair. "He said that I…that I should have been…" He cleared his throat. "He said something awful and I just wanted to get away, you know? So I shoved him to get past. But I didn't mean to *kill* him!"

"Wait." She stared at him. "You pushed him?"

"Yes." His movements were jerky with agitation. "I just wanted to get him out of my *face,* but then he tripped and fell and hit his head on the corner of the hearth. And I *know* I should have called 911, but I couldn't feel a pulse, and there were all those people in the dining room, and I guess I panicked and God, Tori, I am so damn sorry!''

She felt the knots start to unravel, but it was John who said with a much cooler lack of emotion than she ever would have managed, ''You didn't kill him, kid.''

''What?'' Jared turned to stare at Rocket. ''Yeah. I did. I just told you, I couldn't feel a pulse.''

''No, J, he's right.'' The girl with her brother darted over to dance in place in front of him. In a raspy voice that was oddly attractive she said, ''Remember when I told you I saw on the news that your father had been murdered and they were looking for you? Well, they said he was *stabbed*.''

''What?'' He looked as though someone had stabbed him as he struggled to assimilate the news. ''No, that can't be right. I pushed him.''

''But he didn't die from a head wound,'' John informed him. ''He died from blood loss due to a stab wound to the chest.''

''Maybe someone stabbed him after I already killed him.''

''No,'' John said unequivocally. ''I don't know why you couldn't find your father's pulse, but if you'd really killed him his heart would have stopped. There would've been a lot less blood than the records I read indicate.''

Jared blinked. For the first time he really seemed to focus on John and his dark eyebrows furrowed. ''Who *are* you?'' When his voice cracked in the middle of the demand he flushed a painful-looking shade of red.

''I'm sorry, sweetie,'' Victoria interceded. ''I should

have introduced you, but I lost track of everything beyond the fact that you're here and unharmed, as far as I can tell. This is Rocket. John, that is—John Miglionni. He's…an old friend of mine. I hired him to find you.''

''Hired him?'' He glanced at John. ''What are you, some kind of private eye or something?''

John met his gaze with a steady regard. ''Yep.''

''No shit?'' The second the words left his mouth he shrugged as if to invalidate any interest his tone might have suggested. But his shoulders relaxed fractionally as he turned back to Victoria. ''I really didn't kill Dad?''

''You really didn't,'' she assured him.

''Oh, God.'' Legs folding, he abruptly sank to sit cross-legged on the cement path. He buried his head in his hands. ''Oh, God, Tori. I thought I was going to hell, for sure.''

''Look,'' John said. ''We're starting to draw attention and since Jared's not out of the woods yet that's not a situation we want to court before we get everything straightened out. Let's get out of here. We can take this to my office.''

In the excitement of finding him, Victoria had momentarily forgotten that the police still considered her brother their prime suspect. The reminder served to make her glance around and she saw that John was right—this wasn't the best venue for airing their private affairs. ''Good idea.''

The girl with the raspy voice took a few hesitant steps back. ''I guess I'd better be shoving off then.'' She shoved her hands in the pockets of her baggy jeans, hunched her narrow shoulders up around her ears and shot agonized glances at Jared's down-bent head. But when it shot up at her words, she pasted on a bright smile. "Get outta your hair so you guys can get to it and all."

"No!" He jumped to his feet and grabbed her by a slender arm. "You're coming with us."

"Oh, but…"

Without releasing the girl, he turned her toward Victoria. "This is my sister, Tori," he said. "Tor, this is P.J. If it weren't for her I'd have been a lot worse off than I was."

"Naw, that's not true," P.J. disagreed. Her glance locked intently on Victoria. "He's really smart and—"

"She warned me away from dangerous places," Jared interrupted. "Told me where to go to get a shower and food. She kept me *company,* Tor. And if we leave her here, she'll be on the streets all alone. Her damn mother—"

Yanking her arm free, P.J. shoved her slight frame up against Jared's longer, stronger one. "You leave my mother out of this!"

"Yeah, okay, I'm sorry. But you're coming with us."

Victoria watched the interaction with fascination and when the girl gave her a glance rife with uncertainty, the vulnerability and fear in those big golden brown eyes just tore her up. "Better do what he says, P.J.," she advised with a gentle smile. "He can be stubborn as a mule once he sets his mind on something."

"Don't I know it," the girl muttered, but the trepidation faded from her expression. She turned to Jared. "Okay, then, but just for a while."

"Yeah, yeah." He hooked the bend of his elbow around her neck and hauled her in, scrubbing his knuckles against the crown of her Denver Broncos cap.

She jabbed him in the side with her own sharp little elbow and wrested free, tugging the navy-blue bill down to settle the cap more firmly over her hair. "Jeez. Show a little dignity, will ya?"

A muffled laugh escaped Rocket, but when Victoria turned to him his expression was bland. "I'll just give Mac a call and let her know we're coming," he said, hauling his cell phone from his hip pocket.

A piece of her sense of well-being fizzled. *Oh, goody.* Mac again. The woman who ran John's office. The woman with whom he carried on a flirtation. It didn't take much imagination to picture her. She was no doubt some Nordic blonde with a perpetual tan, 40DD breasts and thighs that could crack a walnut. Looking down at her own less-than-pristine T-shirt and dusty sneakers, Victoria wished she'd taken the time to slap on a little makeup this morning.

The kids sat close together in the back of John's vehicle and Victoria got a sense of just how much comfort they must have given each other during their time on the streets. Having seen a little during the past two nights of the life kids made for themselves there, she thought she could appreciate how important it must have been for her brother to have someone to count on. Someone to let him know he wasn't all alone.

Rocket wheeled into a small parking lot that fronted a converted Arts-and-Crafts-style house a short while later. The antique brass sign posted to one of the pillars of the roofed front porch read Semper Fi Investigations.

Somehow, both the beautifully painted little house and the small business district in the upscale neighborhood that housed it took Victoria by surprise. She didn't know what she had expected, exactly, but something more along the lines of a Mickey Spillane book surely. "What?" she murmured. "No seedy hallway? No transom above the frosted glass door?"

John shot her a grin and reached over to give her thigh a squeeze as he twisted around to Jared. "Gird your loins, kid—"

"His name is Jared," P.J. snapped.

He smiled at her. "So it is—my apologies. Gird your loins, Jared. And you too, P.J. You're about to meet Gert."

P.J. unbuckled her seat belt and scooted forward on the seat, all big eyes and interest. "Who's Gert?"

"Gert MacDellar, also known as Mac, is my office manager. My factotum." He sent a sly glance Victoria's way. "My Girl Friday, you might say."

Yeah, yeah, yeah, she thought sourly. *Very droll.* It wasn't that she was jealous…exactly. Well, maybe she was, just a little. The only thing she knew for sure was that she wasn't nearly as speedy as everyone else to climb out of the car. Lagging behind, she paused to slap away some of the dust that had accumulated on her person. It was amazing how much had managed to transfer itself from Denver's alleyways and meaner streets to her.

His Girl Friday was no doubt spotless.

"Good," a voice snapped on the other side of the open doorway, "you're here. I trust you're going to be around more now."

Victoria slowly straightened from brushing off her jeans. *Hello.* What was this? The much-adored Mac didn't possess the dulcet tones she'd expected. Picking up her pace, Victoria climbed the porch steps and walked through the open doorway.

Ensconced behind an enormous oak desk across the room, an older woman with blue-tinted hair and cat's-eye glasses was staring up at John with a militant expression. "Tell me this finally wraps up the Colorado Springs case."

"'Fraid not." He hooked a leg over the corner of her desk and smiled down at her, unaffected by her disgruntled tone.

"Good God Almighty, boy, you gotta wrap it up pretty soon." She waved a fistful of pink slips in his face. "Look at these messages! I've been turning away clients right and left."

"Deal with it, Mac," he said coolly. "This case is more complicated than I first expected it would be and Ms. Hamilton wants me to look into who killed her father now that we know her brother didn't."

"She wants you to look into a *murder* investigation?" The woman turned her fierce blue gaze on Victoria. "Do you have any idea how much that might end up costing you, young lady?"

"Yes. John told me his fee and explained how even paying exorbitant amounts of money wouldn't guarantee me the answers I'm seeking."

"*John* did, did he?"

"Knock it off, Gert."

"Fine." She shot him a look and gave her fifties upsweep a comforting pat. "Close that door," she snapped at P.J., who had been prowling the office and now hung half in and half out the doorway to examine the bird feeder out on the porch. "We're not paying to air-condition the great outdoors."

"Sorry. This place is so beautiful I just wanna see

everything.'' P.J. closed the door as ordered, then skipped over to the desk. ''I love your glasses,'' she said, studying Gert closely. ''And your hair is too cool! It's really tight seeing an old—that is, a senior citizen who knows how to make the most of the retro craze.''

''Glad you approve,'' Gert said acerbically, but her eyes softened as she looked at the young girl.

P.J. indicated Gert's big desk and the office around her. ''So what all do you do here? You must be pretty important, huh? Mr. Miglionni said me and Jared had better gird our loins to meetcha.''

''Mr. Miglionni is a smart-mouthed whippersnapper,'' Gert informed her. ''But he is very good at his job. *My* job is to keep the office working smoothly so he can do it. Not to mention—'' she shot John a pointed look from behind her immaculately polished lenses ''—seeing to it that he turns in his hours on a regular basis, so I can bill the clients, so we can both eat and have roofs over our heads.''

P.J. nodded. ''That's important, for sure,'' she agreed fervently.

Gert froze for a second, then gave the young girl a thorough once-over. ''You're okay, kid.''

''Thanks. My name is P.J.''

''And I'm Gert.''

''And this is Jared,'' John said. ''Now that everyone knows everyone else, let's go into my office and figure out what we need to do to get Jared off the hook and back to a seminormal life.''

''Seminormal?'' Victoria asked.

''He's a teenager.'' John shrugged. ''It's the best we can hope for.''

She smiled and even Jared, who was standing stiffly by her side, dividing his attention between P.J. and Rocket, allowed the corners of his lips to relax.

But John must have sensed his tension, for he said, "My office is this way," and led them down a short hallway with deep gold walls and framed posters of old forties film noir movies.

Victoria divided her time between checking out the rooms they passed—a kitchen, bathroom, and who-knew-what behind a closed door—and admiring the way Rocket's wide shoulders tapered to narrow hips, and the easy, athletic way he had of moving. Then he paused in front of another door and she pulled her attention away from the contemplation of his shiny hair, which he'd braided today. She was rapidly revising the opinion she'd always held that the only men who wore ponytails in this day and age were stuck-in-the-sixties hippies and hit men. Smiling to herself, she glanced at the door he'd stopped in front of.

She stopped dead, as well, and stared at it. For this one had a frosted glass window with an open transom over the top. John Miglionni, Private Investigator had been lettered on the window and, turning, she cocked an eyebrow at him. "Can I call it, or what? This is too good."

A faint wash of color stained his cheekbones, but he gave her a crooked smile. "What can I say?" His shoulders moved fluidly beneath his plain black T-shirt. "It seemed appropriate."

"What did?" P.J. looked up at Jared. "Do you understand what they're talking about?"

''The door,'' he told her. ''In all the old private eye books, the P.I. has an office with a door like this.''

''Huh.'' It didn't take a mind reader to tell she thought they were making a big fuss over nothing.

Within minutes John had them all seated facing his desk. Instead of going around and taking his own chair behind it, he hooked a leg over the corner of the desk nearest Victoria's seat.

She really wished he hadn't. It put his spread thighs and the hard-to-ignore fact that he dressed to the left practically at eye level, forcibly reminding her of the past two nights they'd spent together.

She shifted in her seat, crossing then recrossing her legs.

''The first thing we need to do is get Jared hooked up with a good criminal attorney,'' he said. ''Tori, do you have any objection to my office calling your attorney to request he recommend someone?''

Her face heated. What on earth was she doing, reliving their lovemaking in her mind when her brother was still in trouble? She uncrossed her legs and sat up straight, folding her hands in her lap and primly crossing one ankle over the other. ''Not at all.''

''You have the lawyer's name, Mac?'' he asked.

Victoria twisted around in surprise. She hadn't even realized the woman had come with them, yet there she sat in an old leather chair in the back corner of the room. Gert projected such strength of will that Victoria wouldn't have believed she could enter a room this size without anyone being aware of it. Clearly, though, she could disappear into the woodwork when the situation called for it.

"Rutherford," Gert said now, looking up from a legal pad balanced on the arm of her chair. "I'll give him a call as soon as we're through here."

John turned to Jared. "Okay, here's the deal," he said. "In order to straighten this mess out, you're going to have to turn yourself in to the Colorado Springs Police. The when and the how of it, though, call for strategic handling, so we aren't going to make a move until we have every piece in place. That means keeping you under wraps until we can get our hands on the best damn lawyer in the state. And since you're a minor, you're entitled to have your parents present when the police question you."

"I don't have any parents left," Jared said, shadows darkening his hazel eyes.

"I know," John said briskly. "But I'm guessing Victoria would qualify and what I'd like you to do, Tori," he said, taking his attention off her brother long enough to level his black-eyed gaze on her, "is sign a statement that permits me to stand in for you."

"What?" She sat up even straighter. "No. *I* want to be there."

"I know you do, darlin'. You want to be with him to demonstrate your support when he's questioned, and God knows you deserve to, since you were probably the only one who believed all along in his innocence. But I've met the cop in charge of this case, remember? He's a hard-ass and, if the idea is to clear Jared's name, I have a much better chance of representing his parental interests than you do."

She knew he was probably right, but that didn't stop her from protesting, "It's not as if you were in contact with the detective day after day. You only dealt with him—what?—one time?''

''True. On the other hand, over the years I've dealt with a…shipload…of police departments, in more states than Jared here's got years. It's given me experience in working the system that you simply don't have.''

''And *you* don't have any sort of history or relationship with Jared! Did it ever occur to you that maybe he'd be more comfortable with me there?''

John turned to him. ''Would you?''

Her brother looked at Rocket for several silent moments, then turned to her and said apologetically, ''I don't think I'm going to be comfortable no matter what. Still, if it won't hurt your feelings, I'd like to go with someone who has experience working the system.''

''Oh, sweetie, of course it won't hurt my feelings.'' *Much.* She gave herself a small shake, feeling like a spoiled brat. She had an awful feeling her insistence had more to do with her own guilt at having failed him than the need to offer her support. Reaching over to squeeze his hand, she looked at John. ''I'll sign whatever you say.''

''Thank you,'' he said gently. Then he turned brisk. ''Mac, see about getting a name for a criminal attorney from the family lawyer. Find out where and when he wants to meet us.''

''You got it,'' she said, and left.

In a surprisingly short time she was back. ''Rutherford recommended an attorney named Ted Buchanan. I called his office and he said he'd meet with you all at the Hamilton estate tomorrow morning at eleven.''

"Estate?" P.J. said. She looked at Jared almost in horror, but he merely gave a tiny shrug.

"We might as well head down there this evening then," Rocket said. He turned to P.J. "Which brings us to you."

She froze. "What? No, this ain't got nuthin to do with me. I'm just along for the ride, because J wanted me to."

"You can't go back on the streets, darlin'."

The endearment seemed to fluster her for a moment. Then her chin shot up. "I know. I don't plan to. I'll call my mom."

"And do what if she hangs up on you again?" Jared demanded.

"Your mother hung up on you when you called?" Gert demanded, her blue eyes growing fierce behind her glasses.

P.J. ignored the question, but the old lady simply crossed her arms over her bony chest and stared until the young girl finally shrugged. "Yes'm," she muttered to the floor. Hot color moved up her throat and onto her face.

"But I'm guessing you'd like to go home to her anyway, right?"

"Oh, yes, ma'am."

"Then I'll see to it that you do," Gert said flatly and Victoria for one didn't doubt for a moment that the ferocious old woman would do exactly that. "In the meantime," Gert continued, "you can come home with me."

Raising her head, P.J. gave the office manager a suspicious look. "You're not one of those women who has a thing for girls, are you?"

Gert snorted. "Not likely. Sex with either gender is highly overrated, if you ask me."

"Me, too!"

"Good. Then it's settled."

"No, it's not." The young girl's spine snapped straighter than a plumb line. "I ain't no charity case, lady."

"I never thought you were. The truth is, I could stand some help around here, filing and organizing and such. Do a good job for me and you'll not only work off your room and board, but earn a little spending money to boot."

"Well, okay, then." P.J.'s skin seemed to glow from within at the prospect. "That's different."

"Good. I have a feeling you'll like my house. It's filled with all that—what did you call it? Retro stuff."

John turned to Jared, whose eyes had grown moody the longer he'd listened to Gert make plans for P.J. "Are you okay with that arrangement?" he asked in a low voice as Mac explained a few things to the young girl.

The teen shrugged. "I guess. But why can't she just come home with us?"

"Mac had to work to keep her from feeling like a charity case before she'd agree to stay with her. Your home is a mansion. How do you imagine being a guest there would affect her?"

"Shit." Hands stuffed in his front pockets, the boy hunched his shoulders up around his ears. But he met

John's gaze squarely. "It'd intimidate the hell out of her."

"That's kind of the way I figured it, too. It doesn't mean you can't see her once you've gotten your legal mess straightened out, though."

Jared agreed graciously enough, but Victoria, watching the two of them, could tell her brother wasn't thrilled at the prospect of being separated from his young friend.

She had a feeling Rocket knew it, too, for his voice was less brisk than usual when he said, "Do you mind being left here for a while with P.J. and Gert?"

Jared appraised him for a moment, then shook his head.

"Good. There's food in the kitchen. Help yourself." John turned to her. "Grab your purse," he said heading for the door. "We're going to my place to grab a few things. But first we'll head over to your hotel to pack you up and settle your bill."

Eighteen

Rocket found himself going from professionally impartial to seriously hot and bothered within moments of climbing into the car and he set his jaw as he drove them to Tori's hotel. What the hell was the matter with him? He'd always been the King of Cool when it came to sex, but now, when he should be concentrating on Victoria's brother's situation, where was his damn head instead? On her scent, for God's sake. On the tantalizing curve of her thigh beneath her jeans, which he kept catching glimpses of from the corner of his eye.

He was a real deep guy—clearly there was just no getting away from those Miglionni genes.

Arriving at her hotel gave him the opportunity to get his mind off his fly and on to something else. They went up to her room, grabbed her things and his box of condoms, and were back down in the lobby in record time to take care of the bill. Then they headed for his place.

During the ride over, he worked to keep his focus on what could be done for Jared and by the time he unlocked the door to his apartment a short while later, sex actually wasn't the first thing on his mind. Instead, for some odd reason, wondering what Victoria would think of his place suddenly loomed large in his thoughts.

But when he closed the door behind them, she whirled around, threw herself into his arms and planted a hot kiss on his mouth. That was all it took to send his moment of decorator anxiety and all his high-minded intentions winging straight out the window. Wrapping his arms around her, he swiftly got with the program.

Victoria pulled back a moment later and looked up at him. "*Thank* you," she said with breathless fervency.

"You're welcome." He slid his hands around to the front of her jeans and began unfastening them, meeting her heavy-lidded gaze with a slight smile. "How grateful are you?"

"Oh, very." Her own hands went to his waistband. "Let me show you."

The next thing he knew, his pants were down around his ankles, and he'd stripped her of her jeans and panties. Kissing her feverishly, he stroked her wet heat with one hand as he used the other to don a condom. The instant the protection was rolled into place, he lifted her against the door and sank into her in one smooth thrust.

She moaned, and it only took a few deep strokes to make her come. Emitting breathy sounds that grew increasingly higher pitched, she tightened her grip around his neck and crossed her ankles behind his waist. The slick, muscular contractions squeezing his dick like a languorous fist didn't encourage a leisurely pace.

"God." He was filled with a raft of emotions...only part of which had to do with the imperative need to get off. Bending his head, he opened his mouth against the tender join where her neck flowed into her shoulder and sucked the sun-kissed skin up against his teeth. Feeling her clench even harder around him, his hips began to thrust with more force and speed. He raised his mouth and laved the spot on her neck with the flat of his tongue.

"From the first night we met, you've had the craziest-ass effect on me," he muttered. He pressed kisses from the rapidly beating hollow at the base of her throat up to her ear, where he whispered hoarsely, "I could never hold back with you the way I can with everyone else."

Then he raised his head and stared down into her passion-hazed eyes as his own climax began agitating for release. "You changed me," he said, then groaned as his orgasm roared up his cock. He slammed his hips forward, but just before he gave himself over to the scalding pulsations, he vowed, "You did, Tori. You made me a better man."

Shit, Miglionni, he thought once things had cooled down and they were both slumped bonelessly against the wall. *Could you possibly get any more chatty?* His uncharacteristic loquaciousness left him feeling exposed and vulnerable. When Victoria's ankles uncrossed and her legs started to unfurl from around his waist, he grabbed her by the backs of her thighs to keep her in place and carefully pushed back. "Where do you think you're going?" he growled, feeling the need to reassert his old this-ain't-serious-so-don't-go-getting-comfortable sexuality. He pulled up his jeans enough to keep from shuffling and carried her into the living room, stopping to squat here and there so she could scoop up her discarded panties and jeans.

"Ooh," she said the second time, when her bare ass rested on his thighs for a moment before he surged back upright. "Feeling all those muscles work is very...interesting. It makes me wish I'd taken off more stuff.'' But her cheeks flushed and she ducked her head out of his line of vision. He could feel the heat radiating from her face as she murmured into his ear, "You're still hard. I didn't expect that.''

He laughed and just like that discovered the need to be in control gone the way of his long outgrown love-'em-and-brag-about-'em persona. Victoria had always had that effect on him. ''Enjoy it while you can, because it's fading fast.''

"Ah.'' Smiling, she rested her head on his shoulder. "That must be one of the advantages of being so very, um, long. It takes you a while longer to slip out.''

Reaching his destination, he sat down and for a moment simply held her draped astride his lap. It unnerved him to realize he wasn't even embarrassed to know he could happily sit this way all afternoon.

Too soon she raised her head and straightened in his lap. The movement drove him deeper within her and eyebrows elevated, she looked down at him like a young queen with the village idiot. "I thought you said that thing was going down.''

"It was. But it's kind of excitable and you feel very, very good.'' It was with true regret that he lifted her off of him, scooting her back to perch upon his knees. He smoothed his hand along her hip. "Unfortunately, we don't have time for round two. I don't want to leave your brother cooling his jets in my office too long.''

"No, you're right.'' She straightened her legs and stood, bending quickly to press a fleeting kiss on his mouth before straightening to her full height. "He seemed relieved enough to be going home again, but if he has a change of heart and takes off again I truly don't know what I'd do.''

"I don't think that's something you need to worry about," John assured her. "I just have this thing about erring on the side of caution. Harks back to the days when physical lives hung in the balance." Removing the condom, he tucked himself back into his jeans and gingerly did up his fly as he watched her dress. He had no intention of bringing up their relationship, but when he opened his mouth to tell her that it would take him just a moment to get his stuff together, he instead heard himself demand, "So where do we go from here, you and I?"

The question caught Victoria by surprise and she froze for a moment with her hand stuffed midtuck in the waistband of her jeans. Then she turned to stare at him. He gazed back at her oh-so-casually as he lounged on the couch, his hands crossed behind his head and one ankle propped upon the opposite knee. The slight rigidity of his shoulders and the intensity of his gaze, however, gave her the definite impression that he was very interested in her answer.

She finished tucking in her shirt. She had a feeling she knew what *she* would choose, even if she couldn't quite bring herself to say the words out loud. Once said, they couldn't be taken back, and she'd ruthlessly submerged the impulsive part of her nature years ago. There was also John's reticence about certain matters to consider. "What did you mean when you said your father was a mean drunk?"

His expression closed down. "Just what it sounds like. He was a drunk. I'm not. So what the hell difference does that make?"

"It's the difference between whether you're willing to talk to me about things that matter to you, or you're just interested in getting me in the sack." Looking into his turbulent eyes, she slowly admitted, "When we were together in Pensacola, you set rules of not getting to know each other in more than a superficial way."

"Because that's what worked for me before I met you. And the way you took off without a word, I figured it must have worked just dandy for you, too."

"Would you like to know why I left the way I did?"

"Oh, I think I know, darlin'. You didn't like my rules."

"I went into that arrangement with my eyes wide open, Rocket." She moved closer to him. "But I found myself caring way too much and it scared me silly. It's not a lot of fun being the only one to harbor feelings in a relationship. I was afraid it would hurt too badly if I developed serious emotions for you when your only interest in me was my body."

"I had a jones for a helluva lot more than your body," he said flatly. "I'd always done just fine with the arrangement we had, but I found myself wanting to know every little thing about you. What you loved, what you hated. I hot to know what made you tick. So, hey, if you want to know what a mean drunk is, then I'll be a good little marine and share." He flashed her an easy smile, but his dark eyes were distant when they met hers, as though he'd gone somewhere she couldn't follow. "Mean drunks would rather use their fists when they've had a few too many than exercise the need to think things through or, God forbid, rein in their tempers."

"So your father was a fighter? I'm sorry. I'm sure that must have been difficult and embarrassing." But something in his stillness made the reality of what he was saying sink in and she jerked. "Wait a minute. He hit *you?*"

He shrugged as if it were nothing and Tori's gaze ran headlong into hard-eyed pride that defied her to offer a sympathetic word.

She couldn't even begin to imagine this man she'd known only as a big tough marine getting knocked around by his father. Pushing the shocking revelation aside to mull over later, however, she crossed the room in a flash and climbed back into his lap. She curled her arms around his neck and rested her head on his chest, feeling the strong, rapid thump of his heart beneath her cheek. She ignored the fact that his arms remained stiffly at his side. "That *asshole*. He didn't deserve you."

He laughed, and instead of sounding bitter or mocking or any of the other dark emotions he had a right to feel, it was full of genuine amusement. He wrapped his arms around her, a chuckle still rumbling deep in his chest.

She tipped back her head to look up at him. "What's so funny about that? He didn't."

"You'll get no argument from me, darlin'. It's just…hearing 'asshole' coming from these lips—" he rubbed a thumb over the mouth in question "—strikes my funny bone."

"Well, hey. I'm always happy to amuse." She kept her tone acerbic but spoke nothing short of the truth. She was *very* happy to have driven the shadows from his eyes. "So what do you think," she asked slowly. "Are you willing to take a stab at a real relationship?"

His chest rose and fell beneath her cheek as he inhaled a deep breath and let it out. He tucked his chin to look down at her. "Yeah."

"That means spending more time with Esme," she reminded him. But the words had no sooner left her mouth than she reached up to touch his lean cheek. "You were actually beginning to do that, anyway, before we got the call about Jared."

"Yeah," he said slowly. "Maybe it's not as...tough to do...as I feared it would be. She's easy to be with." He stroked her hair. "But as much as I know you'd probably like to talk it to death and much as *I'd* like to stay in this position for the next several hours, we do have people waiting on us."

"I know. We have to get back." She rapped his head with her knuckles. "But don't think I'm just gonna let that 'talk it to death' crack go by. Be afraid, Miglionni. Be very afraid. Because just when you relax, just when you least expect it, I'm going to make you pay."

"I'm shaking in my boots." He boosted her from his lap again and surged to his feet behind her.

"You do know, don't you," she said a few minutes later as she stood in the doorway to his bedroom and watched him pack more of the silk T-shirts and exquisitely pressed slacks he wore into a small leather duffel, "that once we're back at Father's estate sex between us will be very limited, if not nonexistent?"

"What?" He straightened from his careful packing and looked over at her. "In that case, forget it. This relationship is over."

Her heart sank to her toes, and her dismay must have shown, for he tossed down the shirt he'd been meticulously folding and crossed the room in two giant strides to stand before her.

"God, don't look like that; it was supposed to be a joke." He stroked his palms up and down her arms. "We'll have to forgo the good stuff because of Esme, right? I know it's unrealistic to believe we can continue carrying on the way we have the past couple days with an impressionable little girl running around the house.''

"She has a tendency to climb into bed with me in the middle of the night,'' she said apologetically. "Not every night, of course, but that's just it. I never know when she'll show up.''

"I guess we'll just have to keep our pants on then.''

Oh, man. She was trying real hard to be sophisticated about this, to take her pleasure where she could and not count the cost. But hearing him say stuff like that made her realize that she'd been secretly hoping for exactly what he seemed to be offering: a chance to take their relationship to the next level. His matter-of-fact acceptance of the limits she'd placed on an act he seemed to believe was an integral part of his personality made her want to reach out, grab hold of his implied promise with greedy hands and refuse to let go should he suddenly change his mind about what he wanted out of this deal. And she knew she wasn't sophisticated at all.

Just desperately in love.

Nineteen

Jumpy with nerves, with excitement and unspent adrenaline, Jared slammed through the door to his bedroom Thursday and headed straight for the phone. He punched out the number John had given him for Gert's house. The instant P.J. came on the line, he blurted, "I'm a free man."

She whooped and tucking the telephone against his ear, he flopped back on the bed and grinned up at the ceiling. He felt like he'd been away from home forever and yet, since coming back, it continually caught him by surprise to see that nothing had changed. The disoriented feeling hit even harder after he'd spent the afternoon at the police station.

"Tell me everything," P.J. demanded.

"Okay, give me a sec. I have to figure out where to start."

"It's not brain surgery," she said impatiently. "Just start from the time you left the agency."

He laughed because it was so…P.J. "Okay. We got home about ten Tuesday night, and to tell you the truth, I was wiped. I raided the kitchen said hi to Cook and Mary—"

"Cook? As in *a* cook? A cook who *lives* there? Omigawd! You are so on another planet from me!"

For some reason that gave him a small twinge of

panic. "No, I'm not," he hurried to assure her. "My family merely has money."

"Merely, he says. Not *just*—merely. But forget that," she said and he could practically see her flapping her hand around in a dismissive motion. "Who's Mary?"

"She's the housekeeper. My dad's been married like a hundred times and the stepmothers come and go. But Mary's been here for years and she's always been really good to me. So anyway, I said hi to them and to the current stepmom, who pretended she was thrilled to see me, but who is really pretty underwhelmed, I think. Then I hit the sack."

"Then you got up yesterday…"

"And I played with the pip-squeak until the lawyer arrived. Now *there* was someone who was happy to see me."

"Who's that, your niece?"

"Yeah, Tori's kid, Esme. She's five." He smiled at the thought of the little girl's unconditional excitement at seeing him again.

"And once the lawyer got there…?"

"He drilled me for what seemed like hours on what to say and what not to say once we got to the police station."

"And today you actually went there. Did the P.I. guy go with you like he said he was gonna?"

"Rocket? Yeah, he did."

"His name is Rocket? I thought it was John."

"It is—John Miglionni. But Rocket was his marine handle. Didn't I tell you he was in the marines for like years and years? No, wait, I guess I couldn't have, since I just found out myself yesterday."

"It's kind of a cool nickname," she allowed. "I wonder how he got it."

"I don't know. I asked him, but he just gave me this smile like he knows a secret he's not going to share and changed the subject. Bet it's a rad story, though."

But P.J.'s attention had skipped forward. "So the three of you went to the station. Then what happened?"

"We met with a pain-in-the-ass detective named Simpson."

"First name Homer, y'think?"

"That'd fit him, all right. The guy's an idiot." Jared found his muscles tensing up just thinking about the ordeal the cop had put him through, but he took a deep breath and forced himself to relax. "He'd already made up his mind I was the killer and he sure didn't want to hear anything that didn't fit with his theory. But Buchanan, the lawyer, kept hitting him with the facts and demanding to see the evidence against me. And all that prep work paid off for me, too, because I didn't get nearly as flustered as I would have without it. But it still went on forever until Rocket finally leaned over the table and got right in Simpson's face. He said real quiet that he was tired and *I* was tired and told Simpson that since he didn't have squat to hold me, we were through playing nice. He said if they were going to book me they'd better do it now, because we were going home. I mean, he was so cool, Peej. He didn't raise his voice at all, but Homer backed down and let me go." And Jared wanted to be just like that someday— mature and cool-eyed and tough. Not afraid of anything. "What do you think I'd look like in a ponytail?"

"Dumb. You've got better hair than that guy by miles. And you've already got a boss tattoo."

"Yeah, but did you see his?"

"I know I did, but I don't remember too much about it. Just that it was mostly red with something white inside, right?"

"A skull and crossbones. And it says Silent, Swift and Deadly on three sides of it, with his battalion number across the bottom. He was with a reconnaissance unit until a few years ago. They went in and freed hostages and shit."

"That's pretty tight."

"You know what else? He and Tori are pretending to be engaged so he can get close to all the country-club fat cats and find out who really killed my dad. I bet he does it, too." But the reminder of his father's murder made his euphoria fizzle and he blew out a sigh. "I'm so glad it wasn't me, Peej."

"I know. I am, too."

"I really thought I'd done it—you know?—and it was like acid eating away at my gut one drop at a time." Resolutely, he shook off the remembered horror and the attendant residual guilt. "But enough about me. How are you faring at the old lady's house?"

"You should see it, J. It's got all this great old stuff. Like in the kitchen she's got one of those old chrome tables with the red plastic seats and the kitchen clock is some black cat named Felix, who I guess was famous or something back in the old days. His tail ticks back and forth and his eyes move."

"It sure feels good to sleep in a real bed again, doesn't it?"

"Oh, man, I'll say. And the food! Mac made me brownies last night. No one's ever made me brownies before. I ate *five,* they were so yummy."

He thought about that, the fact that no one had ever made her brownies. For all that his father had been a first-class jerk most of the time, Jared had at least had Tori and Mary and Cook. But knowing P.J. would snap his head off if he offered the slightest hint of sympathy, he merely said, "I know. I haven't been able to stay out of the kitchen since I got home. I don't think I'll ever take a stocked refrigerator for granted again."

Voices yelled outside. They sounded as if they were quite a distance away, but there was a frantic quality to the tone that drew his attention, and Jared climbed off the bed to go see what was going on. He strolled over to the window, stuck his thumb and index finger between the blind slats, and spread them apart. For a second the sun pouring through the window blinded him, but then he saw across the estate to gates that kept the world at bay and his jaw dropped. "Holy shit."

"What?" P.J. demanded. "What's going on?"

"Holy shit, Peej," he repeated, staring at vans that bristled with antennae and at all the people milling around on the far side of the wrought iron. "There's a mess of reporters and one, two, *three* fricking news trucks camped outside my gate. It looks like we're under siege."

Twenty

Siege was the word for it. And after two days spent putting up with the raucous circus going on outside her gate, Victoria finally took refuge in her makeshift studio above the garage. She cranked up the radio to mask the sound of the reporters' voices rising and falling on the other side of the wall. Apparently it was a slow news week, for now that the police had failed to charge Jared, their father's murder investigation was a red-hot story again.

Focused on applying the finishing touches to a Victorian dollhouse, she jumped like a scalded cat a few minutes later when the studio door suddenly slammed against the wall. Esme barreled into the room.

"Hullo, Mummy!"

The sight of her daughter's wide smile instantly elevated her mood and she quickly clamped a freshly glued shingle to the dollhouse roof then set aside her tools. "Hello, sweetie. You startled me." She turned down the radio while taking note of Esme's flushed cheeks and bright eyes. "What have you been up to?"

"I've been playing *Raccoon Ants Mission!*"

Victoria's eyebrows drew together. "Raccoon ants?" She could have sworn she knew every game Esme played, but that one drew a blank.

"Yes! Uncle Jared didn't want to play Barbies with me, so I asked John."

"Oh, Es, sweetheart, he's not here to play dolls with you."

"He *wanted* to play! But he said I have enuff Barbies to ow…to, uh, owf—"

"Outfit," Rocket's deep voice said from the open doorway and an illicit little thrill zigzagged down Victoria's spine when she looked over to see him propping a broad shoulder against the doorjamb.

Crossing his arms over his chest, he gazed back at her, all lean, lazy grace. "The kid's got enough skinny, stacked dolls to outfit an entire platoon."

Esme giggled. "Uh-huh. So we dressed 'em all in trousers."

"Which is much more practical than ball gowns for a reconnaissance mission," John added drily. The corner of his mouth tipped up. "Of course matching all their high-heeled shoes to their outfits, which Esme informs me is a must, sort of put the kibosh to the practicality angle. Her Molly McIntyre would've been better suited, since she at least wears sensible shoes, but Es only has one American Girl doll. And a good recon unit relies on its backup."

"So we played Raccoon Ants Mission with our Barbie ploon!" Esme danced with excitement. "Rapunzel Barbie was a kid napping in the Dream House and the ploon had to get her out."

"Past the Ken soldier with the gold crown and swishy blue satin clothes," John said.

"That's Prince Stefan, Mummy."

Rocket made a face. "The guy's *gotta* be embarrassed to be seen in public in that getup. Although I gotta admit, his sword was pretty righteous."

"Princess Barbie and the Baywatch Barbies crawled on their tummies, and Pop Sensation Ken was the radio offerater."

"Operator," John corrected. "And, I might add, the only one with decent footwear."

"Nuh-uh! Dreamglow Barbie wored slipper socks!" Esme whirled back to her mother. "She had the hangernade."

Tori looked at John. "You outfitted my daughter's dolls with weapons of destruction?"

"Trust me, it was a bloodless coup." He didn't even have the grace to look sheepish. "We whisked the kidnapped princess out from under Swishy Ken's nose without a hitch. Besides, Dreamglow's hand grenade was actually a hairbrush. We had to improvise."

Esme nodded energetically. "Zotic Beauty's knife was a comb, Radio Offerater Ken's oozie was a blow dryer and Mystery Squad Drew had her Morrie code book." Twirling in circles, she spun like a top over to Rocket.

"Morse code, Es. Which I gotta admit was pretty cool, so we used that one the way it was intended. Hell, her shoes were even halfway sensible, once you got past the neon color scheme."

"Freaking neon," Esme said with such pitch-perfect disgust she could only be repeating a direct quote. Leaning against John, she tipped her head back to beam up at him. "Like Dreamglow Barbie's hair, huh, John?"

That made him shoot a sheepish glance at Victoria, but at the same time he smoothed a gentle hand from the crown of Esme's hair down to her nape, where he tugged on one of her braids. "Yeah, baby. Just like Dreamglow Barbie's hair."

Victoria melted. He clearly cared a great deal about his daughter and was putting genuine effort into getting to know her, just as she'd requested. So who was she to complain if his methods were different than those she would have used? Turning to her work space, she capped her Exacto knives with quick efficiency and whipped the clutter into order.

Then she headed across the room toward the other two, laughing as Esme, with her usual easily swayed allegiance, detached herself from Rocket and launched herself at Victoria, hugging her around the legs. She swooped her daughter up and grinned from her to John.

"It's Cook's day off," she said. "So, tell me. Is anybody else in the mood to raid the kitchen for a bowl of ice cream?"

Until today, Jared had been happy merely to be home, but this afternoon an unsettled edginess had begun creeping around the periphery of his contentment. He didn't know where all this itchy restlessness was coming from, but he sure was grateful to hear the sound of voices down in the foyer. He vacated his room without a backward glance and loped down the stairs to find his sister, Rocket and the pip-squeak headed down the hallway toward the kitchen.

Esme, who was dancing backward in front of the others in a way that reminded him of P.J. was the first to spot him. "Hullo, Uncle Jared!" Abandoning Rocket, whom she'd been tugging along by the hand, she raced over to latch onto his. "You're just in time! We're going to have ice cream!"

Tori turned to him with a welcoming smile. "Hey there. Es is right; your timing is impeccable. Come join us."

He allowed himself to be persuaded and sauntered along in their wake, emulating John's easy way of moving. Watching the glide of muscle from shoulder to heel as the former marine strolled in front of him, he wondered if *he'd* ever develop any brawn.

There was so much he liked about Rocket, but probably what he liked best of all was the way he never seemed to say stuff he didn't mean. So far, when John had told him he'd do something, that was precisely what he'd done. And not once had he promised everything would be okay before he'd known for sure that it would be. Jared appreciated that more than he could say.

Still, it was early days yet and he wasn't naive enough to just take things on blind trust. Not anymore. He'd been burned more times than he could count by another man whose approval he'd sought and a distrustful corner of his soul still harbored questions about John's integrity, generating a need to test it for himself.

His attitude had nothing to do with the pip-squeak's account of the Barbie Wars, which he listened to ad nauseam once they'd dished up bowls of ice cream and settled at the table. He wasn't *jealous,* for crissake. He was merely concerned.

"*This* is the way you find out who killed my dad?" he demanded when Esme finally paused to catch her breath after yet another ode to the Fighting Barbies. "By playing dolls?"

Silence fell over the table and his face began to burn. Shoulders hunched up around his ears, he stared down at his ice cream, braced for the acid retort that would slice his ego to ribbons.

But Rocket merely said with easygoing good humor,

"Nope. I thought I'd have better results playing a game of golf."

"You're going to the country club?" Tori asked in surprise.

"Yes, ma'am. Got a ten o'clock tee-off scheduled for tomorrow morning. Apparently your dad used to golf with a foursome every Wednesday and Frank Chilworth arranged for two of the regulars to join us. One of them is Roger Hamlin, who I met at the memorial. Weasely guy who stared at your legs while making a point of telling you how far you'd come from the good old gawky days, if I remember right. The other guy is someone named Frederick Olson." Smiling crookedly, he shook his head. "Frederick. Think I oughtta address him as Fred?"

"Only if you want him to crap his pants," Jared said.

Esme giggled, but when Victoria said his name in an admonishing tone, Jared grimaced apologetically. "Sorry, Tor." He elbowed his niece. "Sorry, Es. Pretend you didn't hear that, okay?"

"'Kay." But she mouthed the offensive phrase to herself.

Pretending he didn't see, he turned back to the adults. "My choice of words might not have been the greatest, but he is president of the country club—and he never lets anyone forget it," he defended himself.

"Yes, he is rather aware of his own consequence," his sister agreed.

Jared shot her a grateful glance before turning to Rocket. "How did you ever get those two to agree to play on a Saturday?" he asked in reluctant admiration. "They and Dad and Haviland Carter always turned up their noses at the idea of golfing any day but Wednesday. It's the sacrosanct Men's Day at the Club."

"I can't take credit for that. Frank made all the arrangements. But I'm guessing simple curiosity has a lot to do with it. You and your sister stand to inherit a huge estate. I'm supposed to be engaged to Victoria. They probably want to know who'll wield the power now that Ford is out of the picture."

Jared's mood, which had been steadily elevating, crashed once again at the reminder of his father's death. "Yeah, well, bully for you," he muttered. "At least you get to slip the leash for a couple of hours."

John leveled his dark-eyed gaze on him. "Is that what you'd like to do? Get out for a while?"

"Hell, yeah." But the very idea made him snort. "Like *that's* gonna happen. I've talked to Dave and Dan on the phone, but it's not like I can go see them in person or join tomorrow's baseball game. Not with all the wolves at the gate."

Esme blinked at him, a ring of melted pink ice cream circling the perfect round O of her lips. *"Wuffs?"*

"The reporters, sweetheart," Victoria said. "Remember the reason I said you need to confine your outside playing to the back gardens?"

"'Cuz of the Nosy Parkers."

"That's right. They're the reporters outside the gate. But Jared's right, as well. They do behave more like animals than civilized human beings."

Rocket turned to him. "You want a day off? I can get you off the estate."

It was Jared's turn to blink. "What?" He stared at the man across the table, who was lazily scraping the last of his ice cream out of the bottom of his bowl.

"You got a case of cabin fever?" he asked without looking up. "You should definitely get out for a while." Then he pushed back his empty bowl and flashed Jared a smile. "Getting you past the reporters is child's play. But you'll have to be ready to come back when I do."

"I can do that! I've got a cell phone you can call me on when you're ready to head back. I was afraid to use it while I was gone, because I didn't know how easy it would be to trace, but it's all charged up and everything."

"Then be down in the foyer, ready to roll, by nine-thirty."

"I will. And I'll let you know exactly where I'm going to be, so you can pick me up when you want to leave."

Rocket leaned back in his seat and stretched out his long legs beneath the table. "You're okay, Hamilton," he said mildly.

And just like that, Jared's vague, unnamed discontent dissolved like so much sugar in the rain, leaving him feeling like a million bucks.

"Are you sure it's a good idea to let him go?"

John turned to see Victoria cresting the top of the stairs. Waiting for her to catch up, he made himself comfortable against one of the bedroom doors. "You saw him, darlin'—he's starting to climb the walls. He's already paid in spades for something he didn't do and he doesn't deserve house arrest on top of it. It'll do him good to get out for a while and talk to some friends, maybe get the chance to play a little ball."

"But what if someone says something hurtful to him?"

"Considering he's going to be in the company of teenagers, no doubt someone will." Reminding himself that women probably looked at things differently than men, he refrained from giving her a negligent shrug as she stopped in front of him. Still… "He'll either take his licks like a man or he won't. But regardless how he chooses to handle matters, it is up to him to deal with it."

She made a dissatisfied sound and he stroked a fingertip down her cheek. "He just spent a couple of weeks living on the street and not only did he survive, he formed an alliance that struck me as being pretty damn tight. You can't wrap him up in cotton batting, Tori, no matter how much you'd like to protect him."

"I realize that. But it doesn't stop me from wanting to all the same."

"I know, but I doubt he'd thank you for it. He's closing in on eighteen, and he's a guy."

"Ergo, the ego."

He laughed. "I don't believe I've ever heard anyone actually say 'ergo' before. But yeah. The famous male ego is especially fragile in the under-twenty crowd."

"Unlike your own, I suppose."

"Mine's solid as a rock," he agreed and wagged his eyebrows at her. "Wanna feel it?"

"You're so crude," she said with well-bred disdain. But she reached out a long-fingered hand and smoothed her palm down the fly of his slacks. Her eyes lit with humor and the corner of her mouth tilted up. "I think I like that about you."

"Yeah? I think I like everything about you, darlin'." Her palm pressing his erection caused a groan to rumble out of his throat and he reached out to pull her to him. It had only been three days since the last time they'd made love, but already it felt like an age. So he took full advantage of the opportunity she offered and lowered his head to kiss her. Sliding his hands into her hair, he held her in place while he tasted his fill.

To his frustration, however, as always when he had her in his arms, he couldn't seem to *get* his fill, and it wasn't long before his hands disengaged from the safe territory of her soft hair to smooth down her neck, over her shoulders and down the groove of her spine. Finally he sank his fingers into the soft, rounded curves of her butt and, bending his knees, he hauled her closer.

They both sucked in a sharp breath when his hard-on brushed the soft cleft between her thighs. He pulled her even more firmly against him and was kissing her with rapidly slipping control when the door at his back suddenly opened.

Only years of honing his reflexes kept him from tumbling into the room behind him. As it was he had to execute some fancy footwork to keep from falling on his ass and dragging Victoria down with him. Catching his balance, he whipped around with Tori securely tucked against his side and saw DeeDee standing in the doorway to the master suite, looking startled.

She quickly gained her equilibrium. ''For God's sake, you two, get a room. There are children in the house.''

As if she gave a damn about the kids. But Tori turned a painful shade of scarlet, so John thought her words had probably served their purpose. She always enjoyed hitting Victoria where she lived and she'd accomplished that. Not pleased, he looked Hamilton's widow up and down.

She was dressed in figure-flattering tennis whites, complete with two narrow diamond bracelets. Her hair looked as if she'd just stepped out of a salon, her fingernails gleamed with bloodred polish and she wore a full complement of makeup. If she was on her way to a match, sweating clearly wasn't on her agenda. Mary's comments from a while back echoed through his mind.

"Off to do the tennis pro?" he asked ingenuously. DeeDee's eyes widened and her jaw dropped open and he smacked himself on the forehead. "Jeez, I'm sorry—where the hell did that come from? Tennis *lesson,* I mean. Off to do your tennis lesson thing with the club pro?"

"Yes," she said tightly. "So if you'll excuse me, I don't want to be late." She pulled the door to the suite closed behind her and stalked off.

He watched her disappear down the stairs before turning back to Victoria. "Don't look like that," he commanded.

She blinked at him. "Like what?"

He pressed a fingertip into her flushed cheek and watched as the white mark it left behind rapidly filled with hot color. "Like you ought to be wearing a big red letter on your forehead."

"But she was right," Victoria argued. "I told you myself that we couldn't make love with Esme in the house, yet what's the first thing I do? Glom onto your, um…"

"Rock-hard dick."

Her color deepened but she nodded and met his gaze head-on. "Precisely. Right out in the middle of the hallway where anyone could have seen us!"

"So, big deal. We'll do better. But you gotta know that DeeDee was just pushing your buttons because she knew she could."

"Probably so." She stared up at him. "But the fact remains, I should've known better. And I have to tell you, you simply cannot solve this mess fast enough to suit me."

Twenty-One

Rumormongers who were willing to dish the dirt
ranked high on John's list of valuable investigational
tools and he hit the mother lode with Roger Hamlin
and Frederick Olson.

But not before a shitload of schmoozing.

Frank played up the fiancé angle as he reintroduced
him to the older men on the first tee. Both had been at
the bogus engagement party and John's suspicion that
they'd accepted today's invitation because they were
dying to find out who'd be handling Ford's estate
proved prophetic. Hamlin and Olson were patently determined to be the first in the know.

It didn't take five minutes in their company to discover they were a couple of dyed-in-the-wool chauvin-
ists and without a qualm he made sure he gave the
impression he was handling matters for Victoria. The
sage nods with which they greeted that little charade
made it clear it was an arrangement they wholeheart-
edly endorsed.

That was the upside. The downside was that they
were a lot more interested in collecting information
than in dispensing it. It took him fourteen holes of
hacking divots in the fairways, muscling golf balls out
of sand traps, and spreading charm like a load of high-

grade fertilizer before he managed to promote even a smidgin of reciprocity.

He wasn't sure what the problem was, because it was clear they weren't adverse to being on the receiving end of a spot of gossip. They hadn't even had to open their mouths for him to know that—it had been obvious the minute he'd realized there wasn't a single caddy attached to the group. Neither man struck him as the kind to eschew a service he clearly considered a God-given right without a damn good reason—and in this case that could only be the desire to discuss subjects they didn't want spreading like a rash through the caddy shack.

Yet avid as they were to hear the latest, it never seemed to fail: every time he managed to get them relaxed enough to start talking freely, their foursome would finish up the current hole. Then the older men would climb into their little golf cart and speed off to the next tee, leaving Frank and John no choice but to get in their own cart and follow.

They reminded him of roosters he'd once seen at a cockfight in the Philippines, strutting and posturing to impress each other with their consequence. The two men took turns driving and it was clear from the way they bickered once they climbed out again that neither was satisfied with the way the other one handled the cart. It took most of the next hole just to get their bristling egos under control once again.

If not for the fact that throwing in the towel ran contrary to his nature, he might have simply declared the day a bust. As it was, he and Frank finally wised up and began ignoring the old men's bizarre ritual, letting them hash it out in their own way, on their own time-table. And apparently the lack of interference worked for the duffers, too, because the arguments seemed to take less time after that.

On the sixteenth hole he actually made a decent shot and grinned at Olson, who gave him a constipated smile in return and generously refrained from saying it was about time. Hamlin said it for him, muttering something about how maybe he and Frederick would make it on time for the bridge game they'd signed up to play that afternoon after all.

Frank rolled his eyes at their humorless attitude and said, ''Nice shot, John,'' as he stepped up to the tee.

He did manage to promote a little further give-and-take from the pair but it was an uphill battle. At one point he caught Hamlin eyeing his ponytail.

The old man, seeing he'd been caught, asked, ''What does Victoria think of you having hair longer than hers?''

''She hasn't complained.'' He fingered the long tail thoughtfully. ''Although I have been thinking lately about having it cut. I only grew it in the first place as a response to fifteen years spent in a marine reconnaissance unit—I wanted to see how long I could get it after all those years of buzz cuts.'' He gave them a wink. ''Then I discovered how much the ladies like it.''

By the eighteenth hole he'd run out of time. He'd tried to work his way gently around to what he wanted to know, but these two seemed to want to talk about everything *but* that. So he might as well just go for it.

Giving them his best sympathetic glance, he said, ''It must have been a terrible shock to find yourself at a dinner party where the host turned up dead.'' What the hell. They'd either take the bait or stare at him like he'd just tossed a rotten herring at their feet.

They took it. In fact they snapped it up and ran with

it with such alacrity it left him wondering why he hadn't simply used it in the first place.

"You have no idea," Hamlin said fervently, launching into an account of every thought and emotion that had crossed his mind upon discovering that Ford had been stabbed to death.

"Yes," Olson interrupted. "At first, when the maid screamed, we assumed she must have dropped the cognac Ford sent her to fetch. After all, she was merely a temporary hire for the night—"

"And you know how unreliable they can be," Hamlin put in.

"Completely and utterly—or so the wife tells me is the universal opinion, anyhow."

"So does mine. God knows domestic help is trouble enough," Hamlin said authoritatively. "But temps— they're simply a nightmare."

A malicious little gleam of glee flickered in the club president's faded blue eyes. "Still, it was quite surprising in Ford's case. He usually insisted on—and managed to procure—the very *crème de la crème* when it came to domestics."

"Yes, but not even the emperor gets what he wants all the time," Hamlin declared with relish.

"In any case," Olson said, "she continued to scream and scream and there was just something about its tone."

"Filled with horror, it was." Hamlin nodded. "Makes my blood run cold just remembering it."

John looked at them. "I imagine everyone ran to see what was going on then?"

Olson opened his mouth to reply, but before he could say a word, Hamlin jumped in, both literally and verbally, as he edged his friend aside. "Yes. And there he was. I'm sure you can imagine our shock when we discovered him lying on the library floor.''

Shooting him an irritated look, Olson took a half step that partly blocked the other man. ''In a pool of blood,'' he added, clearly determined not to be out-done.

''With a letter opener sticking out of his chest!''

The two men glared at each other, but John ignored their game of one-upmanship. ''So who do you two bet on being the killer?''

They turned identical supercilious stares on him. ''Excuse me?'' Hamlin said coolly. Olson looked at him down the length of his nose—a worthy feat considering he was a good six inches shorter than John.

He countered their indignation with a level gaze. ''The way I hear it, the boys in the locker room bet on everything from who's winning what games, to who's likely to die next. You can't seriously expect me to believe that this isn't fodder for the betting pool.''

In unison they turned to glare at Frank, but John said, ''Don't look at Chilworth. My fiancée and I talk. Victoria may have been gone for the past few years, but she grew up here. She knows how things works.''

Hamlin looked unconvinced for a moment, but then gave a thoughtful nod. ''I suppose it is only proper that she tell you everything,'' he conceded.

''Indeed,'' Olson concurred. ''How else could you properly govern her affairs?''

Hoping to hell that Tori never heard about this conversation, he spread the bullshit even thicker. ''Not to mention that you two strike me as a couple of players. I figure if anyone knows the entire scoop, it would be you.'' Victoria didn't depend on any man to see to her needs and he had the feeling she wouldn't appreciate being relegated to the role of a helpless little fluff-brain…no matter now useful the deception might prove to be.

The Odd Couple commenced yet another endless game of I-can-top-that, as each vied to tell him who'd been absent from Ford's dining room during the crucial time span the evening of his death. In this instance, their competition proved useful. Stowing his putter in his bag in preparation for heading back to the club-house, he consigned a number of names to memory to be studied in greater detail later. Hearing one in partic-ular jerked him out of his contemplation, however.

"*Wentworth* was there that night?" He quit shoving the club into the bag, and turned to stare at Roger Ham-lin.

"Yes, yes," the man said impatiently. "Didn't I just say so?"

"You did," he agreed smoothly and flashed a sooth-ing smile at the fussy little man. "I suppose I'm just surprised because I didn't see his name on the list of guests the housekeeper supplied to the police."

"Well, I'm sure I don't know about that. He was a last minute fill-in when Gerald Watson's scheduled Ce-sarian had the bad grace to go into labor early." He glanced at his watch, then back at John. "Now, we really do have to go. I believe this round goes to us, but I trust you'll settle up later. Frederick and I have that bridge game we mentioned."

Several times. Never let it be said a Miglionni couldn't be suave, though. "By all means," he said with a smile, "don't let me detain you. Frank and I will get the bet figured out on our way to the pro shop and catch up with you inside." He shook the two club members' hands. "Thank you for the game and the enlightening conversation, gentlemen. You made me feel most welcome.''

"Yes, it was delightful," Frederick Olson said, suddenly in club president mode. "Be sure to give my best to Victoria."

Hamlin's head bobbed in perfunctory agreement. "Yes, yes. Give the little woman my regards, as well. Tell her I said we must all get together real soon." He glanced at Frank. "You and Pamela, too, of course."

The social niceties satisfied, both men hustled off.

John and Frank watched them go, then simultaneously turned to each other and shook their heads.

"Now there's an offer just guaranteed to make our 'little women' replete with happiness," Frank murmured as they gathered up their bags to hike back to the clubhouse.

"Either that or put 'em in the mood to kick some serious ass once they catch wind of their new title."

Frank laughed and John studied him as they began walking. The other man had keen intelligence burning in his deep-set eyes and John liked his sly sense of humor. "You know," he said slowly, "I didn't fully appreciate before I saw Frick and Frack in action exactly what you'd let yourself in for today—and on a Saturday morning, no less." He held open the pro shop door for the stocky redhead. "Let me buy you lunch. It's the least I can do."

"Damn straight," Frank said. "I've earned the biggest steak on the menu."

John turned in his clubs while Frank shoved his bag into his storage locker, then headed for the clubhouse. They quickly showered and changed in the locker room.

A short while later Frank led the way up the thickly

padded stairs to the lobby. Sunlight streamed in through the windows, illuminating the richly appointed wallpaper and highlighting a few good pieces of art hanging on the wall. A discreet reader board stood by a bank of plants and John only had time to read something about a Cotillion class—whatever the hell that was—before Frank indicated the lounge with a nod of his head.

"What do you say we eat in the bar?" he said. "It's more laid-back than the dining room."

"Sounds good."

A moment later they were settled at a table and Frank handed John a small lunch menu. He looked at him across the top of his own. "So why'd you tell the Dynamic Duo Victoria was the one to rat out the locker-room betting club when we both know it was me?"

John shrugged. "You have to live in this community and I figured they'd take it better coming from the 'little woman.'" He shifted. "Of course if Tori ever hears that I threw her to the lions, I'm probably toast."

Frank studied him. "There's something more going on between the two of you than just this fake engagement, isn't there?"

He merely looked at the other man across the table and Frank gave him a crooked smile in return. "O-kay. So. What do you think of Ford's inner circle so far?"

"That they'd have me believe it was one big love fest, when there doesn't seem to be much love lost between the lot of them."

"Truth to tell, John, I doubt there was a helluva lot of love lost between Ford and anyone. He wasn't the world's nicest guy."

"Yeah. I've been hearing that."

"And from everything Hamlin and Olson had to say

about the people who attended the last supper, damn near all of them had good reason to do him in.''

"Which we pretty much knew already. But I did eliminate several of them from the list today.'' He considered Frank. "I really do owe you for setting this up. I realize it's no accident that we played with the two men who knew practically to the second who was absent from the room during the crucial time.''

"You gotta love the Old Guard. It's a point of pride with them to be in the know.''

The waitress came over to take their order and John automatically flashed her the Miglionni Special before requesting a Corona with lime and the clubhouse sandwich.

She smiled back. "Would you like me to put that on the Hamilton tab, Mr. Miglionni?''

He hid his surprise that people whose names he didn't know at all apparently knew his. "No, thank you, darlin'. I'll pay for my own. And put Frank's on my bill, too.'' He leaned back in his chair and studied her. She was a plump, attractive brunette who looked to be around his own age. "Have you worked here long, Abigail?'' he asked, glancing at her name tag.

"Five years.''

"Yeah? That's definitely a while. So you must like it here, huh?''

Her eyes went cautious. "Sure. I like it just fine, thank you.''

He gave himself a mental head slap for saying something so stupid but flashed her an affable, self-deprecating smile and said easily, "It was a dumb question.'' *Like you'd tell a member your job sucked even if it did.* "So let me pry my foot out of my mouth here.

You got any kids?'' When all else failed, disarm 'em with honesty, he always said.

And it worked, for she visibly relaxed. ''Yes. I have a five and a three-year-old.''

But no husband, if the lack of rings on her left hand was anything to go by. ''Boys or girls?''

''One of each.''

He looked around the bar, which was beginning to fill up. ''I can see you're going to be hopping for a while. But if you have any pictures of your kids and get the chance, be sure to bring them over. I'd like to see them.''

''I'll do that.'' She smiled at him with a mother's pride, took Frank's order, and left.

''Damn,'' Frank murmured. ''You're good.''

John grimaced. ''A large part of this business is simply being able to talk to people, to bring them to a comfortable level where they're willing to talk to you in return. And at least with Ms. Abigail I don't feel like a snake-oil salesman, which I was beginning to feel like with Frederick and Roger before they finally unclenched their sphincters a little.''

He dismissed that with a gesture and returned to the conversation the waitress's arrival had interrupted. ''I knew several of the employees from the hostile take-over were at Ford's that night. But what's the story on the 'cuckolded husband' the duffers were talking about?''

Frank snorted. ''You ask me, it's a rumor that took on a life of its own. George Sanders was at the last supper with his wife, Terri, who was Ford's administrative assistant. According to the locker room pundits, which is where Hamlin got that particular bit of information, Ford was messing around with Terri. People—

and by that I mean bored golfers and the ladies who lunch—started talking when she suddenly got herself a stylish haircut and more attractive clothing and began taking care with her makeup.''

"You don't believe Ford had anything to do with that?''

"No. There's no denying the man had a monster ego and as far as human beings go he was never going to be voted Mr. Congeniality. But this is a tight-knit little society and I've been part of it since the day I was born. And from everything I've ever observed, I'd have to say Ford's relationships were serially monogamous. They didn't tend to last real long, but I honestly believe he remained true to his current lady for the duration.''

"I imagine if he was anything like his golfing buddies, there'd be a snob factor, as well.''

Frank nodded. "Can't say that ever occurred to me before, but it's a definite consideration. His AA would have been beneath his notice, just one more piece of the background on par with the office furnishings. DeeDee is probably the lowest down the social totem he ever traveled, and even she has shirttail connections to the Grants. That sort of thing holds a lot of significance for the older set.'' He raised ginger-colored eyebrows. "Speaking of DeeDee, interesting that she was one of the ones out of the room during the crucial time. Don't the cops always look at family members first?''

"They do. But although it apparently isn't common knowledge, DeeDee signed a prenup and isn't getting enough to make it worth her while to take that big a risk.''

"Do tell.'' Studying Rocket, Frank fell silent a moment. Finally he said, "Hearing that Miles Wentworth was at the last supper seemed to light your fire.''

"Oh, yeah," John agreed grimly. "It did."

"Because he was also away from the dining room around the zero hour, or because he tried to make a scene with Tori at your engagement party?"

"Both. I don't mind telling you that I'd be tickled pink if he turned out to be our guy. But you can rest easy that manufacturing evidence to bust his chops isn't my style." He gave Frank a smile that was all teeth. "He did let slip at the party that Ford may have promised him something. Now, it could be that the old man's death simply dashed Mr. Suave's hopes of ever seeing whatever he aspired to get, so he turned his attention to regaining Victoria's regard. But maybe, just maybe, Ford had the bad luck to tell Wentworth he'd changed his mind about whatever he'd promised and got a letter opener through the heart for his trouble." He shrugged. "It's impossible to know without a deeper look, but it's definitely a thread I want to follow."

"Here you go, gentlemen." Placing a coaster on the table in front of them, the waitress set down their drinks. "Your sandwiches will be a few more minutes."

"Thanks, Abigail." John took a sip of his beer, then raised inquiring eyebrows at her. "Got those pictures?"

She slipped her hand into the pocket of her black slacks and pulled out a couple of wallet-size studio shots.

He looked them over. As little as a month ago it would have been primarily for show—kids having been of zero interest in his life. But that was before. Now that he had one of his own who he was trying to get to know, he studied the photos with genuine curiosity. He touched the edge of the little boy's photo with his fingertip. "This your five-year-old?"

"Yes. That's Sean."

"He looks like a pistol. I bet he's a regular little devil to keep up with."

"Oh, yeah," she said fervently. "He joined a pee-wee league this summer, though, where he's learning to play T-ball. It helps."

"Sure," he agreed. "Gives him an outlet." He gave the other photo a second look. "Now this one looks like a little angel." He shot the waitress a grin. "But I'm guessing she has her moments, too."

Abigail grinned. "She can be amazingly stubborn, all right."

"She like dolls?"

She laughed out loud. "Does the moon pull the tide?"

He smiled back at her with self-deprecating humor. "I seem to be full of dumb questions today."

"Abby," called an impatient voice from a nearby table. "Could we get some service, please?"

"Certainly," she said and swept the pictures up off the table. With a small smile at John she turned away to wait on a quartet of fifty-something women in golf attire.

The men turned back to their drinks and a few minutes later Abigail delivered their sandwiches. John was digging into his when he saw a coterie of little girls in party dresses and shiny Mary Janes and boys wearing dark slacks and white shirts with their conservatively striped ties firmly knotted beneath their Adam's apples, filing past the lounge doorway. He lowered his sandwich, swallowed and jerked his chin toward them. "What's that all about?"

Frank twisted around to see. It only took one glance before he turned back. He grimaced. "Cotillion class."

"I saw that on the reader board out in the lobby. What the hell is it?"

"Debutantes in training and their escorts. They learn to ballroom dance, deportment, that kind of thing."

"Are you kidding me? They can't be that much older than our ki—than your daughter and Esme."

Frank shrugged. "It's all a part of the society they move in."

"Would you gentlemen like another drink?" Abigail stopped by the table.

John raised a brow at Frank. The other man shook his head and he said, "No thanks."

"In that case." She slipped a leather folder off her tray and onto the table. "I'll be your cashier when you're ready."

"Here." Raising one hip, he slid his wallet from his back pocket. "I'm ready now." Pulling out the receipt, he read it then replaced it with a couple of bills. "I don't require change."

"Thank you!" she said, staring at the denominations. "Your fiancée must be thrilled you're nothing like her father." Eyes rounding with horror, she slapped a hand to her mouth, but just as quickly pulled it away. "Oh, my God. I am so sorry. That was a *horrible* thing to say."

"Relax. I never met Ford Hamilton, but I've heard enough about him to know he wasn't a particularly nice guy."

The look on her face expressed fervid agreement, but she clearly wasn't about to dig her hole any deeper.

John smelled information, though, and he gave her a gentle smile. "Please," he said softly. "Won't you tell me your impressions of him? I'd like to understand how he came to be murdered, but I hate to press Tori for details because it makes her so sad.''

She shot a hesitant glance at Frank, who promptly pushed back from the table.

"Excuse me a minute, won't you?" he said. "I need to call my wife to see if she needs me to pick up anything on the way home." Pulling a cell phone from his belt, he headed for the entrance.

Abigail looked at John uncertainly. "There's really not much I can tell you," she said. "Except Mr. Hamilton expected the very best service but didn't tip accordingly. And all the wait staff were nonpeople to him, you know? He treated us like we were invisible."

"That wasn't very smart of him, then, was it? Because you and I know that the people who work behind the scenes are the ones who notice the most about what's going on. I bet the staff even has a pool going on as to who the murderer is."

She flushed, but after a quick glance around admitted in a low voice, "His wife is a favorite."

"Because of the tennis pro?"

She stared at him. "You *know* about him?"

"I heard someone talking about it. Is that what makes her a top contender?"

She shook her head. "She didn't actually take up with the pro until after Mr. Hamilton's death. Mostly she's a favorite because of all the cop shows we've seen or mysteries we've read. They all seem to agree that most murders are committed by family members or friends. But there's also a couple of guys running neck-and-neck for second place."

"Yeah? Who are they?"

She leaned forward. "Well, I heard Mr. Hamilton fighting with a man I don't know. We just call him

Silver Hair, because he had a beautiful head of it. He looked important and he was furious over something Mr. Hamilton was doing to his company. And then Kathy Dugan heard him give Miles Wentworth a tongue-lashing. She said if looks could kill Hamilton would have been stretched out on the dining-room floor.'' She straightened back up. ''I have to get back to work.''

''I know. Thank you for taking a minute.''

''You're welcome, although I don't see how it helps.''

''It just does. I guess it's that knowledge is power thing—it's just better than being completely in the dark.''

He watched her walk off as he absorbed what she'd told him. But his mind soon wandered to the Cotillion kids and Esme. Would she be going to something like that in a couple of years? He knew so little about the workings of his own daughter's life. That wasn't exactly surprising, he supposed, considering the brief span of time he'd even been cognizant he had a kid. But it had to change. He'd been letting things slide because there was so much else going on.

Something about seeing all those little kids getting ready to be turned into Frederick and ''the little woman'' clones, though, did something to him.

And it was time he had a serious talk with Victoria.

Twenty-Two

Jared's day turned out to be both wonderful and lousy. Wonderful was getting out of the house, even if he was forced to leave the grounds hunched down on the floorboard of Rocket's car to avoid being seen by the howling fifth estate. And it was really great to see Dan and Dave and play a little ball.

Other parts of it, though, were not so wonderful. Like the stares of some of the guys at the ball field. Or the sudden silences when he'd join a group. And like the dumb-ass questions several of the kids asked him—all of that was pretty lousy. The way some of them looked at him and the things they said, he might as well be a bug on a pin, because he felt like a goddamn freak. How did they *think* he felt about his father's murder, for crissake? When Rocket called to tell him he was on his way to pick him up, he was more than ready to go.

But when the former marine arrived at the field a short while later and asked him how it had gone, all he said was, "Fine." He closed the door, reached for the seat belt and stared straight ahead.

From the corner of his eye he saw Rocket turning in his seat to assess him and for a minute it felt as if the P.I. had X-ray vision. But just as Jared was on the verge of squirming, Rocket faced forward again and said mildly, "Yeah. Been there." He let out the clutch and roared away from the curb.

For some odd reason that made Jared feel better. So did the way Rocket didn't try to get him to talk about his fricking *feelings*. As if. Instead, the older man ignored him to sing along with the Cherry Poppin' Daddies in a voice that owed more to enthusiasm than great musical ability, tapping out the beat to the parts he didn't know against the leather steering wheel.

They were about a quarter mile from the estate gates when without warning John pulled to the side of the road. He threw the car into Neutral and turned in his seat once again. "You weren't too happy about being on the floorboards coming out," he said. "So how do you want to go back in? The same way is definitely the simplest. But if you'd rather lounge back in your seat and thumb your nose at the lot of them, it's your call."

The attraction of the latter must have shown on his face, for John smiled and said, "Now, how did I know that would appeal to you?" His voice turned serious. "I gotta warn you, though, that the downside to letting reporters know you slipped out right under their noses is that it'll never be that easy to get past them again."

A laugh that was harsh and unamused burst out of him. "So, in other words, unless I ride the floorboards I won't be getting out anymore."

"No, in my exact words, it's simplest." John flashed a smile that was big, white and not particularly civilized. "There's a dozen other ways to get you off the estate."

"Then I think I'll stay right here." He leaned back, stretched his feet out in front of him and clasped his fingers behind his head, spreading his elbows wide. He felt the P.I. study him for a moment, then John dipped his chin in acknowledgment and without another word put the car in gear. He drove back onto the road and gunned it for home.

Jared's bravado faded when he saw the sea of cameras and avid faces that turned their way as they approached. He broke out in a cold sweat when he heard them clamoring for his attention. The two syllables of his name beat in the air outside the estate like the frantic wings of a trapped bird.

But he took his tip from John, who was relaxed and cool, one wrist draped over the steering wheel. Rocket hit the gate opener Tori had given him and slowed down, but he didn't stop. The reporters had dealt with his comings and goings during the past several days and knew better than to stand their ground in front of his approaching car. He'd scattered more than one journalist who'd assumed it would be a good method for making him stop and talk to them.

Staying out of reach of the car's front bumper, however, didn't stop the Hounds from Hell from crowding in on either side. Faces pressed close to Jared's window as they shouted questions. Then the front of Rocket's car passed between the posts and the reporters fell back. The gates, which had just opened their widest, slowly began to close again.

A car suddenly roared up the road behind them, horn blaring. With a quick glance at Rocket, who was looking in the rearview mirror, he craned around to peer through the back window at the fast approaching automobile. It was fire-engine red and headed straight for them like a bullet from a gun. He shot another glance at John and saw a slight smile tilting up the corners of other man's mouth. "Do you know who that is?"

"Yeah. It's Gert." John hit the gate opener again to

reverse its trajectory. "She must have something requiring a signature."

Jared looked back at the speeding car. "Cool wheels," he said. "What is that, a sixty-nine Camaro?"

"Close. A sixty-eight. You've got a good eye."

Unlike Rocket, Gert didn't even bother to slow down for the reporters, and Jared laughed as he watched the ratings-hungry mob that had turned to converge en masse on this newest victim diving left and right to keep from getting run down by her car. Then both vehicles were on the other side of the estate wall with the gates sweeping closed behind them. Grinning, he turned back in his seat. "How cool was that?"

Rocket smiled back. "Pretty damn," he said. "Mac doesn't take crap off of anyone. It's one of the reasons she's one of my all-time favorite people." He parked in front of the garage.

They both climbed out, and Jared looked at John over the roof of the vehicle for a moment. "Thanks," he said slowly. "For—you know—today."

"You're welcome." John looked him in the eye. "I imagine you ran into people who said stupid stuff or just didn't get it."

He shrugged.

"Well, forget about 'em. One of the few good things to come out of bad times is finding out who your real friends are. Don't let the ones who aren't make you feel bad—they're not worth the energy." His gaze went past Jared to his office manager's car as she parked it alongside his and the corner of his mouth crooked up. "Speaking of real friends, look who else is here. It appears I'm not the only one who has company."

Jared twisted around to see P.J. climbing out of the passenger side of Gert's car. With a whoop he headed for her, the last vestige of heaviness tumbling from his heart.

She, on the other hand, didn't even seem to notice him. Mouth agape, she was staring at the back of the mansion and around the grounds. And for the first time since he'd known her, she was totally, unnaturally still.

It unnerved him, so when he reached her he stooped low, got a shoulder under her midsection and surged upright with her firmly flung over his shoulder in a fireman lift. It wasn't until his hand gripped bare skin at the back of her knee that he realized she was wearing a dress.

It stunned him, because P.J. and dresses weren't exactly an automatic association in his mind. For a moment he froze and so did she.

Then, in typical P.J. fashion, she came up fighting, legs kicking and arms failing.

When she started bitch-slapping his head he had no recourse but to set her back on her feet. "Jeez, Peej!"

"Jeez, yourself!" She brushed at the skirt of her thin floral sundress as if he'd covered her in dust. Shiny red-brown hair hanging over one eye, she glared at him. "What's the matter with you?"

"Nothing. I was just glad to see you." He watched as she jerked the dress's straps into place and realized that she had breasts. Really *little* breasts, but still. He'd never noticed that before.

Her head snapped up as if she could read his thoughts and Jared felt a heated flush steal up his throat.

All she said, though, was, "Yeah, well…I'm glad to see you, too. But I got myself all dressed up for this visit, so don't go swinging me around like some sack of smelly old gym socks."

Glancing around, he was relieved to see Rocket and

Gert had disappeared inside. Some of his tension faded with the knowledge that no one had witnessed his less-than-suave technique with the ladies. He looked back at P.J. "I can see that, now the cars aren't between us. You look—" *Man, older than thirteen!* "—really nice."

"Thank you." She smoothed her hand down the skirt of her dress. Then she looked up at him and her uncharacteristic stiffness suddenly disappeared and all the liveliness he was accustomed to seeing blazed forth in her face. "I feel really nice. Gert bought me this." She gave the skirt another stroke. "Ain't it just the prettiest dress you ever seen?"

"*Have* ever seen," he corrected automatically.

Her hands stilled. "What?"

"Nothing. Sorry. I was being rude. Yes, I do believe it is the prettiest dress I've ever seen." But it was too late and as he watched the animation fade, he could have kicked himself. Especially when she wrapped her arms around herself as if she were cold and began humming a song under her breath. The latter scared the shit out of him, for he knew it was something she was particularly prone to doing when she was scared or nervous.

Damn. This was all dicked up. Feeling desperate, he gave her a nudge. "You still singing that country western crap?" She had a surprisingly excellent voice, much clearer and stronger than anyone hearing her raspy speaking voice would expect.

"It's not crap! It's rock and roll with a twang—and better than nine-tenths of that rapper junk you like."

"Yeah, yeah, yeah. Why don't you come on up to my room and convince me?"

"Fine. Lead the way."

They passed through the kitchen and walked down the hallway to the foyer, where P.J. stopped dead. "Omigawd," she said. She stared up at the one-story, unlighted chandelier hanging overhead. "Oh. My. God." Turning in slow circles, she took everything in. "This is so beautiful. This is the most beautiful place I ever—*have* ever—seen in my life. You could probably fit my mama's entire trailer right here." With a sweep of one delicate arm, she indicated the foyer around them. A shadow crossed her face, but then she pasted on a bright smile. "So let's see your room, hotshot. I bet it's bigger than the whosit—that Taj Mahal place—isn't it?"

"Nah. More like Buckingham Palace."

For the rest of the afternoon he saw intermittent flashes of the P.J. he knew. Mostly, though, he got the impression she thought she had to be on her party manners. It was like watching the Anti-Peej as she wandered around his room inspecting things, her hands firmly clasped behind her back as if she feared she'd break something if she actually touched it. The most relaxed she got was when he put on a Dixie Chicks CD he'd ordered off the Internet. She sang along, and her butt, which he noticed had filled out some in the week she'd been getting regular meals, wiggled in time.

When the CD was finished, she plopped down onto the bed next to him. She looked at her nails; she looked at the baseball mitt he'd tossed on the bedpost. Finally she looked at him. "My mama called."

Ice crept through his veins. He'd never met the woman, but he hated her guts anyhow. He kept his voice carefully neutral, however, when he said, "Oh?"

"Yeah. Gert got hold of her. I'm going home to Pueblo." Her expression was both hopeful and scared.

She reached into a little pocket on her dress and pulled out a slip of paper. "That's really why we came down here today—Gert just made up the paperwork-for-John stuff. She said you and me oughtta have the chance to say goodbye in person." She glanced down at the paper in her hand then held it out to him. "I'm leaving tomorrow, but I wanted to give you my phone number so we could still talk." She looked around his big airy room uncertainly. "If you wanna, that is."

"Oh, I want to." He grabbed her chin and pulled it around until she had no choice but to look him in the eye. Ignoring her hands tugging at his and her demands for him to let go, he glared into her feisty, frightened—God, so *vulnerable*—golden brown eyes and reiterated unequivocally, "I want to. I plan to. Count on it."

Victoria looked up from the invoices she was preparing for the two dollhouses she'd shipped this week to see John standing in the doorway to Ford's old office. She saved her work on the laptop computer and smiled at him. "Gert and P.J. get off okay?"

"Yep."

She got up, rounded the desk, and perched her bottom against its front. Bracing her palms on either side of her hips, she curled her fingers around the edge and observed him as he lounged against the jamb. "Didn't you think P.J. seemed subdued?"

He pressed his shoulder into the wood. "Mac located her mother and had a little talk with her. The upshot is P.J.'s moving back to Pueblo tomorrow."

"Oh, boy. I hope that works out for her."

"Me, too. From everything I've heard of Mom, she doesn't exactly sound like Mother of the Year material and I know Jared thinks it's a lousy idea."

"But to P.J. she's still Mama."

"Yeah. And there's nothing any of us can do as long as little Priscilla Jayne wants to go home."

"Is that her real name? Priscilla?" Victoria thought about it for a moment, then smiled. "It suits her."

"Yeah. You might not think so at first, because she comes off as a tough little nougat. But she's got a real soft center, doesn't she?" He shook his head. "She was sure thrilled with the dollhouse you gave her. Wasn't that slated for a customer?"

She shrugged. "I can make another for my customer. I doubt that little girl has been given much in her life."

"It's definitely one gift that's going to be well-loved. She wouldn't hear of Gert putting it in the back seat and was holding it in her lap when they drove away."

Victoria laughed, then changed the subject. "I've been dying to hear how it went today. Did you learn anything new?"

"Yeah. Did you know they make little girls not much older than Esme go to something called Cotillion class?"

She blinked. "What?" It was so not what she'd expected that she couldn't quite wrap her mind around it.

"You shoulda seen it, Tor. Little kids all duded up like miniature adults, marching with a precision I swear the marines would envy toward some class that Frank tells me teaches them to ballroom dance and comport themselves like good little country clubbers." Hands thrust in his slacks pockets, he shoved away from the doorjamb and sauntered across the room toward her. "You aren't going to make Esme attend one of those, are you? 'Cause I'm against it. I mean, manners are great and so is discipline—hell, I'd be the last one to argue with that. But I want my kid to be more than some society princess afraid to scuff her patent-leather shoes or get a bit of sand in her socks. I want to teach her the stuff that counts.''

She crossed her arms over her chest. ''And that would be…?''

''I don't know, something useful like…survival skills! How to find her way out of the woods if she gets lost. How to live off the land. How to—well, maybe not eat grubs, but at least know which berries will see her through and which ones will kill her.''

''Yes, I can see where there's bound to be a great big demand for that in her life.'' She didn't know whether to laugh out loud or swear. On the one hand, he was demonstrating interest in his daughter's life, a basic necessity if he was ever to be an actual part of it. But her foot began to tap. Because on the other hand—

''Uh-oh. Something tells me you're pissed at me.''

He'd moved closer and she had to tilt her head back to look up into his eyes. She used the movement to give him her snootiest nose tilt. ''Hamiltons don't get p.o.'d,'' she said coolly.

''No? Why's that, honey, too vulgar?''

''Much,'' she agreed. ''We are rational and collected. And when we're pushed too far, we become…irate.''

''Irate.'' He leaned so close his breath washed over her lips. ''And are you irate now?''

''A little.''

''Why? You said I should get to know her. Doesn't that mean showing an interest in what she does?''

''Yes, but—'' She took a deep breath. Blew it out. ''Okay, here's the truth. I've gone this alone for nearly six years. The only thing I want to hear from you is what a good job I've done raising her. You don't get to just waltz in here and tell me what is—or isn't—important for my daughter to know.''

''I don't?''

''No.''

His eyes narrowed. ''Now, that's fair.''

''You want fair? Well, what's so fair about you suddenly telling me what to do here?''

He reared back, hands fisting on his hips. ''What the hell are you talking about? I'm not dictating anything. I'm just expressing what I'd like to see as part of her future.''

She went from moderately annoyed to red-hot furious. ''Because you think I'm nothing but a spoiled society princess and you can't stand the thought of her being the same?''

''No! Jesus.'' He thrust his hand through his hair, knocking a strand loose from the rubber band holding it back. He ignored the way it dangled in front of his left eye to pin her in place with his stare. ''Did you attend Cotillion class?''

''Of course.''

''And you had such a great time you can't wait for Es to repeat the experience?''

She considered him, more than a little shocked to realize she was enjoying their skirmishing. And not just because it felt good to hold her ground. While it was certainly true that she was less than thrilled about the thought of sharing the decision-making regarding Esme's future, maybe there was a subtext at work here, as well. One that had more to do with the fact that he was big and hard-bodied, with a slight flush highlighting his cheekbones and his dark eyes liquid with conviction.

And with her sudden acute awareness that it had been several *loooong* days since they'd last made love. She thrust a hand through her own hair.

"I hated Cotillion," she admitted. "But if we end up staying in the Springs it will be a part of Esme's life. Hopefully she'll eventually make friends from all walks of life. But for now she has Rebecca, and you can be sure if Rebecca goes to CC, Es will want to go, too. And I'd rather she make up her own mind as to whether she likes it or not."

He considered it. "I guess that makes sense." Scowling, he took a sudden step back and shook his head. "But, damn. I was really hoping you'd argue."

"Why, so you could argue back just for the sake of arguing?"

"No, darlin'. So I could clear off that nice wide desk behind you and spread you across the top of it."

"Oh." She gripped the wood on either side of her hips so tightly it was a surprise it didn't crumble to dust. "Not a great—" her voice cracked like a thirteen-year-old boy's, and she cleared her throat "—idea."

"I know. But this is hard."

Her gaze instinctively dropped to just below the waistband of his pants.

A bark of laughter escaped him. "Oh, yeah, that, too. But I meant this no-sex stuff. It's really hard, and it's making us both edgy and—"

"Maybe a tiny bit unreasonable?"

"Yes." He shoved his hands back into his pockets and stood with military erectness. "But we said no sex while the kid's around and no sex it is. So, do us both a favor. Go back behind your desk. And I'll bore you with the things I found out during my golf game with Olson and Hamlin."

Twenty-Three

"*We're sorry. You have reached a number that has been disconnected or is no longer in service.*"

Swearing, Jared slammed down the phone. This was the third fricking time he'd dialed the number P.J. had given him and each time he'd gotten the same recording. Why had she bothered to give him a number at all, if the damn telephone wasn't even connected?

Because it was easier than telling you she doesn't like you anymore, whispered a voice in his mind that insisted on reminding him of what he kept trying hard to forget—how uncomfortable she'd been when she'd visited him last week.

"No!" He shoved the thought away and, in an attempt to outrun the icy feeling settling in his gut, left his room with long strides, yanking the door shut behind him with such violence it bounced back open again. Ignoring it, he stormed down the hall.

This wasn't about him. This had something to do with her bitch of a mother, he just knew it, and he was going to find Rocket and hire him to locate P.J. She could come live with them.

But when he turned the corner into the main upstairs corridor and spotted John, shock stopped him dead in his tracks. For the former marine was wrapped around his sister, kissing her as if he were a condemned man and she his last meal. Tori's arms were locked around his neck and John's long fingers clutched her butt.

He must have made a sound, because Rocket's head suddenly lifted and Jared watched his lips form a succinct swear word when he saw him standing there staring at them. Realizing his own jaw must be sagging, Jared snapped it shut so hard his teeth clacked. His worry about P.J. and fury over the operator's electronic message abruptly transferred to his sister and the lanky P.I.

He stalked over to them, his upper lip curling in a sneer when Tori turned to face him and he saw how red and swollen her mouth was, how mussed her clothing. He gave her a slow up and down, but John he ignored entirely. He couldn't look at the older man without feeling betrayed. He'd *admired* him. No, more than that—he'd practically hero-worshiped the guy. And all along the P.I. had only been being nice to him to get close to his sister.

Sickness crawled through him. Because Rocket was a frigging page right out of the old man's book, wasn't he? It was clear he had one eye firmly on the main chance and was looking out for Number One. Victoria was suddenly worth a lot of money and Miglionni had worked fast to consolidate his position.

Jared wasn't quite brave enough to say that aloud, however, and shame at being such a chickenshit added to his fury. Unsure who he despised more at the moment—Rocket, Tori, or himself—he gave his sister his most insolent stare.

"I thought you were trying to *help* me," he said in a low, furious voice. God, if he couldn't trust her, who could he trust? Not P.J., it seemed. She obviously didn't want to be his friend anymore or she wouldn't have given him a bogus telephone number. But Tori was the one person he'd counted on to be unquestioningly on his side.

Yet here he stood, forgotten once again.

It was like all those times with his dad and whichever wife had been in residence. Only this betrayal cut deeper because Jared never in a trillion years expected it from his sister and he lashed out unthinkingly. "I thought you were trying to help, but I guess I was just an excuse to have the studmeister here stay around, wasn't I? Well, hey." He shrugged as if his world wasn't one great big ball of fiery pain. "As long as the big guy here is screwing you regularly, what do my little problems matter?"

Tori's eyes went wide with shock, but before the hurt that replaced it had time to gouge his conscience, she was blocked from view by John's bigger body. The utter fury in his jet-black eyes sent Jared stumbling several steps backward.

"In my office," John snapped. *"Now!"*

Oh shit, oh shit. Cold sweat broke out on Jared's back and trickled down his spine. That was exactly where his dad used to drag him whenever he'd felt the urge to tell him what a loser he was. Wanting desperately to order Rocket to stuff it but afraid to even open his mouth again, he whirled on his heel and stalked down the hallway, impotent fury burning through his veins. He was conscious of the long-legged man striding in his wake as they marched down the stairs and along the main-floor hallway until they reached the office in the rear of the new south wing that Rocket had taken over.

Banging through the doorway, he barreled over to the chair in front of the desk and threw himself down upon it. He folded his arms over his chest and, heart knocking, glared defiantly as Rocket walked around the desk and took his own seat.

"Let's get something straight right off the bat." Leaning his forearms on the desk, Rocket pointed a long, tan finger at him. The skull-and-crossbones tattoo beneath a fan of black hair on his arm shifted with the movement. "You can say whatever the hell you want about me. But you don't talk to your sister—or any other woman, for that matter—that way. Especially not Tori. She believed in you when no one else did. Hell, she disrupted her entire *life* for you, and I'll be damned if I'll listen to you disrespect her."

The look he'd seen on his sister's face already had guilt twisting his gut in knots, but Jared hadn't asked her to do one damn thing for him, so why was he was supposed to take the blame for that?

Stubbornly refusing to admit that anything John said might have a grain of truth to it, he gave Mr-Silent-Swift-and-Deadly his best, go-fuck-yourself look and took the high road. "What the hell are you talking about? How did I disrupt Tori's entire life? Whatever she decided to do, it was her choice."

"Jesus, kid, I know self-interest is the fuel that pretty much drives us all, but do you think you could consider someone besides yourself for five freaking minutes? You are not the sun your sister orbits around. She had a life in England and she uprooted it all—took Esme out of school, left her aunt and her friends, packed up her studio lock, stock and barrel and had it shipped halfway around the world. She did it for *you*, you ingrate, because she cares about you—not because it sounded like a rocking good time."

Suddenly the high road didn't seem so high after all.

"So, who asked her to?" he muttered defensively, but was immediately stabbed with guilt because hearing the words said aloud made him realize that as defenses went it was worse than weak—it was below contempt. He didn't need the look John shot him to tell him that.

Shit. He hadn't even considered that Victoria might have a life that required some serious rearranging in order to help him. He'd just taken for granted that she'd be there. "So, okay," he admitted slowly, "she didn't have to be asked." Shaking with mortification that he'd needed to have it pointed out to him, he instinctively struck back. "But what about you? I suppose your slipping the sausage to my sister doesn't have the first thing to do with your own self-interest?"

John came half out of his seat, rage emanating out of every pore. "Watch your mouth when you talk about her! I'm not going to warn you about it again." Abruptly he seemed to catch himself, for his expression went blank and he sat back down.

Jared noted with satisfaction, though, that John's hands had a slight tremor before he flattened them against the desktop, and it gave him the courage to make a rude noise and sneer, "Like you don't know she's going to be worth a bundle once my dad's will clears probate."

"I don't give a flying fuck about her money!"

"Oh, sure. Her wealth has *nothing* to do with why you're all over a woman you just met a few weeks ago."

John presented him with a noncommittal expression, but Jared saw the pure fury that burned in his eyes. The other man's voice was clipped and neutral, however, when he said, "Not that it's any of your goddamn business, but I didn't just meet your sister. She and I met years ago, and just for the record, E—'' Cutting himself off, he shoved to his feet. "What the hell am I doing, arguing with you about this?" He leveled a finger at Jared once again. "Apologize to your sister. You don't have to like or trust me. But you owe her your respect, not to mention your gratitude. If it wasn't for her, you'd still be begging on the streets."

He walked around the desk and Jared expected him to just keep on going. Instead the tall man stopped in front of his chair and shoved his hands into his slacks pockets as he looked down at him. Jared glowered back defiantly, but his stomach was one big knot of icy nerves. Miglionni's face might not demonstrate anger with anything so obvious as a scowl, but Jared knew he was furious. His shoulders were stiff and his jaw was tight, and Jared braced himself for the parting shot that would slice his confidence to ribbons.

He was caught off guard when Rocket merely said, "If you think Victoria needs money to be attractive to men, kid, you're not only self-absorbed, you're stone-blind."

He blinked. That was it? No: *you worthless little asshole?* No: *your mother should have ripped you out of her body before you ever got the chance to screw up everyone's life?* Just another defense of his sister? It was so far from what he'd been accustomed to hearing from his father that he could only blink like some damn demented rabbit.

By the time he gathered his wits about him again, John had already sidestepped the chair where he sat and strode straight out the door.

Getagrip getagrip, getagrip. The refrain beat time with the temper surging fast and furiously through

John's bloodstream as he stormed along the upstairs hallway toward his room. And he was trying. He was trying like crazy. But sweet, sweet Jesus! Wasn't it bad enough that he couldn't seem to keep his hands off Victoria? Now he'd come within inches of kicking the shit out of her kid brother, as well!

"Great." He slammed open the door to his room. "I'm turning into my goddamn father."

"Oh, I seriously doubt that."

His head shot up. Victoria sat in the striped silk chair across the room, her back elegantly straight, her legs crossed and one foot tapping air. But it was the first inkling he had that he hadn't been paying the least bit of attention to his surroundings and a harsh laugh escaped him.

"Perfect. You know, once upon a time nothing escaped me. I was one of the best—the few, the proud. Now socialite dollhouse designers and punk seventeen-year-olds can get the drop on me without breaking a sweat. What's next—Esme gonna take me down?"

"News flash, pal: you don't have to be on guard around us."

Yes he did. Particularly after the session he'd just had with Jared. He gave her a cool stare. "Look, do you mind? I need a little downtime here."

She didn't budge. "It didn't go too well with Jared, I take it."

His bark of laughter was short on amusement. "No. It didn't go too fucking swell—starting with letting him catch us in the first place. Like I said, I used to be a lot better at this."

"Back when you were a—how did you describe yourself in Pensacola?—a trained killing machine who specialized in covert reconnaissance?"

Had he really been that fat-headed back then? Probably. Still, since the description pretty much covered what he used to do, he gave a curt nod.

"Then give yourself a break," she said. "You must have had downtime, even back then. And I know you were a big popular ladies' man and all, but somehow I doubt you did much heavy necking while you were in 'killing-machine' mode."

He'd been prowling the room trying to burn off some of his temper, but her comment made him stop and stare at her. "Is that supposed to make me feel better? Because, I gotta tell you, baby, it just points out one more way I've screwed up. How many times have I told you I'm going to obey the no-sex rules?" He didn't wait for an answer. "But then every time I see you, I'm all over you."

"I don't recall protesting. As a matter of fact, who started today's episode?"

She had. Still… "That's not the point. It doesn't excuse me breaking my word. I could probably live with it, though, if it was only that. But there's no excuse for physical violence against a kid and I wanted to beat the crap out of your brother!"

"Trust me, I was right there with you in that desire." She shrugged as if the urge was common as dirt. "He's a teenager, John. Who doesn't want to smack them at one time or another?"

"No," he said flatly, looking up from the clench and flex of his fists to engage her gaze. "You don't get it. I *really* wanted to hurt him. I wanted to wrap my hands around his scrawny little neck and squeeze until his face turned blue. I wanted to hit him with my fists. God, Tori, I wanted to mop the floor with his face. I'm no better than my old man." And it scared the bejesus out of him. "I never thought I'd see the day when I'd have to say that, but I just barely hung on to my temper. We're talking by a fingernail, here. I wanted to take him down—both verbally and physically." He scraped his still shaky hands through his hair, digging his nails into his scalp. "You don't *know* how badly I wanted to let go. I'd bet my life it was exactly the way my old man must have felt when he used to let me have it."

She gazed at him calmly. "But you didn't do it, did you?"

"No. But I was *this close.*"

"Close doesn't count." She stood and crossed over to him. Staring solemnly up at him, she reached out to stroke a soothing hand down his arm. "The fact is, you didn't. You held on to your temper and neither told him he was a useless waste of space, the way his own father did, nor hit him."

"This time," he said flatly and stepped away. The trust in her eyes made his gut churn, because God knew he didn't deserve it. She might not fully appreciate what sort of stock he came from, but he did. "Don't break out any medals for me just yet, darlin'. Because who the hell knows what will happen the next time he pisses me off?"

Three days later, Esme came running to Victoria, nearly in tears. "Mummy, John won't play with me!" She threw herself against her mother. "*Again!* I tol' him we could play Raccoon Ants if he wanted, but he said not now!"

"John is not here to play Barbie dolls with you, sweetie. He's here to do a job." Victoria kept her voice placid, but inside she was far from calm. She was, in fact, about ready to tear her hair out by the roots. But reining in her frustration, she held her hand out to her daughter. "I realize it might not be on a par with playing reconnaissance Barbies with John, but why don't you come be my helper in the studio today?"

"I *guess* that'd be okay." Esme wore a long face as she grasped the proffered hand, and she dragged her feet as Victoria piloted her toward the studio. She was by nature an optimistic little girl, though, and by the time they reached the garage she'd begun to skip alongside Victoria and regale her with the details of her earlier telephone conversation with Rebecca. As they let themselves into the studio she provided a word-by-word report of everything her best friend had said to her and her own clever responses.

Victoria um-hmmed and occasionally commented to show she was listening. Her thoughts, however, kept sliding back to John.

God, he was making her nuts. He actually believed that the incident with Jared proved he was on a par with his abusive father and no amount of talking on her part would make him listen to reason. Add in her own inability to concentrate on anything else for more than a minute or two at a time and you had serious ulcer potential.

Unfortunately, unless John decided to quit being an idiot, her stress levels weren't likely to magically correct themselves anytime soon. So acknowledging she wasn't at her sharpest, she got Esme tricked out in a voluminous apron and set her up with one of the scale models, a glue stick, and the package of roofing shingles she'd ordered in the wrong color. The latter could also be blamed on Rocket, since she'd placed that order the day after she'd discovered John Miglionni of Semper Fi Agency was none other than her onetime lover.

The way she felt right now, in fact, damn near everything wrong with the universe could be laid squarely at his long, narrow feet.

Once Esme was absorbed in her task, she picked up the hot glue gun and automatically began applying gingerbread shingles to the dollhouse she was making to replace the one she'd given P.J. Fortunately for her fingers, siding was a job she'd done dozens of times before, because she couldn't concentrate to save her soul.

The day before yesterday Jared had apologized to her. He'd been embarrassed and less than articulate, but she suspected that had quite a lot to do with having to place her and sex in the same context. From what she could glean from his rambling explanation, though, Rocket had spent the entire time he was struggling not to knock her brother's teeth down his throat defending *her*. It certainly seemed to have impressed the hell out of Jared, which she could understand, having seen their father in action.

But would John see that? Oh, no. He was still stubbornly convinced that he was just one argument away from turning into a child abuser. He'd distanced himself from both her brother and Esme, throwing up an emotional wall to prevent them from getting close. He was perfectly civil, but in a distant sort of way, taking extra care to keep both of them safely at arm's length.

Jared didn't seem to mind. The poor kid had learned the hard way not to expect too much from adult males, so any attention he received from John probably seemed like a lot to him. He appeared content enough just to know that the man he was clearly beginning to idolize wasn't mad at him anymore.

But Victoria had specifically removed Esme from her grandfather's sphere so the child would never have to learn the kind of emotional limits that Victoria and Jared had. And she was getting damn tired of seeing her daughter's unhappy confusion over the man who would play imaginative games with her one day, then blow her off the next.

A car engine started up in the garage below the studio and her mouth twisted as she recognized its distinctive growl. *Well, speak of the devil* she thought sourly. The rat was apparently deserting the ship.

Okay, that probably wasn't fair. Still, she glanced over at Esme, afraid her daughter would also recognize the sound of the car accelerating down the lane and have her hurt feelings resurrected. But Es had her tongue caught between her teeth as she concentrated on pressing a miniature shingle next to several others she'd already glued in a lopsided line along the roofline. It wasn't until the reporters outside the gate began clamoring that she looked up.

"Is that the wuffs?" she asked.

"Yes." A slight smile tugged at Victoria's lips. Jared calling the reporters wolves had stuck in Esme's mind.

"Why are they yelling?"

"One never knows with that lot, but I imagine it's because they tend to get excited when people leave or enter the estate."

"Is someone here?" Esme hopped up and shoved her chair over to the window. She climbed up and stood on her tiptoes to peer out the window. When that didn't garner her the results she clearly expected, she started to climb up on its arms.

"Hey, hey, hey! What have I told you about chair safety?" Victoria walked over, scooped her daughter off the chair and set her safely on her feet on the floor. She cupped her palm beneath Esme's soft-skinned chin and lifted it in order to look into her eyes. "You can't see the gates from here, anyway, sweetie."

"But who's here? Maybe somebody came to see us."

"No." She hesitated, then admitted, "John just left."

Esme stared up at her for a moment, then nodded. "'Cause he's gotta work?"

"Yes."

"'Kay." She pushed her chair back over to the worktable. After clambering up to sit on it, she reached for the shingle she'd been applying a smear of waxy glue to before the reporters started yelling. "Good." She slapped the shingle on the roof.

Victoria went back to her own glueing. "Good, huh? Why is that?"

"'Cause maybe he'll want to play with me when he comes back from his job."

"Oh, Es. He still might not have the time."

"Uh-huh. He will so."

Damn John. She and he were going to exchange some serious words if he didn't straighten up and fly right in a big fat hurry. He simply could not persist in this nonsense—not if he wanted to have a place in his daughter's life.

She knew perfectly well he would never strike a child, in anger or otherwise. He had better realize it pretty darn soon, as well, because she would not put up with this. She'd had no choice but to grow up with a father who'd made it clear his time was much too valuable to squander on a mere child, but she could damn well make sure Esme didn't endure the same thing. She bent a fiercely protective glance on her little girl.

Because better no father at all than one who couldn't—or worse, wouldn't—return her love.

Twenty-Four

John spent that afternoon at the club, talking to the dining-room hostess, the pro shop manager and several of the caddies, walking a fine line to ensure his interviews came across as casual conversation. He rounded off his day by nursing a beer in the bar and jawing with the bartender. The tidbits the man let drop were filed away with the others he'd collected, and all of them, he noted, had to do with the quirks of individual personalities. Since it was his experience that information concerning people's behavior often led to figuring out who was likely to do what, he was content with that.

When he finally tipped the bartender and headed for his car, however, contentment was the last thing he felt. Instead, the foremost thought running through his mind was, *What the hell am I doing investigating a murder?*

Being a marine had taught him to go with his strengths, and murder was so far outside his area of expertise as a P.I. it wasn't even funny. It was one thing to have a knack for locating runaway and throwaway kids. Finding a stab-happy killer was something else again. He should have known better than to take the assignment in the first place. Hell, he had known better, but when it came to Victoria, his resistance seemed to be nil. The fact was, though, to be effective he needed the cooperation of the local police, and at the moment he wasn't exactly Detective Simpson's favorite person. So even if he figured out who'd plunged the letter opener into Ford Hamilton's chest, what was he going to do about it, muscle the killer into confessing? A derisive sound slipped out of his mouth. *Sure thing, chief. That's likely to happen.*

He had, as Mac had been calling daily to remind him, a business that needed his attention. And God knew that, so far, the only result of his professional help had been to locate Jared for Victoria. Well, that and generate a bill for her that would probably rival the national debt if one of them didn't get real here pretty soon.

He knew that person had better be him. Although he'd always known on some level that he and Victoria had come from different worlds, hanging around the club really drove home the fact that it was time to quit fooling himself it could somehow be otherwise. He couldn't even say why he'd believed a lasting relationship with her—not to mention being a real father to Esme—had struck him as a possibility in the first place.

The thought of not being a part of their lives, though, gnawed at his gut with razor-wire-sharp, poison-tipped teeth. And he sure didn't look forward to telling Tori. Not after he'd let her think they had the potential to be a unit.

So he'd do what any smart guy would do. He'd avoid her the rest of today and most of tomorrow. They were scheduled to attend a dance at the club tomorrow night—he'd tell her then.

It had nothing to do with cravenness, he told himself firmly. This was merely doing the right thing. The setting would simply give him the chance to help her see reason and put things in perspective while being surrounded by her own people. It was strictly for her benefit.

He wasn't cut out for this one-man/one-woman stuff. He'd known it for years, but for some reason he'd allowed himself to ignore the fact the past couple of weeks. Well, he was through fooling himself. And he sure as hell didn't have to be kicked in the head to realize he was about as far from suitable father material as a man could get. His run-in with Jared had merely strengthened a truth he'd never even thought to question until recently: a man who harbored violent impulses had no business being around kids. It was time he moved on.

Hell, when it came right down to it, he would probably be doing everyone a huge favor by going back to Denver.

Of course, it didn't negate the fact that breaking the news to Tori in a public place was still the wisest move. He had the same abhorrence for messy, emotional arguments as any other right-thinking guy, so why let this turn into an opera if he had another option? His buddies hadn't raised no fool—he knew enough to take advantage of the fact that she was much too polite to make a scene in public. Because God knew neither of them needed any more drama in their lives.

Arriving at his car, he slapped a decisive palm down on its hot metal roof. Yeah. It was much better to keep things simple. It didn't have a damn thing to do with cowardice.

And it sure as hell wasn't as if he were afraid to see her disappointment in him or anything.

The last thing Victoria expected the following evening as she and John were about to leave for the country club was to see DeeDee come tripping out to the circular drive in her skyscraper heels. But the curvaceous blonde yoo-hooed from the entryway and headed straight for them, legs flashing with the motion in the split-to-the-indecent-zone skirt of her gown. Sashaying up to the driver's side of the car, she gave John's window a tap.

"Bum a ride?" she asked the minute the window glided down. "My car has a flat tire of all things and the service station can't send anyone out to fix it until tomorrow."

Victoria had barely caught more than an occasional glimpse of John in the past thirty-six hours and really wanted to talk to him. Her manners were too ingrained to protest, however, when he shrugged his wide shoulders and said, "Sure, why not?"

"Well, now, isn't this cozy?" DeeDee said after John handed her into the back seat of his car. She waited until he shut the door before pulling together the two sides of her skirt.

Victoria had a feeling her face must have reflected some of what she was thinking, for the other woman shot her a malicious smile.

"Oh, don't worry, dear. I'm not planning to horn in on your evening. God knows I don't want to be stuck at a table with you any more than you do with me. I have…plans…for later, too, so I'll catch a ride back with someone else." Then in blatant dismissal, she pulled out a compact and inspected her makeup. She turned her head from side to side until, apparently satisfied, she snapped the compact shut again and tossed it into her tiny evening bag.

Unlike Tori, who avoided making eye contact with the news people outside the gates as they drove past,

DeeDee sat up straight, pulled her shoulders back and thrust out her chest. But she adopted a sad expression as she met the newshounds' avid gazes. Once they were no more than specks in the rearview mirror, however, she dropped the grieving widow expression and leaned forward.

"I have news that ought to brighten up your day," she said to Victoria, who had swung around to watch her act in amazement. "I think it's time I moved out. I plan to find somewhere else to live by the fifteenth."

Tori swivelled back to face front and a tiny smile tugged at the corners of her lips. Well, well. The evening was definitely looking up.

DeeDee was as good as her word when they reached the country club. The moment John brought the car to a halt, she climbed out and headed inside without them, freeing Victoria to pursue her own agenda.

"We need to talk," she said a few minutes later, putting a hand on John's sleeve to stop him from escorting her into the main salon. Music and laughter poured out through its bank of open doors and men in summer tuxes and women in gowns that ran the fashion gamut from classic couture to up-to-the-minute trendy formed a kaleidoscope of constantly shifting colors. The annual Labor Day dance was kicking into high gear.

"I know." John glanced into the salon, then looked down at her. "Let's go find our table. We can talk there."

A table surrounded by partygoers didn't strike her as the ideal place for a serious talk and she glanced around the small reception area. "No," she said decisively, spotting the club manager's small office. "Come with me." She headed across the lobby.

"Tori, wait!"

But she was a woman on a mission and she walked right over to the slightly opened door and poked her head inside. Perfect—it was empty. She stepped in and turned to wait for John.

He followed her but halted on the other side of the door. Shoving his hands into his slacks pockets, he hunched his shoulders and stared at her. "Come on, darlin', let's go into the salon. We can talk there."

"It's too public."

A flash of what almost looked like panic flashed across his face. "Public's not so bad," he said. "We'll talk low." He glanced at the brass name plate on the door. "This is someone's office. We probably shouldn't be in here."

"Right." A skeptical laugh escaped her. "You being a guy who spends so much time worrying about what other people think and all." She reached out and grabbed his forearm, which was warm and hard beneath his tux sleeve, and tugged him over the threshold. "It's here or nowhere, Miglionni."

"Shit." He stepped into the room but left the door open.

Reaching past him, she pushed it shut—then locked it for good measure. Starting to pick up a definite vibe, however, she looked up and met John's hooded gaze. "Why don't you want to be alone with me?"

"I don't know what you're talking about." But he squared his shoulders, slid his hands out of his pockets and slowly straightened until she had no choice but to tip her head back in order to retain eye contact. "Okay," he admitted, "Maybe I do. The truth is, I really hoped to have this talk somewhere you'd hesitate to make a scene."

"*Excuse* me?" She couldn't decide whether she was mortally insulted…or just plain scared. Given the grim determination on his face, it didn't take long for scared to be the runaway favorite. Finding that unacceptable, she scrambled to disguise the emotion by raising her chin and utilizing her iciest tone. "Hamiltons don't make scenes. So why don't you just say whatever it is you have to say."

"I'm going back to Denver."

No! She backed up until her thighs bumped against the utilitarian desk. Gratefully she perched her rear upon it, and not a moment too soon, for her legs suddenly lost all strength. Gripping the edge on either side of her hips, she welcomed the slight sting of wood digging into her palms. "For a day or two?" she asked hopefully.

"For good."

"For good," she repeated without inflection. For a moment a red-hot sea of pain seemed to flood the vicinity of her heart. Then to her relief, icy anger settled over her, forming a numbing seal over the hurt. A host of possible reasons for his sudden defection raced through her mind and she narrowed her eyes at him when one thought abruptly screeched all the others to a dead halt. "My God," she said. "You really played me for a fool, didn't you?"

"What are you talking about?" He gave her the expressionless look she thought of as his military face. "I've never been anything but straight with you and that's all I'm trying to be now."

"Oh, baloney." She shook her head in disgust. "And to think I honestly believed our relationship was somehow different from the week we had in Pensacola. The only thing that's truly changed is my failure to understand how much *you* want to be the one to walk away this time.''

He took a hot step forward before he caught himself. But his cool lack of expression disappeared and he bent a fierce glare on her. ''That's bullshit and you know it!''

''Do I? Well, okay, I will hand it to you—this time lasted longer than a week. But the fact remains, you wanted me for a finite period of time that's apparently over now. What's the story with that, John? Do you have some internal clock or something that tells you when it's time to move on?''

''No!'' John stared at her in frustration. How had she managed to turn everything around? ''Damn, where is this coming from? I've told you before and I meant it—I changed after meeting you. So it's time I return the favor I owe you and get the hell out of your life.''

''How very noble of you.''

Her bitter skepticism flicked him on the raw. ''Just what did you *think* was going to happen between us, Tori?'' Anger wasn't going to accomplish anything, though, so he reeled himself in. He forced his brows to unclench and managed to say with credible lightness, as if he didn't give a good goddamn, ''You're champagne, baby; I'm beer. Not that I don't do pretty well for myself, but I'm sure as hell nowhere in your league. So what did you think was going to happen in the end? Were you planning on giving up the mansion, the country club, the nice cars, to come live with me in my little apartment?''

She surged up off the desk and they were abruptly nose to nose. He jerked back from the fury blazing out of her moss-green eyes.

''You patronizing, arrogant jerk,'' she said, underscoring each word with a poke to his chest. "Until Father died, I lived in a three-bedroom flat—and only had the third room because I needed to combine my home with a workspace! And who said I had a burning desire to live with you, anyway?" An unamused laugh escaped her. "My God. You can't even commit to being Esme's father—you think I'd trust any promise you made for the future?"

"Now wait just a damn minute!" His blood surging hot, fast and furiously through his veins, he got right in her face. No one impugned his honor and just boogied away scott-free.

"No, you wait!" She returned the favor, her high heels bringing her as close as she'd ever gotten to his greater height. "You and I, Rocket? We're adults, and we can hash things out—or not—and if a heart gets broken, we'll pick up the pieces like the supposedly mature people we are and deal with it. But damned if I'll let you jerk around Esme."

"I have no intention of doing that! But if I stick around, then what? Let's say by some grace of God I manage not to knock the crap out of your brother. Can either of us ever trust me with Esme? With my family history? Everyone knows abusers were abused themselves as kids. And I'm sorry if you don't like it, but I'm not about to take a chance with that sweet little girl. It's better that I just leave."

"Better for whom?"

"Everyone!"

"Then do it, by God. But if you do, don't plan on ever coming back."

His gut turned to ice. "What?"

"Make up your bloody mind and do what you have to do. But you can't have it both ways, Rocket. You don't get to waltz out of Esme's life when you feel like it and then waltz back in again when it suits your mood.''

''I never said—''

''No, you've made a *career* out of never saying, haven't you? You don't talk about personal stuff, unless it's someone else's, and you certainly don't share your feelings. Well, fine then, I'll make this real easy and say it for you. Either you're Esme's father or you're out of her life.'' She thrust her nose up under his. ''She doesn't need the confusion, so decide, damn you, and live with the consequences.''

It was one thing, he discovered, to make the decision to walk away himself. It was something else again to be handed an ultimatum. Anger edged with an unfamiliar, humiliating panic he did his best to deny, washed over him. He slapped his hands down on the desktop next to her hips.

She abruptly sat back to keep their bodies from slamming together and blinked up at him, her elegant little jaw agape.

Taking advantage of her failure to close her knees from the militant, screw-you stance she'd assumed, he stepped between them. The voluminous skirt of her gown made way beneath the rough press of his thighs. He stared down at her. ''You don't wanna be offering me ultimatums, darlin'.''

Her mouth snapped closed and her chin thrust up. ''Or what? You'll try to convince me that you're a woman abuser, too?''

''No!'' His brows met over his nose. ''But that doesn't mean you can dismiss my fear of losing my temper and hurting one of the kids. It's a legitimate concern.''

"It's crazy, is what it is. You want to know what I think, John? I think you'd cut off your right hand before you'd ever harm a child. So what's the real story here? You act like Esme and I are important to you one minute, then push us away the next. Is that because you have feelings you don't know how to deal with? Are you clinging to this cockamamie I'm-turning-into-my-dad theory so you won't have to explore those feelings?" She gave his shoulder a soft slap. "Tell me what's going on!"

I think I'm falling in love with you. The unexpected words whispering through his mind scared the crap out of him. No! That wasn't it at all. He was love-'em-and-leave-'em-Miglionni and *falling* in love wasn't in his makeup. Hadn't been six years ago—wasn't now. Sure, he cared about her and Esme. Enough to know that this was the best thing for them. World-class sex could only carry a relationship so far. Victoria could deny it all she wanted, but she was a lady, born and bred, and sooner or later his low-class physicality would disgust her.

Not to mention that his fear of hurting Jared was legit. Ignoring his pounding heart, he pushed back with his hands from the desk and started to straighten up, prepared to bestow a cool smile and a flip rejoinder that would put her in her place once and for all. Something to keep her from poking into places she had no business poking.

But Victoria grabbed him by his bow tie and held him in place. "Did I hit a nerve, John?" she whispered. "*Is* that what this is all about? Do you have some feelings for me, or for Esme, that you're too chickenhearted to claim?"

Her words struck a little too close to the bone and

in an instinctual bid to shut her up, he rocked his mouth over hers. He braced, waiting for her to shove him away. When instead her tongue rose up to return the thrust of his own, every bit of common sense he possessed dissipated like dew beneath the desert sun. His hands came up off the desk to grip her hips and he stepped in closer while jerking her to meet him halfway. They slapped together, hard thrusting sex to soft, accommodating cleft.

She sucked in a breath as her hands tore at the fly of his slacks and the next thing he knew, he was out of his pants and into her hands and he was wrestling yards of slithery gossamer fabric out of his way. He finally got the majority of it up above her waist and, thumbing aside the fragile scrap of lace that was her panties, he let her tug him into place. He sank into her and a low, heartfelt groan escaped him when her hot, wet, slick inner muscles pulled him deep and clamped tightly around him to hold him fast.

Oh, God, she felt so good—she felt like home—and he began to move, withdrawing and plunging, withdrawing and plunging, harder and faster as his hands slid beneath her butt to bring her closer. She crossed her ankles at the small of his back, wrapped her arms around his neck and clung, returning kiss for feverish, fervent kiss.

Then she suddenly ripped her mouth free and her head lolled back. A series of breathy moans stuttered from her throat, starting low and gaining in both volume and pitch.

John's lips drew back from his teeth at the feel of the hard, tight, contractions as she began coming around him. It was the nudge that pushed him over and his fingers sank into her butt as he plunged deep and held, groaning at the way her climax milked his own from his body.

They slumped simultaneously, their lax bodies propping each other up. For a moment John felt as if he were drifting in a pool of golden perfection and he closed his eyes to focus on the feeling. His arms tightened when Tori shifted against him, but she merely tipped her head to press a kiss on his shoulder, and the corners of his lips curved up.

Then he felt her stiffen, heard her whisper, ''Oh, my God, what have we done?'' and the golden moment popped. Reality returned with a crash and, flattening his palms on the desk, he straight-armed himself away from her.

''Now do you see what I've been saying?'' he demanded. ''Didn't take you long to regret it, did it?''

''We didn't use birth control, John!''

His heart slammed up against the wall of his chest and he jerked back, pulling out of her. Staring down to where they'd been joined he saw his seed begin to trickle out of her and whipped the faultlessly folded handkerchief from his breast pocket. He pressed it between her legs. ''I'm sorry,'' he said. ''God, Tori, I'm sorry.''

The knob rattled on the door behind them and he broke off the rest of whatever he might have said. Watching Victoria carefully pull her panties back into place over the folded handkerchief, he tucked himself back into his slacks and zipped up. Knuckles rapped on the door.

''Who's in there?'' a male voice demanded. ''Open up! This is the manager.''

''Give us a second!'' John snapped without looking away from Victoria. ''We had a little emergency here, and need a minute. We'll be out as soon as we get it straightened out.'' Whenever the hell that might be. They needed to talk.

But Tori, who five minutes ago had been raking him over the coals for never talking about his feelings, rose to her feet from the desk and shook her floaty purply blue skirt back into place. She smoothed her upswept hair, then reached past him for the lock on the door.

He intercepted her hand. ''Darlin'—''

''Don't.'' She pulled her fingers free. ''I can't talk about this right now. We had the excuse of a faulty condom in Pensacola, but we don't have a good excuse for this.''

''Doesn't mean we don't still need to decide—'' What? He didn't know *what* the hell the next step was supposed to be.

As if reading his mind, she echoed, ''What—how we handle it *this* time if I turn up pregnant again? Oh, God.'' She stepped around him to reach for the lock again, but instead of turning it, she rested her forehead on the wooden panel of the door. ''It's not like we just resolved anything, John. Maybe you had the right idea. Maybe it is time you went back to Denver.''

It was what he'd thought best for everyone ten minutes ago. So why didn't it make him feel any better to hear her agreeing now? Why did it instead seem to increase the sick feeling in the pit of his stomach? ''That's what I was trying to tell you,'' he said, but being right did nothing to prevent his heart from feeling as if someone had used it to mop up the floor.

Well, screw that, he thought as he watched her turn the lock on the door. But he had to fist his hands to keep himself from running a finger down her nape where it was exposed by her upswept hair and he forced extra crispness into his voice to compensate. "I don't know about you," he said briskly, "but I'm in no mood to go out there and make the big announcement that our engagement is off. How about we try to get through tonight without giving the Springs a new scandal to serve up with their morning Wheaties?"

She turned her head to look at him and for a moment she looked so defeated he wanted nothing more than to pull her into his arms. But even as he watched, her spine snapped erect and her chin raised. "Sure." She shrugged her smooth shoulders. "I can if you can."

"Hell, yeah," he said. "Not a problem." And with pride stiffening his own backbone, he reached past her to open the door.

Twenty-Five

*I*diot, *idiot*, *IDIOT!*

Standing amidst the partygoers, Victoria smiled and chatted and pretended everything was fine. That *she* was fine. But one shallow scratch beneath the carefully erected surface was a virago who wanted to scream and kick and tear her hair out by the roots. A heartsick fool who wanted to curl up into a ball of misery and cry an ocean of tears.

How could she have been so *irresponsible?* Not only with her heart, which when it came to John Miglionni couldn't really be helped, but with her body, which certainly could have been. While she would never regret the decision to have Esme and refused to apologize for the circumstances of her daughter's birth, neither had she ever intended to bring another child into the world outside the sanctity of marriage. She'd be damn lucky, however, if rolling around on the desk with John this evening didn't result in a sibling for Es nine months down the line. Heaven knew they'd been fertile beyond belief when they had practiced birth control. What were the chances of avoiding another pregnancy in the wake of such blatant carelessness?

God. What was it about Rocket, anyway, that made her abandon all sense of propriety? Somehow the fact that she was madly in love with him didn't strike her as a sound enough excuse for losing all semblance of good sense. Yet deep in her heart she couldn't help but feel it was his fault her brain fried whenever he touched her.

His fault for not being smart enough to love her back.

A woman wearing enough jewelry to subsidize a small nation finally wound up the anecdote she'd been relating and Victoria smiled and murmured a perfunctory response. For some reason the woman looked shocked, but before she could summon the energy to discover why, John offered the woman their excuses and gave Victoria's elbow a light tug. She drifted away in response to his guiding hand.

He bent his head to hers as he steered them toward the bar. "'Lovely' probably wasn't the best response to being told her pet poodle had died," he murmured.

"Um-hmm," she agreed vaguely. For just a moment the fog lifted from her brain and his face came into focus. His dark eyes were hooded, his eyebrows drawn together over the Roman thrust of his nose as he stared down at her, and she noticed he didn't appear any happier than she.

Her heart squeezed. As much as she'd love to assign all blame for this mess to him, in good conscience she couldn't. He hadn't asked her to fall in love with him and she'd certainly contributed her fair share to tonight's debacle. Perhaps even more so than him, if one went strictly by the facts, since she'd been the first to put her hands where they didn't belong. And she hadn't even had the grace to regret it—not until the realization of their failure to use a condom had exploded into her consciousness.

"Maybe trying to stick out the evening isn't such a hot idea after all," John said quietly.

She nodded. The chance to escape and the opportunity for privacy to deal with her tumultuous feelings was suddenly too attractive to pass up. "Yes. Let's go—"

"Ms. Hamilton," a soft feminine voice interrupted them. "Hello."

She blinked and turned to the young woman who'd brushed soft fingers across her forearm to get her attention. "Please," she responded automatically while her brain tried to process where she'd seen the sandy-haired woman and her stocky escort. "Call me Victoria." Then the facts clicked into place. "How are you, Mrs. Sanders? Are you enjoying the dance?"

"I'm fine and please, do call me Terri. The party is lovely."

"Yes, it is, isn't it? Have you met my fiancé?" Without awaiting an answer she turned to Rocket. "John, this is Terri Sanders and her husband, George. Terri was my father's administrative assistant. Terri, George, please meet John Miglionni."

"How do you do?" John shook hands with the couple. "If we were already introduced at Ford's memorial please forgive me," he said with an easy smile. "Between that and tonight's dance, I've met so many people my head is beginning to swim. So I'm officially declaring a break. Please. Won't you join us at our table? Allow me to buy you a drink."

An automatic protest rose in Victoria's throat. But she swallowed it. There was something about his white-toothed, megawatt smile as he poured on the charisma that served to pull her scattered thoughts together and she abruptly realized that Terri Sanders might well have information about her father. She had to get a grip on her wandering mind. A memory scratched for attention as John smoothly ushered everyone to the linen-draped table and she gave him a curious look. "Did you say something about a poodle?"

A faint smile crooked his lips. "Yeah. We'll talk about it later."

She managed to hold up her end of a superficial conversation while John collected drinks from the bar, but it wasn't until he'd returned and was emptying the tray onto the table that a substantive thought struck her. She reached out to touch Terri's hand. "I'm sorry," she said. "I never even thought to ask if you were laid off when my father died. I know there's a new CEO in place, I'm afraid I've been so caught up with my own concerns that I failed to follow through on the ramifications of Father's death for his other employees. You must think me terribly rude."

"Of course I don't," the other woman insisted. "And as it happens, very few jobs were lost. Your father ran a tight ship and he believed in delegating, so the infrastructure was in place to continue without him. I stayed on to tie up as many loose ends as I could and I actually had the opportunity to keep my position with the new CEO, but I accepted another offer from Soundhill Investments instead. They're a corporation your father often dealt with, so they were familiar with my work."

"She's the best," George added, smiling at his wife with pride.

"I have him trained to say that."

John and Tori laughed and he leaned forward, flashing an attentive, charming smile at the young woman.

"It sounds as if Soundhill's gain is definitely our loss. When do you start?"

"Three weeks from Monday. After a vacation to Ireland that George and I have had planned forever."

Victoria sat back and listened as John questioned Terri so skillfully that neither the young woman nor her husband appeared to have the slightest clue she was being interrogated. He drew from her the names of the current CEO and several others in the company who appeared to have benefitted from Ford's death. It was clear from Terri's responses that she had been a valuable employee and John played to that, as well, making much of her contribution and lamenting the fact that the company had let her services slip away without making more of an effort to retain them.

Victoria leaned toward the other woman. "John's right," she agreed softly. "My father was extremely lucky to have you. Doubly so, considering how difficult he could be to deal with most of the time. I doubt anyone would say he was an easy man, so working for him couldn't have been all roses."

"That's a fact," George Sanders said. "You, however, are a nicer person altogether." He draped his arm along the back of his wife's chair and strummed his fingertips up and down her upper arm. "Tell them about the bonuses, honey."

Terri bit her lip and glancing from John to her and back again. Finally she took a deep breath, softly exhaled, and straightened her shoulders. "I'm not sure if you're aware of this, but several years ago, for all intents and purposes, Ford moved the company headquarters to the Cayman Islands. Right after that he made a private agreement with the board to get his bonuses in bearer bonds."

Victoria blinked. "Yes?"

John apparently saw some significance, however, for after a moment's silence, he sucked in a breath, sat a little straighter, and pinned the AA in his sights. "Because a Cayman-registered business doesn't require that the bonds be reported to the IRS?"

"Yes. I made copies of the transactions and it would be a great relief to turn them over to you. While I know it's none of my business, those bonds are virtually the same thing as cash and since Ford's death I've never once heard them mentioned. I don't like the thought of them just floating around out there." She shot them an apologetic grimace. "I realize I should probably have reported this to the police myself, but I hesitated to make Ford's private finances public."

"I respect your loyalty." John was quiet for a moment, then said, "When do you leave for your trip to Ireland?"

"Well, that's the thing. Our flight leaves tomorrow afternoon."

"Where are the copies now?"

She hesitated, then blew out a breath and admitted, "I took them home with me when I left."

John's expression remained nonjudgmental. "Then why don't we follow you on our way home and gather whatever you want to give us? That way you can leave for your vacation with all the loose ends tied up."

"You wouldn't mind?"

John raised his eyebrows at Victoria, who smiled at the young woman. "Not at all," she said. "Just say the word when you're ready to go."

"Well, if you truly mean that, we were actually about to leave when I spotted you and thought I should say hello. We still have a great deal of packing to do."

"Excellent." She rose to her feet with alacrity. Maybe this night would finally end after all.

As soon as she and John climbed into his car, her sense of well-being vanished. The atmosphere between them grew tenser by the minute as they followed the Sanders to their home.

John turned to look at her at the first red light. "Tori, listen—"

The last thing she could bear was a rehash of their problems. They'd already said everything that needed to be said and it had netted them nothing but pain. "It was good of Terri to inform us of Father's bonds, wasn't it?" she said coolly, her eyes on the car in front of them.

"You think that was from the goodness of her heart?" He laughed shortly. "Sanders strikes me as bright enough to know when to cover her ass."

She turned in her seat to look at him directly. "What do you mean?"

"I have a feeling she's not as sure about the legality of those bonds as she claims and wants it on record that she did her best to inform someone in a position of authority—in this case you—should the situation ever come back to bite her on the butt."

She stared at him openmouthed. "My God. Nothing cynical about you, is there?"

"I prefer to call it realistic. She had the opportunity to tell the police herself—but what do you imagine it would've done to her job search if it had been all over the news that she'd spilled her former employer's private business?" He shrugged and fell silent, following the Sanders' car to an attractive middle-income neighborhood several miles from the club. A moment later he pulled into a driveway off a tree-lined street behind the other couple.

They followed Terri and George into a neat little brick house and down the hallway to a home office, where Terri opened the drawer of an oak filing cabinet. She extracted a slim file.

Turning, she handed it to Victoria and then smiled brilliantly. "I feel free for the first time in a long while. Now I truly can enjoy our vacation."

They exchanged a few pleasantries, then Victoria and John climbed into his car and drove away. The instant they turned the corner out of sight of the young couple's house, however, he pulled over to the curb, killed the engine, and turned on the overhead light. Victoria leaned over the console so they could both examine the copies of her father's bearer bonds inside the folder she'd flipped opened.

"Holy shit," he breathed a moment later and sat back in his seat. "Six-point-five million a year for the past five years. That's pretty good compensation." He looked at her. "Were any of the actual bonds accounted for when you went through your father's things?"

She'd been slow about a lot of things tonight, but she, too, had figured out that they should have been with her father's effects or at least listed on the asset sheet the lawyer had given her. "No."

He swore softly, turned off the overhead light and twisted around once more to gaze at her across the console. "You know what this means, don't you?"

"That absolutely anyone could have killed my father and walked away with a fortune in bearer bonds?"

"Yeah." His dark eyes gleamed enigmatically in the dim, diffused light that filtered through the windshield from a standard on the other side of the lot. "And that

I'm not going anywhere until we know for damn sure it wasn't anyone living in your house.''

John felt as if a huge boulder had been lifted off his chest and he didn't even try to pretend otherwise. Despite his insistence that it was time to leave, he'd felt lousy ever since the words had left his mouth. The feeling had only grown stronger in the face of Victoria's refusal to talk to him—or even look him in the eye if she had the least opportunity to do otherwise.

So having a legitimate reason to stay was the good news. The bad news was this case was seriously screwed up. Ford's having had a fortune in bearer bonds was purely overkill. The man'd had enough enemies as it was—throwing in a bundle in bonds that were cashable by anyone who got their hands on them merely made the possibilities too numerous to count.

The only thing he knew for certain about this mess was that he wasn't prepared to leave Tori and his kid alone to deal with it. He might not be worth a damn for their emotional health in the long run, but in the short run he was at least another bulwark to stand between them and whoever had killed Ford.

Victoria hadn't responded to his announcement one way or the other, and he turned to look at her leaning back against the passenger door. She looked shell-shocked and worn to a nub as she stared back at him.

He gripped the steering wheel to keep from reaching for her. ''Do I have your permission to search the mansion for the bonds?''

She nodded jerkily.

''Anyone could have taken them,'' he admitted. ''But there's no sense speculating who until we've done our best to make sure they aren't simply tucked away somewhere in the house. Once we have, I suppose we'll have to take the information to the police.''

''Dear God,'' she said, looking even more tired, ''you plan to do all that tonight?''

''No,'' he said, although in truth that had been his initial impulse. ''First thing in the morning.''

As it turned out, he didn't sleep worth a damn. Betting that Victoria hadn't, either, he rousted Jared out of bed at eight the following morning and the two of them were outside her rooms by eight-oh-seven. He knocked on the door to her suite as he finished explaining the situation to the teenager. The door swung open almost instantly, but no one was there. Then he adjusted his sights downward and found Esme beaming up at him.

''Hi! Have you come to play with me, then?''

''No, sweetie,'' Victoria's voice said from within the room. A second later she, too, was at the door. ''We're going to search for some missing things of your grandfather's. Hello, darling,'' she said to Jared, leaning forward to give him a peck on the cheek. ''I didn't expect to see you.''

''I thought he should be here,'' John said. ''Seeing as he's got the most to gain or lose from this latest development if we can give the cops another suspect to investigate.''

''Yes, he does,'' she agreed, barely sparing John a glance. ''I should have thought of that myself.''

''It sounds like looking for the proverbial needle in the haystack to me,'' Jared said a bit sullenly. ''Still, I suppose I'm game if everyone else is.''

''I'm game!'' Esme bounced up and down on her toes. ''I want to look, too, Mummy. Can I look for Grandpapa's things, too?''

"Sure. But this is not a game, Es, so I don't want to hear about it if you grow bored."

"'Kay."

John dragged his gaze away from Victoria and his daughter. Part of him wanted to claim them, to mark his territory so anyone who might have other ideas—including Tori, herself—could just think again. Another part of him, however, urged him to get a grip. Allowing himself to feel possessive was just begging for trouble. He knew better than to put himself out there where people were free to examine him and find him wanting.

The way his father always had.

But that kind of thinking was a fast track to nowhere and shoving his personal doubts behind a shield of professionalism, he said briskly, "I did some research on the Net last night. Bearer bonds have no registered owners, so the paying agent—in this case Ansbacher Cayman Limited—won't be able to say who the owner is. They can identify the party who received the last interest payment, but that's not of particular help at this moment, since the bank won't be open again until Tuesday morning. Meanwhile, it occurs to me that three spots in the house are more likely than others to have been used by your father."

"His offices and the master suite?" Victoria asked.

"Exactly."

"Then we're already screwed with a full third of our options," Jared said flatly. "Because DeeDee never moved out of Dad's suite, did she?"

Victoria shook her head, looking as discouraged as her brother.

John, however, merely shrugged. "So we'll ask her permission to search it."

"And if she says no?" Jared asked doubtfully.

He reined in his impatience at the continuing pessimism. "You and your sister are the legal owners," he said in a level tone. "As long as you give permission, we don't really need DeeDee's. But before we just write her off, why don't we go see what she has to say in the matter?"

"Don't like DeeDee," Esme muttered.

A slight smile tugged up one corner of Victoria's mouth and she reached down to lightly grip her daughter's shoulder. She met John's gaze over the little girl's head. "Do you mind if Esme and I start in Father's old office?"

"Not at all." He turned to Jared. " C'mon, kid. It looks like it's you and me."

He studied the teen as they strode down the corridor to the master suite. He'd been so busy worrying about controlling his own temper around the boy that it had taken him a while to notice Jared's mood, too, had been steadily deteriorating. "Everything okay with you?" he asked.

"Just friggin' swell."

O-kay. Precisely the opposite, it appeared. "Your friends giving you a bad time?"

"Some of them," Jared admitted with a lack of rancor that told John it probably wasn't the problem. "Most of them are cool, though." His mouth twisted. "Well, maybe not most of them," he admitted. "Since most seem to have a thing about asking stupid questions like what it's like to be accused of murder. Still, the ones I give a good goddamn about have been pretty cool."

"Like little Priscilla Jayne." John smiled at the thought of her. "How are things working out for her back home?"

Jared stiffened. "I wouldn't know. The number she gave me is disconnected."

Ah-hah. And therein lay the rub, he was guessing. "Mac wasn't real impressed with P.J.'s mom," he said slowly. "You want me to look into their whereabouts for you?"

For just a second, the teen looked as if he'd like nothing more than to accept the offer. Then a sullen, screw-you expression settled over his features. "No. If she wanted to talk to me, she would've given me a working number in the first place."

"Could've moved."

"Yeah. But I haven't, so she also could've called me with the new number. The hell with her."

He thought the kid was making a mistake but merely nodded. "You're the boss," he said mildly. "Let me know if you change your mind."

They arrived at the master suite then and he rapped on the door. Silence greeted his knock and he waited a moment, then knocked harder. When there was still no answer, he gave up all pretense of subtlety and pounded. "DeeDee!"

"Wha?" Her voice sounded sleepy and faraway.

"Open up. We need to talk to you."

"Come back later," she said blearily.

"No. Now."

"Oh, for—" The oath was cut off and dimly, behind the closed door, he distinguished the faint sound of bare feet slapping against the hardwood floor. A second later the door was ripped open and DeeDee stood glaring up at him.

She was the next best thing to naked.

Twenty-Six

John glanced at Jared, who was staring without blinking at DeeDee's lush breasts through her diaphanous baby-doll nightie. She obviously subscribed to the Frederick's of Hollywood school of lingerie, which leaned more toward showcasing a woman's assets than hiding them, and the kid's eyeballs were all but bugging out of his head.

His total absorption carved a slight smile into the corners of John's mouth. "You might wanna roll your tongue back into your head before we're called upon to move our feet," he advised drily. "I'd hate for you to trip and fall on your face. And you," he added sternly to Ford's widow, "go put on a robe or something. I think you've given Jared here all the education he can stand for one morning."

"Not true," Jared disagreed, his gaze eagerly taking in every exposed inch of the blonde's impressive curves. "I can stand a lot more."

But DeeDee gave John's crotch a quick once-over, shrugged, and turned on her bare heel to pad back to her room.

"Dang," Jared said wistfully. "She looks as good going as coming." He watched until his father's fifth wife, in her practically nonexistent top and teensy thong undies, had disappeared through a doorway.

Then he turned and jabbed his elbow into John's side. "Did you see that? She was checking you out to see if she'd given you a boner." He rocked back on his heels and slid fisted hands into his pants pockets to make his own incipient erection less noticeable. "She didn't even bother to see what she'd done to me."

"You're seventeen." John bumped shoulders companionably with Jared, understanding better than most how beneficial good old-fashioned teenage lust could be for what ailed a guy. "Something would have to be seriously skewed if she couldn't give you a hard-on."

"I suppose. Still, you're a guy and you're not *that* old."

"Yeah." He gave the boy a rueful smile. "I hardly creak at all when I move."

"So how come it didn't work with you?"

"Hell if I know. It's not as if I didn't enjoy the view as much as you. I guess I'm just a few years beyond allowing the sight of a naked woman to drive me into a frenzy of lust."

"Oh, man, not me," Jared said and he grinned, looking suddenly more carefree than John had ever seen him. "But feel free to bring on the nudie girls until I get as ho-hum about it as you."

DeeDee returned a few moments later wrapped in a red satin kimono. John noticed she'd taken the time to brush her hair, as well, and to apply lipstick and mascara. "Now," she said, looking at them without smiling. "What can I do for you gentlemen?"

"Victoria and I learned last night that Ford took his yearly CEO bonus in bearer bonds. They never showed up on the estate's asset list and before we turn the information over to the police, we want to make sure they're not merely filed away somewhere in the house.

To that end, we'd like your permission to search your suite."

She shrugged and stepped back from the doorway where they'd been politely waiting permission to enter. "Knock yourselves out," she invited. As if realizing how indifferent that sounded, she pasted on a sorrowful expression. "I haven't been able to bring myself to go though the dear man's effects, so everything is just as he left it. You can start in here, if you like, while I go get dressed."

Jared didn't look nearly as admiring as he watched her leave the room this time. "I don't get her at all," he said. "She's like Split-Personality Girl. One minute she acts as though my dad was the big love of her life and the next as if she could care less that he's dead."

"Yeah, she's a tough one to get a fix on, all right. I haven't been able to figure out what her story is, either. Maybe she's one of those people who just plain needs to be in the spotlight." Dismissing her, he thrust a forefinger at the small desk in the corner of the room. "How 'bout you start with that? I'll take the books off the shelves and go through those."

"Sure." But for a moment Jared merely stood in the same spot and stared at him. "What does a bearer bond look like, anyhow?"

"Excellent question." He pulled a sheet of paper from his hip pocket and snapped it open before passing it to the teen. "Here. This is one of the bond copies your dad's AA gave us last night."

"Fricking hell." Jared blew out a breath. "That needle in the haystack I mentioned earlier would probably be easier to locate. This is going to be a major pain in the butt."

He nevertheless buckled down to looking and John

was impressed with both the kid's work ethic and his willingness to continue the thankless job when an hour and a half later they'd finished searching the sitting room and were ready to move on to the bedroom. DeeDee had long ago left for the country club, leaving them free to divide the new space and Jared started inspecting his section without complaint.

Together they were lifting the king-size mattress to check between it and its matching box springs when the outer door in the other room suddenly banged open. *"John!"*

Victoria's voice was laced with such panic that man and boy exchanged one rapid-fire look and dropped the mattress. Before John could even round the end of the bed, the bedroom door slammed open and bounced off the inner wall as Victoria barreled into the room. Halting abruptly, she stared at him, wild-eyed.

"Oh, God, John, oh, *God*." Her moss-green eyes filled with tears. "Esme's gone!"

Sick with fear, Victoria could only stand rooted in the middle of the floor, breathing in ragged, panicked gulps, as she watched Rocket vault the corner of the bed, then eat up the distance between them with long strides.

Pulling up short in front of her, he reached out to grip her shoulders. "What do you mean gone?"

"As in *not where she ought to be!*" Her voice rose perilously close to hysteria. "As in *can't be found!*"

"Okay, shhh. I'm sorry, that was a stupid question. Take a deep breath, darlin'. Now let it out nice and slow—*that's* my girl. Now." His voice went from warm and crooning to authoritative and cool. "When did you see her last?"

The change made her blink back her tears, swallow her terror and concentrate. "Around nine-twenty," she said. "As I suspected, she grew bored with the search for Father's bonds, so I took her to Helen."

"And Helen discovered she wasn't where she was supposed to be when?"

"I don't know, maybe twenty minutes ago." She shook her head. "At least that's when she came to me. But of course she searched on her own for a while first."

"Had they done anything out of the ordinary before Esme went missing?"

"No. Helen said they played dolls for a while and that Es talked to Rebecca on the phone. Then she told Helen she was coming back to help me again."

"And she just let her go?" John demanded incredulously. His mouth twisting, however, he promptly shook his head. "Of course she did—Esme was in the house and going to join her mother." He tightened his grip on her shoulders. "Tell me every place you've looked for her already."

"Everywhere we could *think* to look within the house, including the kitchen and Cook's and Mary's rooms. We even searched the basement, despite the fact that Esme hates it and would never voluntarily go down there. I've looked up in my workshop and all the places on the estate where I've allowed her to play since the reporters started hanging around the front gate."

"How about the front part of the grounds?"

"No. There was no point since I've told her repeatedly not to—" She cut herself off. "Oh, God. How stupid can I be? Of course that's going to make it more attractive to her." Abandoning the discussion, she wrenched free and sprinted for the door.

He passed her before she'd even reached the top of the stairs. By the time she hit the foyer at the bottom, he was already out the door and headed down the main drive. The distance between them widened even farther as he suddenly left the road and disappeared into the live oaks and pine trees dotting the grounds.

John slowed down as he hit the trees. He sucked in and expelled slow, careful breaths to regulate his pounding heart. God, he could barely hear above the sound of his own harsh breathing and to his surprise he realized he was almost as panicked as Tori.

Allowing emotions free rein served only to screw up the efficiency of an op—he knew that better than most. So to discover himself doing exactly that was not merely a shock, it was an unacceptable departure from his usual cool-headed effectiveness.

Identifying the problem and doing something about it were two separate issues, however. No way in hell was this a standard op. It concerned his kid, she was just a little peanut of a girl, and she was missing.

All the same he forced himself to stand still, quiet his breathing and open his ears. Behaving like a raw recruit would benefit no one.

The minute he settled down he heard what he should have heard earlier. A man's voice mumbled in the distance, near the wall that provided the estate's privacy. Quietly, John headed in that direction, but it wasn't until he'd gone about a hundred feet that the words turned from an indistinguishable drone into distinct words.

"Hey, there, little girl," he heard an artificially jovial voice murmur. "Look over here. Your name's Esme, right? You sure are pretty, Esme. Can you smile for the camera? C'mon, girlie, look this way."

Anger percolating in his veins, John moved silently toward the cajoling voice. The trees had thickened here but he followed the sound to a place where they formed a clearing. And there, in the dappled sunlight on the estate side of the wall, squatted a middle-aged man wearing a good white shirt and a bad comb over. He was aiming a high-end digital camera at Esme, who stood stock-still in front of him, clearly too scared to move, while he alternately flattered and tried to wheedle her into looking his way as he snapped off frame after frame.

John's first inclination was to rip the man's head from his body in the most painful manner devisable. He took a step forward to do exactly that before it occurred to him that Esme was already terrified. He drew a calming breath, because the last thing she needed was to witness an act of violence carried out by a man she trusted. He became aware of Victoria and Jared calling her name as they crashed through the grounds behind him, but so far neither his daughter nor the reporter appeared to notice. Hearing the two grow closer, however, solidified his own decision between going in like Rambo to snatch Es from the jaws of danger, or adapting a more covert approach.

There was really no choice. The "jaws" weren't all that dangerous and rushing in might send Esme into a panic. Hunkering down, he duck-walked from tree trunk to tree trunk until he was as close to her as he could get. "Es," he called out softly.

Her head came up and she swung in his direction, her big, dark eyes searching wildly through the shadows beneath the trees.

Still in a crouch, he eased a leg's-reach away from

the trunk so she could see him and held out an inviting arm. "Come to Daddy, darlin'."

"Wuffs!" she shrieked and hurtled her sturdy little body across the distance separating them. She threw herself into his arms just as Victoria and Jared burst into the clearing. John surged to his feet with her clinging to his neck and everyone spotted everyone else at once. Victoria and Jared called out Esme's name, Esme yelled, "Mummy!" and stretched her arms out yearningly toward her mother and the reporter bit off a succinct swear word and began to sidle away.

"Oh, no, you don't," John said grimly. He thrust Esme into Tori's reaching arms and ordered Jared to get them out of there. The teen's instant compliance freed him to take off after the rapidly departing photographer.

He caught up with him just as the other man was about to clamber over the stone wall. Reaching out, he seized him by the back of his shirt and yanked him down. The reporter's camera swung in a wild arc as he tumbled to the ground and, bending down, John grasped it by its long lens. He ripped it off over the man's head, not particularly worried when the strap momentarily caught around the photographer's neck before it wrenched free.

The man rolled over and began scrambling away on his hands and knees. Slinging the camera around his own neck, John reached back down to grasp the reporter by the back of his shirt and the waistband of his pants. The guy screamed like a girl, but John ignored the shrill racket as he lifted him and turned toward the wall.

The noise attracted the attention of the other reporters and they stampeded down from the gate to see what was happening. The first of them arrived just as John was hoisting the reporter chest-high. He braced himself and flung the man over the wall.

They scattered to get out of the way and as their comrade landed with a thud at their feet he raked them all with a contemptuous gaze. "The next bloodsucker to climb this wall will get a helluva lot worse than your friend there," he said, yanking the camera off over his head. Holding it by its woven strap, he swung it with all his strength at the stone wall and was filled with grim satisfaction when it smashed into several pieces.

Shouting in outrage, the photographer picked himself up off the ground. "You son of a bitch!" he yelled in a voice that was several octaves higher than it had been when cajoling Esme to look his way. "That's destruction of private property. I'll *sue* your ass!"

"You do that," John said. "I'll countersue for trespassing and harassment of a minor. Or maybe I should just talk to the police about charging you with attempted kidnapping. For all I know that's why you were skulking around trying to get a little girl to come to you in the first place." Ignoring the man's sputtered protest, he widened his attention to include the rest of the fifth estate. "Broken cameras will be the least of your worries if I ever catch any of you messing with my daughter again. *Nobody* terrorizes my kid and gets away with it." His gaze traveled back to the man who'd done exactly that, and this time he allowed all the blood lust he'd managed to tamp down to flare in his eyes. He smiled narrowly when the man jerked back as if physically threatened.

"You got off easy," he told him flatly. "Be grateful, because if you'd harmed one hair on her head I would've snapped your neck without blinking an eye."

Ignoring the spate of questions and frantically whirring cameras, he turned on his heel and strode from sight into the trees.

It wasn't until he reached the smooth expanse of the lawn and saw Victoria coming toward him that he realized what he had just publicly revealed. Swearing beneath his breath, he picked up his pace to give them a moment's privacy before Jared, too, who was strolling in Victoria's wake with Esme riding his shoulders, reached them.

"Is Es okay?" he demanded the moment they met.

"Yes. She was rattled to find herself in the woods with a man she didn't know, but she's got that child's ability to bounce back. How about you?" She touched his forearm. "You looked pretty grim when we left you back there. Are you all right?"

"Well, there's good news and there's bad news about that. The good news is you were right."

She blinked. "That's always a happy circumstance, of course. What exactly was I right about this time?"

He hesitated a second, but couldn't deny the rush of protective feelings that had come over him in the woods. "That there's no way in hell I will ever hurt that little girl. Esme's adventure drove that home like nothing else could. I really wanted to rip that guy's head from his body, Tori. But I knew it would only further terrorize Es, and the fact that I didn't even have to think before putting her feelings first made me realize that I have a lot more control around kids than I thought. So I guess I'm not like my father after all."

"Damn straight you're not," she agreed fiercely. Then her expression gentled and she stroked soft fingertips along the raised veins on the back of his hand.

"I'm gratified you finally understand that. Does this mean you're ready to claim her as your daughter?"

"Well, that's kind of the bad news." He studied her face for a second, hating to admit what he'd done. But there was no help for it and he finally said, "I just did that in a very public way."

"What do you mean?"

"When I picked up the photographer to toss him back over the wall, he screamed like one of those chicks in a horror flick and all the other newshounds came running. I said in front of them all that he was lucky I didn't break his neck for messing with my kid."

"Tell me they didn't capture that on film!" She looked at him in horror. "Wait, maybe they'll think you were speaking generically—sort of an I'm-going-to-marry-the-mother-therefore-her-kid-is-my-kid thing. But, God, Rocket, if anyone digs deeper—"

Her obvious desire to keep his parentage under wraps was like a swift kick in the balls and suddenly his moment of feeling okay about the Miglionni genes evaporated. For the first time he acknowledged that his feelings for Victoria went so much deeper than sex it wasn't even funny. He had to face the fact that he'd been kidding himself for a long time. From practically the get-go, he'd known his feelings for her were different than anything he'd ever felt for any other woman. But his image of himself had been formed early, and deep in his heart he had feared that no matter how far he'd traveled from his roots he might never be good enough for her.

The fact that she agreed—that she was horrified by the very thought of the world learning he was Esme's father—cut to the quick. *So this is love. Hurts like a son of a bitch.*

His back went militarily erect. *So, what'd you expect, fool? You pretty much knew last night that in the long run an uptown girl like her would never be content with a guy like you.* His gut felt overcrowded with frozen knots, but he managed to give her an amiable nod. "'Fraid they did."

"We have to tell Es ourselves before word of this starts making the rounds."

"Well, I'll tell you—I was just one *hell* of a chatty individual today, because I may have done that already, as well. I don't remember exactly what I said to her in the woods, but I think it was along the lines of, 'Come to Papa.'"

"She must have been too shook up to notice," Victoria said. "Either that or she thought it was an extension of the pretend-engagement game, because she didn't say a word about it to me."

Yeah, she's probably as thrilled by the idea of having me in her life as you are, he thought with a touch of bitterness. Understanding on a fatalistic level, however, that he was too late to claim mother or daughter, he forced himself to say with professional equanimity, "As you say, then, ma'am, we'll tell her together."

"Ma'am?" Her jaw dropped, but she immediately firmed it up and shot him a crooked smile that said she was wise to his teasing. "Don't you think we've come a ways past ma'am?"

Not nearly as far as I assumed we had, apparently. Jared and Esme were only a few steps away, though, so he merely looked at her.

Victoria gave him a puzzled stare. "Are you all right, John?"

"Hell, yeah," he said briskly. "I'm…fine. Absolutely dandy."

Twenty-Seven

"Look, Mummy! Up here! I'm up in the tree!"

Victoria stopped short beneath the black walnut tree that shaded the new south wing of the mansion, her head jerking back to peer up through its dark green leaves. Helen had informed her just moments ago that John had taken Esme out for a walk. She doubted he'd try to talk to their daughter without her present, but he'd been oddly distant ever since he'd returned from dealing with the reporter in the woods. So she had set out after them, a vague uneasiness nipping at her mood.

The last place she'd expected to find the two of them was on a fat branch high up in a tree, sitting side by side with their legs dangling into space. Her heart lodged in her throat when Esme leaned forward to grin down at her, but John casually stretched a strong arm in front of her, bracing his palm against the tree trunk to form a bridge for their daughter to hang over.

Their daughter. She still wasn't accustomed to the idea of that.

"Me and John climbed up here!" the little girl crowed and Victoria marveled once again at her daughter's lightning-fast powers of recuperation. She'd half expected Es to stick to her like glue for the rest of the afternoon, but within fifteen minutes of being rescued from her scare in the woods, she'd been off and running.

"Come up, Mummy! John was just going to tell me sumpin important."

She gaped at him, dumbfounded. He *was* going to tell Esme he was her father! Without her. She subjected him to a hard stare, but if he felt the least bit embarrassed to be caught cutting her out of the process it didn't show. He merely looked back at her with that infuriatingly blank, noncommittal expression she hated.

What was his problem? The way he was acting you'd think *she'd* done something wrong. But it wasn't her who'd told the world he was Esme's father before the two of them could even tell their daughter. It wasn't *she* who had then vanished.

"Come up, Mummy!"

"Oh, I intend to," she said grimly, studying the intimidating gap that stretched between her and the first branch. "Just as soon as I figure out how."

John sighed and turned to Esme. "Scooch over, little darlin' and hug the tree trunk there real tight while I go help your mama."

Gazing at him as if he were a god descended from on high, the child did as he commanded.

"Now don't budge an inch, you hear?"

"'Kay."

When John appeared satisfied she'd do exactly as instructed, he swung lithely down through the branches until he stood on the bottom-most limb. Squatting, he glanced up to make sure Esme hadn't moved, then anchored himself with one hand and leaned down to extend the other to Victoria. "C'mon," he growled impatiently when she didn't immediately reach out to grasp it. "We don't want to leave her unattended a second longer than necessary. Grab hold with both hands.''

And then what? She wasn't exactly Miss Petite to be lifted one-handedly from that position. Still, such was his air of command that she reached up to do as he said. And even as she wrapped her hands around the hot, hard strength of his wrist and forearm, his physical power wasn't what she questioned aloud. Instead, she heard herself demanding in a low voice, ''Why are you acting this way?''

Not bothering to answer, he latched onto her forearm and pulled her up as if she weighed nothing at all, grasping her other arm and rising to his feet as he brought her level with his branch. She was still gasping from the shock of her rapid ascent when he disengaged her hands from his arm and placed them on a limb above their heads. For just a second they stood chest to breast, arms stretched overhead, touching from wrist to elbow, his hands tough-skinned and warm as they settled her grip around the limb.

He stared down at her, his expression unreadable. ''Got your footing?''

She nodded, aware of him in every cell of her body. Then he was gone, swarming up the tree to reclaim his seat next to Esme.

She climbed much more cautiously, but a moment later she gingerly edged her bottom onto the thick branch next to her daughter. Digging her fingers into the limb's bark, she gazed around and remembered when this tree was set away from the house. Now, with the new addition, if she leaned a little to the right she could see down into the kitchen. Fascinated by the perspective, she watched Mary polish silver at the big worktable as she talked to Cook, who was working at the stove. The closed windows that accommodated the air-conditioning prevented Victoria from hearing the actual words being said and her attention drifted until she found herself gazing down at the set of windows almost directly in front of her. Everything looked so different from this vantage point that it took her a moment to realize they looked into her father's new office. The one Rocket currently used.

"Isn't this super, Mummy?"

"Yes, it's very interesting," she agreed, smiling down at Esme. "I don't believe I've ever climbed this tree before." She wasn't up here to admire the view, however. Looking past her daughter, she studied Rocket's closed face. "Where did you disappear to after Esme's big adventure?"

"I wanted to give Terri Sanders a call before she left on her trip. It occurred to me she might have some ideas about Miles Wentworth's dealings with your father."

"And did she?"

"Yes. Apparently Ford promised to put Miles in charge of the European division. So he lost out bigtime when your father died."

"Which means—" she cut her eyes toward Esme.

"Exactly. My favorite suspect had no motive."

Esme wiggled impatiently and Victoria sucked in a breath until she saw that Rocket's arm was behind the little girl's squirmy bottom, providing a bulwark between her and the long drop to the ground. Her daughter turned impatient eyes on her.

"I don't care about the mile man. John has sumpin important to tell me." Folding her hands in her lap, she turned to Rocket. "Go ahead, then."

"Yes, John," Victoria said pleasantly. "Do go ahead."

He didn't even spare her a glance. Focused on Esme, he cleared his throat. "You remember how your mama told you that your daddy couldn't be with you?"

"Uh-huh. But God wanted Mummy to have a special little girl, so He sent *me* to her." She turned to Victoria. "Didn't He, Mummy?"

"Yes, He did."

"Yeah, that's pretty much the story I heard, too."

Esme may not have heard the sarcasm in John's voice, but Victoria did, and she stared at him over her daughter's head as he tweaked Esme's braid to redirect her attention back to him. She didn't get it—what did he have to be so miffed about?

"Anyhow," he told the child, "since God did such a good job the first time around, He decided to send you your father, too."

"Huh?"

"That would be me. I'm your daddy."

Her little eyebrows pleated, then as if she suddenly understood, her brow cleared and she gave a decisive nod. "My pretend daddy," she said, clearly remembering their talk of make-believe engagements. She flashed him a great big pleased-with-herself smile.

His own dark brows gathered over the thrust of his nose and Victoria thought that father and daughter looked so much alike it was a wonder no one had ever noted the resemblance before.

John made an obvious effort to erase his frown. He rubbed a hand over the back of his neck. "No, sweetheart. Your *real* father." He looked over her head at Victoria. "Are you gonna just sit there, or do you want to help me out here?"

He looked a little desperate, but five minutes ago he'd been perfectly willing to go behind her back, so she wasn't feeling particularly charitable. She rounded her eyes at him. "Oh, you need *my* help?" she inquired sweetly. "And here I thought you wanted to handle everything on your own."

Then guilt ruined her nice moment of self-righteousness. This probably wasn't the best time to get bitchy. It was Esme's future that would ultimately be affected—not to mention that her daughter had turned to her in confusion. She gently brushed a wavy strand of hair from Esme's eyes.

"It's true, sweetie," she said softly. "John is your real daddy."

The little girl blinked big, puzzled eyes up at her. "But how come he didn't come 'til now?"

"We didn't know how to find each other, so there wasn't any way to let him know about you."

But it hit her suddenly that she *had* possessed a way of finding him. She'd had his tattoo to go by. God knew she'd spent enough time during their week in Pensacola fiddling with it, tracing it with her fingers, outlining it with her tongue. And while the words *Swift, Silent* and *Deadly* were the ones most burned into her brain, *2nd Recon Bn* was also inscribed across the bottom. She could have taken that knowledge and his marine handle and tracked him down. It would have been embarrassing and it would have taken some effort, but if she'd really, truly wanted to involve him in Esme's life, it could have been done. She glanced at him with a dawning sense of guilt that she hadn't been fair.

It was a feeling that increased as she saw the tenderness on his face as he gazed at Esme, who had turned her attention back to him.

"You been here a long time," the little girl said. "How come you didn't tell me you was my daddy?"

"Your mom—that is, *we*—wanted to be sure I had the ability to be a good parent before we said anything. No sense getting your hopes up if I turned out to be a dud."

"You're not a dud," she said indignantly.

"Yeah, that's what we finally decided, too. That—" he cleared his throat again "—I'm good enough to be your papa, after all."

Victoria's heart melted.

Esme's must have also, for she stared up at him with shining eyes. "You're truly my daddy?"

"Yeah."

She bounced on the branch. "So you're gonna be with Mummy and me forever and ever?"

"No!" He seemed to realize he'd rapped out the word like a drill sergeant, for he gentled his voice. But his tone was no less resolute when he reiterated, "*No. I'm your real daddy, but the engagement is still just pretend. And I know it's confusing, baby, but you've got to keep that part to yourself.*" He drilled Victoria with a hard-eyed look over Esme's head.

She felt as if he'd reached across their daughter and backhanded her. *Well. You certainly can't ask for a plainer message than that.* Clearly she was good enough to sleep with, but he was letting her know loud and clear that he still wasn't the marrying kind and she'd be wise not to get any ideas to the contrary.

She couldn't believe how much it hurt and she angled her body slightly away from them as Esme began bombarding John with questions. Staring through the leaves at the first-floor section that comprised Ford's new office, she forced her face into a neutral expression that wouldn't give away the world of misery his words had thrust her into.

She tried to collect her thoughts, but they kept spinning in a kaleidoscope of choppy words and broken images that shifted and altered and refused to form any kind of coherent whole. A flash here said she shouldn't be so surprised—it wasn't as if they'd ever promised each other permanency. But a jumbled recollection there reminded her of John's protectiveness toward her. Her rebellious memory briefly taunted her with a glimpse of the look he always wore when he was inside her. Scalding pain radiated along every nerve ending, because she'd truly believed what they had was so much more than sex, that it had meant something to him, too, not just her. And, oh, God. She hurt.

She hurt.

She hurt.

After what felt like a lifetime spent staring at the side of the house as she eased breaths past the ball of fire in her chest, an aberration began to niggle for her attention. There was something…not right…between what she'd swear were the inside dimensions of Father's office and what she was currently looking at and she seized the distraction gratefully, using it as a focal point to keep all this clawing agony at bay. Then little by little, the architect in her began to think independently of her anguish. Her mind had registered an apparent discrepancy. But what was it and what could account for it? She studied the area and stared in the windows. She ran measurements in her head. And suddenly it sank in.

"Oh, my God," she said. "*That's* why that room has always bothered me." Turning to Esme, which meant facing John once again, as well, she forced composure where she felt none. "I'm going to go down now, sweetie. I'd rather you didn't stay up here very much longer, either. It's almost time for lunch." She cast a glance at Rocket, but the pain crashed back over her in a red-hot wave and she quickly jerked her gaze away again.

"Be careful," she told her daughter and saw with a little wash of bitterness that she wouldn't be missed for Esme had already turned back to chat animatedly with John. Taking her own advice, she made her way down to the bottom branch, where she stared in dismay at the considerable drop to the ground.

"Wait a sec," John called down. "I'll give you a hand down."

"No!" God, no. She didn't think she could bear to be touched by him right now. Not when she knew it wouldn't hold close to the same meaning for him that it did for her. The instinctive denial had come out too abruptly, though, and she flung a vacuous smile in his general direction. "That is, no, thank you. I'm sure I can handle this."

For a moment, she merely stared down at the limb beneath her feet and wondered how the hell she planned to do that. Disliking the helplessness of that mind-set, however, she forced herself to concentrate. She was an intelligent woman and this was hardly nuclear fusion. She crouched down and straddled the branch. Slowly she lay along its length on her stomach, and wrapping her hands and ankles around the limb, she eased herself over the side.

And suddenly she was on the underside of the branch, looking up. *Oh, shit.* She could see John and Esme's feet and legs overhead, but luckily they couldn't see her hanging upside down, clinging to the branch like a damn monkey. At least she hoped they couldn't.

Either way, she couldn't stay here all day. Uncrossing her ankles, she let her legs drop and gripped the branch with all her might as she prepared to hang by her hands. She intended to get as close to the ground as possible before letting go.

That was the plan, anyhow. But she overestimated her upper body strength or underestimated the weight-velocity ratio of her dropping legs or figured *something* wrong, because the next thing she knew she'd garnered a nasty case of bark-burn on her palms as her body weight ripped them from the tree, and the ground was rushing up to meet her. She landed in a heap.

"You okay down there?" John inquired in an aloof voice.

She picked herself up. "I'm fine," she said, dusting herself off. *Like you care.* "Just had a little trouble sticking the landing." Gathering her tattered dignity, she hobbled toward the back corner of the house.

By the time she reached the kitchen door, however, she knew she was more shaken by the fall than bruised. And by the time she reached Father's new office, she'd shoved her unruly, roiling emotions into the darkest closet her mind could produce and slammed the door. She'd deal with them later. Right now she had to find out if her theory was correct. She had to see if there truly was a false wall at the west end of the office.

Something had always disturbed her about this room and now she knew what it was. Its inner length was shorter than the outside wall suggested. While she'd never consciously observed the discrepancy between exterior and interior measurements, her mind had apparently made note of it at one time or another and had been trying to feed her the information whenever she'd had occasion to be in the room.

She crossed to the floor-to-ceiling bookcase at the far end of the room and visually examined it. The whole unit must swing out somehow, she decided. Stepping closer, she felt carefully along the outside edge of its ornate molding, palpating it inch by inch in hopes of locating some kind of pressure latch. When that availed her nothing, she went over the same ground again, only this time along the molding's surface.

It wasn't until she applied pressure against the recessed paneling forming the interior of the built-in that she felt something give beneath her fingers. She'd found a buried latch, but the bookshelves didn't budge. Maintaining steady pressure on the spot, she continued feeling her way up the interior of the case with her free hand. That didn't garner results, so she inched her fingers along its ceiling. And suddenly she found a second pressure point. The case still didn't move, but she realized the surprise of finding the second latch had made her relax the pressure she'd been applying against the first, and she firmly pressed both.

The bookcase swung silently open.

"Oh, my God." Despite her newly realized belief that there had to be a secret space behind the wall, she was startled to actually discover it. It was simply too Nancy Drew and people didn't just step into girl detective books.

There was nothing the least bit fictional about the hidden bay, however—the space behind the bookcase was incontrovertible. It was only about eighteen inches deep, with a narrow shelf at the top that contained a single box. She reached out and opened it.

She fully expected to find the missing bearer bonds

by this time and she did, but after mentally adding them up two times, their sheer cumulative value still made her whistle. She put them back in the box, closed the lid, and stood back. *Now* what did she do?

She knew she should take them straight to John, but her heart ached at the thought of facing him. Yet, what other choice did she have? Depressed, she closed the bookcase.

"Father must have hidden them," she muttered in an attempt to cheer herself up. "So at least everyone in the house is off the hook."

"Well, now," said a dry voice from behind her. "As much as I'd love to simply leave it at that, I've worked too damn hard for those babies to let you add them to the estate fund where I'll never see a penny."

Startled, Victoria whipped around. To her surprise DeeDee stood not five feet away. The other woman was dressed in her tennis whites and sneakers, one of the rare times Victoria had ever seen her without her signature sky-high heels. Her hair was twisted up in an artful froth of curls, her face was fully made up and two diamond tennis bracelets glittered at her wrists.

But it was the accessory at her side that commanded Victoria's full attention. For her father's widow held a knife in her hand that had the longest, wickedest looking blade she had ever seen in her life.

And DeeDee gripped it like she meant business.

Twenty-Eight

"Are you talking about these?" Victoria gave the box of bonds on the shelf at her back a quick glance over her shoulder, then turned her attention back to DeeDee. Her gaze drifted instantly to the knife, which fascinated her in much the same way a snake might. Forcing herself to look away, she peered into DeeDee's face. "What do you mean you worked too hard for them?"

Then she wished she hadn't asked, because only one thing made sense. She was very much afraid she already knew the answer, and like an idiot, she just blurted it out. "Dear God. You killed Father, didn't you?"

Her voice emerged as little more than a horrified croak, but DeeDee clearly heard her all the same. The other woman shrugged, patted the blade of the knife against the open palm of her free hand and said conversationally, "You really are the biggest pain in the ass, you know that? I pulled off the perfect crime—although that seems a pretty harsh word for it since—as that song in *Chicago* goes—he had it coming. Still, you gotta admit I was good and in a week or so I would've been out of here and home free. But, no. Oh, no. You just had to go poking around and discover the secret closet, didn't you? How the hell did you find it, anyhow?''

Victoria gathered her wits and launched into an explanation that she intended to be full of detail and most importantly *long*. ''It was more a feeling than anything concrete. Every time I was in this room something just felt…wrong. I kept thinking it ought to be lighter, or taller, or longer, or somethi—''

''Never mind,'' DeeDee cut her off. ''I don't care. The only thing that matters is that you managed to screw everything up. And isn't that just my luck?'' She shook her head, her blond curls bobbing and an edge of bitterness crept into her tone. ''You know, I really thought I'd hit the jackpot when your father married me. I was so happy to have money again and be in the company of the movers and shakers that I didn't even care about the prenup he made me sign. At least at first.''

The reminder, from Victoria's point of view, was unfortunate, since it made DeeDee's eyes darken and her mouth twist. With clear, sinister intent, the woman took a step toward her.

''But then you had to live with him,'' Victoria hastened to interject. *Keep her talking. Just keep her talking while you figure out how the hell you're going to wiggle your way out of this.* ''That can't have been easy. He was a difficult man.'' Oh, God. Where was John when she really needed him?

Luckily for her, DeeDee apparently wasn't immune to sympathy. What's more, she clearly wanted someone to know and appreciate how clever she'd been, for she stopped and nodded. ''Right. Then I had to live with the bastard. The funny part is, I knew going in that I could put up with his crappy temper and power plays.

What I didn't count on was having to sleep every damn night of the week with a man old enough to be my father.'' She shuddered. ''That just about killed me, let me tell ya.''

Victoria really wished she hadn't used that particular description, for the word hung in the air between them and seemed to strengthen DeeDee's determination. Her father's widow—*no, face it, Tori, his killer*—squared her shoulders and took another step in her direction.

Victoria backed up, holding out her hands, palms out. ''You don't want to do this, DeeDee.''

To her surprise, the other woman stopped once again. ''No,'' she agreed in a tone suggesting she wasn't particularly happy about it, ''I don't—or else I would've stuck you before you even knew I was in the room. You're such a goody two-shoes, it makes me wanna barf, but you let me stay after Ford's death when you could've kicked me out. Of course, that would have given me the excuse I needed to leave with the bonds without raising suspicion.'' That apparently recalled her annoyance, but she shrugged it aside. ''Still, you didn't have to be so decent to me.''

''So why didn't you simply take the bonds in the first place? Why kill Father?''

''Are you kidding? Surely you knew him better than that. It was pure chance that I even saw him open the bookcase one night and I gotta tell you, when I came back later and discovered what he'd hidden here, I just knew I'd hit the mother lode. But the more I thought about it, the more I realized that no way in hell would Ford just roll over and quietly accept my taking them. There might not be a damn thing he could do about it legally, but when did that ever stop him from getting what he wanted? Ford wasn't one to give up what was his and he'd probably have a contract out on me quicker than you can say, 'Put that on my tab.'" A new thought clearly disgruntled her. "Worse, he had contacts all over the world, so he'd sure as hell make certain everyone knew I'd stolen from him. Even if I lived long enough to spend the bonds, no one who counted would have welcomed me the way they should have. So I put it off."

Her face hardened. "Then the night of the dinner party, Ford told me he was divorcing me. That bastard virtually said he expected me to be the perfect little hostess for his fucking soiree, then pack my stuff and start looking for a new place to live because he was *tired* of me." She glared at Victoria, the flat of the knife blade slapping rapidly against her palm. "*He* was tired of *me*. So, you know, I didn't plan what happened. But when I found him in the library where the kid had knocked him out, and he woke up and demanded a hand up as if I were his goddamn lackey...well, it was the last straw."

Victoria believed her and the fact that it hadn't been a cold-blooded execution gave her a moment of hope. "So just take the bonds and leave, DeeDee. I won't tell anyone."

The other woman's eyes narrowed. "Do I look stupid to you?"

"No, of course not. But you want to get away with the money, *I* want to live and—"

"Ten seconds after I'm out the door you'll be yelling for the Italian Stallion."

A bitter laugh escaped Victoria. "Right. As if *he'd* give a rip."

"Get out!" DeeDee shot her a look rife with skep-

ticism. "You two have something hot and heavy going."

"Yeah, so I thought, too. But John made it plain as
could be today it was a temporary fling that's now
over." Not liking the gathering resolution she saw on
DeeDee's face, she rushed to ask, "Why did you push
that phony engagement between us, anyway? I mean,
you knew what no one else did—that John's only reason for being here was to find Jared and clear his name.
I would've thought, given the secret you were hiding,
you would have wanted him out of here."

"Yeah, that was a mistake. It bugged me that a guy
so young and hot seemed to prefer you to me. And it
was clear that the two of you had some hang-ups about
each other. So I shoved you together because I could
and then got all caught up enjoying my private little
joke. Too caught up, as it turns out. I thought I was so
smart to be pulling a fast one right under everyone's
noses—*especially* your darling P.I.'s. But I guess I mis-
calculated. I assumed *he* was the one I had to keep an
eye on—not you. My mistake."

Victoria glanced covertly around the office, looking
for something, *anything,* she might use to help her out
of this predicament. "Even so, I'm impressed with the
way you resisted rushing your exit. That was smart."

It turned out to be the wrong thing to say, for the
other woman's eyes went hard as diamonds. "Yes,
dammit, I handled the situation brilliantly. Until *you*
had to go ruin everything. So let's quit screwing around
here. We both know the only way I'm ever going to
get out of this with both my bonds and my freedom is
if you aren't running around kicking up a storm. So be
a good girl. There's the closet just waiting to conceal

a new secret. Do us both a favor and get in without a fuss.''

''Sure.'' Victoria held her hands up in a hey-I'm-not-arguing-here gesture. ''Whatever you say.'' Better to spend time in a stifling closet until someone came to let her out than be stabbed. Putting on a face to show how well she was cooperating, she took a baby step backward.

Her thoughts must have somehow shown, however, for DeeDee gave her a smug smile.

She stopped dead. ''What?''

''Did I mention it's soundproof?''

Victoria started to panic at the thought of slowly suffocating in a small confined space, then saw the pleased-with-herself expression on DeeDee's face and forced herself to relax. ''Why are you doing this? I thought you didn't want to hurt me.''

''Yeah, well, maybe I changed my mind. Maybe the more I think of the way you torpedoed all my hard work, the less charitable I'm feeling.''

''Someone will find me.''

''You think? Didn't you say you and John weren't on the greatest terms? So probably not, dear, especially after I tell him you had an emergency in London. But hey, he does seem fond of the brat for some damn reason, so just to show you how big-hearted I can be, I will let him know you wanted him to watch her for you.''

Victoria's anger and determination rose with every word DeeDee uttered. One way or another, it appeared, the other woman intended for her to die. If it was bloodless and DeeDee didn't have to watch, she probably figured it didn't really count. Well, she'd always said DeeDee wasn't too bright. For if she had been, she would have kept her mouth shut. Victoria had been willing to take her chances with the closet until the bitch had painted it as a death trap.

"Or maybe I should just leave the brat with Helen," DeeDee continued, clearly enjoying having the upper hand, or perhaps simply the thought of messing with her mind. "Because, honey, I'd sure like a piece of that man. And if you're out of the picture and he's unencumbered…well." She slowly stroked her free hand down her curves. "Um-um. Might as well show him what a real woman can do."

All right. Tori's chin shot up. *That does it!*

Twenty-Nine

John would have sworn he knew females, but Esme was a revelation. Apparently an event wasn't an event for a little girl until it had been talked over with her best friend. With a bemused smile, he left his daughter punching out Rebecca's number on the phone and headed outside.

This had been both the best and the worst day of his life. If anyone had told him six weeks ago he'd be thrilled to be a father, he would have laughed in that person's face and invited him to have his head examined. Yet here he was, reeling beneath the weight of emotions he never even dreamed existed and he liked it. No, "liked" was too weak a word. He flat-out loved it.

Yet today he'd also realized he was in love with Tori and neither had he known it was possible to hurt as badly as he did. Knowing that she didn't return his feelings was like a knife buried in his heart. He brooded about it as he headed down toward the woods where he'd discovered Esme and the reporter.

He kicked aside a pinecone. Well, hey, her loss. If she was too big a snob to see what a good deal she'd be getting in him, the hell with her.

Except…that didn't sound right. He came to a stop, hands thrust deep in his pants pockets as he stared into space. If he'd learned anything during his time with Victoria, it was that she was far from a snob. So, why the hell had she acted so horrified that he'd informed the world he was Esme's dad?

Well, okay, there might be the fact that the news Nazis would do their best to turn the information into a three-ring circus. A minor little detail, but you know women—they could be funny about these things.

He rolled his shoulders uneasily. All right, not such a minor detail. Still, he'd been hyperaware of her up in the tree and he hadn't missed the fact that she was pissed.

Of course, that might have something to do with the way he'd been preparing to tell Esme he was the kid's father without her, which he had to admit hadn't been the brightest idea he'd ever had.

She didn't want you touching her, Ace.

Yeah. There was no getting around that one. He understood a categorical ''no'' when he heard it. Never mind the little bread-and-butter display of manners she'd put on to cover it up—it was tough to ignore the fact she'd rather fall out of the frigging tree than accept his help.

Shit. He hunched his shoulders and kicked a few more pinecones. Love sucked.

But at least he had Esme. Turning, he slowly sauntered back toward the mansion, replaying their conversations in his head.

''You gonna be with Mummy and me forever and ever?''

He stopped again. What had he said when she'd asked him that? He'd been caught by surprise and still smarting from Tori's earlier rejection when she'd learned he'd shot off his big mouth to the press and he'd just snapped out a no as unequivocal as the one that had given him such a sting a short while later. He tried to remember now if she'd been standoffish before then.

Damned if he could remember. There had been his mood at the time, her less-than-thrilled attitude at discovering he was cutting her out of the process of informing Es of her parentage, and at this point he didn't know *what* was what.

So is this the kind of uncertainty you want to hang your future on, Ace?

He snapped to attention. No. *Hell,* no. If love meant putting yourself on the line, even if it turned out the other person didn't feel the same way as you, so be it. Better at this point to chance getting his teeth kicked down his throat than to torture himself trying to second-guess what Victoria felt. At least he'd know one way or the other.

With renewed determination, he picked up his pace. She hadn't been in her rooms when he'd turned Esme over to Helen, so there was no point in looking for her there. In the tree he'd heard her say something about a room that had always bothered her. The only one he remembered her ever mentioning in that context was the one he used for his office. It seemed unlikely she'd go there, but he'd check it out, all the same.

It was at least a place to start.

Sheer possessiveness gave Victoria a fresh surge of power and the distracting fear abruptly cleared from her head. She'd already made up her mind it was better to die trying than to docilely accept certain death by stepping into her father's secret closet. But DeeDee had made a big, big mistake when she'd taunted her about Rocket.

"Screw you," she snapped. "I left John once before without fighting for him. Damned if I intend to do it again." While the other woman gaped at her, she stepped back, swept the box from the shelf and, clutching it to her chest, quickly stepped around the front of the bookcase to prevent DeeDee from trapping her behind it. Giving the other woman, who stood foursquare between her and freedom, a quick assessment, she came to a decision. DeeDee wanted a war of words? She could do that. To hell with manners—she had good cause to know nice girls finish last.

"Look, Big D," she taunted. "I've got the bonds. You want them, come and get them—if you can." She gave the other woman an insolent once-over. "Put on a few pounds lately, haven't you?"

"You bitch! You'd better watch your mouth, because I've got the knife, and it won't take much to make me use it."

Victoria shrugged as if it were a minor consideration. "You'll need it, Chubs. I'm younger and fitter."

DeeDee's mouth opened and closed several times before she finally sputtered, "You're kidding me, right? I'm only a few years older than you and I play tennis every day!"

"Big deal. I chase after a five-year-old. And face it, both of us know we can count your age in slut years. Besides, I've got news for you, Blondie—I've got a much longer reach and I can run circles around a rolypoly little thing like you any day of the week. More importantly, I'm smarter. Oh, and Big D—?"

"Quit calling me that!"

She shrugged. "I was merely going to say that you

could present yourself to John stark naked on a silver platter and he wouldn't look twice. Father truly was more your speed.''

DeeDee screeched and launched herself at Victoria, but Tori was ready for her and sidestepped the charge, dancing away from the bookcase when the other woman crashed into it and inadvertently slammed it shut. The knife dropped from DeeDee's hand.

Victoria didn't know whether to go for the weapon or make a run for it. *So much for smarter,* she thought sourly when she decided on the latter and found she'd hesitated a second too long. She really wished she'd run while the running was good when she saw DeeDee dive for the knife, because no way on earth would she voluntarily present her back to the other woman. Leaping forward, she kicked at the knife just as DeeDee reached for it.

The other woman got her hand wrapped around it anyway and rolled onto her back where she started slashing wildly, preventing Victoria from kicking again. Victoria back-pedaled as fast as she could, but realized she had underestimated DeeDee's speed when the woman scrambled to her feet. Swearing under her breath, Tori threw the box at the blonde as hard as she could.

As she'd hoped, DeeDee dropped the knife to catch the box of bonds. Taking advantage of the other woman's momentary preoccupation, she whirled and ran for the door. Before she could reach it, however, it opened and she ran smack up against a hard surface.

She let loose a single eardrum-piercing scream of shock. Long arms wrapped around her and although she'd managed to keep her wits about her up until now, she abruptly lost it and began kicking and struggling. Oh, God. DeeDee had an accomplice.

"Tori, calm down," said a firm, no-nonsense voice. "I've got you."

She knew that voice and its familiar lack of sentimentality sank into her panicked mind and calmed her as nothing else could have. She tipped her head back to stare up into John's face, her gaze traveling over every beloved centimeter as she curled her fingers in his shirt. "Oh, God, Rocket, oh, God. I thought I'd never see you again. It was DeeDee. She killed Father and I found the bonds and she wanted to steal them and lock me up in the wall and we fought and, and—"

She was babbling like an idiot, but John apparently understood. His eyes narrowing, he abruptly set her aside and crossed the room in a few long strides. Reaching down, he grabbed hold of the knife that DeeDee had once again managed to pick up, wrenched it from her grip, flipped it in the air and caught it by the tip of its blade. He sent it winging, embedding it with a solid thunk in the spine of a book on the second-to-the-top shelf. Then he snapped his fingers around her wrist like a handcuff.

She looked down at his long, tanned fingers, then slowly raised her head. Her shoulders went back, her breasts lifted and licking her lips, she rubbed up against his side. "I've got a fortune in bonds here," she said giving the box clutched to her side a little jiggle. "Help me get rid of Victoria and you and I can have a real good time spending it."

"Let me get this straight. You want me to—"

Victoria made a rude noise. "Kill me."

"No, no." DeeDee pressed closer yet, looking up at him with choirgirl eyes. "I wouldn't ask you to *kill* her. Just shut her up long enough for us to get away. It's not like you two are an item anymore or anything. She told me herself that you dumped her this afternoon.''

He turned to stare at Victoria, who raised her chin slightly. His face was expressionless and she didn't exactly hear him rushing to deny it.

''She told you that, huh?''

''Yes, she did. So I'm offering you a two-fer. Here's your chance at the brass ring *and* the best sex you've ever had.''

John didn't even glance down at the female nestled next to his side. ''Tori was mistaken. I was under the impression *she* dumped me.'' His jet eyes bored into Victoria's. ''Call the cops, darlin'. Then you and I have got some serious talking to do.''

''*No!* You *bastard!*'' Spewing obscenities, DeeDee kicked out at him, twisting to pull free of his grasp and snapping at his arm with her teeth when his hold didn't loosen. John did something to her wrist that put an immediate stop to her struggles. The box tumbled to the floor, spilling its contents, and she sagged against him. Staring down at the bonds scattered across the hardwood floor, tears began to trickle down her cheeks.

Victoria simply stood and stared, until John looked over at her and repeated, ''Call the cops.'' Then he gave her a big white grin. ''Darlin'.''

She turned to do his bidding, but even as she punched out 911 on the phone's keypad, the only thought she could seem to hold on to for more than three seconds running was: *he thought I dumped him? When?* They did have to talk. Then the memory of that killer Miglionni smile and the second, deliberate *darlin'* floated across her consciousness and the corners of her lips curled up.

Of course, it was too much to expect that the situation could be handled either quickly or quietly. The police arrived with sirens blaring, which the detective who showed up with the surly Detective Simpson admitted had sent the reporters at the gates into a frenzy. And everyone in the household came running to see what had caused the ruckus. Victoria let Jared stay but sent Esme back to Helen and the staff about their business. Finally, however, after Victoria and John had explained discovering the existence of the bonds and she'd told the police over and over again how she'd come to realize there was a secret space and demonstrated how the closet worked, they took DeeDee away and the room finally cleared of everyone but her, John and Jared.

John turned to her brother. "I know you probably have more questions, but would you mind giving your sister and me a few minutes? We've got some things we need to hammer out and they've been put off too long already."

"Sure." Jared headed across the room, but turned at the door to look back at them. A smile transformed the soberness that too often had been his natural expression lately. "This is going to be all over the news, isn't it."

It wasn't really a question, but John nodded anyway. "Yeah. Your name's going to be publicly cleared, buddy. That's a good thing."

"Yeah." Jared's smile grew wider. "That's a real good thing."

Then he was gone, slamming the door exuberantly behind him and John turned back to Victoria. He trailed a tough-skinned fingertip over her cheek and she registered the touch all the way down to her toes.

"Are you all right?" he asked.

She nodded.

He shifted slightly, shoving his hands into his pockets and balancing on the balls of his feet. "Tori—do you love me?" He promptly grimaced and shook his head. "Sorry. You don't have to answer that. I'm going about this backward. I was specifically looking for you, you know, when I walked in on your little catfight with DeeDee."

"You were?"

"Yeah." He moved closer. "Because I realized today that I love you—and I figured I owed it to you to at least tell you…without expecting anything in return."

Joy, in its purest form, burst inside her like a brilliant, multicolored pyrotechnic. It was like the Fourth of July and her birthday and the way she'd felt the first time she'd held Esme all rolled into one, only multiplied a hundredfold.

"I've always made a point of playing it safe when it comes to women," John went on in a low, hoarse voice. "But I don't want to do that with you. Whether you return my feelings or not, I want you to know you're the only one for me."

"I do, though. I love you, too."

"Otherwise it's just…what?" A slow, whiter-than-white smile spread across his face. "Yeah?"

"*Oh, yeah.* I love you so much, John, and I'd sort of started to assume we were headed somewhere with this relationship. I felt like dying when you told Es there was nothing between us."

"Because I thought it was what *you* wanted! You

were so pissed when I told the reporters I was her dad
and—''

"We hadn't even told *her* yet, and I didn't want
some enterprising yellow journalist looking up her birth
certificate and broadcasting the Father Unknown from
here to kingdom come!''

"Yeah, I figured that out once I actually thought it
through, but at the time I had it in my mind that you
were ashamed of me, that you didn't think I was good
enough to publicly acknowledge as the father of your
kid.''

Stepping close, she smacked him on the chest with
the flat of her hand. "When are you going to realize
who I am?''

"I did, darlin'. Earlier, I did just that. I figured out
once and for all what I knew instinctively in Pensacola
but kept forgetting here—that you've never been and
never will be that kind of elitist. I know that if you
don't like something I've done or don't want me for
whatever reason, I can trust you to tell me up front.''
He jerked her against him and looked down the length
of his nose at her with the arrogance she both loved
and deplored. "So, we're gonna get married for real,
right? I think we oughtta. And soon.''

She blinked up at him. That was his big apology?
That was his *proposal?* Then she smiled crookedly and
looped her arms around his neck. *What the hell.* John
was like a cat who'd come late to hearth and home:
almost domesticated, but not quite. Maybe that would
improve as he learned to trust in her love for him—or
maybe he wouldn't ever be entirely tame. She was
pretty sure he'd never be a Hallmark card kind of guy.
It didn't matter, because in all the ways that counted
he showed his love. He was the man who hadn't hes-

itated to put his heart on the line for her—with no expectation of getting anything in return.

She kissed him, hard and quick, then pulled back. "Soon works for me. You want a nice big society wedding?"

"God, no! That is—that's not what you want, is it?" His eyes narrowed as she grinned up at him. "Ah. You're jerking my chain. Very cute."

Her grin widened. "Admit it, when it comes to anything society you're just too easy to tease—although in all honesty I think *you* fit in better with the country-club set than I do." He laughed and she kissed him again. When they came up for air this time, she said, "Something small and private would suit me. Just you and me and Jared and Es, with a few family and friends. That sound more your style?"

"Much." He eyed the desk covetously, then set her loose and stepped back. "We'd better get out of here," he said with patent reluctance. "Much as I've developed a lech for you on desktops, we've got a couple of kids who are probably dying of curiosity. If we want to satisfy it—and more importantly, avoid putting on a show the entire household will hear—we've got to deliver me from temptation."

They were laughing when they left the office, but paused to kiss a few yards down the hall. It had just begun to heat up when Jared's voice intruded. "Jeez, you two."

John pulled back and turned to give the young man an unabashed, ear-to-ear grin. "Hey. I'd like you to be the first to know your sister has just agreed to marry me."

Jared's smile froze. Then, eyes shadowed and posture stiff, he nodded politely. "That's nice. Congratulations. I'll, uh, start looking for a new school."

It broke Victoria's heart that experience had accustomed her brother to expect nothing else. Father's marriages had equalled getting shipped off to school.

Before she could open her mouth to reassure him, however, John said, "Yeah, maybe you should do that."

Her head jerked up and she stared at him in dumbfounded betrayal. "Rocket!"

He stepped away from her toward her brother. "Start looking in Denver," he advised over her protests. Hooking his elbow around Jared's neck, he hauled him in, scrubbing his knuckles atop the boy's head, which was nearly on a level with his own. "That's where you'll be living, with us."

Oh, God. She should have known better and she loved him, loved him, *loved* him so much it hurt.

Esme's radar must have been working overtime, because she came clattering down the stairs and within moments the entire household was assembled to hear the details of DeeDee's arrest and learn of their plans to wed. The latter called for an impromptu ice-cream party in the kitchen.

It was a good hour and a half later before Victoria finally got John to herself again. She followed him into his bedroom, closed the door, then launched herself into his arms. Laughing, he waltzed her over to the bed and dipped her until they both tumbled onto the mattress.

Victoria gazed up at him solemnly when he propped himself over her, his forearms on either side of her shoulders and his lanky body looming over hers. His ponytail slid over his shoulder to pool on her chest and she reached for it, wrapping it around her hand. "You just had a taste of the chaos that's going to be your life from now on. You still willing to sign on for this?''

''Hell, yeah. I grew up without much in the way of a family—I'm really gonna dig belonging to one.'' Lowering his head, he nuzzled along her jaw. ''And make no mistake about it, darlin', you all are mine.''

''Good.'' She arched her neck. ''Have any opinions about adding to it?''

He raised his head to look down at her. ''Have more babies, you mean?'' His eyes lit up. ''Sure. What the hell. Let's build us a dynasty.''

''A dynasty? Why, Mr. Miglionni.'' She batted her eyes at him. ''Do you think you're up to the task?''

Lowering himself over her, he wiggled his hips.

''Oooh. I see that you are.''

''Oh, yeah,'' he said. ''What do you say we get started?''

''Now?'' She let her thighs fall apart and sighed when he immediately made himself at home between them.

''No time like the present, darlin'. I believe in giving one hundred percent to any project. And if the first effort doesn't take, you know what they say.'' He kissed her until her bones felt like warm candle wax. Then he pulled back to gaze down at her. His smile was lopsided, his eyes full of love and his fingers were gentler than a summer breeze as they traced her damp, swollen lips. Lowering his head, he whispered in her ear. ''Prac-tice, prac-tice, prac-tice.''

Epilogue

For the first time in hours John found himself alone. Propping his shoulders against a wall of the intimate Brown Palace banquet room he and Tori had rented for their wedding reception, he savored his happiness. He tapped his foot in time with the four-piece band playing at the other end of the room, surprised no one was dancing on the minuscule floor. Attendance in the room, however, was momentarily sparse. His bride had slipped away with the women and even Coop and Zach, who'd been having a grand time toasting and roasting him, had disappeared a few minutes ago. He had a sneaking suspicion they were out in the parking lot messing with his car. He'd probably find all kinds of embarrassing crap tied to it when he and Tori left. You'd think they were teenagers instead of grown men, but Jared acted more mature.

No sooner had the thought popped into his head than his new brother-in-law materialized in front of him, wearing a faultlessly tailored tux and the biggest cheese-eating grin John had ever seen, forcing him to revise his previous opinion. Great. Obviously, his friends had managed to corrupt the kid already.

"Your buddies are so cool! Zach told me Coop is actually James Lee Cooper. I've read *The Eagle Flies*! How rad is that?"

"Pretty damn. His stuff is great, isn't it?"

"Man, I'll say. Coop said Zach got the handle Midnight in the marines because he sees really well in the dark and Zach told me Coop was called the Iceman because the tougher the situation, the steadier his nerves always got. But when I asked why they call you Rocket, they just laughed and said to ask you. So why do they?"

"Because I've got a dick like a suborbital transportation system."

Jared laughed. "Yeah, right. How come, really?"

John grinned. What the hell. When truth is stranger than fiction, make something up. "Good with munitions." Suddenly remembering the card in his pocket, he said, "Hey, while it's just the two of us, I have something for you."

"You do?"

"Yeah." Reaching inside his tux, he pulled out the index card and extended it to the teen. "I located P.J. I know you weren't interested the last time I asked, but I thought if you ever change your mind about contacting her, you'll at least have her current address and phone number."

Jared took the card and looked down at it. "She's in Wyoming?"

"Yeah. Her mom's working nights at a truck stop."

The boy stared at the card for several silent moments. Then he slid it into his tux pocket and looked back at John. "Thanks." He paused, then asked slowly, "Rocket, do you know how I'd go about getting a hundred bucks from my inheritance before it clears probate?"

"Nope, but I'd be happy to float you a loan in the meantime."

"You would?" Jared stared at him as if waiting for the catch. Finally, he asked, "Without knowing what I want it for?"

"Sure. You've got a good head on your shoulders. I'm sure you've got an excellent reason."

"I do," the boy said eagerly. "There's this lady in Denver who gave me money she couldn't afford just because she was decent…and because I reminded her of a son who'd died in Iraq. I want to send it to her."

"She gave you a hundred bucks?"

"No, she gave me and Peej three, but I saw into her wallet and she only had five to begin with, which made me feel doubly crappy about conning her."

"You've got style, kid. Forget the loan—I'll write you a check right now. Consider it a small thank-you to the lady from your sister and me." Suiting action to words, he pulled his checkbook from the same inside pocket where he'd stored the index card, scribbled out a check, and ripped it from the book. He handed it to his new brother-in-law.

Jared stuffed it into his pocket. "Thanks." He hesitated, then said, "I'm really glad Tori married you."

"You and me both, buddy. I'm pretty jazzed about getting you for a brother, too. You're one of the good guys."

The teen looked both delighted to hear it and terrified the sentimentality might suddenly run amok. Luckily, before the moment could grow emotionally sticky, Esme's excited voice called, "Look, Daddy, look at me!"

He turned to see her riding Coop's shoulders, her hands clutching the big blonde's spiky hair, looking thrilled right down to her little ruffled socks but a little nervous at being so far up off the ground. His heart clutched at the sound of "daddy" from her lips and at the sight of her, all flushed and bright-eyed in her little party dress and patent-leather shoes, with her hair wild and wavy down her back. "Yeah, look at you," he said. "How'd you con the big guy into giving you a ride?"

"He offered! Mr. Blackstock has a niece and her name is Lizzy and she's a coupla years older 'n me and he says someday we'll have to visit them!" She tugged on Coop's hair and leaned over to peer into his face when he tipped his head back to look up at her. "I want down now, Mr. Blackstock."

"I wish you'd call me Coop, Little Bit." His muscular shoulders shifted beneath his suit jacket as he reached overhead to lift her off them and again as he swung her to the ground. He bent and gently straightened the mussed skirt of her flower-girl dress, his dark brows furrowed with concentration.

Esme flashed him a big smile. "Thank you for the ride, Mr. Coop. It was super! I hafta go tell Rebecca and Auntie Fiona." With a swirl of rustling violet fabric and stiff white petticoat, she spun and raced across the room.

Victoria, who had paused to watch from a few feet away, walked up to the two men. "I sure do like your friends, John."

Rocket turned. "Hey, there you are!" He wrapped his arm around her and hugged her to his side, moving her veil aside with his chin in order to nuzzle her ear. "That's better," he breathed. "We haven't done this in, oh, ten minutes or so; I was starting to go into withdrawal. Where've you been?"

"Getting to know Ronnie…and Lily, whom I'm embarrassed to admit I was a little put off by at first."

Coop grinned. "It's the Marilyn Monroe hair and that bodacious body."

Victoria smiled at him. "Exactly. She's a bombshell, which under ordinary circumstances I like to believe wouldn't have got me all puckered up. But I'm sure you've heard all about DeeDee by now and she and Lily share a very similar look. Of course, it only took two minutes of watching her take care of your wife in the rest room to realize that the only thing those two have in common is massive sex appeal. Lily's a genuinely nice woman. And very kind."

Coop's black brows drew together. "Ronnie's throwing up?"

"Yes, I'm afraid so." She reached out and squeezed his forearm. "I understand congratulations are in order, although I must warn you your name was taken in vain between her bouts of hanging over the toilet."

"You're gonna be a dad?" John slapped his friend on the shoulder. "That's great news—congratulations, Ice!"

Pride cloaked Coop like a mantle, but his gaze drifted toward the ladies' room. "Thanks, we're real excited. Except Ronnie's been miserable with morning sickness, which doesn't even have the decency to confine itself to morning. She's almost into her second trimester, though, so we're hoping it will go away soon." His bittersweet chocolate-colored eyes suddenly lit up and, excusing himself, he stepped past Victoria, who looked over her shoulder to see the women they'd been discussing walking up to them.

"Hey, sweetpea," he murmured to his wife. "You all right?"

"Yes." Ronnie swept her shiny black hair away

from her damp forehead and smiled. "I feel much better."

"You look pale, princess."

John gave his friend a quizzical look. "How can you tell?"

Tori elbowed him in the side, but secretly thought he had a point. Ronnie had the whitest skin she'd ever seen and Victoria couldn't see a discernible difference from the way the other woman had looked before her stomach had gone wonky.

Pam and Frank joined them as the band segued into a jazzy tune. Pam and Ronnie discussed the injustice of morning sickness and Victoria was telling Lily about the large Craftsman-style house they'd just purchased in Denver when the petite woman suddenly stared past her. She saw the blonde's jaw drop.

"Oh, my gawd. Look at Zach!"

Tori turned to see him swing dancing with John's business manager. The tall black-haired man swung Gert out, and both kicked their left legs exuberantly fore and aft before he snapped the older woman back in and bent to dance cheek to cheek with her while they executed several complicated steps.

Smiling in delight, she looked back at his wife and friends and found them equally delighted. When the dance came to an end, John and Cooper stomped, whooped and shouted their approval.

Zach executed a snappy salute in recognition of their appreciation and escorted Gert over to the group. Bending down, he gave his wife a quick kiss on her still startled mouth. "Sorry, sweet thing, but I'm gonna have to demand a divorce. Me and Gert are running away to dance up a storm in Jamaica."

"Now don't go teasing an old broad, boy." Gert

gave him a swat, but then patted her blue updo in an appreciative feminine preen. "My pacemaker can only handle so much excitement."

Everyone laughed, but Lily continued to stare at Zach as if bedazzled. "Where did you *learn* that?"

"I took lessons Tuesday nights when I told you I was teaching the Special Ops course. You said you wished I liked to dance. Turns out I do." He stroked a gentle fingertip down her cheek. "I wanted to surprise you."

"Ohmigracious, Zachariah, you certainly did that!" She grabbed his hand and tugged. "Come on. Show me what else you've learned."

Jared, who had just rejoined the group, stared after Zach. "He teaches?" he asked, a hint of disillusionment tinging his voice.

"There comes a day when you're too old for recon, kid," Cooper said sternly. "Besides, he doesn't just teach—he's one of the best damn instructors the MOUT facility at Camp LeJuene has ever had, teaching the Urban Warrior program."

"What's MOUT?" the youth asked.

"Military Operations in Urban Terrain," John explained. "Modern warfare is beginning to be fought more and more within cities and the Urban Warrior program is a series of exercises that the Corps Warfighting Laboratory puts on to examine new urban tactics and experimental technologies. We'll have to take a trip to North Carolina before Zach musters out next year so you can check out the place for yourself. It's awesome."

Jared's eyes lit up. "Really?"

"You bet," John replied.

"Damn straight," Coop agreed and launched into a

story about one of the exercises he'd witnessed. Victoria watched as all three males ended up lying on their stomachs on the old rug, sighting down phantom weaponry.

Seeing her brother blossom under the men's attention, she counted herself one lucky woman. Not only had she captured the heart of the only man to ever engage her own, but in one fell swoop Esme had gained a dad, Jared a big brother and all three of them an expanded circle of friends.

John rolled over and sat up, grinning sheepishly when he saw her watching. "You can take the boy out of the marines, darlin', but you'll never take the marines outta the boy." He jumped to his feet and came over to her. "Have I told you how beautiful you look today?" He fingered her white veil. "I wanna see you wearing nothing but this tonight." Slicking his long hands down the sides of her slim satin-and-lace gown, he gave her a crooked smile. "Okay, and maybe those white thigh-high stockings and heels you've got on under this."

"Oh, God, John, I love you so much."

"Hey," he crooned, "what's this?" He captured a single tear sliding down her cheek and brought it to his mouth, where he sipped it off his fingertip. Bending his knees, he peered into her face. "You having one of those girly sentimental-fool moments, darlin'?"

She punched his arm. "You are such a chauvinist."

"And proud of it," he agreed, grasping her hand and running his thumb over the three-stone diamond band on her ring finger. "You won't catch *me* getting all dewy-eyed." His dark gaze, however, told a different story as he stared down at her with such naked love it made her breath catch.

Then he flashed a cocky smile, picked her up by the elbows, and planted a hard kiss on her lips. He set her gently back on her feet. ''But look at it this way, darlin'. You've got years and *years* to reform my wicked ways.''

**In a matter of seconds everything can go wrong…
And then there's no turning back.**

ALEX KAVA

**A line has been crossed.
Suddenly there's nothing left to lose.**

Melanie Starks and her seventeen-year-old son, Charlie, have been running
one con job or another for as long as she can remember. But Melanie is
getting sick of that life and wants out.

Then her brother, Jared, reappears in her life. There's something different
about Jared since his release from a life sentence for murder—a new,
dangerous edge. He has the perfect plan for a big score and he needs
Melanie's and Charlie's help. Deciding this will be the last job she ever
pulls, Melanie agrees to Jared's plan to rob a local Nebraska bank.

But then everything goes terribly wrong….

ONE FALSE MOVE

Available in August 2004 wherever books are sold.

USA TODAY bestselling author

JOAN WOLF

White Horses

January 1813—the British army is preparing to cross the Pyrenees and advance against Napoleon's army. Only one thing stands in the way—funds. It will take two people masquerading as lovers to carry out a dangerous plan....

"The always-awesome Joan Wolf proves she is a master in any format or genre."
—Romantic Times

Available August 2004 wherever paperbacks are sold.

If you enjoyed what you just read,
then we've got an offer you can't resist!

Take 2
bestselling novels FREE!
Plus get a FREE surprise gift!

NEW YORK TIMES BESTSELLING AUTHOR

HEATHER GRAHAM

Toni MacNally and her friends have hit on the ultimate moneymaking plan. Turn an ancient run-down Scottish castle into a tourist destination complete with a reenactment combining fact and fiction, local history, murder and an imaginary laird named Bruce MacNiall.

So when the castle's actual owner—a tall, dark and formidable Scot who shares Bruce MacNiall's name—comes charging in, Toni is stunned…because he seems eerily familiar. And when the group is drawn into a real-life murder mystery, Toni is plagued with sinister lifelike dreams in which she sees through the eyes of a killer….

THE
PRESENCE

"Graham has crafted a fine paranormal romance with a strong mystery plot and a vibrant setting."
—*Booklist* on *Haunted*

Available the first week of September 2004,
wherever paperbacks are sold.